THE
CHEF

A totally addictive psychological thriller
with a shocking twist

ROBIN MAHLE

JOFFE
BOOKS

Joffe Books, London
www.joffebooks.com

First published in Great Britain in 2024

© Robin Mahle 2024

Cover art by Nick Castle

ISBN: 978-1-83526-461-4

PROLOGUE

He forced the animal into a corner. That animal was me. My fingers tightened around the steering wheel, feeling the coolness of it against my skin. Ahead of me, a never-ending strip of black asphalt, interrupted by the occasional streak of headlights passing by.

On either side of the highway lay rolling hills with the crisscrossed patterns of the many vineyards that painted the Napa Valley landscape. But the moon's silvery light wasn't enough to reveal their beauty. Too many clouds shrouded the night sky. What was clear? The murderous thoughts that ran through my mind as I listened to my passenger. His arrogance, his self-satisfaction, growing bigger and bigger until it filled the entire car.

"I really do appreciate the lift home tonight," Ray said, his cheeks puffing out as he spoke. "And I'd just changed that battery too. I must've left the lights on or something. Maybe it's the alternator. Who knows?"

I could hardly stand to listen to him anymore. If only he would just shut the hell up. After almost six months, this blowhard, who looked like a heart attack would take him before he hit forty, had finally pushed me to my limit. It was a shame, because I'd hoped things would be different here.

"Don't worry about it. It's no problem." I looked at him, wearing a taut smile. "It's on my way home." As if his battery had died of its own accord. This kind of thing took planning. Opportunities didn't just present themselves. They had to be fashioned.

"Just take this exit here." Ray pointed ahead. "Tonight was a tough shift, and don't worry about Zach. He doesn't hold you to the same standard as he holds me."

Ignoring Ray's backhanded comment, I drove on. "I get it." The off-ramp was just ahead, but I continued past it.

"Hey, you missed the exit." Ray shot a glance over his shoulder. "You have to pay attention. It's what I always tell you, right? Keep your eyes on the clock. Pay attention to every detail. I didn't think I had to tell you that applied to driving, too. Jeez."

"You're right. Sorry about that. It's been a long night. I'll take the next exit and circle back." Was I going to do that? No, I don't think so.

"Sure, yeah," Ray replied. "It's so important to stay on top of things."

I nodded, pressing down on the gas just a little harder. He droned on, but I stopped listening. Instead, I fixed my gaze at the darkness of the road ahead, the pedal almost to the floor now. We were about a quarter of a mile before the next exit. This looked like a good spot, so I peered into my rearview mirror. Tiny dots of headlights were well behind me. And as I started to veer right, toward the shoulder, I heard Ray sigh.

"What are you doing? Is there a problem?" he asked, his meaty palms upturned.

"You know what, Ray? I think there is." I reached the side of the road and came to a stop. My mid-sized Toyota SUV tilted slightly as it straddled the shoulder and the soft earth that led down into a ditch. "Get out."

A crease formed in between Ray's beady eyes as he let loose a chuckle. "What?"

"I said, get out." I reached under my seat, my hand searching for the gun I'd tucked in there before going into work tonight. My fingers wrapped around the handle, and I retrieved it. "Get out — now."

Ray scrambled, his eyes bulging, his cheeks reddening. He used his legs to push against the passenger door. "What the hell are you doing?"

"What needs to be done." I released the safety. "Now get out, or I'll shoot you right here."

His right hand searched for the handle, and he opened the door, tumbling out onto the cold earth below. I killed the headlights and stepped out, surveying the highway. I had a few moments before other cars would reach us, enough that I could remain concealed in darkness while they drove by. I walked around to see Ray struggle to get to his feet.

"I don't know what you want, but I'll do it, all right?" he said, his hands raised in surrender.

"The only thing I want . . ." I trained the gun on him. "Is for you to be dead."

The gunshot rang out, echoing through the hills. Funny . . . it was louder than I'd expected, and I whipped around, spotting headlights in the distance. "Shit."

Ray had collapsed to the ground, his rotund form teetering on the edge of the ditch. I squatted low to avoid being seen. I noticed his breath was labored and his eyes locked onto mine.

"Why?" His voice gurgled while his chest spilled blood.

I leaned closer to him, taking in the damage I'd caused as the life drained from Ray's body. "Guess Lilibell's will be looking for a new head chef."

CHAPTER 1: KIRA

We were crazy to want to do it, but a couple of ex-New Yorkers moving to LA to open a restaurant were probably already a little crazy. When Dante and I told everyone we were moving to LA to sink every dime we had into this place, my father had reminded me of the statistics. "Sixty percent fail in the first year," he'd said. We were well aware of that, but it didn't deter me, or my husband. La Bianca's had been open for about a month now. In the heart of downtown LA, we had stiff competition. And we'd faced every hurdle imaginable to make it here.

With only hours before dinner service, the line cooks were busy prepping the dishes. Our kitchen wasn't exactly state-of-the-art, but it functioned well enough. Our head chef, Eric Castor, stood at his station. Sous chef Naomi Gatz was next to him. Amy Rodriguez was our pastry chef, and Manny Madura our butcher chef. They'd all come to us with relatively little experience, except for Eric and Naomi. But we couldn't afford to pay for the best, so we had to help turn them into the best.

My job was mostly to handle the books, an unpleasant task when we weren't making any money. But I also worked with the vendors and scheduled deliveries, and one had just arrived. I walked through the kitchen, wearing dress pants, a cotton blouse, and my most comfortable shoes.

Upon stepping through the rear exit, the delivery truck had opened its doors and prepared to unload the packages of meat. I had expected the sun to shine in my eyes, but it was overcast on this early spring day. Seasons didn't seem to mean much here in Southern California. Not like in New York. Here, tepid dry weather was the norm virtually year-round.

"Sorry I'm a little late." The young male driver, dressed in blue coveralls, jumped into the back of the truck to grab a box. "Damn traffic."

I'd been here two years and knew all about LA traffic. Still, it wasn't exactly a surprise to most. "That's all right. I understand."

I glanced at our small employee parking lot, the two dumpsters off to the right, and the unsightly view of the back of a bank. When the driver re-emerged with hands full, I ushered him toward the back door.

He carried the packages through the kitchen, setting them down on a nearby table. Once he finished bringing in the rest of the order, he handed over the invoice. "I just need you to sign here, ma'am."

"Sure." I double-checked the total before signing. Dante would be pissed I'd spent so much. "Thanks, and we'll see you in two days." I closed the back door behind him as he left, then headed toward Manny, who'd already begun to unwrap the roast at his station. The sounds of vegetables being chopped, pots of broth bubbling on the gas burners, and 90s pop music filled the kitchen "We're running out of time to get that in the oven," I said to him.

"I'm on it, Mrs. Lucini." Manny, a stocky twenty-seven-year-old with the best smile I'd ever seen, knew how to grill a steak better than anyone.

"How many times have I told you to call me Kira?" I watched him as he removed the white paper and kitchen string. It was the smell that hit me first. My hand covered my nose. Something was wrong.

Manny took his knife and sliced into the beef. The rancid smell grew worse by the second, and then, the maggots spilled out. They squirmed over the raw meat, and blood pooled onto the counter. "What the . . . ?" He dropped his knife and jumped back.

My stomach turned and I felt bile rise in my throat. "Oh my God."

Eric lumbered toward us. "What is it?" But I didn't have to explain. "We have to clean this up right now." He yanked the towel from his broad shoulder. "Manny, get the blue towels." He looked at me. "Kira, grab the bleach."

I ran back into the storage room and pulled the cleaning supplies, including the bleach solution, carrying them into the kitchen. The rest of the staff rushed in to help contain the spill of blood and squirming maggots that had fallen to the vinyl floor and crawled over the utensils.

"I'll get Dante," Naomi said, running through the kitchen, disappearing into the dining room.

Dante generally stayed out front, helping set up the dining area, but we needed all hands on deck to contain this disaster.

Naomi returned with Dante behind her. He looked at me. I didn't know what to say. My mouth opened, but the words wouldn't come.

"Dinner service is in three hours," he shouted, marching toward us. "This beef just came in?"

We'd been married for six years. Dante had been blessed with striking features. Olive skin, a sharp jawbone, thick black hair. It was the Italian in him. New York Italian, to be exact. And his accent got extra thick when he was stressed, or angry. Right now, I believed he was both.

"It was on the truck minutes ago," I replied. "This has never happened before." I stood frozen, stunned by what looked like a scene from a horror movie. "We have to take the roast off tonight's menu, Dante."

He raked his hand through his hair, watching the staff scurry to help clean. "It's our best seller."

"I get that. But we can't serve this."

"Obviously," he replied before turning to Eric. "You think you can come up with a special tonight to make up for it?"

Eric scratched his full but clean-shaven cheek, appearing to consider his options. "Yeah, I think I can."

"Good. Do it." Dante turned back to me. "Get on the phone with the vendor and get our money back."

"I'll check the rest of the order first with Manny," I replied.

Dante vanished, leaving the rest of us to pick up the pieces. Fine. Whatever. I walked over to Manny.

"I've looked, Kira," he began. "Everything else appears good."

"Thank God for that." I tightened my ponytail and smoothed down my rogue strands of hair, disheveled by the commotion.

"I have no idea why they would bring this to us," Manny said.

"They must not have known."

He looked at me with pursed lips, his thin mustache curling. "We both smelled it. They had to have known."

"Let's just do our best to get through tonight." The back door opened and caught my attention. Eric had walked inside. I hadn't realized he'd stepped out.

He returned to his station. Naomi glanced at him and then at me. That was odd. I walked over to him. "How are we coming along? Back on track?"

"Soon. I just needed to catch my breath," he replied.

"Yeah, sure." I studied him for a moment as he gathered his supplies. One of the carrots he'd had at his station rolled off and fell to the ground. I walked behind him. "I'll get that." I bent down to pick it up.

"Don't bother, let me." Eric swung around as I stood again.

The knife he'd been holding sliced my right forearm. We stared at each other for a moment, as though we weren't sure what had just happened. I looked at my shirt, and blood began to seep through my sleeve. My eyes widened. And then the pain hit.

"Oh my God. Jesus, Kira, I'm so sorry." Eric grabbed his towel and covered my arm with it. "Dante?" He called out. "Go get Dante!"

I'd grown dizzy and my stomach turned. I felt like I was going to . . .

* * *

Nurses looked down at me, concerned, as I lay on the gurney. I hadn't been all that worried until I saw their expressions. But then, I didn't think the gash in my arm had been deep. Maybe they knew differently. On glancing at it again, there did seem to be a fair amount of blood seeping through the gauze Dante had applied before driving me to the hospital.

The wheels rolled along the hallway floor, the sound echoing in my ears. The lights in the ceiling passed by in a blur as I stared at them.

Dante jogged alongside me, his hand resting on my shoulder. His face, too, was masked in worry. "Just hang tight, babe, you'll be okay."

"He's right," the nurse beside me added. "We'll get you fixed up."

My heart thumped in my ears, slow and steady. They said I briefly lost consciousness on the way over. Maybe that was why I was on this gurney. It hadn't seemed real, all that had happened today. First the rotten beef, then getting stabbed by my head chef. All right, I wasn't exactly *stabbed*, but it still hurt like hell. I was just grateful nothing happened to the staff. We couldn't afford a claim on our insurance. As it was, I had no idea how we would pay for this hospital bill.

As they continued to roll me through the corridor, I noticed a clock on the wall. "Oh no. What about dinner service?" I asked Dante.

"Don't worry about that. Naomi and Eric have everything under control," he replied. "We'll get you stitched up, and I'll take you home. You're going to need a lot of stitches."

"Great." I closed my eyes thinking about the scar that would remain. "Don't blame Eric for this, okay? I should've been more careful."

Dante looked down at me. "He had no business holding his knife like that. You could've been hurt a lot worse."

"But I wasn't," I insisted. "You should go back to the restaurant. I'll be fine."

"Not a chance. I'm not leaving you here alone. It's you and me, okay?"

That was one of the first things Dante had ever said to me. I'd been working at a Manhattan restaurant called Michael's. That was where we'd met. I was a server; he was the butcher chef at the time. Several of the staff had called out sick during a bad flu season. I was one of three servers that night. Dante had to step in to help the head chef. I remember him winking at me, raising a corner of his lips. "*It's you and me, okay? We got this.*"

Things between Dante and me had been rocky since we bought the restaurant seven months ago. Renovating it, creating the menu, hiring staff. Maybe this would help bring us together — me almost getting killed. I chuckled.

"What's that, babe?" Dante asked.

"Nothing."

They rolled me into what looked like a small operating room, except there weren't all the big overhead lights and equipment and stuff like they show on TV. It was like a sort of triage room.

Two orderlies, a nurse, and a doctor hoisted me onto the bed. They raised my back to an upright position. The movement made me feel light-headed, as though all my blood rushed from my brain to my arm.

"Just relax." The doctor, whose face was hidden behind a mask, looked at me with kind eyes. "We're going to take care of you now, all right? This will all be over soon."

"Okay," I said before turning back to Dante.

He'd kept his focus on the doctor and watched him prepare a table of instruments. And then I thought to myself — *Yeah, that's what I'm afraid of.*

* * *

We'd settled on two days' rest. My injury was hardly debilitating, and I needed to be at the restaurant. It was Friday, and our weekend reservations were only now starting to take off. Dante didn't push back. Our experience in this business forced a reckoning. We understood the reality of our situation.

The dining area was awash in a soft amber glow when I began my final inspection. The bandage on my arm was hidden under a long-sleeved blouse, and no one was any the wiser that I'd had fifteen stitches put in the other night. I wasn't going to lie, though: the throbbing in my arm was just barely tolerable as I walked around.

The overhead lights reflected off the brass contours embossed in the ceiling. They shone down onto the half-moon-shaped booths. Modern pendant lights hung over black tufted leather seating. Square tables with black walnut tops lined the center of the room. And large windows that offered stunning views of the downtown Los Angeles skyline glimmered.

As I looked around, I knew this place would become a success if we survived these first few painful months. A good write-up in the *LA Times* — something nice about our authentic Italian cuisine with a Mediterranean flair. These would be the marks of greatness; however, incidents like what happened with me, and the disastrous beef delivery, couldn't get out. Our reputation would be tarnished before it even began.

I returned to the kitchen and found Dante brushing off a speck of fluff from the lapel of his black Armani suit. We had money troubles, and his suits were part of that. But he insisted that he had to play the part of the restaurateur, and he did so impeccably. The son of Italian immigrants, he was born and raised in Brooklyn, New York. His parents had owned an Italian bakery, where he and his older brother had worked since they were kids. Unfortunately, both parents were gone now, and so was the bakery.

I had been out of college for a couple of years, and I quickly came to realize that my NYU degree in literature was going to get me nowhere, except maybe a decent teaching gig. But that wasn't what I'd wanted. I'd wanted excitement, and when I met Dante, he gave that to me.

He found me working as a server in a Manhattan restaurant. He said he was drawn to my strawberry blond hair, fair skin, and most of all, the freckles that bridged across my nose. I wasn't sure about that. I have since come to know his weakness for women like me, petite with ample breasts. One look at Naomi made that clear.

I stood next to Dante in the kitchen, and he kissed me on the cheek. "You sure you don't want to rest at home?"

"I'm sure," I replied. "I feel fine, really."

"All right. I'd better go check on Angelo." He started toward the door that led to the dining area. "You know what he's like."

I did. Angelo was Dante's older brother. A leech. A hanger-on. And if he wasn't the funniest alcoholic I'd ever met, I might have had a problem with him. That wasn't an entirely fair assessment, however. I did love him, and he hadn't begun to drink until his parents died shortly before we left New York.

Dante disappeared into the dining area, or front-of-house, as we called it. I looked back to see that the staff was operating like clockwork, so I walked to the swinging door, pushing it open to glimpse the two brothers at the bar.

Angelo, a hefty forty-year-old, sat on his stool and sipped on a glass of red wine from a bottle he'd taken off our well-curated, and highly expensive wall display.

Dante approached him. "At least make it look like you're doing something."

"I'm tasting the wine," Angelo replied. "That is doing something. I saw Kira a minute ago as I was coming in. I'm surprised she's here."

I let the door close again, returning to the back-of-house and walking into the manager's office. Angelo had a good heart, and Dante had always had a soft spot for his brother. I'd quickly realized he'd become a permanent fixture in our marriage, and I suppose I'd been pretty okay with that so far.

The computer screen in front of me had been opened to the nightly receipts. I sat down at the desk and added tonight's page, ready to enter the take at the end of shift. And as I prepared to finish one of the many reports I ran on a daily basis, I heard a knock on the door.

"Come in," I said, not bothering to look away from the screen.

"Hey."

The voice, I easily recognized. "Hey, Eric." I looked over at him. "Everything all right?"

He meandered inside, tucking his hands into the pockets of his chef's jacket. "Yeah, sure. We're all set for opening. I just wanted to come and see how you were doing."

I glanced at my arm. "Fine. I don't really have much pain anymore." That was a lie, but no point in making the guy feel worse than he already did.

"That's great news. You know how sorry I am about all that, right?"

"Of course I do. Look, we were busy. Things got a little chaotic, what, with the whole meat thing. It was my fault, Eric. I shouldn't have been walking behind you."

"It's me who messed up," he replied. "I wasn't thinking."

"Look, accidents happen in the kitchen. We all know that," I assured him. "Please don't think twice about it, okay, Eric? Let's just make tonight different. I'll stay out of the way. I promise."

He nodded, but his face was still masked in guilt. "Yeah, okay." He jerked back his thumb. "I should get back to it."

"Yep. We'll have a great night, Eric. I know we will." I watched him turn around to leave, as he'd left my door open. But he didn't return to his station. Instead, he pushed outside through the kitchen's back door.

Eric was a big, beefy guy, and seeing him that way, almost childlike in his expression, I'd really felt for him. So, I'd let him take a few minutes to clear his head and take in the evening air. After that, I'd need him on top of his game.

CHAPTER 2: DANTE

Since Kira and I bought this place, my smoking habit had gone from half a pack a day, to a pack a day. As the dinner service prepared to get underway, I needed a quick break and headed outside through the back exit.

I reached for the pack of cigarettes tucked in my jacket pocket and noticed Eric a few steps away. "Hey." With the pack in my hand, I held it out for him.

He waved me off. "No, thanks, Chef."

"Suit yourself." I lit up my cigarette as I stood near the back stoop. "You doing all right, man?"

"Yes, Chef." He walked toward the building again. "Just taking a quick break. Better get back to the grind."

"Good luck tonight." I gently grabbed his arm as he headed away. "Listen, I know you still feel like shit over what happened to Kira. Don't, okay? She's good. Accidents happen."

"Not to me, Chef. Not usually."

He returned inside and when the back door closed again, I was alone. Staying out here for too long would be noticed, but I needed a minute to myself. I knew what was coming, and I knew I had to play it cool. Did I like it? No, not particularly. But it was a necessary evil.

The sound of LA at night, especially where we were, comprised loud music from nearby bars, heavy traffic, typical of just about everywhere around here, and chatter from people on the street. I couldn't have picked a better location for our restaurant. Of course, we'd gotten lucky because the building had been foreclosed on, and the bank had owned it.

I'd begun my career at Michael's, an upscale steakhouse in Manhattan. Kira had worked as a server. It was where we'd met. I worked my way up, eventually landing the head chef position. It was the owner, Michael, who mentioned this place to me. Said he'd heard it had been foreclosed on and that if we were really interested in making a move, this would be a great place to start. So, that was what we did, Kira and me.

I'd grown up working in my parents' bakery, eventually heading off to culinary school. Michael had given me my first job as a line cook, though I still helped out my folks when they needed it. When my parents died, my wife and I packed up, dragging along my older brother, and came here to make a go of it. I supposed the timing happened to work out well enough because here we were now.

As I looked around, knowing money was flying right out the door every night, I wasn't sure we were going to make it. It had been hard on both of us, personally and professionally.

I dropped my cigarette, snuffing it out with my three-hundred-dollar dress shoes, and noticed the back door open again. Naomi stepped out and smiled at me.

"Dante, what are you doing out here?" she asked.

"Same as you, no doubt. Is it getting too hot in that kitchen?" I asked, trying to sound funny, but probably coming off like a douche.

"No, it's okay. I was just taking a quick break." She walked toward me, her eyes on my pack of cigarettes.

"Want one?" I asked.

"Why not?"

I took one out, lighting it for her when she put it between her lips.

She inhaled deeply and blew the smoke up into the night sky. "Thanks. I needed that."

"Anytime." I watched her lips wrap around the cigarette again. I couldn't deny Naomi was a beautiful woman. Young. Younger than me, anyway. No one needed to tell me how dangerous it was for me to let thoughts of her roam around in my head. I already knew.

Her talent had exceeded my expectations, but sometimes, I noticed her ambition getting in the way. She wanted to be the best, and I knew remaining a sous chef for long wasn't in the cards for her.

"Whatcha got going on after shift tonight? Anything?" I asked, regretting the question the moment I asked it.

She tilted her head. Her brunette hair was pulled back in a bun. I imagined what it would look like cascading down in soft waves framing her face. Her big blue eyes and full lips enhancing the color.

Shake out of it, Dante.

"Nothing tonight. I know it's Friday and all that, but it's been a long week. I want nothing more than to run myself a hot bath. Grab a bottle of wine and some candles, and then just soak the night away."

"Sounds perfect," I said.

The back door opened, and a voice called out. "Naomi? We need you—now."

"Coming." She put out the cigarette and smiled. "See you inside. And thanks for the smoke."

When she returned inside, I exhaled, chuckling a little, then I walked toward the dumpster to toss the now empty pack of cigarettes. From the corner of my eye, I spotted a parked car. Right there on the curb just outside our parking lot. Someone was inside. It was dark and the driver was cast in shadow, but who the hell was it?

I approached the vehicle, feeling like maybe this was someone casing the joint. Blame the Brooklyn in me, but I could go old-school at the drop of a hat, like right now.

"Yo," I called out.

When I got closer, the headlights flicked on, blinding me where I stood. I raised my arm to shield my eyes and the car just took off.

"The hell?" I stood there a moment, trying to make out the vehicle as it drove away. All I noticed were the taillights, possibly from an SUV, and that it was a dark color. Could've been a thief. Could've been competition, too. Someone looking to see how busy we were.

I swatted my hand. "Who the hell cares." I'd been out here too long anyway and needed to get back inside before the missus cracked the whip.

Stepping through the back door, I smelled a busy kitchen — it never got old. Savory and sweet. A hint of dishwasher detergent and cleaner. And sweat. Our people hustled like no one else. And as I looked around at my crew, I knew we were going to make it. We wouldn't be part of that sixty percent who failed in the first year. Eighty percent who failed in the first five years. Those figures had been pounded into my head by everyone I knew. So screw 'em. That wasn't going to be us.

"There you are," Kira said, approaching me. "I finally got an email back from the butcher."

She motioned for me to follow her to the office. Kira worked there most of the time while I stayed busy with the guests out front, ensuring service was top-notch. "What'd he say?"

We stepped inside and she closed the door, sitting down at the desk. "This is the email. He apologized, but said the beef didn't come from him."

"No?" I asked. "Then where the hell does he think it came from? Did you email the pictures we took?"

"I did." Kira turned her chair to face me. "Dante, he's not going to give us a refund. That slab cost us almost four hundred dollars."

"Yeah, I know. And close to a grand in retail sales." I shook my head. "Then I guess we have to find another vendor. To be honest, we should shop around anyway. We're spending a ton of money we don't have."

Kira rubbed her arm that was still bandaged.

"You okay? Is that hurting?" I asked.

"No, I'm fine. It's just — none of this makes sense. I mean, why isn't he fessing up to this? The delivery came straight off his truck. Now he's denying it? Dante, we can't afford to go toe-to-toe with any of these guys. Word gets around we're difficult, and no one will want to work with us."

"For Christ's sake, Kira, we aren't using that guy again," I said. "He should be forking over that refund. Let me handle this, all right? I'll take care of it."

I opened the door, knowing that the longer I stayed there, the more likely we'd start arguing. And we were too busy for that right now.

I stepped out of the office and stopped cold when Naomi crossed in front of me. "Whoa. Sorry about that. Almost ran into you."

"Maybe next time?" She winked and carried on to her station.

Kira tapped my shoulder. "Everything okay?"

I spun around, her touch scaring the shit out of me. I hadn't even heard her step out of the office. And her asking if everything was okay meant she'd heard the exchange between Naomi and me as well. Everything was most decidedly *not* okay by the look in her eyes.

"Yeah, all good."

CHAPTER 3: KIRA

It wasn't the first time I'd seen Dante and Naomi flirting. He used to flirt with me like that, and I'd loved it. I'd felt special, like the only woman in the room. I thought back for a moment to New York. To the holiday party we'd attended when Dante had been promoted to head chef at Michael's. We'd been married for a couple of years. Things had been pretty great.

Christmas music played softly in the background. The laughter and jangling of glasses filled the elegant Upper East Side loft belonging to restaurant owner, Michael Lombardi, who'd hosted the party. The lights of the city glittered through the floor-to-ceiling plate glass windows, and I was mesmerized. Dante turned to me.

"You ready for another glass of champagne?" he asked, noticing my empty flute.

"Yes, please. Thank you." I watched him walk away, heading toward one of two open bars when behind me, a man brushed against my hip. His hand gently touched my shoulder. I turned around.

"Excuse me," he said. "I should really watch where I'm going."

The three glasses of champagne loosened my inhibitions. I leaned into him, placing my hand on his chest, running my fingers down the ridges of his tuxedo shirt. He was somewhat ordinary. Didn't seem particularly confident around women. Kept pushing up the glasses from his nose. "It's okay. I should pay more attention."

"Not at all." He tilted his head. "You work at the restaurant, don't you?"

I opened my mouth, ready to speak, when Dante returned with glasses in hand.

"There's my beautiful wife," he said, his eyes fixed on the tall, willowy man.

My cheeks flushed because his words came off like a proclamation. Dante set down the glasses on a nearby table, grabbed me and dipped me as though we'd just danced a tango. I laughed, bumping into the man behind me.

Dante pulled me up again, and we both giggled. I turned around to apologize to the gentleman, but he'd already headed away from us. I regarded Dante, feeling flattered by the obvious marking of his territory. "May I have my champagne?"

I missed the way he used to be just a little jealous of how other men looked at me. I know it should've bothered me, but now . . . now, it was me who was jealous of the attention he'd lavished on Naomi. I was afraid of losing him. We'd been here before, and I couldn't go through that again.

However, tonight, I was going to set aside my marriage troubles, because the doors had opened, and we were slammed.

The noise of the kitchen kept my attention, and I hadn't noticed Angelo hurrying inside.

"Kira?" he said in a raised tone. His hair was already fully gray. He wore it short and spiky, reminding me a little of Guy Fieri.

I noticed the look on his face. It sent a momentary shot of adrenaline through me. "What happened?" The restaurant was in full dinner service and I, of course, feared another terrible incident, only this time, maybe it concerned one of the guests. "Is everything okay?"

"You won't believe who's out there," he said.

"Who?"

"Otis Oliver."

Angelo looked at me like I should know who that was. I did. I knew exactly who he was, and why he was here. "Where's Dante?"

"Front of house. I think he spotted him too, but he was talking to some guests. I didn't want to interrupt," Angelo said.

No sooner had the words left Angelo's mouth did Dante rush into the kitchen. "Otis Oliver is here. He just walked in."

He'd said it loudly enough so that the entire kitchen heard him. They didn't need to be rattled by this, and I watched their faces fill with terror.

"All right." I raised my hands. "It's going to be fine." I noticed Eric stiffen in response. "This is exactly the reason why we aren't supposed to know when these people come in." I looked over at Dante. "You recognized him? You know for sure it's Oliver?"

"Of course I do," he shot back. "He's at table eleven."

"We have to give him VIP treatment," Angelo said.

I walked between the brothers. "We all know they look down on that. They want to be treated like regular customers. For all we know, he's been here before, and we didn't spot him." My words seemed to do little to settle the nerves of the staff, or my husband. "We've been open for a month. We knew this time would come eventually."

I walked over to Eric's station, shoulders back, feeling confident. "You know what you're doing. Just do it. Don't think about whose table it's going to." I then moved on to Naomi. "Same goes for you. You're here to do your job."

"Yes, Chef," she replied.

"Okay, then." I walked back to the brothers. "We keep going and whatever happens, happens. We just have to do our best."

"Yes, Chef!" the team shouted in unison.

Dante leaned into my ear and whispered, "We can't afford to mess this up."

"I know. They know it, too."

Only moments passed when the order for table eleven came through. Pappardelle Mimmo was a restaurant favorite, and Otis Oliver had ordered it. A flat, wide pasta, the dish was served with scrumptious scallops and buttery lobster.

The added sage and truffle topped it off, giving it an earthy finish. It was our specialty.

Eric used his towel to wipe the plate clean and ensure his presentation was perfect. He fixed his gaze on it for several moments, while the servers appeared to grow anxious. Finally, he nodded. "It's ready."

I couldn't deny my anxiety level was at a ten. Dante's was, too, as I watched him approach Eric and inspect the dish.

A smile danced on Dante's lips. "Perfection." He patted Eric on the shoulder and eyed the young servers dressed in black, their hands clasped behind them as if standing at ease. "Jonah, you take it."

"Yes, Chef."

Jonah Evans was our most experienced of the servers on staff. His resume, albeit short, was impressive. The twenty-three-year-old folded his towel over his arm and held out his hands.

Eric offered a final nod, and Jonah reached for the dish. "Thank you, Chef." He spun around on his heel, almost like a military march, and made his way to the door.

Dante opened it for him. "You got this."

A small corridor lay between the back and front of house. I stood out there alongside Dante, both of us cast in shadow. We watched Jonah make his way to the table of the food critic, who may not have understood he'd been recognized.

"Pappardelle Mimmo, sir." Jonah set down the plate, and as he removed his hand, his pinky finger nicked the wine glass filled with a luscious red.

It wobbled a moment, and I clutched my chest, praying it wouldn't spill into Otis Oliver's lap. I could see the whites of Jonah's eyes as he looked on in terror.

Everything slowed down as the scene unfolded. Jonah glanced at Oliver, who'd raised his hand, preparing to catch the glass before it landed on the table and wine traveled down to his pants.

But the glass settled again. Disaster averted. I let out my breath while Dante grabbed my shoulder. We both looked at each other wearing a grin. I almost burst out laughing with relief. Luckily, I didn't.

Jonah looked relieved as well. "Is there anything else I can get you, sir?"

"No, thank you." Oliver reached for the wine glass and moved it to the other side of his plate.

"Of course. Enjoy." Jonah retreated, wearing a pleasant smile, but as he reached the darkened corridor, he noticed we stood in his way. "I'm sorry, Chefs."

Dante patted his back. "It's all right, Jonah. Nothing happened."

"Yes, Chef. I just need a breath of air."

When Jonah walked through the kitchen door, I turned back to Dante, noticing he couldn't take his eyes off Oliver. "Relax. He'll love it, Dante. Let's go back inside." I entered the kitchen and noticed Jonah had left out the back exit. I turned my sights to Eric's station. "Where's Chef?"

Naomi raised her eyes to me. "He went outside a few minutes ago. He was nervous."

"He needs to be in here keeping us on schedule." When Dante trailed me, I captured his attention. "Eric stepped out. I'll go check on him and get him back in here. We can't afford to let things fall apart now."

"Okay, babe," he replied.

I carefully walked through the kitchen, calling out my intention as I passed by each station. "Walking behind. Coming through. Behind you." I wasn't about to get cut again.

I opened the door that led to the back of the restaurant. The evening air felt lukewarm. The noise of cars and people came from every direction. However, my senses quickly ran afoul of the dumpster as I walked down the concrete steps into the parking lot.

Jonah was off to the right, several feet away. He stood with his back to me, facing the other buildings that surrounded our restaurant. Movement caught my attention. I heard rustling behind the dumpster and walked around to investigate. And what I saw was the last thing I expected. "Jesus, Eric."

Eric spun around, wiping the white residue from his nose. "Kira, I–I . . ."

"What the hell are you doing?" I knew what he was doing, but that wasn't exactly my point.

"My nerves — I was — I don't have an excuse. Please, it was just this one time."

I observed the sweat that beaded his heavy brow. His pupils that were dilated. I took in a deep breath and folded my arms, but the pain reminded me of the cut Eric had inflicted and I returned them to my sides. "Really?"

"Yes, I swear it. I was nervous about Otis Oliver. I know what getting a good review will mean for the restaurant."

Car horns, sirens, and the occasional screeching of tires rang in my ears as Eric froze next to the dumpster. The smell of it still wafting in the air. Spoiled food, uneaten meals, and other kitchen waste were piled high, keeping the lid propped open.

"Are you going to tell Dante?" Eric asked. "I need this job, Kira. I'm a good chef, you know that."

"Yeah, I do know that."

Jonah approached us. He looked at me with a strange expression. Almost as if he realized I now knew what maybe everyone else already had. And yet, no one had said. "Go back inside, Jonah. Make sure Oliver is taken care of."

"Yes, Chef." He glanced over at Eric, smoothing his black button-down and adjusting the small apron at his waist.

When he disappeared inside, I looked again at Eric. "Were you high when you sliced me with your knife the other day?"

"No, no, I wasn't. Kira, come on. You know me."

"I thought I did." I glanced back at the door, my head swimming with various scenarios as to how the rest of this evening would play out. Let Eric return to work and finish his shift, hoping nothing else would happen, but then fire him later. This would keep Dante happy and probably the

23

customers, whose service would go uninterrupted. I could fire him right now and force him off the premises. He might make a scene, drawing unwanted attention from guests or Otis Oliver, jeopardizing the review. Or I pretend none of this happened and go on about the evening.

That last option was the most appealing, but I knew I couldn't let this slide. I couldn't put the rest of the staff at risk, especially after what happened to me. So, only one option remained.

"Collect your things and leave, Eric," I said. "If you make a scene, I'll make sure you never work at another restaurant in this city again."

CHAPTER 4: DANTE

All Kira and I needed was a good review from Otis Oliver. The restaurant would be booked for weeks on end. Who would've thought a kid from Brooklyn, raised by Italian immigrant parents, would one day own his own successful restaurant? Not this Brooklyn kid.

I made another pass around the customers, stopping at Oliver's table. "Good evening. How's everything for you tonight?"

Oliver, a thin, balding man with frameless glasses dabbed his lips with the napkin. "Wonderful. Thank you." I nodded and prepared to return to the kitchen. Kira had already gone to check in on Jonah after the wine glass mishap. It was time for me to keep this ship on its course.

As I turned around, I saw my brother sitting at the bar, sipping on another glass of wine. One day that man would drink me into bankruptcy. But I loved him, and since our parents died, we were all we had. Well, I had Kira. Angelo didn't have anyone else.

This had to be kept on the low, so I walked over to Angelo and stood next to him. "Look, man, you gotta leave. I can't have that critic seeing you over here just mooching."

Angelo set down his glass. "You think I'm mooching, fine. I'll leave. I'll go back home."

"I didn't say you had to leave the restaurant. Just go in the back or something, would you? Hell, take the bottle with you for all I care."

"I believe I will." Angelo snatched the bottle and walked into the kitchen.

I rapped my knuckles on the sleek marbled bar top and eyed my bartender, Gavin, a young guy with mad mixology skills. "Thanks for entertaining him."

"No problem, Dante. He's no trouble. I got brothers and sisters, and they're all pains in my ass," he added.

I smiled and tossed a nod over at the critic. "You think we'll get a good review?"

"I hope so, boss. We're doing good and all that, but it can't hurt, right?"

"Can't hurt at all." I returned to the kitchen. The hustle put a smile on my face. Mostly because it meant I was making money instead of watching it fly out the door, as had been the case lately. Kira and I had spent a fortune to get this place open. A second on the house. Credit card debt up to our armpits. With a good review from Otis Oliver, we might get out of the red.

I stopped dead in my tracks, the kitchen door swinging behind me. Something was going on. "Naomi, what the hell are you doing?"

"Kira asked me to take over for Chef Eric."

"What?" I set my sights on the office where I assumed Kira was holed up. She appeared in the doorway, and I furrowed my brow. "What the hell is going on?"

"We need to talk."

She walked over to me, took my arm, and led me into the office, closing the door behind her. "Jesus, Kira, we have a dining room full of guests. What's going on with Eric? Where is he?"

"He's in the locker room, packing up his things."

Had I heard her right? My head chef was quitting in the middle of his shift, and not only that, the most important shift of my goddamn career? "Eric quit on us?"

"I fired him," she said.

Her words echoed in my ears. I paced the office, my arms crossed tightly over my chest. "Why the hell did you fire Eric? Are you insane? Do you know how busy it is out there?"

"Yes, I do, and it would be nice if you would just hear me out a second, all right?"

My palms had begun to sweat. "Fine. I'm listening."

"I went out back to check on Jonah when I heard some noise behind the dumpster. Dante, it was Eric. He was doing coke. I saw the powder on his nose."

"For Christ's sake." I raked my hand through my hair. "You're serious?"

"Of course I am. I don't think Jonah saw him, but when I told him to go back inside, it was like he knew. Like maybe everyone knew," she replied. "I couldn't let him come back and work like nothing had happened. Dante, what if I was hurt because Eric had been high the other day, too?"

She had a point. Still, this couldn't be happening. "What the hell are we supposed to do now?"

"I've taken care of things. Naomi will finish the shift. She's a good sous chef. She'll be fine. You can help her manage things, if you feel it's necessary."

It had been months since I'd cooked. Of course, I knew our menu like the back of my hand — I created it — but I hadn't cooked any of the dishes in a while. Eric had been with us since before the beginning when we were still renovating. "You couldn't just let him finish out tonight? Otis Oliver is out there."

"I know that, Dante. Sorry if I was more concerned about our staff's safety," she shot back.

The last thing I wanted was for this to blow up into another full-fledged argument. We'd had plenty of those over the past few months, but right now, I was pissed. "Fine. I'd better get out there and make sure we don't fall apart." I reached for the door handle but stopped. "You said Eric's in the locker room?"

"Yes."

My face heated with anger at both Kira and Eric. They were screwing with the status quo tonight, of all nights. I marched back into the kitchen. The eyes of the staff were on me. "Get back to work," I barked, immediately feeling guilty for projecting onto them.

I brushed past a couple of the servers. Jonah was nowhere to be seen. The locker room was straight ahead, and I walked inside. There he was, tossing his things into a grocery bag. "What the hell, man?"

Eric turned around, shame masking his face. "I'm so sorry, Dante. I–I messed up. I know that. I didn't see Kira come outside."

"Tonight, man? With Otis Oliver out there, you do this shit tonight?" I gestured toward the door as if Oliver waited on the other side. "I told you to keep that shit away from the restaurant, didn't I?"

Eric dropped onto the bench. "I got so freaked out, wondering if that critic was going to like my dish. I know what this means to you and Kira. I didn't want to screw it up."

I pressed my hands against my waist and looked down at him. "So you snorted coke in front of my wife?"

"That's not how it went down, I swear it. I needed to take the edge off. I walked outside, saw Jonah, and just went around the dumpster."

I was at my wit's end. Anger boiling over. "You promised that shit was under control. I can't defend you on this, you get that, right? Kira will have my ass if she finds out I knew about it."

"I won't say anything. You know me," Eric replied.

"Yeah, I thought I did." My chest tightened like I couldn't get enough air in my lungs. Stress wasn't something I handled well. Probably should've considered that before opening my own restaurant. Before mortgaging my house to the hilt. "Just go, man."

Eric got to his feet and grabbed the grocery bag. In his hands, he held his chef's jacket. As he walked toward me, he handed it over. "I'm sorry, Chef. I really am."

When I returned to the kitchen, Kira was already addressing the staff. They obviously had seen Eric leaving out the back in the middle of dinner service. I listened as Kira went on.

"We'll get through tonight with Naomi at the helm. Dante and I will put a plan together so that we can continue to operate while we search for a new head chef."

For a moment, I let the scenario play out in my head. Kira packing a bag for me and kicking me out of my home. That was exactly what would happen if she found out that I knew about Eric's problem — and the other stuff. I should've asked him at the time if he'd been high when Kira was injured. But I didn't. I swept it under the rug.

She stopped speaking and looked over at me. "In the interim, Dante will step in and help Naomi assume the head chef position. But right now, we have to get out these orders. Our quality cannot suffer. I know I speak for Dante, too, when I say that we have an incredible team here. I know Eric will be missed, but you all are just as talented. So, let's get through tonight."

I didn't feel the need to elaborate, so I walked over to Naomi. "You think you can do this?"

She glanced at the clock on the wall. "Yes, Chef. I got this."

"Good." I walked toward the front of house when I spotted Jonah returning from the dining room. "Is everything all right?"

"Yes, Chef," Jonah replied.

"Mr. Oliver? Is he enjoying the meal?" I continued.

"I think so, Chef."

I squared up to him, sensing he had more to say. "Then what's the problem?"

"Nothing, Chef. There's no problem," Jonah said. "I better go. I have more tables."

* * *

The restaurant had closed. The staff had gone home. Only Kira and I remained. We perched on the concrete steps outside the back of the restaurant. The street still bustled with cars and people. Lights shone from the several bars around us. LA never really slept. I used to love that about this city, but my age was catching up with me. Christ, I was in my late thirties; what the hell was I talking about? Guess the stress made me feel older. That, and lying to my wife.

"We had a good night," Kira said, pulling the ponytail band from her thick hair.

"Till we had to fire our head chef." I flicked the ashes from my cigarette that dangled between my fingers.

"He didn't give me a choice, babe." Kira clutched my arm as she pulled in closer to me.

"You did the right thing," I assured her. "And Naomi can handle things until we find someone else."

"I guess. But when Oliver comes back, and you know he will, what if he doesn't like the food? We know these guys stop by two or three times before they do their write-up."

I chuckled. "Who's to say he enjoyed tonight's meal?"

She rolled her eyes at me, but when I saw a smile tug at her lips, I knew all would be forgiven — until she learned the truth. I puffed on my cigarette once again, turning my head to blow the smoke in the other direction. "We need La Bianca's to do well."

"And it will. We just have to stay focused. We'll get through this." Kira leaned in to kiss my cheek. The warmth of her lips felt inviting. "We always do."

"You should go home." I thumbed at the back door. "I'll give the place a once-over and see that we're locked up. Get some rest. With that arm, you shouldn't have been here in the first place."

Kira stood, her slim figure silhouetted against the backdrop of the city's lights. I saw her disappointment, but as usual, chose to ignore it.

"Okay, babe." She nodded. "I'll see you when you get home."

* * *

Kira padded into the kitchen, dressed in a long T-shirt, and looking half-asleep. I sat at the breakfast table inside our home in the hills and watched her pour a cup of coffee. My phone lay on the table in front of me, but I turned my gaze back to the rising sun that pushed through the smog-filled skyline. I'd been up for an hour already. Couldn't sleep after all that had happened last night.

"Good morning," she said.

"Morning. Coffee's still hot," I replied, taking a sip from my mug.

Kira spooned in her sugar substitute and stirred. "You've been up for a while, huh?"

"Couldn't sleep."

Her phone lay on the kitchen island, and she picked it up. "You don't suppose . . ."

"I've been checking, but haven't seen anything yet," I replied.

She grabbed a handful of her hair and flicked it onto her back before scrolling through her phone.

When her eyes widened, and she shot a look at me, I realized she'd found it. "Where?"

"The *Times*," she replied, carrying her coffee to the table. She sat down next to me. "Oh my God, it's in the *Times*."

I quickly opened my phone to the website and found the article. We both read it, neither speaking for several moments. The silence was finally broken by her squeal of delight.

"It's a fantastic review," she said. "I can't believe it. All of our hard work, the long hours, and the sleepless nights . . . Dante, they've finally paid off."

31

My head raced with thoughts as to what this could mean for us, for the restaurant. "We'll be booked for weeks, if not months."

"It means we're going to be okay," she replied.

Then, reality hit me. "No, it doesn't."

"You mean because of what happened with Eric?" she asked. "We'll find someone else."

The sun's rays bounced off the metal patio furniture outside the window, forcing me to squint. I looked at Kira. "Maybe I should bring him back. Just get him some help or something. Don't we owe him that much?"

"Owe him?" she asked. "First of all, we can't afford to get him help, Dante. We can barely afford to replace him." She held up her still-bandaged arm. "And this? You remember how this happened, right?"

"I do, babe, but maybe with this review . . . I don't know, maybe we'll find someone else quicker. In the interim, it's going to have to be me," I said. "And we will be busy after this."

Kira donned a smile that I hadn't seen in a long time. Too long. She took my hand.

"This is the best thing that could've happened to us, Dante. We needed some good news and now we have it."

I placed my hand over hers. "So long as we don't screw it up. It's do or die from here on out."

* * *

The restaurant opened for prep work at 10 a.m. I arrived ahead of Kira. We usually drove separately because I stayed late to close, and she often needed to drive to the market to shop for fish and produce. Anything that we didn't have delivered daily from one of our usual vendors. But I wasn't the first to arrive. Sous chef Naomi was already at her station.

"Good morning," I said. "Are you the first one here?"

Naomi set down her knife and regarded me with a smile, but underneath it, seemed to lie apprehension. "So far."

I held up my phone as I made my way toward her. "You saw the review?"

"I did," she replied. "Is Kira happy with it?"

"We both are." She looked at my hand as I placed it on her shoulder. I pulled it away and cleared my throat. "I should get to work before Kira gets here." As I headed into the manager's office, Naomi called out.

"Dante?"

I stopped and turned back. "Yeah?"

"What are we doing tonight?"

"Don't worry. I'll be your backup. You good with that?"

Naomi smiled. "Yes. I think I am."

"Good. I just need to take care of a few things first, and I'll help you and the rest of the team prep." I entered the office, setting down my laptop bag on the floor next to the desk. The office door was still open, and I glanced back at Naomi. She'd come from a good culinary school and had worked in the business for only a year, but she was talented. It was exactly the reason I'd hired her. And she and Eric had worked well together. But could she handle being head chef? I wasn't sure. I turned away when she caught me watching her.

The computer was up and running and I scanned through my emails. Lots of congratulatory words from my peers. Yeah, it felt pretty good getting that review from Otis Oliver. Despite all that had gone down with Eric, and the injury to Kira, I felt we were over the hump now. But a lot would depend on how we performed from here, without our head chef.

An incoming call captured my attention. I snatched my phone that lay on the desk. "Shit." I answered it. "Eric, how are you?"

"I just wanted to congratulate you and Kira on the Otis Oliver review," he said.

"Thank you. I appreciate it, and I do know that it was because of your talents." A line could easily be crossed right now, and I had to choose my words carefully. What I didn't want was for Eric to go public with the fact he was no longer La Bianca's head chef, and regardless of the review, the quality of the dishes might suffer. "I want you to know that Kira and I wish only the best for you, Eric. We want you to get the help you need."

"Sure, yeah, I get that," he began. "Listen, I thought I should call to offer my congratulations, but also to say that, you know, things are going to be tight for me for a while. Despite all that went down, I'd appreciate a letter of recommendation from you."

I closed my eyes and rubbed my forehead. "I'm not sure that's going to fly with Kira, after the knife incident and then her seeing what she saw."

"Here's the thing, Dante. And I'm gonna need you to hear me on this." He paused and inhaled a deep breath. "If you don't write that letter, I'll tell Kira you knew all about my habit, you feel me on this?"

Motherfucker. "Yeah, I feel you, man."

"Oh, and another thing . . . you do this for me," Eric continued, "I'll make sure to keep my mouth shut about the money, too. I'll meet you after closing to pick up the letter. Man, I really appreciate it, Dante."

If that son of a bitch was standing in front of me right now, I'd punch his face. Then again . . . "Sure, man. No problem."

CHAPTER 5: KIRA

For the first time since we signed the papers on the restaurant, I believed that we were going to be okay. So much so, in fact, that I let myself enjoy the morning sun driving with the top down on my Mercedes. I felt free. I wrapped my hair in a silk scarf and donned sunglasses. I couldn't deny that vintage Hepburn coming out of me. This was LA, after all.

Despite the fact that the stitches on my arm had begun to itch, I enjoyed the drive into work, relishing the good fortune that had come our way. And on my arrival, I spotted Dante's black Porsche Carrera. I'll admit, we'd fallen hard into that trap of keeping up with the Joneses — in other words, our peers who also owned restaurants. I wondered whether they, too, were in as much debt as we had been. If so, they didn't show it.

I turned into the parking lot, feeling like the load had been lightened. Yes, we had challenges ahead of us, particularly finding a new head chef, but no one was going to dampen my mood today. Not when we'd gotten such a fabulous review.

Stepping out of my car, I pulled off the scarf and tousled my hair. I walked through the rear entrance. "Good morning." Naomi stood at her station and the other line cooks appeared to have just arrived. I removed my sunglasses. "Where's Dante? Shouldn't he be helping?"

"In here," he called out.

He stood in the doorway of my office. *Our* office. "Hi."

"Hi," he said. "You want to go over last night's receipts?"

"Sure." I carried on through the kitchen and into the office. "I see everyone's busy. How's Naomi taking things?" I closed the door behind me.

"Seems fine so far. We'll go through this, and then I'll jump in and give the guys a hand."

"Okay." I sat down at the computer, sensing that something had changed in Dante. As though the shine from the glowing review had already tarnished. "Is everything okay?"

"Fine, yeah. It's just going to be a little crazy around here."

It would take a moment to check the reservation system to see whether we were going to have a full house tonight. I held my breath. The screen populated and there it was, the reservation list for tonight.

"Oh, my God. Have you seen this yet?" I subdued my giddiness and gauged Dante's reaction. "We're fully booked. Tonight. Tomorrow night. Monday night. We are booked solid, babe."

"That's great news," he replied.

I looked at him with a pinched brow. "Maybe you should tell that to your face."

"It's just a lot of pressure." He stepped closer. "Can you pull the receipts? I want to see where we landed last night."

"Yeah, okay." I supposed he wasn't ready to count his chickens, unlike I had. My fingers clicked on the keys and soon, more information came up. And as I scrolled to the bottom of the page, the numbers in bright red stood out. "Damn it."

"Son of a bitch." Dante lowered his gaze and rubbed the back of his neck. "How the hell did we lose money again?"

"Everything's expensive," I said. "We're still disputing that charge from the butcher. But you need to look at the bigger picture. Things are bound to turn around now."

"We didn't break even. Why not? What the hell do you keep buying?"

He'd raised his tone at me. I felt my cheeks flush with irritation. "I buy what's necessary to make the dishes you created, all right?"

"You have to find other vendors, Kira." He tapped his index finger on the screen hard enough to shake it. "We can't keep spending like this. Good review or not, we'll never get ahead this way."

"You think I don't know that?" Now my voice was raised, and everyone was going to hear us. "And now we have to find another head chef."

"Naomi will do fine in the interim." He stood in defiance.

I smirked at him, ready to take another jab. "I'm sure she will." Dante didn't think I noticed the way he flirted around her. What an asshole.

He thrust his hands in the air. "What the hell is that supposed to mean?"

"Nothing. Just go. I have to finish this." I turned my back to him, pretending to study the screen, when I was really just waiting for him to leave. Soon, I heard him stomp away, slamming the door behind him.

"Goddamn it." I shook off the tension that had built up. "He's under a lot of pressure. Cut him some slack." That was what I had to keep telling myself, but the stress of it all was affecting our marriage and had been for some time.

The only thing I could do was to try to find other vendors, cheaper vendors who maintained the kind of quality we needed. That review could easily be updated to reflect a downward change. I couldn't let that happen.

I picked up the phone and started making calls. My mind raced with all the things that needed to be done. In the background, Dante's voice carried as he barked orders at the kitchen staff. I almost couldn't hear the guy on the other end of the line. "Thank you, yeah, I'll come take a look this morning. I appreciate it. Bye."

My notepad was next to me, and I jotted down the list of potential new vendors. It was the perfect excuse to get the hell out of here for a while. When Dante got like this, he couldn't be reasoned with.

I grabbed my keys, making my way out of the office and through the kitchen to the dining area. No one said anything to me, least of all, my husband. Angelo had arrived and had already made himself at home in the dining room.

Gavin was setting up the bar and Angelo had a drink in his hand.

"Kira," Angelo smiled, setting down his Bloody Mary. "Good morning, sweetheart. How are you today? I saw the review. Good news, yes?"

"Very good news. Good morning, Angelo." I didn't say anything about the drink. What was the point? "Dante wasn't happy about the receipts from last night, though, so any good vibes we had are gone now."

"I'm sorry to hear that." Angelo removed the celery stalk from the drink and took a sip. "You know my brother. It's always something. He never could appreciate what was right in front of him. Fuck him, right?"

I chuckled. "Yeah, fuck him."

* * *

The nearest farmer's market was about ten miles away, on the edge of the downtown area. The drive was necessary for me to clear my head, and I was grateful for it. The palm tree-lined streets. The blue sky dotted with fluffy clouds. I reminded myself that things would be better soon, and that I needed to see this through. Walking away wasn't an option.

As I arrived, it seemed there weren't many cars, so I wondered if the produce had already been picked over. Most of the restaurant owners came here, some to another market to buy their daily produce. But I was here to scope things out, pick up what we needed, and maybe look at saving a buck or two by rubbing elbows with some of the newer suppliers.

A few people still milled around as I made my way inside. Maybe I wasn't the last to the party. The colors always amazed me. Fruits, vegetables. All beautifully presented. I decided on a booth and smiled at the man behind it.

"Good morning. What can I get for you today?" he asked, wearing a grin on his weathered face.

"I'll take two dozen heirloom tomatoes and eight bunches of asparagus, please," I replied, eyeing the vibrant red and yellow tomatoes on display.

"Which restaurant are you with?" he asked.

"La Bianca's. Downtown," I replied.

"Of course. Congratulations," he added, still packing my order.

I was a little surprised word had gotten around so fast. "You saw the review?"

"Of course, I did. For a restaurant open barely a month, I'd say you're doing all right." He walked to the register and keyed in the numbers. "That'll be $108.65, please."

I handed over the company credit card, which was nearly maxed out. "Here you go." When he swiped it, my heart stopped for a moment, praying the transaction would go through. When the machine spit out a receipt, I felt relieved. "Listen, if you know of anyone looking for a head chef position, I'd love to hear about it."

He handed over the receipt. "What happened to yours?"

"Quit last night. Just up and quit." It was a risk putting this out there, but I needed references and fast. Thought I'd leave out the whole snorting-coke thing, though.

"I'm sorry to hear that, and especially after the review. I'll keep my ears open." He glanced at my card, ready to hand it over. "You have a good day, Ms. Lucini."

"Thank you. You, too."

As I returned to my car, I realized there was one other stop I'd wanted to make. A block over, a building had been under renovation. I'd seen it before, but today, I'd noticed a sign had been posted on the front window. Turned out, it was going to be a restaurant. Always wanting to keep abreast of the competition, I wanted to scope it out.

The windows were covered in brown paper, and the large sign posted read, "Sunset 717 Restaurant Coming Soon." Good name.

The front door was partially exposed, and I cupped my hand over my brow, peeking inside. The walls were adorned with intricate murals, but otherwise, it appeared far from completion. I was lost in thought, and didn't notice the man standing behind me until he spoke.

"Can I help you?" he asked, his voice deep and smooth.

Startled, I turned around as though I'd been caught red-handed. For what, I had no idea. The man was at least six feet. Appeared well-built under his form-fitted black T-shirt. But what struck me was how green his eyes were. Jesus, had I ever seen eyes so green? "I was just . . . um . . . looking." *Stop staring. Stop staring.* "You work here?"

"This is my restaurant. As you can see, we're not open yet," he replied.

"Right, of course. I'm sorry to be so nosy." I stepped away when he called out.

"Hey."

I stopped cold and slowly turned around to face him again. "Yes?"

"Are you in the restaurant business?"

"I am. Is it that obvious?" I asked.

"To be completely honest with you . . ." He walked toward me. "I saw you at the market buying a lot of produce. Figured you were one of us. Why don't you come in? I'd love to pick your brain if you have a few minutes. I have coffee."

I agreed without a second thought. "Sure. I guess I have a few minutes."

He keyed the lock and opened the door, holding it open for me to enter. So I did. The interior was rustic with wooden tables and chairs stacked together. The smell of fresh paint nearly knocked me over. "I don't know what you have planned, but it looks like it's taking shape."

He walked over to the unfinished bar and the coffee pot that rested on its top. "Slowly but surely. You must know all about that." He gestured to a nearby table. "Have a seat."

"Thanks." I pulled out a chair, feeling awkward as he poured my coffee.

With two mugs in hand, he headed toward me. "My name's Marco."

"I'm Kira."

He joined me at the table. "So, Kira, you were at the market and saw this place?"

"Uh, yeah, I guess I did. I own La Bianca's. It's an Italian place downtown. Well, my husband and I own it. I saw the renovations here and thought I'd look for inspiration," I replied, sipping on the strong brew. "We just went through this, so I can relate."

Marco raised an eyebrow. "La Bianca's? I've heard of it. In fact, I'm sure I just read something recently." He grabbed his phone.

"The review," I cut in. "The Otis Oliver review in the *LA Times*. Yeah, that was us. Just came out today, as a matter of fact."

"Then why are you looking for inspiration? You should be the one inspiring others," he said with a grin.

Guilt was getting the better of me, so I confessed. "Look, I'll be honest with you, I was here for the market, but when I saw this place, I guess I wanted to check out the competition."

Marco surveyed the unfinished dining room. "We're far from being your competition. Not only in distance, but clearly, we're not even open yet. I do, however, appreciate your candor."

I jerked a thumb over my shoulder. "I should probably head back. I need to get the produce to the kitchen."

Marco nodded as he stood to join me. "Of course, I understand. But promise me you'll come back when we're open. I'd love to get your thoughts."

I looked around the restaurant, taking in the details of the decor. "I'd love that. What's your specialty going to be?"

He walked over to me. I took half a step back as he stood unexpectedly close. A grin played on his lips as he leaned into my ear. "I make a mean risotto."

CHAPTER 6: DANTE

The clock on the kitchen wall displayed 3 p.m. The sound of chopping, pans clinking, and oven timers going off brought home the reality that we would open in just a few hours. I double-checked my watch to be sure, and wondered where the hell Kira was. She'd only gone to the market. If she had bought anything, it was too late to be used tonight. Might as well burn the money she spent instead.

Dressed in my black suit with a dark gray shirt, I smoothed out any wrinkles and walked to the front of house. We were set to be fully booked tonight, and it was the first time since we'd opened that I had felt so nervous. The dining room windows overlooked the street and I saw Kira's Mercedes pulling into the rear parking lot. "Finally."

I returned to the kitchen when the back door opened, letting in light from the afternoon sun. Kira emerged from the rays behind her. Her hair captured them, making it appear platinum blond instead of strawberry. And it wasn't pulled back the way it had been when she'd left earlier. Her hands were full, and I caught up to her. "Let me get one of those for you."

"Thanks, I got it."

She walked by me, straight into the pantry, and set down the items. I trailed her. "I expected you back sooner. We won't be able to use any of this tonight."

Kira turned around, blowing the hair from her face. "It'll keep for a day. I got caught up at this new restaurant near the market. I met the owner."

"Oh yeah?" I rocked back and forth on my heels, casually shoving my hands in my pockets. "And that's where you've been for the past three hours, knowing what we're up against tonight?"

That look appeared on her face. The slight tilt of her head. Exasperation mixed with disappointment. Gotta be honest, for a minute, I wanted to slap her. It's not in my DNA, so I never would, but that didn't change the fact I wanted to.

"I needed some space, Dante, all right? I needed to clear my head. Besides, I wasn't there the whole time. I did do some shopping and got information from a couple of potential new vendors."

If I took this farther, it would only result in another clash, and we were too close to opening. "Forget about it. We can't afford to blow this. People have seen the review. You only need to look at the reservation list to know that."

"I'm well aware, Dante."

I raised my hands in surrender. "Then let's just get back to business."

"Fine by me." Kira nodded.

There was something in her eyes that I couldn't ignore. Like she was done with me or something. Maybe I had pushed her too far. After all, she wasn't solely to blame for the restaurant losing money. And she wasn't to blame for Eric either.

She stayed in the pantry, meticulously organizing the ingredients she'd just purchased. I had nothing else to say and time was short, so I returned to the staff and finished preparations. Still, I wondered what the hell she'd been up to.

* * *

Dinner service had gone off without a hitch. Naomi came through, and so had the rest of the staff. To say I was relieved would be the understatement of the year. If only that had been the last of my worries.

Secrets could destroy a marriage. But if Kira ever learned that I'd made a deal with Eric, writing him a recommendation so he'd keep his mouth shut about the money, my marriage would be as good as done. Oh, and the whole thing in regard to me knowing about Eric's habit? Could I give her a better excuse to leave me?

Kira leaned into the doorway of the office. Her bag over her shoulder. "I'm taking off. See you at home?"

"Yeah, sure. Drive safe." I should say it. I know I should. It might not help much, but it wouldn't hurt. "I love you," I called out as she walked away.

"Love you, too."

She didn't even look back. I raised my gaze to the ceiling and inhaled a deep breath. "This too shall pass."

"What will?" Angelo appeared, holding a glass of wine. His bloodshot eyes suggested he'd had several already.

"Nothing," I said. "I have a few things to finish up, and then I'll drive you home."

"I have my car," he replied.

"You think I'm letting you get behind the wheel? Think again, pal."

Angelo donned a crooked smile. "I didn't know you cared so much."

"The fuck I do. I just don't want to get sued if you kill someone." I waved him off. "Give me twenty minutes." Harsh words, but he'd caught me at a bad time. I learned long ago that I wasn't going to change my brother. And he sure as hell wasn't going to change himself.

When you're told your entire life that you'll take over the family bakery, then your mom and pop die in that very bakery in a fire, it tended to mess with your head. Angelo never recovered. Neither had I, but I stayed sober. That was the only good thing I could think about myself.

I glanced into the kitchen. Everyone was gone. The place was clean. Angelo had gone back to the dining room for another drink, no doubt. I was alone and I walked to the safe inside an electrical closet in the office. We kept cash in there in case of emergency, like if we ran out of stuff to make marinara or some shit.

The combination was easy. Ma's birthday. I punched the numbers and the little green light flashed, and the click sounded. I opened it to see two bundles of cash inside. Kira knew the combination too, and we hadn't needed to get into this for a while. But I couldn't exactly write Eric a check, now, could I? Son of a bitch wanted cash. I considered having him arrested, but we didn't need the bad press, so I was going to let him blackmail me. And hope he didn't come back for more. Things might turn ugly if that happened.

I grabbed one of the bundles and counted out the bills. A cool grand was what he'd asked for. Not a lot of money to some; a shit ton to others. For me, it stung, more for the principle of the thing than anything else. And Eric knew we were broke, so I guess he figured he would cut me a break. But if Kira noticed it was missing, she'd come at me with a cleaver to my balls. A regular Lorena Bobbitt situation. I laughed, but knew secretly, it was possible.

The safe clicked again as I closed the door. Now, I had to wait for Eric. He was due to arrive in about five minutes. Guess I'd better head out back and wait. Just get this shit over with so I could go home.

The night air felt warm on my skin. It took some getting used to, this Southern California weather. I almost missed the snow — almost. The stars were barely visible. It was too bright here to see them. And when I spotted headlights, I figured it was Eric. Was this the right way to handle things? Only if I wanted to keep the status quo and get this damn restaurant off the ground.

Eric stepped out of his Cadillac Escalade. All of us were guilty of playing the part — looking successful even if we weren't there yet. It was the LA scene. Take it or leave it.

I sniffed and ran a finger under my nose, acting like this was about to be some kind of mafia deal, and I was Tony Soprano. Eric walked toward me. "Hey."

"Hey," he replied, shifting his gaze. "You have it?"

"I said I would, and I do." I pulled out the envelope that contained the recommendation and another that contained the cash. "You did this to yourself, man. I don't know why I'm even going through with it."

"Cause you don't want Kira to find out what you did." He took both envelopes. "I'm sorry it had to be this way. I really am. I love you like a brother, Dante; you should know that."

"My brother's a raging alcoholic, but he'd never stab me in the back like you're doing right now. Listen, uh, good luck, all right? But you should know I don't want to see you around here anymore, got it?"

"I have no intention of coming back."

Eric sized me up and I thought for a minute, he might throw a punch. "What you did to Kira the other night, that shit's on you," I said. "And the fact you're doing this shows me your true colors."

"I didn't mean to hurt her, Dante," he replied. "Look, it's done now. We don't have to see each other anymore. Take care, man." Eric turned around and headed back to his Escalade.

I watched him climb inside and start the engine. A moment later, he was gone. And when I turned back toward the restaurant, I saw Angelo standing in the doorway of the rear exit. The look on his face hinted that he'd seen more than I would've preferred. "You ready to get out of here, or what?" I asked him as I approached.

"Ready when you are, brother."

* * *

Our home was cast in darkness and shadow when I entered. The living room windows let in the lights from the city down the hill, but hardly enough to see my hand in front of my face. It felt peaceful, though. Maybe I needed a little of that after tonight. But it was over now, and we could move on. I'd dropped off Angelo at his condo and took the long way home. It was two in the morning. Kira was probably sound asleep by now.

I set down my keys on the entry table and slipped off my dress shoes. I hadn't had to cook like that in a long time, and even though I wore my apron, my shoes looked worse for wear from all the shit I spilled. "Damn cheese sauce." Not to mention, my feet were sore as hell. It felt good — for a while. Then I remembered how tough a job it was.

Finding another head chef was going to be a bitch, and we didn't have time to mess around looking. I needed to call on acquaintances to see if they knew of anyone looking for work. One more thing to put on my list for tomorrow.

The tile floor felt cool under my sweaty socked feet. I pulled off my suit jacket and laid it over one of the dining chairs. It'd be nice to sit outside and enjoy the breeze, but I was exhausted and needed sleep. Tomorrow would come whether I wanted it to or not. So, I shuffled down the hall toward my bedroom.

The door was slightly ajar, and I pushed it open to see Kira laying on her side with her back to me. She was just a silhouette. Her tiny figure, curved inward. Her hands tucked under her head. Her hair fanned out on the pillow. I took off my shirt and pants and slid quietly under the lightweight covers. A ceiling fan blew cool air on my arms, and I exhaled.

Kira rustled a little, turning over to face me. "It's late."

"I know. I had to take Angelo home."

"Figures," she said as she moved in closer to me. "I'm sorry about today. I should've helped you get everything ready, not taken time for myself."

"Sometimes it's necessary. I get it," I replied. And then I felt her pull in even closer, laying her hand on my hip. "Your arm," I said.

"I'll be fine." She pressed her warm lips against mine, a slight moan sounding from her. My hand slipped from her cheek to her shoulder and then to her bare breast. I closed my eyes as my groin tingled. It had been weeks since we'd made love. I wasn't going to stop because I was tired.

47

"I love you," I whispered.

She climbed on top of me. "I love you, too."

* * *

Kira had left early this morning. She was gone before I was out of the shower. We didn't say much to each other last night, but I'd hoped that our being intimate meant a clean slate today. I would soon find out as I drove to the restaurant and arrived with the sun hovering over the high-rise buildings. The sky looked clearer today. A good sign the rest of the day would go well. That was what I told myself, anyway.

When I walked in through the rear entrance, I saw the light on inside the manager's office. No staff had yet arrived. I'd half-expected to see Naomi. After last night, I'm pretty sure she had hopes of an offer for the head chef position. As much as I'd love to give her that shot, I knew she wasn't ready for it.

"Good morning," I said, standing in the office doorway. "I didn't hear you leave the house earlier."

Kira looked at me with worry in her eyes. "Sorry, I wanted to get in and start making some calls. We need a replacement, Dante. I'm freaking out about this."

I walked inside and perched on the edge of her desk, unbuttoning my suit jacket. "It's okay. We have Naomi. She did great last night. We can go for a while until we find the right person."

"And how long can you burn the candle at both ends?" she asked. "You're trying to run front of house and be head chef? It's not sustainable."

I could see her vulnerability, and a part of me wanted to take her in my arms. But I knew my wife, and I knew she would take it as though I didn't think she could handle the stress. To be honest, it wasn't her strongest suit either.

"We'll make some calls this morning and find out who's looking. That's how we have to play this right now and keep our fingers crossed."

She nodded but looked about a million miles away. "I feel like our hope of a Michelin star is getting pushed farther and farther away. Like it might be unattainable altogether."

"That has been our goal, yes," I began. "But that was a far-off goal to begin with. It could be years. We both know that, but I have faith that we will get there. Otis Oliver's review is a good start."

My attention was drawn to the back door as staff began to arrive. "I see Naomi. I'd better get with her about tonight's menu." I stood up and noticed Kira's phone ringing. The caller ID displayed "Unknown." She caught me looking at the screen and I suddenly felt like I'd intruded on her privacy. "I'll catch up with you later, babe."

She answered the call as I walked out of the office. Her voice was high-pitched, as though she was speaking to a friend she hadn't heard from in a long time. I didn't turn back, and instead, headed toward Naomi.

"Good morning," I said to her.

"Morning, Chef," she replied.

Her long brunette hair was pulled back in a ponytail, exposing her high cheek bones that were dusted with a soft shade of pink. When she smiled, her entire face lit up. I soon realized I'd been staring at her and cleared my throat. "So, let's go over tonight's menu, and we'll start getting everything ready to prep, okay?"

"Yes, Chef. Ready when you are," Naomi replied.

I donned my chef's jacket and walked around next to her. "I thought we'd work on something that goes back a ways in my family."

"Sounds great. What is it?" she asked.

I noticed Kira emerge from the office and walk over to us. She appeared happy. Maybe it had been the phone call.

"Someone's coming in to interview for head chef," she said, appearing hardly able to contain her excitement.

"Oh, you're bringing someone in without discussing it with me first?" I asked.

Kira raised her hands in defense. "This was unexpected. That call I just got? It was a recommendation from the owner of Brindi's. He'd heard we were looking—"

"How?" I interrupted.

"I asked around yesterday at the market. I assume word got out that way. But what's important here is that we have someone, right?"

"I guess so." I felt Naomi's stare, but kept my eyes on Kira. "Okay, so when is this person coming?" I looked at the clock. "We need to keep moving."

"Yeah, I said that, but he can be here in about an hour." She raised her shoulders. "What do you think? I mean, this is good, right? Brindi's is an amazing restaurant. A recommendation from them means something."

"He? Yeah, no, you're right," I stammered. "Okay, I'll get Naomi set up and be ready to talk to this guy in an hour."

"Great. I'll call back to confirm." Kira spun around and marched back to the office.

Naomi had busied herself with prepping the ground sausage. When Kira was out of sight, I looked at her. "Should we get back to it?"

"Yes, Chef," Naomi replied.

Her tone had changed. I knew then we were going to have to talk about this, and that I would have to explain why she couldn't be considered for the job. But as usual, I chose to sweep it under the rug and grabbed the list of items for tonight's special.

Our words were kept at a minimum for the next hour. And now, I had to get ready to meet with some chef I had no idea about, but that Kira seemed excited for. I removed my jacket. "I'll let you keep going while I take this meeting."

"Yes, Chef," she replied.

I sighed, but kept it low enough that she didn't hear. At least, I didn't think she did. The kitchen was busy once again, and I noticed Angelo push through the kitchen door. "Can't talk right now. Kira arranged an interview for a new chef."

50

"That's great news, but I was really just wanting to say that you're out of pinot noir."

I stopped dead. "We are? Damn it. How about you make yourself useful then, and when Gavin comes in, let him know, so he can re-stock before we open."

"You got it. And good luck." Angelo disappeared into the dining room again.

I reached the office and leaned in. "Should we meet out front in one of the booths?"

"That's what I was thinking." Kira grabbed a folder.

"What's in there?" I asked.

"Our menu. Some questions I wanted to ask him. Stuff like that." She walked out ahead of me.

"Okay. Good." I pulled on my suit jacket from the back of her chair and trailed her into the dining room. Angelo was at the bar, sipping on a white. "Hey, Ang . . . you mind getting lost for a while? We're going to interview this guy out here," I said.

He turned up his palms. "Where the hell you want me to go?"

"I don't know, man, just go to the back office or something," I said, brushing him off.

Kira set down the file at one of our larger booths near the back, one with a nice view of the streetscape outside. I grabbed a pitcher of water and three glasses, carrying them back to the table. "Just in case."

"Good idea," she said. "I think I see him now." Kira walked to the door with the keys in her hand. She unlocked it and her face changed.

I narrowed my gaze as the man walked inside. I had no idea who he was, but I had a feeling Kira knew him.

She showed him to the booth, still wearing a strange look.

I stood up with an outstretched hand. "Hi, I'm Dante Lucini. Nice to meet you."

She gestured to the guy. "Dante, this is Marco Devaney."

He had a firm handshake, which I respected. Good-looking guy. About my age, I'd guess. Maybe a little younger. "Thanks for coming in. Have a seat."

"Appreciate it." He unbuttoned his jacket and slid into the booth.

I gestured for Kira to slide in the other end, and when I moved in after her, I looked at the two exchanging a glance. "I'm sorry, but I have to ask, do you two know each other?"

CHAPTER 7: KIRA

When I saw his face, I couldn't believe it was him. Dante had waited near the booth; I had unlocked the front door and immediately recognized Marco as he approached. How was this possible? The man said he owned that restaurant and hadn't given me his last name. Why would he be here now, and under a recommendation from one of the best restaurants in town?

Marco looked at me after Dante posed the question. I should've jumped at it, preempting any response from the man who now sat across from us. Instead, I froze.

"Well, you know, I met Kira yesterday, actually," Marco began. "She walked into a restaurant that was under renovation, and I was there to offer my insight to the owners, who I'd known from way back. I'd asked if she wanted to have a look around."

"And so I did," I cut in. "It was that place I told you about, Dante. Remember?"

"Vaguely," he replied. "I thought you'd said you'd met the owner, though."

Marco placed his hand on his chest. "Well, that was my fault. It was a complicated situation, and I thought it was just easier to say that I owned it, rather than explain why I had a key and what I was doing there."

I couldn't believe what he was saying. Was any of it true? "I get it. I was just some strange woman peeking through the door. It's fine. I'm glad you're here." I touched Dante's arm. "We're glad you're here. You come highly recommended by the owners of Brindi's."

"I've known them for a long time," Marco said. "They're the true owners of that new place near the market. It's their second location, but they'll be opening under a new name, Sunset 717. I spoke to them after you and I talked, Kira, and you mentioned you and Dante were looking for a new head chef."

"So they said they'd put in a good word," Dante added. "Fantastic. How about we get started, then?"

I could tell by Dante's voice that he was a little taken aback. To be honest, so was I, but here we were now. Maybe what Marco said was true. He didn't know me. Didn't think he had to explain everything. I guess it made sense. And we really needed the help. From glancing at Marco's resume, he was highly qualified for the position. "I'd just like to cut in a second," I said. "Your resume says you were the sous chef at Lilibell's in Napa Valley. That's a Michelin star restaurant."

"Yes, it is," Marco replied, appearing humbled. "As you can see, I was there for only about seven months. Of course, it was after they'd received their star. I only helped them keep it."

"Why did you leave?" Dante asked.

"Creative differences, I guess you could say. And when their head chef position opened up, they went another way, unfortunately. It wasn't the first time that'd happened to me."

I noticed his eyes darken a little and a slight tic in his lower lip. "What do you mean?"

Marco kept his sights on Dante, but now donned a pleasant grin. "I'm sure you've been there. In this business, it's kill, or be killed. I've seen a few casualties in my time." He shifted his gaze between Dante and me. "Is that your goal here? For La Bianca's to get a star?"

"Someday, yes. Absolutely," Dante replied.

Marco laced his fingers on the table. "Well, maybe I can help make that happen."

To have a chef with his reputation in our employ would enhance our chances of getting that star. La Bianca's was on its way up after the Oliver review. This was our shot at keeping the momentum. But I had to remind him that we weren't Lilibell's. We weren't Brindi's. La Bianca's was still an upstart, and our budget for head chef reflected that.

"We couldn't match what you were making at your previous restaurant," I began.

Dante nudged my arm. "What Kira means to say is that we'd have to come to an agreement. We would have to start you off with less than you're used to, but, if in the next year, you could help put us on the map, well, we could start talking about percentages of sales."

Marco surveyed the dining room. His lips turned down as he seemed to assess the details of this potential arrangement. I wasn't sure about Dante's proposal, but it would solve our immediate problem, assuming he agreed to the salary, which was yet to be stated.

"I'd be thrilled to work with you and your staff," Marco finally said. "I like what you've done here. I'm impressed by the review."

And then Marco did something strange. He looked at me, *through* me, actually. Those green eyes. I had no idea if Dante picked up on it, but I felt a jolt of electricity from head to toe. I had to shake off the feeling as I turned to my husband. "Well, what do you think?"

Dante raised his chin, eyeing Marco for a moment, when a smile seemed to tug at his lips. "I say, if you're available, let's see what you can do tonight. You'll get a chance to see how we operate. Sample the dishes. See if it's a place you want to be. I'll pay you a consultant's fee. And if you decide to stay on, and we're all happy with the team, then we move forward."

"What do you say?" I asked Marco. "Are you free tonight?"

He extended his hand, offering it to Dante. "Yes, I am."

* * *

In a kitchen with two other line cooks, a butcher chef, pastry chef, and all the rest that made a kitchen run, bringing on a new Chef de Cuisine, or head chef, took finesse. Egos were fragile in a kitchen. Ours was no exception.

We introduced Marco to the staff, and all of them seemed skeptical, but it was Naomi who seemed most reluctant. Dante and I had already discussed promoting her, but neither of us believed she was ready. And I can admit that part of me was happy to keep Dante out of the kitchen and let Marco do the job.

The doors opened and the dining room was full. We were booked solid once again. I knew we were tempting fate letting Marco prove himself only days after receiving the glowing review, but how better to test his mettle than to throw him into the fire?

As I emerged from the back office, I noticed Dante looming over the stations, inspecting each plate, ensuring absolute perfection.

"Hey," he said to Expo. They're the guys who prep salads and other such things.

"Yes, Chef?" The young man carried a steel bowl and stopped in front of Dante.

Dante peered into the bowl. "What are you going to do with that shredded cheese?"

"Uh, I was going to rinse out the bowl, Chef," he replied.

Dante raised his brow, and I watched the Italian in him come out. "I could make a whole pizza with what you got left in there. Don't throw that out."

"Yes, Chef. I mean, no, Chef, I won't." He hurried away from Dante, back to his station.

Orders were being called out. Marco seemed to slip right into the shoes left vacant by Eric. And I couldn't help but notice how he seemed to charm Naomi.

She smiled more than I'd seen her smile in a long time, especially during dinner service. I felt a twinge of envy, wondering what it was like to stand beside Marco, working together with him.

My senses were aroused by the enticing aroma of oregano, garlic, and olive oil, hinting at the culinary delight to come. I watched him. With a skilled hand, he selected the ingredients. Vibrant tomatoes, fragrant basil, and portabella mushrooms lined up on the cutting board as he expertly diced and chopped. He sliced the fresh mozzarella, placing it on a towel to dry.

He drizzled the olive oil in the pan, a sizzle filling the air. Marco's focus was unwavering, his culinary prowess on full display. He moved with grace and precision, adding the arborio rice to the chicken stock. A dash of sea salt to the pot.

I looked on in amazement. Eric had been an excellent chef, but this . . . this was the work of a master. I lost myself in his movement, but when I felt a hand on my back, I was startled to see Dante.

"What do you think so far?" he asked.

"He's amazing," I replied, glancing back at him. I noticed how Dante kept his eyes on Naomi — his mouth downturned, his hands clasped behind his back, offering a disapproving glance. "What's wrong?" I asked.

"Nothing." He thumbed back. "I'll see how things are going out front. I'm sure Angelo is already three sheets, you know?"

"Okay."

He walked through the door and looked back at Naomi. She turned away and I realized she had been watching Dante, too. Marco then caught sight of my gaze and smiled. He tipped his head, and I nodded in reply.

The tickets spit out of the machine that lay at the server's station near the door to the front of house. Jonah pushed inside and headed straight toward it, peering at the orders as if double-checking they were correct.

I was only a few feet away when he came through, stopping a moment where I stood. "How's it going out there tonight?" I asked him.

"Great. Everyone seems happy and we're busy," Jonah replied.

That was when I noticed a sort of hesitation in his expression. His lips parted as if ready to speak, but no words came. "Is there something else you wanted to say?"

"I was just wondering why now?" he asked.

"Sorry?" I pinched my brow. "What do you mean?"

"Firing Eric. We really needed him. He got us that good review. And you guys chose to fire him. It's not like we didn't all know what he was doing."

I tilted my head, eying Jonah. "Everyone knew?" It was then that I surveyed the staff, who were all busy doing their jobs. Had they all known, and had Dante and I been completely in the dark? Were we so out of touch with our own people that we'd missed it?

"Well, yeah," Jonah continued. "I guess we assumed you guys did, too."

He grabbed a pitcher of water and returned to the front of house. I stood there, stunned by his admission. He had been outside that night when I saw Eric, but I didn't think he'd picked up on what had been happening. But it made me wonder — had Dante known too? He was the one who helped the staff close out each night. I went home most nights as soon as the last table was served.

It was a question that begged to be asked, but I knew if I did, and I got an answer I didn't want, it would only create more problems. The last thing Dante and I needed were more problems. I peered at my arm, still bandaged. And the thing that hit me the most was if Dante knew, and Eric was high when he did this to me, then he knew he was risking the safety of all of us.

My thoughts carried me away for several moments before our pastry chef captured my attention. "Yeah, sorry, Amy, what's up?"

Amy Rodriguez had been hired on just before we opened. She was twenty-eight with short blond hair worn in a pixie cut. Her cannoli rivaled Dante's mother's, which was the precise reason she'd been hired.

"My brother just texted me." She wiped her eyes that had suddenly reddened. "My dad's in the hospital. I'd like to go see him. I'm so sorry, Kira, I know we're right in the middle of service."

"Hey, no." I gently took her by the shoulders. "You go, all right? We'll be fine. You have everything prepped. I can take over."

"Are you sure? I'm so sorry about this," she said, growing more distraught.

"I'm sure. Now go. Take as much time as you need. Just maybe send me a text tomorrow and let me know what's going on, okay?"

Amy nodded, wearing a rueful grin. "Thank you so much, Kira. Thank you." She removed her jacket and handed it to me. "I'll let you know as soon as I know anything."

"Okay."

She started to walk away, and I called out, "Amy, do you need a ride?" I wasn't sure she should drive in this condition.

"No, thank you. I'll be okay. The hospital's only a few miles from here."

I nodded as she exited through the back.

"Are you taking over for Chef Amy?" Naomi called out.

I pulled on the jacket and started toward the pastry station. "Yes, Chef."

Whatever thoughts I'd had about Eric and what Dante may or may not have known were quickly locked away in the back of my mind. It was time to focus on helping the team get through service. I knew little about what Amy did, but luckily, the girl was on top of her game. She'd prepped all the desserts, and it was only a matter of garnishing with whipped cream or the occasional chocolate sauce. And I had to admit, it felt good being on this side of the fence again. So much so, that I hadn't noticed when Dante approached me.

"Hey, what happened? Where's Amy?" he asked.

"Family emergency," I said. "Her dad's in the hospital. She was pretty upset and asked to leave. I didn't think it would be a problem."

"No, of course not." He eyed the station. "Looks like she's got everything ready to go anyway."

"Yep. I've just been garnishing, so all's good." This wasn't the time to bring up Eric, so I held my tongue. "How are we looking out front? The orders have been going out on time."

"Yeah, no, everything's been going great."

I noticed him glance back at Marco and Naomi.

"They're working well together as a team," Dante continued. "We should count ourselves lucky that he fell into our laps."

"I agree. Listen, I'm good here. You go on — do what you need to do. We're almost through service anyway."

"You sure?" He placed his hand on my back.

"I'm sure." I smiled in reply.

"Okay, then."

He disappeared once again, doing whatever it was that he did. I never really kept track of what he did out front, knowing a lot of it was probably keeping Angelo in line. Dante was the public face of the restaurant, and I let him take that role because I had no interest in it. In fact, I preferred to remain behind the scenes.

I was startled when Marco appeared next to me. "Oh, hi."

"You look like you've done this before," he said, hovering a little close.

"I step in when necessary. Amy had a family emergency."

"Oh, well, I'm so sorry to hear that." Marco glanced back at Naomi. "You have an excellent sous chef back there. She's been showing me the ropes."

"So you've been happy with how tonight's gone?" I asked.

"Absolutely."

His hand slid across my lower back as he stepped closer. I felt both uncomfortable and slightly aroused.

"I'm so happy I met you yesterday, Kira Lucini. I believe this could be the start of something amazing."

* * *

Finally it felt like things were turning around. The review, the bookings, and now we might have found a remarkable chef that could help us achieve our dreams. Money was still a problem and would be for the immediate future. But when I left tonight, I could see it in Dante's eyes too. It was as though we'd made it over the hump. Time would tell, and so would tonight's receipts, but I wanted to enjoy this moment, even if it might not last.

I entered the foyer and switched on the lights. It was midnight and I'd stayed longer than usual. Dante, however, wouldn't likely be home for another hour or two. I'd been so busy that I hardly said two words to Angelo. It was a nice break, actually.

Our bedroom was down the hall, and I slipped off my low-heeled boots. My feet were killing me. I wasn't used to standing at a station for hours. Had I known that was what I'd be doing tonight, I would've chosen more sensible shoes for the job.

After changing into a tank top and shorts, I headed back toward the kitchen and grabbed a bottle of water from the fridge. I stared through the kitchen window at the city lights below. God, I loved it here. The city had its problems, and maybe at some point those problems might creep into our lives. But for now, this was where I wanted to be — to see our restaurant get that Michelin star.

Our overstuffed cream sofa sectional called my name. I dropped onto the cozy seat surrounded by decorative pillows. Dante hated the pillows. Said they got in the way. I said they were necessary for the pop of color. His response was to roll his eyes at me.

With my phone in my hand, I searched Yelp for any new reviews. It was part of my nightly routine. Nothing new posted, but that also meant nothing negative had been posted either.

The night had gone well, all things considered. My thoughts turned to Amy, and I wanted to text her, but it felt like an intrusion. She said she'd contact me, and I had to let it lie.

My attention turned to the front door when keys jiggled in the handle. I checked the time. One a.m. Dante was home early. Was that a good thing or a bad thing?

He walked inside and noticed me looking at him.

"You're still up?" he asked.

"I only got home a little while ago. I didn't expect you to be back so soon," I replied. "Everything okay?"

"Yeah. Marco and I hung around after everyone left. Sat and talked for a bit."

My throat dried and I forced a smile. "Oh, yeah? What about?"

Dante continued inside, dropping his keys into the bowl at the entry table. He slipped off his shoes and padded in socked feet to the kitchen. "Just about his experience. How he thought the night went." He grabbed a bottle of water.

"Oh, and what did he think about how we run things?" I asked, as he walked back to the living room and sat down next to me.

"He thought it was great. Said he had some ideas on how to improve on what we've done, but that we ran a tight ship and he'd be happy to join us." Dante took a drink. "Any word on Amy yet?"

I glanced at my phone that lay on the coffee table. "No, nothing yet. I'm sure she'll text tomorrow."

"I hope her dad is okay," Dante said.

"Me, too."

He looked at me and, in his eyes, I saw regret. "What's wrong?"

"Nothing." He placed his hand on my cheek. "Tonight was a good night. One I hope to repeat. But I have to ask you something."

"Sure." My pulse quickened.

"We don't keep secrets from each other, right?"

CHAPTER 8: DANTE

The only reason I had even entertained the idea of telling Kira
about the money I'd taken was because I was afraid she'd find
out on her own. Tomorrow, she would audit the cash. It was
the end of the month, and the books needed to be balanced.

I'd planned on putting it back, the three grand I'd paid
Otis Oliver to write up the review. Other reviewers had flat out
rejected the suggestion. I never directly came out and offered
to pay them. I only alluded to it, in the event my efforts came
back to haunt me. And now, it seemed that they had.

Eric knew what I'd done. He'd overheard a phone conversation, and I tried explaining to him that I thought it was
a necessary evil. And it wasn't like he was going to spill his
guts because, of course, I knew all about his habit. Mutually
assured destruction kept both of us quiet. Until now.

He also knew that I had taken out a line of credit with
the bank without Kira's knowledge in order to do so. The
money he'd demanded to keep quiet was petty cash from the
safe. Kira would discover it had gone missing. More importantly, the bank wanted payment for the line of credit. She
would figure that out too.

So, that was the real reason I'd stayed behind tonight.
Marco left shortly after Kira had. Soon, they'd all gone home,

and I was left with my brother. But when I realized I had no other means by which to replenish the stores, I knew I'd have to say something to her tonight.

I took Kira's hand as I sat beside her on our sofa, the lights from beyond our windows shining through in shimmery ambers. Admitting to what I knew about Eric was only going to make things worse, so I had to figure a way to say this without mentioning him, or what he'd done.

"Let me start off by saying that I never thought I'd have to do something like this, Kira. You have to know that."

She curled up her legs onto the sofa. "Okay. You're starting to scare me, Dante. What is it?"

"I took out a line of credit without your knowledge." I kept my eyes fixed on her. Nothing about Eric. Nothing about the bribe to Oliver. I just needed to explain away the money. The rest, I could keep to myself. "I had to pay for the stove repairs, the electric bill . . . I'm sorry, I should've told you."

She pulled back. "How much are we talking?"

"Eleven thousand. I paid back a thousand as the first payment. And I'd taken it from the safe." That wasn't true. It was ten. A grand to Eric taken in cash. Three grand to Otis Oliver for the bribe. And I had used the rest to pay for the things I'd mentioned. I wasn't a complete liar.

Her eyes widened, and she leaped off the sofa. "Oh my God. Another eleven thousand dollars? Jesus, Dante. What the hell were you thinking? We already owe one-twenty-five for the first loan. The second mortgage on this place? And that was after the money from Angelo. Now, you borrowed even more without telling me?"

She paced the room, her hands rubbing her forehead. "I assume you're telling me this now because it's the end of the month."

"Yes. I know you'll look in the safe tomorrow when you start on the books. The money's not there. And you'll see the bank statements."

Her shoulders dropped in what appeared to be utter defeat. I felt like a piece of garbage. I *was* a piece of garbage. "I'm so sorry, babe. I should've come clean."

Kira looked up at the ceiling, her hands on her slim hips. The tank top she wore without a bra clung to her full breasts. She was pissed and I was sorry, but I still found her attractive. "I swear to you, babe, it won't happen again. We'll figure out a way to pay all this back. You've seen how busy we are since the review. We're booked for the next two weeks." I moved toward her, sliding my hand around her waist. "I did what I thought I had to do, and I knew I needed to tell you."

"You only said something because you knew I'd find out. If you could've covered it up, I think you would have."

"Don't say that." Now, I really felt like a piece of shit because she had no idea all that I had kept from her. But with Eric out of the way, this was going to work. "I'm asking for your forgiveness. Please, Kira. I screwed up. It won't happen again." I kissed her neck. She resisted, but only for a moment.

"What about Marco?" she whispered. "I want him to stay."

I kissed her lips and then held her gaze. "Do you think he'll give us what we need to get past this? To get that star?"

She bit her lower lip. "Yes, I do."

* * *

Once again, Kira was already gone by the time I woke up. Part of me felt relieved, because at least I'd explained away the cash and the bank. I wouldn't have to deal with that at the restaurant when she opened the books.

I threw off the covers and swung my legs over the bed and onto the cool tile floor. I glanced at our bedroom window. The curtains were still drawn, but light from another sunny day shone around them.

It didn't take me long to get cleaned up. I showered, shaved, and put on my suit. We wouldn't open for hours, but I always wore a suit. I felt I had a part to play, and I'd play it as well as I could. The staff looked up to me, for now. And with Marco coming onboard, I was sure that our fortunes would turn for the better. He seemed all right, even if I was pretty certain he had an eye for Kira. But I wasn't a jealous man. A lot of men found my wife attractive.

I left the house and drove to the restaurant. Kira's Mercedes was in the parking lot and another car, too, that I didn't recognize. Marco's? Guess I'd find out soon enough. I stepped out of my Porsche and entered through the back, as I usually did. Turned out, I was right. That car must've belonged to Marco, because he was at his station, prepping food.

"Good morning," I said. "I didn't expect to see you here yet."

"Just getting a head start on the day. You don't mind, do you?" he asked.

"Not at all. Kira here?"

He nodded. "In the office, I believe."

"Great. Thanks." I carried on, glancing over my shoulder to see that Marco was watching me. Maybe he was admiring my suit. Didn't matter. I knocked on the office door and opened it. "Just me."

"Hi."

It didn't take a genius to see she was already stressed. Her shoulders were raised, her back was hunched over the desk, and her fingers rubbed her right temple.

"That good, huh?" I asked, trying to lighten the mood.

She looked over her shoulder at me, appearing exhausted and fed up. I'm sure a lot of that was directed right at me.

"I'm not sure we can afford to pay Marco what we paid Eric," she said.

I closed the door behind me and crossed my arms. "Why not? I don't think we can get away with paying him any less. The guy comes from good stock."

"I know, but we're so far in the hole, Dante, I don't see how we're getting out."

"But we're booked," I pleaded.

"We are, yes, but unless those who've booked want to pay for their meal up front, we have to find a way to cut costs, especially so we can afford to pay back that line of credit you took out."

And there it was. I should've guessed that played into her equation. "What about cutting staff?"

"No. I'm not laying off anyone. First of all, we'd have to pay unemployment, and secondly, we need each and every one of them. We have a great team. They've only been with us a couple of months. That's not an option."

"Then we need to cut elsewhere," I added. "What about the new vendors you talked about?"

She nodded. "That'll help, but I don't think it'll be enough."

Kira's phone rang. I noticed the caller ID, but didn't recognize the name. She answered the line.

"Hello, this is Kira."

I watched as she listened to the caller. And then she glanced over at me, raising her index finger. I nodded and stepped out of the office. By this time, Naomi had arrived and was with Marco. They were in conversation, each of them smiling at one another while they worked. I walked over to them. "Hey, Naomi. What's going on?"

"Good morning, Dante. Marco and I were just talking."

I suddenly felt as though I'd intruded on a private moment. An inside joke. "Cool. I should probably get to it."

"Anything else you need from me, Chef?" Marco asked.

"Nope. Looks like you two have things under control." I made my way to the back and stepped outside. The sun was in my eyes, and I squinted, which made it almost impossible to see the SUV that approached. It took a moment when I realized who it belonged to. "Shit. What the hell are you doing here?"

Eric stepped out of his Escalade. I firmed my stance as he approached. "What are you doing here, man? I thought our business was settled."

"I heard you found my replacement," Eric said.

"Yeah." I shoved my hands in my pockets. "You had to know that would happen."

"Oh, I figured as much." Eric took a few steps closer. "I had that shit under control, Dante. You knew it. Why didn't you tell Kira?"

"Wouldn't have mattered if I had, Eric. She would've insisted you be fired. And look, I have to think that what happened with her arm was because you were high."

"I had it under control," he insisted.

"Yeah, well, you hurt my wife. Look, man, you need to leave. We settled our business. Don't make this worse than it already is." My attention was drawn to the back door. I hadn't noticed Marco standing there smoking a cigarette.

"Damn it," I whispered. I did not need that guy knowing anything about Eric, let alone seeing him standing here with me. If Kira found out . . . "Hey, man."

"Sorry, am I interrupting?" Marco approached Eric with an outstretched hand. "I'm Marco Devaney. The new chef."

Eric laughed. "I see. Good to meet you, Marco. I'm Eric."

They shook hands, and I felt this wasn't going to end well for me.

"Nice to meet you too, Eric. Are you one of the suppliers?" Marco asked.

"No." Eric shot a look at me. "I used to work here. Listen, I'll let you both get back to it. I know it's gonna get crazy in a bit, so you got your hands full."

"Take care, Eric. Pleasure." Marco walked back inside.

"So that's him, huh?" Eric asked.

"Yeah, I should get back inside." I spun around when Eric called my name. I lowered my gaze and turned back around to him. "Yes?"

"I'm not gonna come back here again, all right, man?" Eric said. "So you don't need to worry about that. I just came to tell you to watch yourself."

I marched toward him, heat rising under my collar. "What did you just say to me?"

Eric raised his hands in defense. "I'm saying you should watch yourself. I've gotten to know Naomi well, all right? The woman has a thing for you and trust me when I say, she wanted my job. Forget what went down between us."

"Forget you blackmailed me?" I asked. "That might be tough."

"All I'm saying is that I've seen the way you are around her — Naomi, I mean. Just watch yourself. You'll fuck up more than just this restaurant."

"Appreciate the marital advice, but it's not needed." I made my way to the door and walked back inside. It took a minute for my eyes to adjust to the room again. I heard Eric's V8 engine rev up and then fade away. He was gone.

I looked at Naomi, who was nudging Marco as if she'd just told him a joke. I wondered why Eric warned me. What had he stood to gain by doing so? Did he know something I didn't?

"So that was the previous chef?" Marco asked me.

Clearly, he'd said something to Naomi and mentioned Eric's name. "Yeah, he was," I said. "We didn't leave on the best of terms."

"I heard," Marco said. "That's too bad. Seems like a nice guy."

* * *

Dinner service was winding down. It had been another successful night. We had been fully booked, and the actions I'd taken to make that happen seemed a distant memory now.

As the last table was leaving, I offered a wave and a smile. "Thank you for coming. Enjoy the rest of your evening."

"Loved it. Thank you," the man replied.

Angelo was sitting near the far end of the dining room at a two-top. I unbuttoned my suit jacket and grabbed the chair across from him, taking a seat. I noticed his eyes were glossed over. His cheeks, flushed from the alcohol. It had been a rocky week and things had started to look up, but I couldn't ignore my brother's worsening condition. "Angelo, look, man, you gotta start making some changes, here."

The corner of his mouth tilted up. "What do you want me to do? I got nothing to offer you or anyone else."

"That's not true, all right? Look, I can put you to work."

Angelo scoffed. "Doing what? You got a pastry chef. I only do desserts, you know that. And I haven't baked in years. Not since . . ."

"Not since Ma and Pop died." I leaned over the table. "I love you, Ang. You know that. Kira loves you, too. We want you around, but I gotta be honest, here, things are tight right now. Like really tight. You're drinking two bottles of wine a night. Expensive bottles. Drinks during the day. Man, I can't let you keep doing that. Not to mention what it's doing to your health."

Angelo reached into his pocket and pulled out his wallet. "You want me to pay for it? Is that what this is about?" He threw a credit card onto the table.

I knew that card was probably maxed out, and I wasn't going to take money from my brother anyway. "I don't want your damn money. I want you to clean yourself up. Get a job. Man, you got talents I don't, and you sit here every night drowning them in booze." I reached for his hand. "I'm scared for you, brother."

Angelo got up from the table and started toward the exit. I jumped up. "Don't think I'm going to let you get behind the wheel."

"I'm getting an Uber. Fuck off." Angelo pushed open the front door and disappeared.

I stared at the door for a moment, wondering if I should stop him. I don't know why I said anything. It has never made a difference, and only makes things awkward between us. "Damn it."

"Everything all right?"

I shot around to see Marco heading toward me. "Yeah. Sure. Everything's fine."

"Was that your brother who just left?" he continued. "He's a funny guy. I had a chance to talk to him earlier."

"He's funny, all right," I said.

"Uh, listen, we got everything buttoned up back there," Marco continued. "Thought I should let you know that we were heading out."

"We?" I asked.

"Yeah, I'm going to grab a drink with Naomi." He cocked his head. "That all right?"

"Of course. It's none of my business what you do outside this place," I said, feeling that twinge of jealousy in my gut.

Marco took a step back, but stopped and raised his index finger. "Oh, there was something . . . I was talking with Kira and happened to mention that I'd met Eric earlier today. She seemed kind of surprised. I hope I didn't overstep."

My cheeks felt a sudden rush of heat. "No, man. Of course not. Have a good night."

"You, too. I did ask if Kira wanted to join me in checking out a couple of wineries up in Napa sometime soon. When she has the time, obviously."

"Okay," I replied, with some hesitation.

"I just figured . . . well, I knew you guys were looking at some new vendors to help save on costs. I know a couple of distributors in Napa who I could get you a good deal with. But I thought Kira would want to meet with them personally first."

"Yeah, no, I think that would be great." I donned a tight-lipped grin. "Have a good night, Marco, and I'll see you tomorrow."

"Yes, Chef."

CHAPTER 9: MARCO

The LA scene was exactly my style, so when Naomi asked me out for a drink after my first shift as the official head chef, I figured, why not? She was cute. Smart. Why not see where this went? It was clear during my first shift at La Bianca's that Naomi was into Dante. I was certain I wasn't the only one to notice. Maybe the only reason she asked me out was to make him jealous.

The inner workings of this restaurant eluded me, for now. It wouldn't take long to pick up on the important things, pushing aside the ones who couldn't or didn't want to help me. As I sipped on my glass of red wine at the bar, Naomi fixed her gaze on me. Behind that gaze appeared to lay some suspicion.

"You look like you want to ask me something," I said to her.

"Just wondering where you came from," she replied, resting her chin on her hand.

"What do you mean? I live in LA. Most recently worked in Napa. Trained a little in Europe and New York." I kept my eyes on her while taking another sip from my glass of wine, knowing I needed to pivot this conversation. "What about you, huh? La Bianca's hired you to help get them off the ground. That's impressive. What did you do before this?"

"I've been in the business for about a year. Started right out of culinary school," she began. "Dante and Kira have been good to me, so far."

That was when I figured her out. She was sizing me up, wondering how long I'd last. Wondering how much longer it would be before she got her shot. "Were you close to the last head chef?"

"Eric?" Naomi tucked a swath of her dark hair behind her ear and donned a closed-lip smile. "He was hired a few months before me, while they were still renovating. The Lucinis brought everyone else onboard about six weeks before opening. Trained us up. Put together the menu. It was fun." She raised her glass to her lips.

Naomi had great lips. And when she set down her glass, they'd been stained a dark red, just like the merlot she drank.

"So, yeah, Eric and I got pretty close. Honestly, I was surprised it took them as long as it did to fire him."

"Why is that?" I asked.

Naomi scoffed. "Everyone knew Eric had a problem with coke. At least, I thought everyone knew. But he was a hell of a chef, so I guess they decided to turn a blind eye."

I took another drink before continuing, "But he was fired, so was it because of drugs?"

"I wasn't there, but Jonah was. Apparently, Kira caught Eric doing a line. That was the end of Eric."

"So, clearly she didn't know about the drugs," I said.

"I guess not."

"That means you think Dante did," I added.

She cocked her head. "Oh yeah. He knew." Naomi threw back the last of her wine.

"Do you think Dante would hire him back if he got help?"

"I don't know. Maybe. But you're here now." She eyed the exit. "Hey, you want to get out of here? I live down the street."

I retrieved my wallet and dropped two twenties on the bar. The bartender approached and I raised my hand. "Keep

73

the change." I looked over at Naomi, who was already standing. "Let's go."

We walked outside into the balmy late-night air. Or was it early morning? Hard to say. The streets still buzzed with well-dressed people and luxury cars. And as I took in the vibe, I realized I was among my people. LA at night was alive with an energy distinctly different from the daytime hustle. Like vampires, we were drawn to this nightlife. Inhibitions disappeared, and the pulsating rhythm of clubs and bars was a powerful lure for those seeking to lose themselves in the after-dark world. And Naomi? She was one of us too. I knew it the moment I laid eyes on her.

"What about my car?" I asked, having parked next to her.

"We can walk back later." Naomi offered her hand.

I took hold of it, feeling the heat between us rise. We walked along the street. Younger, scantily dressed women, moved in packs around us, their faces illuminated by the soft glow of smartphones. Young men in loose jeans and tight T-shirts attempted to worm their way into the packs but seemed to fail miserably. But my only thought was what I would do to Naomi.

Within minutes, we'd arrived at her high-rise apartment building. "This is your place, huh? Nice."

"Thanks." She used her key to unlock the main door.

I trailed her inside, walking toward the elevators when she pressed the button. The doors opened and she stepped in.

"Are you coming?" she asked.

"Yes, I am." I quickly joined her. The doors closed and I noticed she'd pressed the tenth floor button. It only went to twelve. "How long have you . . ."

She swooped in front of me, pushing me backward against the elevator wall, her lips firmly against mine. The handrail along the wall dug into my lower back, but I didn't move. Instead, I clutched her hips and yanked her against my groin. I went hard in an instant. Naomi grabbed my crotch and started kissing my neck. My hands gripped the bar, and I leaned my head back, taking pleasure in her touch.

The elevator doors parted, and she pulled away. I opened my eyes, wondering if anyone stood on the other side. Not that it would've mattered much to me, but this was her building. She might have been embarrassed by that. Then again, Naomi didn't seem to be the type of woman who embarrassed easily.

She led the way down the corridor, and I followed, my head spinning about what awaited me when we stepped into her place.

"This is it." Naomi keyed the lock and opened the door to a darkened room. "Come in." She switched on the light and closed the door.

"This is a great apartment." My gaze wandered, noticing the tidy living room and kitchen. But what struck me as odd was that I saw no picture frames. Friends, family. Nothing. "How long have you lived here?"

"Just after I was hired. The location was perfect." She dropped her keys onto the living room side table. "I moved from New Mexico where I'd gone to school."

"I see. Good to know you do have a past," I replied. The key was to let her take the lead. I could tell that was the way she liked it, and it would be better for me to get what I needed from this encounter.

We moved toward each other, Naomi picking up where she'd left off in the elevator. Her lips still tasted like the merlot, then again, mine probably did too. I let my hand slide down to her breast. She moaned a little as I squeezed.

Naomi unbuttoned my pants and pulled down the zipper.

"Should we take this into the bedroom?" she asked.

I swept her off her feet and carried her to the couch, laying her down. "I can't wait that long."

She pulled off her pants and underwear. I laid down on top of her, stripping down and then sliding into her with ease. Her face twisted with pleasure. And I wondered, was she thinking of me, or Dante? Either way, I would get what I wanted.

* * *

A soft gray hue seeped in through Naomi's closed window blinds. Dawn must have been close. I'd moved to the floor while Naomi slept on the sofa. She was a decent lay, but I'd had better. I surveyed the living room in what scant light came through, searching for her purse. I noticed it on a small table next to the door. I looked to her again.

Naomi snored lightly and she had one arm over her eyes and the other, hanging down off the couch. Now was my chance.

My right leg was asleep, so when I stood, pins and needles shot through it, nearly forcing me down again. I stumbled a little, then regained my balance. Naomi slept through the shuffle. I padded softly to the table and opened her purse.

Her phone rested on top of her wallet. I grabbed it, cupping my hand around the screen and pressing the Home button. It was locked, of course, but I did see notifications of text messages she'd received. And one of them was from Eric. I could only read the first two lines. He'd warned her to be careful around me. That could present a problem. I needed her on my side.

Naomi was still asleep when I glanced back, so now was my cue to leave before she awakened. I grabbed my shoes behind the sofa and, with quiet steps, made my way to the door.

Stepping out into the hall, I closed the door behind me, wincing when it clicked shut. My car was only a few blocks away at the bar where Naomi and I shared a drink. I hadn't expected her to ask me out, let alone take me home. And it was the best possible outcome. Naomi had her own agenda, but so did I.

As I headed outside, I checked the time. Three a.m. Eight hours before my shift was set to begin. My car was exactly where I'd left it and I stepped inside, driving out onto the street ahead. Several minutes later, I arrived at the restaurant near the market. The soon-to-be Sunset 717. The very place I'd met Kira only days earlier.

With the key in hand, I unlocked the door and stepped inside. The granite had been installed on the bar and I noticed an envelope laying on top of it. As I approached, it was my name that had been written on it. I slid my finger under the flap and tore it open, retrieving the note inside. "*We're square now. Leave the key and lock the door behind you.*"

"Not quite, Tom. Not quite."

* * *

The I-10 was a disaster as I drove into work. Worse than usual, and that was saying something. The sun shone in my eyes, and the traffic was snarled at the onramp. I fucking hated LA traffic.

By the time I made it to the restaurant, I recognized the two cars parked in the back lot. They belonged to Kira and Dante. A Porsche and a Mercedes. "Typical." I stepped out, locking my humble Toyota SUV, and headed inside. "Good morning," I said, as Kira walked by.

"Good morning, Marco. Right on time," she replied.

"It was hit and miss for a while with traffic, but I made it." I walked to the lockers and pulled on my coat. I changed into my kitchen shoes, which were essentially orthotics so my back wouldn't scream at me by the end of the shift. I wondered where Naomi was, figuring she might've already arrived. But no sooner had that thought crossed my mind and I returned to the kitchen did she walk in.

This was where I had to act like I was happy to see her. Like I was interested and cared about her. "Morning, Naomi."

"Chef," she replied, carrying on toward the lockers at the back.

Seemed a little cold. I shrugged and carried on preparing the meat. We had a slow-roasted Italian beef over top of a creamy polenta. The roast took several hours, and I needed to get it into the oven quickly.

When Naomi returned, it was like she flipped a switch. She smiled at me, and when she reached her station, she touched my shoulder. "Good morning, Marco."

I noticed Dante had walked into the kitchen. That explained things. "Morning," I said, with an eye on Dante.

"I had a great time last night," she said, loud enough for Dante to hear.

"Yeah, me too," I replied, noticing Naomi had gotten what she'd wanted — Dante's attention. I saw it in his face. He was jealous.

I hadn't known him long enough to ascertain his level of insecurity. But I suspected he wouldn't take well to the idea of his head chef and sous chef in a relationship. For a moment, I considered whether Naomi and Chef Eric had also been an item. Regardless, I was her weapon of choice now in the battle for Dante's affections, and I would use it to my advantage.

Dante seemed to linger with an ear toward us, so I indulged him by stepping closer to Naomi. Close enough to rub shoulders. She was preparing stock for the polenta, and I leaned in to whisper. "You up for a drink at my place after work tonight?" My words were too low for anyone but Naomi to hear. And the smile on her face said it all. I grinned, raising my gaze to Dante, who'd been glancing over at us.

I pulled back and returned to my task, looking on to see Dante disappear into the manager's office. He and Kira seemed to have a tumultuous relationship. I could see that from the moment I met Kira. But I wondered, too, how far I could push her.

* * *

The dinner shift had started an hour ago. The restaurant was booked solid once again, thanks to the Otis Oliver review, no doubt. I noticed Kira step out from her office. Now was my time to show her just how good I really was.

I peered over at the sliced brisket, ready to plate the dish. The scent of the fresh rosemary, thyme and oregano filled the air. The tomato sauce, created from ripe, juicy tomatoes, bubbled in its pot. I glanced at her, parting my lips just a little, ticking them up into a sly grin.

She continued watching me as I readied the course-ground cornmeal that I'd turned into a creamy and flavorful polenta. The broth Naomi made enhanced the depth of the dish. On the side of my station lay the Parmigiano-Reggiano, finely grated, ready to add a nutty, salty kick to the polenta.

As I added the beef to the tomato sauce, I glanced at her again. Kira's eyes were locked onto me. I knew then that she was mine for the taking. A final sprinkle of fresh herbs and a drizzle of extra virgin olive oil completed my masterpiece.

Her gaze pulled away, turning to Dante as he approached. Alas, she was taken from me, but I knew it wouldn't be for long.

Dante had gestured outside and appeared agitated. I wondered if something had gone wrong. The noise of the kitchen made it impossible for me to hear them, so I decided a trip to the pantry would bring me close enough to get the gist of the conversation.

"I need something from the pantry," I said to Naomi.

"Have Expo get it for you," she replied. "What do you need?"

"It's fine. I'll just be a second." I didn't give her another chance to stop me and headed toward the office. Down the hall, before the lockers, was the dry pantry. And as I approached, I slowed down and glanced at the couple. They'd stopped speaking while I passed by. I entered the pantry and quickly grabbed a bulb of garlic. I had no need for it, but it was close and easy to take.

With only a moment to spare, I headed back out into the hall and stopped short. Dante and Kira had continued their conversation. This time, Dante's voice had raised enough to be heard just above the kitchen staff.

"I don't know what he wants, Kira, but he's waiting for me outside," Dante said. "If I don't go out there, he'll come in and we don't need him making a scene."

"Fine. Just get him out of here," she replied.

I heard Dante's heavy footfalls as he walked through the kitchen. I stepped out with the bulb of garlic in my hand. Kira offered me a curt nod and returned to her office.

Ahead of me, I watched Dante step out the back. None of the staff seemed to take notice. I didn't know who was out there waiting for him, but it was clearly someone neither of them had wanted to see. I returned to my station, setting down the garlic, before I clutched my stomach and moaned a little.

"Are you okay?" Naomi asked.

"I feel a little nauseous. How are we doing? Do you think I can step out for a quick breath of air? I'm sure that'll help."

"I think so," she began. "But don't be too long."

"Thanks." I headed toward the back door and opened it, quietly stepping out when I noticed Dante standing next to a man in a large Cadillac SUV. *Eric.* The two were several feet away in the staff parking area. Neither had noticed my arrival, so I slipped into the shadow of the building, close enough to listen in on their conversation.

Dante was upset. His tone, firm. "I already gave you money. I told you not to come back here."

"You gotta give me back my job, man," Eric said. "I swear to you that I'm off the stuff, all right? I'm getting clean."

"I gave you the letter of recommendation, Eric. And the cash. I have nothing else to offer," Dante continued. "You know Kira will never allow you back. She thinks you were high when you cut her arm."

Kira hadn't gone into how her arm was injured, but it seemed clear to me now that Eric had been involved. As the argument grew heated, I debated whether to step in, but that might backfire. No, I couldn't risk it. I'd seen what I needed to see and returned inside.

As I arrived at my station, Naomi looked at me. "Feeling better?"

"A little, but I think I'll take a rain check on drinks tonight." I noticed Dante return inside and the two of us locked eyes. "I might be coming down with something."

CHAPTER 10: KIRA

The pounding on our front door forced me up from our bed. I pushed the hair from my face and looked at my phone through blurry eyes. The pounding continued, and I turned to Dante, who finally stirred. "Dante, someone's at the door. Wake up." I got up and pulled on my robe, securing it around my waist. "If you don't go out there, then I will."

"I'm up. I'm up." He flung away the covers and hunched over on the edge of the bed. "What time is it?"

"It's six in the morning." I paced our bedroom. "Who could be out there? Should we call the police?"

"No." Dante stood, hiking up his boxer shorts that had slipped below his waist. "I'll go see who it is." He snatched his T-shirt that hung over the bench and put it on before raking a hand through his hair.

My nerves were on end as I watched him head into the hallway. I followed but stayed in the shadows as he emerged into the living room. The knock thumped again.

"Who is it?" Dante shouted.

"LAPD."

My heart jumped into my throat, and I clutched my robe. "The cops? What the hell are they doing here?"

My voice must've carried because Dante turned around and waved his arm, motioning for me to get back. I didn't budge.

He peeked through the security lens, and then unlocked the door. If it was the cops, then what did I have to fear? *Bad news.* "Angelo." I rushed through the hall to join Dante as he opened the door.

Two officers stood on the other side.

"Mr. and Mrs. Lucini?" the officer asked.

"Yes, I'm Dante. This is my wife, Kira. What's going on, Officer?"

We stepped back, allowing the officers into our home. My mind spun. I hadn't felt this afraid since Dante got the call about his parents. *Please, God, don't let this be about Angelo.* If he was gone, Dante would be lost.

"I'm sorry about this, Mr. Lucini, but do you know an Eric Castor?"

"Yes, sir, I do. He used to work for me." Dante thumbed back. "My wife and I own a restaurant downtown, La Bianca's."

"He wrapped his vehicle around a tree early this morning," the officer began. "I'm afraid he didn't survive the accident."

I gasped, placing my hand over my mouth. Dante pulled me close.

"It's okay, babe."

The officer glanced at me with compassion in his gaze. And when he looked back at Dante, he continued, "His vehicle was equipped with OnStar, and we were able to find him, unfortunately not in time. We retrieved his driver's license for his address, but when we went to his home, no one answered. You were listed as his employer, and he had this as the address."

Dante looked at me, his eyes imbued with sadness. "Probably because we hadn't opened the restaurant when he was hired."

"OnStar provided us with his GPS locations over the past twenty-four hours. It appeared he was at your restaurant last night around 9 p.m."

"Yes, sir, he was. I'd talked to him outside in the parking lot," Dante replied. "What are you saying?"

"Anyone else speak to him?" he pressed.

"No, sir."

"Well then, Mr. Lucini, it seems that you might have been the last person to see Mr. Castor alive."

* * *

I'd followed Dante to the police station to make a statement. Daylight had emerged and we'd been here too long. I knew I had to get to the restaurant. It still hadn't hit me — the reality that Eric was dead. Dante had taken it harder than I'd expected. Despite Eric's issues, he was a good person, and I couldn't help but wonder if the cause of the accident had been drugs.

I gazed through the window near the desk where we sat. "Officer, I really have to get to our restaurant. Do I need to stay?"

"No, ma'am. You're free to go. Both of you." He raised his index finger. "However, I reserve the right to ask you to come back if new information comes out of this."

"Yes, sir," Dante replied. "Thank you."

He stood up and I joined him. We started toward the door when the officer called out.

"Mr. and Mrs. Lucini?"

Dante and I turned around as the officer headed toward us.

"I did want to ask you about one more thing," he said.

"Of course," Dante replied, looking at me with an odd expression. I couldn't be sure, but it looked like he'd wanted to say something.

"Mr. Castor was found with drug paraphernalia in his vehicle," he began. "I assume that will lead us to finding drugs in his system when the toxicology report comes back. That said, had you been aware that Mr. Castor was a drug user?"

"No. No, sir, I wasn't," Dante replied.

My lips parted, but I stopped myself from saying a word. Dante had just lied to the cops. Why?

"Okay, I'll be in touch." The officer tipped his head and turned around to leave.

As we walked outside and reached Dante's car, I stepped into the passenger seat, waiting for him to get inside. After he slipped behind the wheel and pressed the ignition, I turned to him. "Why on earth did you lie about Eric?" He slammed on the gas, and I lurched back into my seat. "What is wrong with you?"

"Well, let's see, our former head chef just died. The cops think I was the last person to see him, and we have a restaurant to run. So, forgive me if I'm a little on edge."

"Well, lying to the cops wasn't the best move." I peered through the windshield, irritated that we'd finally started to see some real gains only to be brought down by something so awful. I had been angry at Eric, but that didn't mean I wanted him hurt or dead. "We'll just have to get through this like everything else."

"What about the staff? Do we tell them?" he asked.

"Of course we tell them," I replied. "They worked with him too."

Dante sighed as he seemed to raise his foot from the pedal, slowing down the car. "Yeah, you're right. Of course, you're right. We'll do it when we get back."

I considered the impact this would have on our staff. Marco was the only one who didn't know Eric. Maybe that was a blessing in disguise. He could help keep up morale as the restaurant grew busy. And maybe I could enlist Angelo. He was a kind soul, despite his own struggle with addiction. But one thing I knew for certain — had I not caught Eric doing drugs, he wouldn't have been fired. And maybe he would still be alive.

We returned to the restaurant. Dante wanted to go in through the back and just tell the staff straight away. But I wanted to see Angelo first, and I knew where he would be.

It was already pushing ten o'clock, and everyone would have arrived by now, except for the servers, of course.

I gripped the door handle of Dante's car and turned to him. "Angelo should know first, anyway. He was close to Eric. Closer than either of us."

"All right." Dante opened his car door. "We'll go in through the front and talk to him."

The sun felt warm on my face. The sky was, surprisingly, a clear blue today. I inhaled a deep breath, steadying myself for the grief that lay in wait. I would shoulder it all. Theirs, mine, Dante's. A part of him carried the weight of Eric's death as I had. Both of us bore some responsibility, even if we never admitted it out loud.

We walked inside. Angelo was sitting at a table with a bottle of wine in front of him and a half-full glass in his hands. He must've sensed a problem as we entered, pulling up in his chair, and wearing concern on his face. Something in me clicked. My eyes reddened and tears welled. I looked back at Dante, who placed his arm around my shoulder.

"For God's sake, someone better tell me what happened," Angelo said, darting his gaze between us.

As we moved toward him, the grief swept over me. I hadn't even known Eric for that long, but this hit hard.

"Eric died in a car accident early this morning," Dante said, his face unyielding.

"Oh, my God." Angelo walked around the table and pulled me into an embrace. I sobbed into his large, soft chest.

"How did you find out?" Angelo asked.

"The cops came pounding on our door at six this morning," Dante replied. "We were listed as his employer. They went to his home, but of course . . ."

"Eric had his problems, but he was a good kid, and a great chef. Christ," Angelo sighed. "What are you going to tell the staff?"

I pulled back, dabbing at my eyes with my fingertips. I hadn't showered. I had on no makeup, and I wore a T-shirt and shorts. I didn't exactly look like the spine of the operation. I turned to Dante, knowing it would have to come from him.

"The truth," Dante said. "It's all we can do."

* * *

Dante and I had stood together to make the announcement, though the words came from him. Some of the staff had asked to go home after hearing the troubling news. What could we do but say yes? But that meant we were going to be shorthanded. Dante and I would step in and cover the shifts. Amy had returned, knowing her dad was going to be okay. Despite feeling terrible about what happened to Eric, she had agreed to stick it out tonight.

So, I would help cover appetizers and garnishes. Easy for me, but then I wasn't a chef. Dante was the chef in the family. He was the entire reason I was here right now.

As I organized my station, Marco approached. I looked at him with a forlorn smile. "Hi. Everything going all right?"

"Fine for me. I'm not sure I can say the same about you, though." He placed his hand on the middle of my back.

"I'm doing all right. We've had to overcome a lot lately, but I'll be the first to admit that this will be the most difficult."

Marco removed his hand, clasping them behind his back. "I do feel like an outsider at the moment. Not knowing Eric and being the one who replaced him."

I set down my cloth and squared up to him. "No one expects you to feel anything, Marco, okay? Obviously, you're a good person and I know you feel sorry about what happened, but you didn't know Eric. Just do your best to run things tonight, but also, as much as possible, try not to push them too hard." I raised my hands. "I know that's your job, and your reputation is on the line, so I understand that can only go so far. But I guess what I'm saying is—"

"Be sympathetic," he cut in. "Yeah, I get that. And I will."

I smiled and returned to my task, but he stopped and raised a finger. "You know, I saw them talking last night," he began.

"Who?" I asked him.

"Dante and Eric. I was feeling a little off, so I went outside for some fresh air for just a moment. I saw Dante talking to Eric. It looked to be a heated conversation, and I heard something about money or whatever. I don't know, but I felt like I was eavesdropping, so I returned inside." He shrugged. "For what it's worth . . . just thought you should know Eric seemed troubled at the time. I have no doubt Dante was trying to help him."

When he walked away again, I felt an itch in the back of my brain. I knew Eric had turned up last night. Dante and I almost had an argument over it. But what money was Marco talking about?

* * *

It didn't take long for the orders to start coming in. Dante was filling in where needed, but Marco took the lead, alongside Naomi, who also stayed. I was impressed by his skills as a chef and now as a leader. Even while ordering the staff, a certain quality came through in his tone. I couldn't help but be impressed.

By the end of the shift, we'd all felt it. A comradery that even while Eric was here, hadn't been this strong. I removed my apron and walked over to Marco's station. "Great job tonight."

"Thank you," he replied. "But clearly, I didn't do it alone." He gestured out to the cooks and nodded at Naomi. "These guys are great. Even though they're hurting, they came through."

"Yes, they did." I touched his shoulder and donned a smile. "I'm glad you're here."

"Me, too, Kira."

As I started back to my office, I felt Dante's stare. He followed me in and closed the door behind him.

"I have no idea how we got through that service," I said. "Marco did a great job tonight. So did Naomi. They all did."

"I agree," Dante replied. "Listen, why don't you go home? I'll stick around and help clean. You don't need to, especially with that arm."

It had improved, but the stitches still bothered me. "Yeah, okay." I walked toward him, standing on tiptoes to kiss his lips. "I don't know what happened with Eric when he came here last night. Marco said it was something about money or whatever—"

Dante pinched his brow. "What's that?"

"I guess he'd gone outside after needing some air last night and briefly noticed you two talking. Thought it was a little heated, and that it had something to do with money. Did we still owe Eric backpay?"

"No, uh, no, he was all paid up. I'm not really sure what Marco was referring to."

"Oh. Maybe he misunderstood." I grabbed my keys. "I'll see you at home. Try not to work these guys too hard."

"I won't. Drive safe, babe."

I started out toward the front of house. Saying good-night Angelo was at the top of my list. He'd come through for us with the staff, standing at our side while we relayed the difficult news. Everyone loved him, for all his faults.

"You're still here?" he asked me.

"I'm leaving now. What about you? You need a lift?" I was pretty sure he'd had at least two bottles tonight. Maybe three. But I wasn't going to give him grief about it right now. I didn't have the energy.

"No, I'm okay. I think I'll stick around with Dante and see if I can help out." He stood from the table, swaying a little on wobbly legs. "How are you holding up?"

"I'm okay. Feels like a dark cloud has been hanging over us for so long, and then we get that review, but then this . . . you know?"

"I know. But you'll get through it. Dante will too."

"A lot of that has to do with you, Angelo," I said. "The staff loves you. We all do."

He looked back toward the kitchen. "Yeah, well, I have my demons, just like Eric did."

"Don't we all?" I carried on outside, walking around the building toward my car parked out back. I noticed Marco outside smoking a cigarette. "Hi, again."

He dropped it onto the ground, snuffing it out with his shoe. "Nasty habit, I know."

"In this business, it's pretty normal. Don't worry about it. I was just leaving after stopping to say goodnight to Angelo." He caught up to me as I opened my car door, his eyes locked on mine.

"Listen, uh, we don't know each other that well, but if you need to talk — I'd be happy to listen."

And the way he looked at me. It was like the day we met in that restaurant. Deep green eyes that made my heart jump into my throat. "Thank you, Marco. I appreciate that."

He placed his hand on my arm, rubbing it slowly. "You and Dante will do great with this place, of that, I have no doubt. And I'm happy to be going along for the ride."

I looked at his hand and he pulled it away. "I'm glad to hear that. Good night, Marco." I sat in my car for a moment while he returned inside. The undeniable spark between us was — unexpected. Playing a game this dangerous would have consequences. Was I prepared for them?

CHAPTER 11: DANTE

The smoke break Marco had taken lasted longer than I'd expected. I noticed him return to the kitchen when I'd finished tipping out the servers. It was like this guy had a hard time being where he was supposed to be, and yet, always seemed to turn up where he wasn't wanted. Case in point, my conversation with Eric last night. How the hell had he even known Eric was here?

"Thanks for all your hard work, Jonah." I handed him three hundred dollars. "It was a good night. You would've made Eric proud."

"Thank you, Dante. I'm off tomorrow, which, all things considered, I suppose I'm grateful for. So I'll see you the day after." He nodded and went on his way.

As I closed out, my gaze drifted to Marco and Naomi. He appeared to be comforting her, and I felt that twinge again. Trying to shake it off, I turned away and headed back into the office.

The sight of Marco and Naomi getting along so well taunted me. Stupid and irrational, oh yeah, but I couldn't help myself. As if I didn't have bigger problems. My former head chef, who — by the way — had been blackmailing me, was now dead. And the cops said I was probably the last

90

person to have seen him alive. If they found evidence of this blackmail? I was sorry about Eric, really, but if they made that connection, I was toast.

According to Kira, Marco had been outside listening to my conversation with Eric last night. He must've heard Eric talk about the money I'd paid him to keep quiet about the bribe. Why didn't he tell Kira that? What was his angle?

I had to take control of this situation right now. Confront Marco and clear the air before any other misunderstandings arose. So, I stepped out of the office and made my way into the kitchen. Marco watched me approach and greeted me with a smile. There was something under that grin that made me question this man's intentions. Paranoia? We'll see about that.

Naomi was still at her station, and I turned to her. "Would you excuse us a moment?"

"Sure." She disappeared into the hall, probably heading toward the lockers.

Marco wiped his hands on his apron, still wearing that grin. "I think things went well tonight; all things considered. Don't you, Chef?"

"Yes, all things considered," I replied. "Listen, can we talk in private for a minute?"

He looked around. "Looks like we're alone. Shoot."

I rubbed my chin a moment, gathering my thoughts so I wouldn't sound like a paranoid freak to my new head chef. "Look, Marco, I know you caught a glimpse of Eric and me last night outside talking. Maybe even heard a thing or two. I just want to make it clear that whatever you heard . . . I mean, look, what happened to him was an accident."

Marco's smile faded, and he deadpanned. "I never thought anything otherwise. And, honestly, I wasn't paying much attention. I didn't know the man or why he was there."

He was lying to me. He'd made it clear to Kira that he knew about the money — some money, anyway. Maybe he didn't think she would tell me, or he planned on using the information to undermine me. Either way, I wasn't going to sit back and let him do that. "You know, Kira thinks highly of you, Marco." I folded my arms over my chest, feeling defensive now.

"Is that so?" he nodded. "And what do you think of me, Dante?"

"I think you're a damn good chef." I raised my chin and steadied my gaze. "But I also think you might have a soft spot for my wife. I've noticed how you are around her."

At this, Marco flashed a bright-white smile. His green eyes seemed to sparkle. "How *I* am or how *she* is?" he replied.

The smug look on his face forced a ball of anger to form in my stomach. My fists clenched under my crossed arms. Was this guy seriously suggesting my wife was after him?

Marco raised his hands in surrender. "I'm sorry, Dante. That was completely out of line. I respect you and your wife and I'm grateful to be here. Please, it's late and I'm exhausted. Please forget what I just said."

My blood pressure lowered a little, and I couldn't help but feel that he wasn't wrong about Kira. I'd seen it. "Listen, doesn't matter, all right." *The hell it didn't.* "I just want to make sure you know that what happened between me and Eric had nothing to do with the restaurant or anything else."

Marco nodded. "I have no doubt about that. I mean, I may have overheard something, but I get it. Doesn't mean I'm going to go running to the police about it."

"The police? Who said anything about the police?" There was that ball of anger rising again. "What exactly is it you think you heard, Marco?"

He hesitated for a moment, looking like he was about to reconsider, but finally continued, "I heard something about some money he wanted or whatever. That's all."

Reading faces wasn't my specialty, but I knew when someone was bullshitting me. He had heard all of it. I was sure of that now. But I couldn't let this blow up in my face. I needed Marco and I think he knew that. "It was his backpay."

"Yeah, of course," Marco said. "I figured it was something like that."

"Yeah, so, you know, Eric left on good terms. No hard feelings. And that's all you need to know. Am I making myself clear?" I pressed.

Marco locked eyes with me. His expression hardened. "Crystal — boss."

"Good." I patted him on the back. "Go home and get some rest. I'll see you tomorrow."

"Yes, Chef." Marco retreated into the hall.

Naomi passed him by on her way into the kitchen. She wore her street clothes and tennis shoes, looking prepared to head home. The two of us gazed at one another, and I recognized the look on her face. Desire. But what had she desired: me or Marco's job? I wasn't blind to her ambitions. I knew she was disappointed we didn't offer her head chef. But damn if it didn't look like she was trying to leverage Marco against me. Or was this more of my own paranoia? My fear of the truth about Eric and the bribe getting out?

I took a deep breath, trying to shake off the tension that had built, pinching my shoulders and neck. I returned to the office and prepared to shut down.

Naomi appeared in the doorway. "Is everything okay, Dante?"

"I'm fine," I said. "Just dealing with a few . . . complications."

Naomi nodded, her eyes glancing at my mouth. "If you ever need someone to talk to, Dante, I'm here for you."

"I appreciate that. All good here. Go on home. It's been a tough day for all of us."

"Okay. Good night." Disappointment masked her face as she walked away, heading out through the back exit.

I stayed until everyone had gone home. Despite the fact that we'd been booked solid and made good money tonight, Eric's death clouded all of it. I was pissed at him for what he'd done, but the man was dead now. It put things into perspective.

When I was sure I was alone, I headed out of the office and walked into the dining room. "Ang? What are you still doing here? I thought you hitched a ride with Kira?"

"I was gonna take an Uber, but the driver never showed."
His eyes were bloodshot and even though he was sitting
down, he swayed in the chair.

"Christ. And you've been sitting out here ever since?" I
headed toward him. "How about I drop you off at home?" I
stood at his table, offering a hand to help him up.

"I got it. I'm not that drunk," he said.

"I beg to differ, my friend. Is this because of Eric?"

"Is what because of Eric?" Angelo asked as he rocked.

"The reason why you're still here. Still drinking. Look,
I know you liked the guy, but it was an accident. Nothing
either of us could've done."

"No?" Angelo asked. "You sure about that?"

"What are you saying?" I stepped back while he moved
toward me, appearing ready to tumble to the ground. Angelo's
drunkenness made me uneasy. I hadn't seen him this bad in a
while.

"I'm saying that it wasn't an accident." His words spilled
out in an incoherent mess. "Eric's death was no accident, and
you know it." He aimed his finger at me.

"The hell you talking about?" I rocked back on my heels.
"You saying I had something to do with it? Are you crazy, or
just drunk off your ass?"

"I'm talking about murder, Dante," Angelo said, grabbing onto my shirt with both hands. "You think I don't
know what goes on around here. I do. I know."

I tried to pull away, but Angelo's grip was surprisingly
strong. "Get the fuck off me. You're not making any sense."

"No?" He scoffed and stormed outside.

I had no idea what had just happened, but I suspected
that Marco Devaney had something to do with it. Had he
been talking to my brother? Whispering lies about me? This
guy tries to get in good with my wife, and now my brother?

I stepped outside, securing the door behind me. As I
reached my car, I saw Angelo already in the passenger seat.
I peered at him through the windshield before climbing

94

behind the wheel. Pressing the ignition, I pulled out of the back lot and headed toward Angelo's place.

After several minutes, I felt Angelo's eyes on me. "What? You want to apologize?"

"What went down with Eric?" he asked.

My grip on the steering wheel tightened. "Who's been saying stuff to you, huh? Kira? Marco? Kira's devastated about this, all right? She thinks I knew all about Eric's problems and that I didn't do shit about it. And now the guy's dead."

"You did know. We all knew."

"I'm sorry he died, all right, Ang? I still liked the guy, despite his flaws. Like any of us is perfect. We all knew what kind of problems he had, and it was fine until—"

"Until your wife found out," Angelo cut in.

"Until she got hurt because of Eric. Is that what you want to hear?" I shouted. "Eric could've done some serious damage to Kira, and I knew the man was getting high. I just didn't know how bad it got."

Angelo was quiet again.

"What I should be focusing on now is the restaurant," I added. "Let the cops figure out what happened to Eric. They gotta do what they gotta do. I got nothing to hide. It's just—" I stopped cold, recalling Marco's words.

"What?" Angelo asked.

"Nothing." It occurred to me in that moment that maybe it had been Marco who tipped off the cops. Somehow sending them pounding on my door, thinking I had anything to do with what happened. That would have meant Marco knew about the accident. But Eric had a sister. Why wouldn't the cops have gone to her house first? I noticed Angelo's apartment building appear in the distance. "Listen, just let me figure this out, all right? And for Christ's sake, keep your mouth shut about it, would you?"

* * *

95

When I arrived home, I walked into our house to find Kira curled up on the sofa, her head leaning on one of the arms and her eyes closed. I walked toward her, gently placing my hand on her shoulder. "Babe? Babe, let's get you to bed."

Her eyes fluttered for a moment and finally opened. "I didn't realize I'd fallen asleep. What time is it?"

"Late. I had to take Angelo home, and I just got back," I replied.

"Again?" she asked.

"Again." I reached for her arm to help her off the couch. "Come on, let's get some sleep."

As we walked down the hall, Kira looked at me. "I'm scared, Dante."

"Of what?"

"I'm starting to feel like things are falling apart," she replied. "I thought that after that review, things would be different. But now Eric's dead."

"I know, babe. And things are different. We are doing better because of that review." I wondered what would happen if she knew about the bribe.

"We're so deep into this restaurant that any one thing could happen, and we could lose it all," Kira continued.

I rubbed her back. "But it won't. We won't lose anything."

She stopped and squared up to me. "I feel like outside forces are trying to pull us apart, Dante."

"What do you mean?" I asked.

"Naomi, for one. She's angry we didn't give her the head chef job. I know you see that," Kira said.

"I suppose I do," I whispered.

"Then you also see that she's trying to get close to you. I don't know why, but she is."

I placed my hand on her soft cheek and held her gaze. "No one will tear us apart, Kira, I promise you. You don't need to worry about Naomi. I can handle her." We walked on again and I stopped in front of our bedroom door. I knew I should keep my mouth shut, and put this to bed, but it gnawed at me. The same way Naomi must've gnawed at her. "And Marco? Are you attracted to him?"

Kira hesitated, a soft groan emanating from her. "I see. No, Dante. I'm not. I can't deny that he's a force in the kitchen, and he's rallied the cooks around him. We need that after this whole Eric thing. But, no, I don't want him. Only you. It's always been you."

I leaned down to kiss her, my hands on either side of her face. "Good. I trust you," I said. "And we'll handle everything together. We're a team, Kira."

She nodded, her eyes shining with tears. "I love you, Dante."

"I love you, too." I pulled her into a tight embrace before we both stripped down to our underwear and crawled into bed.

As we lay there, I couldn't help but think about Naomi. Kira was right: she was trying to get close to me, and I could feel my attraction to her growing stronger by the day. But I couldn't let that happen. Kira meant everything to me, and I'd be damned if I let anyone come between us.

CHAPTER 12: KIRA

The dread I'd felt over the loss of Eric still weighed on me, but clearing the air with Dante last night had lifted some of that weight. That was, until I arrived at the restaurant this morning. A man in a crisp white shirt and tie was leaning against his black sedan in the customer parking lot. He pressed his hand on the trunk, his other hand in his pocket. My first thought? He was a cop, and this was about Eric.

I continued around back, but I knew he'd seen me. When I parked and cut the engine, I steadied myself, knowing I was going to have to talk to him. Dante had lied to the cops, and I had a feeling this guy was here for the truth.

Finally, I stepped out of my car. The light breeze cooled my skin as the cloudy sky blocked out the sun's rays. I gathered my courage and walked around to the front of the restaurant, facing the man who was here to get answers from me. "Good morning. Can I help you?"

He reached into his pants pocket and retrieved a badge. "Good morning. You must be Mrs. Lucini."

"Kira, yes. And you are?" He wasn't the officer who'd taken Dante's statement the other night. This man was older, late forties, at least. His hair was short and black, tamed by heavy product. Not particularly handsome, he looked worn down and tired. A slight bulge at his midsection.

"Detective Ed Lyman, LAPD. I'd like to speak to you about Eric Castor." He looked around as if searching for someone. "Is Mr. Lucini here?"

"No. He doesn't usually arrive until about ten," I replied. "You're welcome to come back—"

"I'd still like to speak with you, if you have a few minutes," he cut in.

I gestured toward the entrance. "Of course. Why don't we go inside? If we can keep this brief, I'd appreciate it." I unlocked the door and walked in, heading to the keypad near the hostess station to deactivate the alarm. "The rest of the kitchen staff will be here soon, and with everything that's happened, I'd rather they not get distracted by you being here."

Lyman raised his hands. "I understand completely."

"Would you like a cappuccino?" I walked toward the bar where we kept our espresso machine.

"As lovely as that sounds, it won't be necessary." He pulled out a chair and sat at one of the tables. "Mr. Castor's vehicle is in our forensics department. Because the responding officer discovered drug paraphernalia inside, it's standard procedure to search for drugs or alcohol that might have contributed to his accident while we await the tox screen."

"I'm not sure how that pertains to my husband and I, but all right." I joined him at the table. "What can I answer for you then, Detective?"

"Among Mr. Castor's possessions inside the vehicle, two envelopes were discovered. Both were found lying on top of the passenger floor mat. Inside one of them was a letter of recommendation signed by Mr. Lucini. The other contained a money wrapper. No cash, but that piece of paper had one thousand printed on it. So, I'm left to assume that envelope had once contained cash."

"I see." That must've been what Marco was talking about. He'd mentioned that Dante and Eric discussed money. Why hadn't Dante told me about this? "You should know that I had discovered Eric doing drugs while he was on the clock. That was the reason he was fired. He wasn't the man we thought he was." While that was true, I felt guilty for disparaging a dead man, who I'd considered a friend.

Lyman rested his elbows on the table and leaned in a little. "Mr. Lucini was asked that question, point blank, by Officer Browning. Your husband denied any such knowledge."

"He'd asked Dante whether we knew Eric had a problem," I said, trying to work my way out of this. "We didn't know, until I caught him."

"Fair enough. And I could write off the cash as drug money, however, it's the letter that drew my concern."

"Why is that?" I asked.

"Why would your husband recommend a man who clearly had a drug problem?" He pulled back, tilting his head. "That doesn't square up with me. Even more odd is the fact that a matching envelope seemed to once contain a good amount of cash."

My hands trembled in my lap. I had no idea about any letter, and now I feared saying anything else that might shine a brighter light on Dante, or me, for that matter. The restaurant didn't need this kind of attention. "My husband considered Eric a friend. I have no doubt he had offered some money, or it was possibly backpay, and that letter, so that Eric might have a fresh start somewhere else. That's how my husband is. He's very good to people." I don't know where I pulled that from, but it sounded good. "And may I ask, I thought what happened to Eric was an accident, yet you're here asking questions. Do you believe it wasn't?"

The detective glanced at my arm. I noticed part of the bandage had been exposed under my blouse, and I quickly pulled down my sleeve.

"What happened to your arm, Mrs. Lucini?"

"Minor kitchen accident. It happens sometimes." Mentioning Eric's culpability was probably a bad idea in

100

light of what this detective already seemed to suspect — that Dante had something to do with Eric's death.

He raised an eyebrow but didn't press further. "Well, Mrs. Lucini, if you remember anything else about Eric or if you come across any information that could be helpful to the investigation, please don't hesitate to contact me." He stood up, and I joined him. "Oh, and one more thing," he said, turning back to face me. "Can you think of anyone who might have had a grudge against Mr. Castor?"

"No, no one comes to mind. Eric was well-liked. I imagine he would've stayed on, if not for the drugs. Especially since we'd gotten such a wonderful review of our restaurant based on his food."

Lyman nodded. "I don't think I'd been aware of that. So, he helped you and your husband?"

"Yes."

"Was this recent?" Lyman asked.

"Yes, sir. The review was published only a couple of days ago," I replied.

"Hmm. That's too bad." He sucked on his teeth for a moment, peering off into the distance. "Thank you for your time, Mrs. Lucini. Have a good day."

When he stepped outside, I called out to him. "Detective Lyman?"

"Yes, ma'am?" He stopped and turned back to me.

"You didn't answer my question. Do you believe Eric's death wasn't an accident?"

He grinned and glanced down at his feet. "I wouldn't be here otherwise, Mrs. Lucini. Take care now."

* * *

Two hours had gone by, and my mind had reeled with thoughts of where Dante had been in the early hours before the cops came to our door. I'd been asleep when he'd gotten home. He didn't wake me, claiming to have taken home his brother.

"Stop," I said, rubbing my temple as I sat at my desk.

My computer screen displayed last night's receipts as I tried to run my reports. I couldn't focus. This detective made me doubt my husband. Was he right? Should I ask the question?

But the rest of the staff arrived, and I held my tongue about Detective Lyman for the time being. Not until I could get it straight in my head whether I believed my husband could've somehow been responsible or involved in Eric's death.

He'd told me about taking the money, but said it'd been to pay bills, and then the line of credit. Nothing about giving Eric anything. But in the grand scheme of things, a thousand bucks was hardly worth harming someone. I knew it wasn't backpay. That wasn't how we operated. And the letter of recommendation?

"Okay, just stop. You can't think about this anymore."

I stepped into the kitchen where Naomi and Marco were already hard at work, chopping, slicing, and stewing. Soon, I moved on to see how Amy was doing. She seemed better since her father's heart attack, but with the loss of Eric, it was hard to gauge her mood. As I approached her, a loud yelp cut through the air. I spun around and saw Naomi cradling her hand. "What happened?"

Naomi stumbled back. "I touched the pan. I didn't know it was hot."

"Damn it." I rushed over to grab the first aid kit from the wall in my office and ran to Naomi's side. Marco had already taken Naomi's hand and held it under a faucet running cold water over the burn.

"I got it. I got it." I nudged my way between them and took her hand, examining it. "It's not great, but I don't think you need urgent care. How did this happen?"

"I grabbed the pan," Naomi began. "I had no idea it was on the fire. I was sure the burner was off. Jesus, I was sure it was off."

"Let's get some ointment on this and wrap it up," I said. "I think you'll be okay, but maybe sit down for a few minutes, all right? Take a breath."

"Yeah, okay," Naomi replied.

While I worked to treat her hand, Marco attempted to comfort Naomi. "What were you doing, Marco?" I asked him. "I mean, when Naomi reached out for the pan? Had you been using it?"

"No, I wasn't." His voice raised. "Maybe I knocked the burner knob and turned it on. I don't think so, but I suppose it's possible." He looked over at Naomi. "I'll keep a closer eye and make sure we aren't getting in each other's way. I'm sorry that happened to you, Chef."

Naomi waved him off with her other hand. "It's fine. I'll live."

I noticed Dante approach, his face masked in concern. "I heard a noise in the dining room. Is everything okay?"

He looked directly at Naomi, and then her hand, as I continued to wrap the bandage around her palm.

"I'm okay," Naomi said. "It was a miscommunication."

I noticed her glance at Marco and thought I should chime in to keep emotions in check. "She touched a hot pan. It's not too bad," I said.

Dante raised a sympathetic gaze to Naomi. "Take all the time you need. I'll step in and help prep."

"Yes, Chef," Naomi replied.

Her tone was cold and harsh. She was angry, maybe a little embarrassed too. "Okay, you're all set. Go sit down in my office if you'd like," I said.

"Thanks, Kira." She stepped into the office and closed the door.

I looked at Dante. "I got this. You should head out front. We're good here." I watched him and Marco trading glances as though a pissing match was about to get underway.

"Yeah, all right." He walked to the door that led to the dining room.

"I'm so sorry about this, Kira," Marco said. "I–I didn't think . . ."

"It's okay. Naomi's going to be fine. We just need to pay better attention."

"Yeah, of course." He folded his arms and cleared his throat.

I sensed he wanted to say something else. "What is it?"

"Nothing, I guess — this probably isn't the best time, but I was thinking that maybe we should take a trip to Napa to check out some of the local wineries."

Where was this coming from? It seemed a strange request, and I wasn't sure how to respond.

Marco raised his hands. "I know how busy you and Dante are with things around here. But I know some people up there who could probably give us a deal for some high-end stuff. I think it would raise the profile of the restaurant. Of course, you're the decision-maker, so if you think it's a waste of time—"

"It wouldn't be a waste of time, Marco," I said. "But now probably isn't the *right* time."

Why was he bringing this up after what just happened? It was like he blocked it out and moved onto the next thing. No remorse. Even if he wasn't responsible, for God's sake, his sous chef was injured.

"Just an overnight trip," he pressed. "We could talk to some of those people and maybe bring back a few cases to test out. From there, if they sold well, you could place an order for shipment."

"Like I said, with everything going on with Eric and all that, you know . . ." I trailed off.

Marco reached out for my shoulder. "You know what . . . think about it. Maybe we can work it in in the next few weeks or so? If not, I get it. It's a tough time right now, Kira. But I want you to know that I'm here for you, and I want to do what's best for this place, and for you."

"Okay, I'll think about it. I'll talk it over with Dante." His gaze appeared sincere, and I suddenly got the feeling that being alone with Marco might not be the best idea.

I was then reminded that maybe now was the right time to tell Dante about the detective coming here this morning. Something about the way Marco looked at me just now sparked that feeling in me again that outside influences were at play.

And guilt bore down on me for even considering my husband could have had anything to do with Eric's so-called accident.

I headed into the dining room and spotted Dante at the podium. "Hey, can we talk for a minute?"

"Sure."

Angelo had already made himself at home at the bar, and I nodded to him. "Good morning, Ang."

"Morning, sweetheart," Angelo replied. "Dante."

The curt nod from him toward Dante was unusual. The brothers shared a closeness I had never known myself, being an only child. But with that closeness came the protection of family secrets known only to the brothers. I would never be part of that world, and I'd come to accept that.

"What is it, Kira?" Dante asked, taking a seat in the corner booth. "We're slammed as it is."

"I know." I slid in across from him. "A detective came here earlier this morning looking for you."

"For me?" He thumbed at his chest.

"Yes." I leaned in and lowered my tone. "They found two envelopes in Eric's Cadillac. One they believe had once contained cash, thanks to a money wrapper inside, and one that contained a letter of recommendation from you. The wrapper denoted a grand, the exact amount of money you said you'd taken from the safe to make a payment on that line of credit. Dante, did you give Eric that money? And why would you write him a letter?"

I watched his face lose all expression. His fingers fidgeted on the table. I waited for a response. When none came, I continued, "That detective thinks you had something to do with what happened to Eric. And after what they found? They don't believe this was an accident."

"I can explain." Dante took a deep breath. "Eric was having financial troubles, and he came to me for help. I gave him that money as a loan."

"A loan?" I asked. "We're in the red, borrowing off this line of credit, and you gave him a loan? Did you forget that he got fired because he was doing coke out back? Or how about the fact that he cut my arm so badly I needed fifteen stitches? Jesus, Dante. You should've told me this."

"I know. And I'm sorry. I realize we couldn't afford it. As for the letter, I felt I had to write it so he could get another job. No way would anyone hire him after what happened."

"No shit," I snapped back. "Why didn't you tell me any of this that night?"

Dante looked away. "I didn't want to involve you. I thought I could handle it on my own. That I could find a way to get the money back quickly enough."

I felt exasperated. "It's no wonder that detective wanted to ask you questions." And then it occurred to me that Angelo was at the bar. Whether he heard us, I couldn't tell, but I didn't think so. His face was buried in a bottle. "Angelo?" I called out.

He turned around. "Yeah?"

"Did Dante give you a ride the night before last? The night before Eric's car accident?"

Angelo looked up as if in thought. "I think so. My memory is a little fuzzy."

"I'll bet." I turned back to Dante. "Please, tell me the truth because this affects all of us, our entire business. And now the police are involved. Tell me you had nothing to do with Eric's accident."

"I swear I didn't. Come on. Where is this coming from?" he pleaded. "I know I messed up, but I promise I'll make it right. I'll talk to the detective and explain everything."

I leaned back in the booth, taking a deep breath. "If any of this gets out—"

The sound of a shattering plate rang out from the kitchen. "For God's sake. What now?" I stood up, ready to head back, but Dante grabbed my arm. I looked at him.

"Wait, Kira. I need to know you believe me. I had nothing to do with Eric's accident."

His eyes held guilt. I'd seen the look before. The question remained, was it guilt for lying to me, or something worse?

"If the cops thought this was an accident, they wouldn't have come here, Dante. Whatever is going on, you'll have to be the one to fix it."

CHAPTER 13: DANTE

We'd been busy again tonight, and it was all because of what I'd done. I should've felt proud of our success, but pride was the farthest thing from my mind. I couldn't bring myself to tell Kira yet. We had maintained an awkward silence throughout the evening, avoiding each other as much as possible. She clearly wondered how all this tied back to me.

Only Otis Oliver, Eric, and I knew about the bribe that had been arranged. Marco may or may not have overheard enough to piece it together himself. Though he knew at least enough to stir Kira's anxiety. His reasons for doing so weren't hard to imagine. Regardless, the detective was likely to come back soon, and in order to preempt Kira's further involvement, I needed to go into the station in the morning with an explanation. This detective had reason to suspect I'd had a motive for what happened to Eric, giving him money and a letter to make him go away.

I couldn't put off going into the kitchen any longer. Angelo was still at the bar, and I eyed him as I entered the hallway toward the kitchen. I didn't have the energy to deal with him right now. Kira was the only person I needed to confirm was still on my side.

As I made my way to the kitchen, I noticed Kira and Marco standing together, drinking a glass of wine. Marco's presence overshadowed that of everyone else in the kitchen. For some reason, the two seemed to have a connection that I couldn't explain. I'm not sure she even knew it existed — or at least, to the extent that it had. They were lost in conversation and didn't seem to notice me watching them from a distance.

When Kira finally looked up, and our eyes met, their conversation came to an abrupt halt.

"Dante, we were just getting ready to close out." She walked over to me, glancing back at Marco. "We had a good night."

"So I noticed." I shifted my gaze between them for a moment. "Can we talk?"

"Sure."

I stood at the office door, waiting for her to enter. And when she did, I looked out at Marco, nodding before I closed the door behind me.

Kira sat down in her desk chair. "I hope you don't mind that I was taking a break. It's been a long night, and everyone was pretty much finished cleaning anyway."

It wasn't like her to ask for permission, especially when she didn't need it. She was avoiding the inevitable conversation as much as I was. "That's fine, Kira. You own this restaurant too. If you want to take a break, you're allowed to do that."

I tucked my hands into my pants pocket, unsure of what to say, exactly. "Listen, about what we discussed this morning . . . I'll go see Detective Lyman first thing in the morning before coming in."

Relief shrouded her face. "Thank you. Yes, that's the best thing, Dante. Just get it out of the way, and they can do whatever it is they need to do without coming around here anymore."

"My thoughts exactly." A knock sounded on the door, and I turned around to open it. Naomi stood on the other side, her hand still bandaged. "Hey, what's up?"

"I'm sorry to bother you guys, but I was heading out to my car and noticed I had a flat tire. Like I haven't dealt with enough shit today," she sighed. "Anyway, don't suppose I could get a ride? I don't have a spare."

"I can give you a ride," Marco called out from his station. "You should've said something, Naomi."

"There you go," I said. "Problem solved. I can run out with you tomorrow to pick up a new tire or help you get it towed. Whatever you like. It'll be fine here tonight."

I noticed the look on her face. Was it fear? Anger? I didn't know exactly what'd happened earlier with her hand, but it seemed she didn't want Marco to take her home. Hadn't they gone out for drinks the other night? Why the hesitation?

"Yeah, sure. Thanks." Naomi replied to Marco, disappearing around the corner.

I closed the door again. "That was weird."

"What was?" Kira asked.

"The look on her face. It didn't look like she wanted Marco to take her home." Then I noticed Kira appeared hesitant. "What? What is it?"

She looked down, drawing in a deep breath. "I don't know exactly, but . . ." Kira looked up at me again. "All this stuff that's been happening lately?"

"Yeah?" I asked, waiting for her to elaborate.

"Is it me, or does it seem like we're cursed?"

I raised a shoulder, chuckling a little. "Maybe we are."

* * *

It was a rare day that I awakened before Kira. But I'm not sure I even slept at all last night. My thoughts had been consumed with Eric and the possibility that someone had caused his death.

He'd only been with us for a few months. And even though I picked up on his bad habit early on, I suppose I had no idea the kind of people he had in his life. Maybe he owed someone money, and that was why he'd blackmailed me. As pissed as I was forking over that cash, the man was dead. It was hard to be mad at him at this point.

The only problem was that now I had to insist to the cops that I had nothing to do with what happened, regardless of what I'd given Eric to keep his mouth shut about the bribe — something they knew nothing about.

I headed out of our house quietly with a travel mug full of coffee. My car was parked next to Kira's, and I slipped onto the black leather seat.

Daylight had pushed through the night sky, though the streetlights still burned under the grayish brown hue. I pulled around the circular driveway, and headed down the hill, into the city, leaving behind our highly leveraged castle in the sky. That was what we'd called it when we first moved in. But if things didn't turn around soon, it would be the bank's castle. Not ours.

That was two years ago, one year after my parents burned to death in that fire. I worked almost every day as a kid in their bakery; so did Angelo. I then went off to culinary school, but soon came back to help while I worked on gaining experience in various New York restaurants.

Angelo came out to LA after resolving my parents' finances, their home, and business. He came back with a lot of money he'd received because of their life and business insurance. As the oldest, he'd been charged with handling all of it.

The fire had been deemed an accident, and so their payout was made in full. Angelo offered me half, and, using his half, we both put it into renovating the building we eventually opened as La Bianca's. He'd never asked to be a part-owner, or for any sort of payback, so it was hard for me to give him so much grief about drinking at the restaurant. Hell, he'd paid for a lot of it.

I weaved in and out of traffic, finally reaching the police station. I stepped out of my car and buttoned my coat, figured it would help if I looked like a respectable businessman. Someone who had far too much to lose to risk it all for a thousand bucks. Never mind that I'd lost a friend.

The glass doors parted, and I stepped inside to a hectic scene. I'd been here the other morning, so this marked the third time I'd been inside a police station. Three times too many, you ask me. But before this place, I'd been inside the Brooklyn station after my parents' bakery burned down. This place dwarfed that station in both size and the volume of people coming in and out. A long counter was only steps away, and when I reached it, I cleared my throat to garner the officer's attention. "Hello, good morning."

"What can I do for you, sir?" the officer asked.

"I'm here to see Detective Ed Lyman. I'm Dante Lucini."

"I'll call him up for you."

"Thanks." I stepped away, pretending to admire the awards that hung on the walls. I don't know why I felt defensive and angry. These guys were only doing their jobs, but when their attention was directed at me, my attitude changed. Go figure.

"Mr. Lucini?"

I turned around at the sound of my name and noticed a man in a blue suit approaching. "That's me."

"I'm Detective Lyman. I spoke with your wife yesterday." He offered his hand. "I appreciate you coming in. We can talk in my office."

I followed the man with jet black hair, short and slick. He stood a few inches shorter than me and was a little broader as well. It was clear that he'd been around the block more than a few times. Either that or being a cop in LA made him age faster than most.

"Right through here. Take a seat." Lyman gestured to a chair in front of his desk.

"Thanks." I sat down, surveying the office. It looked different than I would've expected. Several books covered the shelves. Mostly crime and law, by the look of them. A few pieces of modern art hung on the walls. Okay, so the guy had moderate taste.

"So, Mr. Lucini." Lyman took a seat. "Why did you give Eric Castor money? And did you have anything to do with his murder?"

* * *

111

The word still clamored in my ear. *Murder*. I drove on toward the restaurant after listening to Detective Lyman tell me about how they knew Eric had been followed in the early hours that morning. Two sets of tire tracks had led to the side of the road, one ended at the tree.

Where the hell had he been going at five in the morning? And who knew where he would be? I supposed it still could've been accidental. A distracted driver, road rage, a host of things. But Lyman believed whoever had been following Eric ran him off the road, intentionally leading him toward the tree.

My mind spun with thoughts of Eric and how terrified he must've been. Yeah, the guy had a drug problem, and he'd resorted to blackmail, but he was still a human being. Dying that way . . . I could imagine it, because I'd lost my parents in a horrific fire.

When I made it back to the restaurant, I saw Kira's car and called her on my cell. She answered. "Can you come out back and talk? I don't want to see everyone like this."

"I'll be right there," she replied.

Moments later, the back door opened, and Kira emerged. My eyes welled as she approached my car. She must've noticed because when she stepped into the passenger seat, concern lingered in her gaze.

"What's wrong? Are you okay?"

"I'm fine." I took a breath to calm my nerves and settle my rising emotions. "Kira, the cops think Eric was followed and run off the road. That's what the detective told me."

"Oh my God. He's sure?" she asked.

"They have these forensic people, I guess, and they said that there were tire tracks on the road behind Eric's vehicle, but that they didn't match his Cadi . . ." I couldn't go on. She could probably have figured out the rest.

Kira covered her mouth, her own eyes reddening. "Do they think you did it?"

"I gave him my phone, which showed my location, and proved I was at home with you. But you're going to have to back me up on that." She was quiet for a moment, which sparked my concern. "Kira?"

"Yeah, of course. So, then, who do they think it was?" she pressed.

"That's what they have to figure out. I mean, it could've been anyone. Who knows the kind of people Eric hung out with? He only worked for us a few months. We didn't know him that well." I kept my gaze on her. Her face lined with worry. Her eyes still glistening from tears. "The thing is, I had to tell him why I gave Eric that money and the letter."

"Okay." She tilted her head, waiting for the answer.

"Eric was blackmailing me, Kira, because he knew I'd bribed Otis Oliver. And he'd threatened to tell you that I knew about his habit, too." I looked away, ashamed of what I'd done, believing I had to for the success of the restaurant. "That wasn't what I'd told Lyman. I told him the money was a loan, and the letter was to help him out. But I can't lie to you about this anymore."

She went quiet again. I could see her chest rise and fall, faster and faster. "Kira, babe, I know what you're going to say—"

"Oh, I don't think you do." Her face became heated. "You bribed a food critic to give us a good review, and our head chef found out? Now he's dead." She turned away, laughing an insane laughter I didn't recognize.

"Kira, please—"

"No." She raised her hand to stop me. "Do you have any idea what will happen to us if that gets out, Dante? We'll be ruined. Completely and totally ruined." She leaned back against the seat. "Oh my God. What have you done?"

I noticed the back door open. "For Christ's sake. Does this guy have the worst timing or what?"

Kira glanced through the windshield. "He's just taking out the trash, Dante."

"I don't like the way he looks at you," I said. "I know what you told me, but—"

"Don't," she said flatly. "Don't try to change the subject. At least Marco tried to warn me what you'd done. He saw you two standing out here that night, and clearly understood the ramifications of what was being said."

I shot her a look. "Funny how he seems to turn up everywhere, don't you think? Like a goddamn bad penny." I knew our voices would carry through the car and I stopped, fixing my gaze on Marco as he tossed the bag into the nearby dumpster. He looked at me, too. The kind of look that might as well have been a warning.

When he walked back inside, I turned to Kira. "Look, I'm sorry, okay? It is my fault. I know that. The important thing is that I've talked to the detective and—"

"Lied to him," she shot back. "How much did you give Oliver?"

"Three," I whispered. "Three grand."

She placed her hand on her forehead, and a sound came from her that was part laughter and part sobbing. "Oh my God."

"I just need to figure out if I should talk to Oliver and warn him," I said.

"Warn him about what?"

"About what happened to Eric." I gripped my car door handle. "I don't know how to stop this thing from snowballing, Kira. I can't risk Oliver being confronted about this if Eric told anyone else, and then Oliver denies the story."

"Which he will," she jumped in. "Are you kidding? He won't have a choice unless he wants to ruin his career." Kira looked away for a moment. "If Oliver says a word, we can kiss everything we've worked for goodbye."

CHAPTER 14: KIRA

It was hard to enjoy the artistry before me as I observed the kitchen at its peak. Standing outside my office, I watched Marco prepare the food, announce the orders, and run the shift like he was the orchestrator of the New York philharmonic.

But recent events had cast a cloud over what should have been our rising success. My husband, who was in the front of house, dispensing pleasantries to the guests, had undermined all we'd worked toward. I was angry with him for jeopardizing it all. And the tragic loss of our former chef — well, I hadn't yet come to terms with the reality of it.

The restaurant hummed with activity as the dinner rush hit full steam. Waitstaff darted in and out of the kitchen, delivering plates of exquisitely prepared dishes. The clinking of cutlery and the murmur of diners wafted into the back each time the door swung open.

Sweat glistened on Marco's brow as he choreographed the kitchen's activities, his voice rising above the sizzling pans and clattering pots. "Manny, where's that order for table twelve?" he barked, his eyes darting across the line of chefs.

"Two minutes, Chef," Manny replied as he adjusted the flame beneath the pans.

Alex was our food Expo, a young and ambitious culinary student doing an internship. He frantically assembled salads with practiced precision.

Amy created delicate desserts that were works of art. She swirled the spun sugar into an intricate web, gently plating it before adding a drizzle of chocolate sauce for design.

In the back corner, Ryan, one of the dishwashers, worked with methodical efficiency. He scrubbed plates and pans, sending up clouds of steam.

I watched as Marco surveyed the chaos with a sense of satisfaction, his sharp eyes catching every detail. Something else lay beneath those eyes, something that was most noticeable when he set his gaze on me. I couldn't deny feeling it, too. And then I recalled his question. I had dismissed it once, but now, looking back at him, I wondered . . .

Smoothing down my ponytailed hair, I walked toward Marco's station. Naomi seemed to keep one eye on me as I neared. I already knew her game. Shame Dante hadn't picked up on it. Or if he had, he thoroughly reveled in the attention.

"Everything looks amazing, Marco," I said, feeling Naomi's eyes on me.

"Thank you, Chef," he replied. "Service! Plates up for table twelve!"

Junior server Marie trailed Jonah as the plates were whisked away.

I had only moments to speak to him, knowing his next dish would be prepped quickly. "Can I have a brief word?"

Marco wiped his hands on his apron and nodded at Naomi. "I'll only be a minute."

He followed me back to my office. When we were steps apart, I said, "When?"

He knitted his brow. "When what?"

"When do you want to go?" I added. "To Napa."

The look on his face was a mix of surprise and joy. "Whenever you can get away. Maybe over a Monday and Tuesday, since we're not as busy." He thumbed back to Naomi. "I'm sure she can hold down the fort along with Dante."

"Perfect," I said. "Let's plan on a flight Monday morning." I smiled. "I'll book something now."

The smile on his face spread from ear to ear. "Great. I'd better get back to my station."

Dante entered the kitchen, appearing pleased, appearing as though everything was business as usual. It wasn't. In fact, it was far from it.

"Great shift, everyone," he said, clapping softly. "Tonight was the busiest we've been since opening, and I couldn't be prouder of everyone in this room."

I wanted to be happy. I should have been, but the weight of it all bore down on my shoulders. It was as though Dante didn't realize the damage he'd done both to the restaurant and to our personal reputations. He walked toward me, sliding his hand around my waist. I felt an almost sickening feeling at his touch as I glanced at Marco. The look he returned was like we'd shared a secret.

"I hope you can enjoy this too, Kira. Despite all that's happened," Dante said to me.

"This is all just a mirage now." I slipped away from his grasp and returned to the office to grab my things. On my way out, I saw Dante had already disappeared. Probably returned to the dining room to usher out the last of the dinner guests. I said my goodbyes, heading toward the rear exit when Marco caught up to me.

"Mind if I walk out with you?" he asked.

"You're leaving too?" I looked back and noticed his station was clean.

"I asked Dante if I could bail early to meet with a friend of mine. He didn't seem to have a problem with it. Do you?"

I opened the door. "No, of course not." I headed toward my car while Marco walked beside me. I fiddled with my keys as I reached the driver's side. "Listen, I had a chance to really see you tonight, and I'm amazed by you, if I'm being honest."

He shoved his hands in his pants pockets and glanced at his feet as if embarrassed by the compliment. "You have an excellent kitchen staff. Every one of those guys knows what they're doing. It wasn't just me."

"I appreciate you saying that." I glanced over at the back door, wondering who might step out, and how much time we had to ourselves. Dante's actions — his underhandedness — emboldened me. I reached inside my purse and grabbed a pack of cigarettes.

"You smoke?" Marco asked.

"Sometimes." I shook one out of the box. "Want one?"

"Hell, yes. Thanks."

The lighter was in my hand, but he reached out for it. "Let me do that." He lit my cigarette, then lit his own before handing back the lighter.

"Thank you." I took a long drag and felt a burn that made me cough. "I guess it's been a while." My cheeks turned pink with mild embarrassment.

He smiled at me, a quiet chuckle escaping between his lips while his cigarette dangled. "Tonight was a strong night."

"It was." I exhaled the smoke and watched it drift into the late-night sky.

"But?" Marco pressed.

"No buts, just uncertainty."

He flicked away the ashes. "About going to Napa?"

A part of me wanted to say, *hell, yes,* but I wasn't ready to show him my cards. "No, it's just us getting off the ground, you know?" I inhaled again, coughing a little less this time, but still looking like an amateur. "Can I ask you something?"

I was afraid to confide in him. Well, not so much confide, because he'd already known what happened, or most of it, anyway. But simply talk to him about it. Get a sense of direction, because I had no idea what to do. "You saw Dante with Eric the night before Eric's accident," I said.

"I did, yes. Only briefly, though."

"Right." I flicked away the cigarette ash and watched it float to the ground. "But you saw enough."

Marco licked his lips. "I suppose I did."

"You told me they'd discussed money, but I think you know it was more than that." I tried to read his face. "What do you plan to do with that information?"

"I make it a point to keep my nose out of other people's business, Kira," he replied. "It's a rule that's served me well so far. One I don't plan to change."

"What did you do after overhearing their conversation?" I asked, brushing aside his comment.

"I went back to the kitchen. Why are you pressing me? I have to think we're both on the same side here, meaning the side of the restaurant and its success."

"I'm afraid word might get out. I'm afraid that someone actually murdered Eric, and the worst part is that I don't know who or why."

"Maybe it's not for you to know," he added. "The man had a problem. Those kinds of problems tend to involve unseemly types, if you take my meaning."

I shrugged. "I suppose so. I just — I don't know how long I can hold it together, you know?" I felt my eyes sting.

Marco placed his hand on my arm. "Look, I don't pretend to know what you and Dante are going through, but maybe a day or two away from here is what you need. Clear your head. And if it helps the restaurant as well, then all the better, right?"

I looked up at him, surprised by his kindness. He wasn't the one who bribed Oliver. He didn't know Eric, or the fact that the guy was a drug addict. Did he deserve blame? No, that was me looking to point the finger at anyone other than my own husband.

"Thank you, Marco. And you're right. A day or two away from here will help." Butterflies. I actually felt butterflies in my stomach as I gazed into his eyes. I looked at his hand still resting on my arm. He began to slide it up to my shoulder. The spark between us surged.

He smiled at me, his green eyes glittering in the dim light of the parking lot. "I think it'll be good for us both."

His lips parted ever so slightly as he moved in. The shuffle of his feet on the rocky asphalt drew him closer. Thoughts of what Dante had done — what he had risked — swam in my head. The way he had flirted with Naomi. The financial and emotional strain this restaurant had placed on us. God, it was too much to think about, especially when this man, whose lips were inches from mine, so clearly wanted me. For a split second, our lips touched, and then I pulled away. Not because I'd wanted to, but because I feared being seen.

I dropped the cigarette butt from my fingers and watched it fall onto the asphalt. With the tip of my shoes, I squashed any remaining embers. Looking up at Marco again, I continued, "I'm sorry. I should go."

He opened my car door for me, saying nothing. "Thank you." I stepped inside. "Goodnight, Marco. I'll see you tomorrow."

"I hope so. Goodnight, Kira." Marco closed the door and walked to his Toyota parked nearby.

He stepped inside and with a smile back at me, drove away. The smile was confirmation that we now shared a secret. The kiss, though brief, sent waves of desire through me. The anger I'd felt toward my husband, now replaced. I pressed the ignition and pulled out onto the road, but when I drove on, passing by the exit to our home, I realized I needed to do something else.

I wanted to see where Eric crashed his car. When Dante and I went to the police station that morning to make our statement, the officer told us where it happened, so that was where I was headed.

As I drove, I felt compelled to check my rearview mirror. Several times, in fact. I don't know what I was looking for, but I felt an odd sensation that a car followed me. I slowed down, hoping to confirm or dismiss my fears. No lights approached. No one was there at all. Dismiss it I would, then. Nevertheless, the unease persisted.

When I arrived at the spot, I saw the damage to the tree. Skid marks appeared on the road. I got out and walked closer, the dirt of the shoulder clinging to my shoes. The tires that gouged the dirt from the weight of the vehicle ended just before the tree. It was splintered, cracked as though it might fall over. The bark was gone where the SUV struck it.

I looked around as though I was a detective on the hunt for clues. Something left behind by whoever drove him off the road. But I was no detective, and I saw nothing of the sort. I supposed I was simply looking for someone to blame. Maybe the only person to blame was Eric. If he hadn't come back to blackmail us, we wouldn't be in this position now. And he might still be alive. But could I truly let Dante off the hook so easily?

I wiped a tear that fell down my cheek, struggling to contain my emotions over this, over Marco, over Dante. Still, this was a fruitless endeavor, so I returned to my car only feet from where my friend had perished.

As I sat inside, my headlights aimed at the damaged tree and the faint skid marks that remained, I couldn't help but think about Marco. The way his lips touched mine. It had been too long since I'd felt a spark like that. But to consider what I was considering would change everything. Yes, Dante lied. Was this the answer to that? To become what he was?

My phone lay propped in the center console. I glanced at it, then at the clock on my dash. I had about two hours before Dante got home. Pushing away every good and decent thought, I called Marco.

"Listen, uh, I was wondering if you wanted to meet for a drink? Talk about the vendors we want to see in Napa." I waited for him to answer, instead, I was met with silence. "Marco?"

"I'm here. I'll text you the address of a place I've been wanting to try. They're still open."

A hint of a smile played on my lips. "Okay. I'll see you soon."

* * *

I knew this place. It had been a long time, mostly because I didn't often frequent bars anymore. But Dante and I had been here once more than a year ago. Must've been around the time we got the financing approved for the restaurant. Now, here I was again, teetering on the edge of right and wrong. Then again, it seemed my husband did the same thing willingly, and without regard for what it would do to me.

Several cars lined the parking lot, but I noticed Marco's right away. His Toyota was down the next row, so I pulled up next to it. He was still inside. We must've arrived at the same time. I walked around to his driver's side as he opened the door. "Hi."

"Hi," he said, stepping out. "I was surprised to hear from you."

I glanced down, shrugging my shoulder. "Yeah, well, I thought we could iron out the details of this trip before I bring it up to Dante."

"Fine by me." He placed his arm on the small of my back. "Let's go sit down and talk about it."

He opened the door for me, and I stepped inside the mid-sized bar. Plenty of people inside. Music was a little loud, but the ambiance was nice. Velvet booths. Sleek light fixtures. A stunning bar with more kinds of booze than I could possibly know. I always noticed these things now — now that I had my own restaurant.

Marco led us to a booth at the back. "This okay?"

"Perfect." I slid inside, double-checking the time again. He must've noticed as he'd laughed a little slipping next to me.

"Don't worry. Just a quick drink is all we'll need to figure this out," he said.

"Of course," I replied, dropping my phone into my purse.

A server took our orders. I kept it simple. A nice glass of red. He ordered a beer. "Sorry it's so late. I guess I wasn't ready to go home just yet." I thought about telling him where I'd been, but figured it was best not to. I don't know why. Too personal, maybe?

"Hey, I'm a night owl, so it's fine by me," he replied.

We went on to discuss the mundane things. Logistics of the short jaunt north. Who we would venture out to see.

What we would bring back. It was all very professional. Until it wasn't.

Marco placed his hand on my knee as he took a drink from his glass of beer. This was what I'd wanted. I made the call to him. Not the other way around. And after the kiss earlier, could I be angry with him for making the move?

I let him slide his hand up as he reached my thigh. We kept talking as though none of this was happening beneath the table. But it was, and I didn't know if I wanted to stop it. I felt a gentle squeeze on my inner thigh.

That was when he kissed me. Only this time, I didn't pull back. I let his tongue search mine. The scent of lager hung on his breath and mixed with my Cabernet. His hand squeezed my thigh and then slid a little higher. Enough to make me feel faint.

Who are you? I wondered. *Why are you here? Should I be afraid, or should I give in?*

When his other hand cupped my breast, I returned to my senses. "Hang on. Hang on." I leaned back, removing his hands from me. "I'm sorry, Marco. I thought I could do this, but I can't. Things are . . . complicated right now. I don't want to make them worse."

"It's okay, Kira. I understand."

And the look on his face made me want to believe him. "I need to go home."

"Of course." He took cash from his wallet and dropped it onto the table. Sliding out from the booth, he offered me his hand. "Come on. Let's get you to your car."

We didn't speak after that. I felt embarrassed, ashamed. I was his boss, after all. Is this what Dante had done with Naomi? Did he kiss her? Touch her thigh? Her breast? I didn't know. I only knew what I'd done.

Marco walked me to my car and as I unlocked it. He called out.

"Don't worry, Kira. This stays between us. We can keep this professional, okay? It's fine. Even in Napa, I promise, I won't try anything. I'm sorry for making you feel uncomfortable."

123

Napa, I thought. Christ, was I still going to go through with that now? "Thank you, Marco. Good night."

As I stepped inside and closed my door, I noticed my phone chime with an incoming text message. I waited for Marco to reach his car before I checked the screen again. "Unknown." So I viewed the message.

He's a dangerous man. One you can't trust.

The vague but ominous message sent my mind to worry. What man? Otis Oliver? Detective Lyman? But why would this sender keep his identity concealed? Could this be about Dante?

I typed my reply. *Who are you?*

No answer. And now I felt like I was being watched once again, the sender knowing where I was, and what I'd just done. A few cars went by me in the parking lot, but no one looked at me at all. This wasn't a message to scare me. It was a warning.

* * *

The hour was late when Dante arrived home. I heard him enter our bedroom, shuffling around as he prepared for bed. He climbed in, not at all subtle in his efforts to keep from awakening me, even if I hadn't been asleep. I was still angry over what he'd done, but was I any better? I loved him and wondered now more than ever if he'd crossed that line with Naomi as I now had with Marco. Were we in denial now about who we were and what we believed our marriage to be? I turned over to look at him. "Goodnight."

In the darkness of our bedroom, I noticed his face. While it was shadowed, I saw his worried brow, his parted lips. "What's wrong?"

"Naomi," he said.

"What about her? Is she okay? Please don't tell me she quit."

Funny how I didn't think to ask whether he'd slept with her, instead growing more concerned about the impact to the restaurant.

"She's sick. Really sick."

Admittedly, I felt relieved by this news. It was far better than what I'd expected. "Oh, okay. I hope you told her to stay at home tomorrow and get some rest. We can't afford for her to get anyone else sick."

"It's not a stomach bug, Kira. I've been doing this long enough to recognize food poisoning when I see it."

I shot up in bed and turned on the lamp on my night-stand. "Oh God. What did she eat? Did we serve something bad? Have we heard if any of our guests are sick?"

"I haven't heard, but it's late, so it's impossible to know."

"No, no, it's not impossible." I pulled my knees to my chest. "Have you checked our social media pages to see if anyone's commented about being sick?"

"That was the first thing I did." Dante sat up against the headboard, holding his phone. "I can check again." He opened Facebook.

I leaned in to see the screen, forgetting, at least momentarily, my betrayal. "I don't see any mention of anything, thank God. What about the others?"

Dante opened our other pages, and there was no mention anywhere of anyone getting sick tonight from our food.

Relief swelled in my chest. "Then it wasn't us."

Dante looked at me as if a terrible thing had just dawned on him. "It was something Naomi ate. She said there was a little bit of Chicken Alfredo left over, and she ate some of it just as we closed. And not long after you left, maybe an hour or so, she was hovering over the toilet, puking her guts out."

"Jesus." My head spun, and I couldn't ignore the timing. The flat tire. The hot pan she didn't know about. And now this? What was happening, and could we do anything to stop it?

As we sat there in silence, I wondered what else could go wrong. It seemed like our barely thriving restaurant was now a ticking time bomb, and it was only a matter of time before it exploded. My mind raced with all the possibilities, including one I had considered earlier, but brushed aside as my desire took over. I turned to Dante, holding his gaze. "What the hell is going on?"

"I wish I knew. Goddamn it. All this started when I bribed Oliver." Dante pushed his hand through his hair. "I knew it was wrong, but I thought, you know, we needed a leg up. We've played by the rules with everything, Kira, and we've still been screwed. So I made the choice, and this is what we get in return."

This was his fault, and now I could blame him for my own weaknesses. "No, I don't think this is on you. Not all of it." I grabbed my phone and opened the message to show him. "I got this earlier."

He snatched it from me and viewed the screen. "What? Who sent you this?"

"I have no idea," I replied. "But whoever did is warning us."

"About what? About who?" Dante asked.

"At first, I thought, maybe it was about you," I said sheepishly.

"Kira. I would never—"

"But then I saw the look in your eyes just now. I know you, and I let myself doubt you. I'm sorry. I know you didn't do anything to hurt Eric. But now . . ." I shrugged. "What are we supposed to do?"

And when I fixed my gaze on his, I saw the answer in his eyes. The very same answer I had. Only one possibility existed, no matter how hard I tried to ignore or deny it. And maybe it started to make sense now — the way I'd let myself succumb to my desire for him. A desire driven from anger. I couldn't tell Dante about it. Another time, yes, but not now. I was afraid he would climb out of this bed, and I'd never see him again. And yet I was torn, wanting to know if he'd done anything with Naomi. Why had he still been there tonight? Taking care of her? Was anyone else there with them?

I shook my head, telling myself to stop. Shouting in my mind to stop. "Babe, I know it was my suggestion to bring on Marco Devaney." I swallowed hard. "And I can't be sure any of this is about him, but it's hard to ignore the timing."

"So, we're on the same page?" Dante pressed.

"That maybe it's time we learn more about our head chef?" I asked. "Yeah, we are."

CHAPTER 15: DANTE

The trick was to be discreet. Looking into Marco Devaney without him figuring it out would take finesse. Why had this man come to us? Would he try to ruin the very place he now worked, and in the most prestigious position? The investigation into Eric's death seemed a good place to start digging. Eric hadn't known Marco, or at least, hadn't admitted to it, but was there another connection?

I could admit that I'd wanted a reason to let him go, regardless of how much we needed him right now. His skills were unparalleled, and Kira had been attracted to him. I knew it the moment she denied it. I thought I wasn't a jealous man because I didn't believe Kira would ever leave me. I wasn't so sure anymore. I had lied to her about the bribe, and Eric. I had no idea how much more she could take. The only way out now was to find out just who we were dealing with in Marco Devaney. And hope to God all that had happened pointed back at him, and not me.

I headed back to the LAPD to talk to Detective Lyman again, while Kira went about business as usual at the restaurant this morning. No one would miss me for a couple of hours. Enough time to gather more information. Naomi had texted me with a message that she was feeling better, thank

God. Problem was, if Marco had been responsible for making her sick, would he do anything else to her or the other staff? To my wife?

As I headed inside, the sun's reflection on the glass doors caught my eyes, temporarily blinding me until I reached the front desk. "Good morning." I blinked a moment to clear my vision. "I'd like to see Detective Lyman, if he's available."

A young female officer, not more than twenty-five, looked at me with some wariness. I wondered if I looked guilty of something.

"What's your name?" She set her gaze onto the computer screen in front of her.

"Dante Lucini. I'm here about the detective's investigation into the death of Eric Castor."

She reached for the phone, and, keeping an eye on me, spoke into the receiver. "Detective, there's a Dante Lucini here to see you."

A long pause followed, and I wondered what Lyman was telling her.

"I'll let him know. Thanks." She hung up the phone. "He'll be up in a minute. Take a seat over there."

She pointed a finger toward the rows of hard plastic chairs and so I took a seat, feeling even more guilty somehow. Technically, I was. Last I checked, bribery was a felony here in the great state of California. But so was blackmail.

My wait was short-lived when, from around the corner, I spotted Lyman in his cheap suit approaching me. I stood from the hard chair, my ass the worse for it.

"Good morning, Detective." We exchanged a firm handshake.

Lyman tilted his head and narrowed his gaze at me. "You're here about Eric Castor's death. I thought you'd said everything there was to say on the matter, Mr. Lucini. So, imagine my surprise to find you here this morning."

"Yes, sir, I'm sure this is unexpected," I said. "However, I've learned a few things since we last talked, and I thought it best to come see you."

"All right. Follow me."

I trailed Lyman into the long corridor, past an open bullpen where cops hurried around, and then past offices that belonged to higher-ranking officials, captains and lieutenants. A few eyeballs were aimed in my direction, but I carried on until we reached the detective's office.

"Take a seat, Mr. Lucini." Lyman gestured inside. "Can I get you a coffee?"

"No, thank you." I'd been here before, and somehow felt more at ease this time around. Familiarity, sure, but also knowing that I was about to offer information that would drive the investigation away from me and toward Marco Devaney.

Lyman took a seat at his desk. A steaming mug of coffee already sat in front of him. "Okay, Mr. Lucini, go on and tell me why you're here."

I cleared my throat, then I went into it. "Well, Detective, I have reason to think that my new head chef, Marco Devaney, might've had something to do with Eric's murder."

Detail here was key, so I elaborated. Telling him about Kira's text message, the incidents with Naomi, and how all of this seemed to point to Marco. Leaving out, of course, the fact that Marco knew Eric was blackmailing me and that I'd bribed an *LA Times* food critic. I thought it best to keep those tidbits of information to myself.

Lyman listened carefully, sipping his coffee as I spoke. When I finished, he leaned back in his chair, his gaze fixed on me. "Just so I understand things. You're accusing your head chef of running Eric Castor off the road, resulting in his death, based on a text message and the fact that your other chef suffered some sort of food poisoning episode?"

I swallowed hard. It sounded like BS when he put it that way, but it was all I had to go on. "I know it sounds far-fetched, Detective, but I have a gut feeling about this. There's something off about that guy. He just showed up out of nowhere."

"Nowhere?" Lyman leaned over his desk, appearing serious. "Mr. Lucini, I appreciate you coming forward with this information. But I need hard evidence, not a feeling. And as far as I can see, you don't have any evidence."

"So, what, I should wait until something else happens? Maybe to my wife?" I stood from the chair. "I'll be sure and get back to you when this guy comes at me or something." I headed toward the door when I heard Lyman call my name.

"Mr. Lucini?"

I turned around, irritated. "Yeah?"

"If you want to know more about this man you hired," he began, "then I suggest you do your homework. Maybe that was something that you ought to have already done? And then, if you feel the need, come back to me, and we'll talk again. In the meantime, I'll continue with my investigation."

"Sure thing. Got it." I nodded curtly at him and headed back into the corridor, no longer caring what the top brass in the glass offices thought of me as I walked by. I was angry. Lyman wasn't going to help, so it would be up to Kira and me to figure out who Marco was and why he'd come into our lives.

As I drove away, I called Kira, wondering if she'd arrived at the restaurant. When she answered, I began, "Hey, I'm leaving the station now. Where are you?"

Her voice sounded through the speaker. "In the office, going over receipts. How'd it go?"

Anticipation laced her words, but before I delved into it, I had to know she was alone. "Who's there with you?"

"Naomi, Marco, and Manny. No one else yet. My door is closed. What did Lyman say to you?"

The sun caught my eye, and I dropped down the visor. I almost didn't see the light turn red on San Bernardino Drive, and I braked hard to stop. "Holy shit."

"Dante, are you okay?"

"Yeah, sorry. Anyway, Lyman said he couldn't do anything for us. That we had nothing to make him think Marco had anything to do with Eric's death. Which, I don't know, maybe he's right. Maybe this is too much of a stretch, Kira."

"Look, this isn't over because he won't help." Her breathy response revealed her frustration. "We need to make up some excuse that both of us have to take off today."

"Who's going to run things?" I asked.

"Angelo."

"Are you serious? Look, babe, I love my brother, I really do, but the man's drunk most of the time. We can't—"

"He'll do it, Dante. You're going to have to trust me on this. You're right about his drinking, but when push comes to shove, you know you've always been able to count on him."

"Okay, fine. But what are you going to tell the staff?" I asked.

"I don't know . . . that we had a family emergency, or something."

I listened as she unleashed another heavy sigh. "What about your mom? Tell them she's in the hospital, and you're trying to get hold of her doctors back home."

"I won't lie about something like that, Dante. Putting that out there in the universe."

"Right." I rolled my eyes, knowing full well how Kira felt about karma, and the universe, and all that shit. But I had to respect it. We needed to be a team now more than ever. "It's none of their business why we can't be there today. We own the place, all right? So, you don't have to go into detail. I'll call my brother and, like you said, he'll come through for us. At least tonight."

"Where do you want to meet?" Kira asked.

As I drove along the highway that was still crammed with commuters, I realized I had no actual plan to deal with this. "I guess the first thing we should do is call the restaurants he listed on his resume. See what kind of reaction we get. It's a start. Meet me at home, okay? We'll take it from there."

"Yeah. I'll be there in an hour."

Kira hung up on her end, and I clasped the steering wheel with both hands. I was going to have to ask Angelo to step up. And I wasn't entirely sure he could, but I had to give it a shot.

The next call was one I hesitated to make, but one which I had to, if any chance existed that Kira and I could put an end to what seemed like an unraveling of our lives.

I pressed the Bluetooth and he answered. "Ang, it's me. Where are you?"

"At home. It's 9 a.m. Where the hell you think I'd be?"

His words were clear. No evidence that he was already hammered. This was a good sign. "Yeah, right. Listen, Kira and I have to take care of some stuff today. Would you mind stepping in at the restaurant in our absence?"

The only sound on the line I could hear was Angelo's breathing. "You know I wouldn't ask if I didn't really need you, bro."

"Yeah, I know, which is why I'm concerned," Angelo continued. "What's going on?"

"It's a long story. Kira's mom." I would respect Kira's wishes and not jinx her mother's health, leaving it at that. I had to hope Angelo wouldn't ask further. "It's only for today. And with Marco and Naomi, you'll just be overseeing things. No big deal."

"You remember what happened the last time I was in charge, right?" Angelo said.

"It won't be like that again. I trust you, Ang. You know that. All I ask is that you cut down on the drinking tonight. I wouldn't do this if I didn't really need the help."

"And if the staff asks questions?" Angelo pressed. "What do I tell them?"

"Same as I told you. Kira's family issues. That's all you know, and that's all they need to know."

"But her family's okay, right?" he continued.

"Yeah, of course," I said, hoping to placate him. "Kira's heading home now and we'll be out for the day. You can reach either of us by phone, but I'd prefer if you handled things on your own."

The line went quiet again until Angelo finally spoke up. "I'll do my best."

"I know you will, man. Oh, and hey, don't let Marco bully you, all right? You're the one in charge. Not him. Talk to you later." I pressed the end call button and rubbed my temple for a moment.

Two problems down; one big problem to go. Kira and I could be going after someone innocent. Fair enough. And I couldn't forget my part in this, but it was more than that, and we both knew it now.

I arrived home and noticed Kira's car in the driveway. Perfect. I stepped out, walking up the sidewalk to our front door. On opening it, I called out. "Babe, it's me."

The echo of Kira's footsteps suggested she was in the kitchen. I closed the door behind me and headed there. "Hi."

Kira stood before me, worry masking her face.

"Do you think you raised any suspicions about leaving?" I asked.

"No. I don't think so. What did Angelo say when you asked him to cover for us?"

"He's up for it. I think." I reached inside the fridge and grabbed two bottles of water, handing one to Kira. "We'll contact the restaurant in Napa. Lilibell's. That was where he listed his last job."

Kira opened the water bottle, taking a long sip before responding. "I think we should also try to talk to some of Eric's friends. Maybe there's something they know that could help us."

"I figured Lyman would've already done that, but he wouldn't have asked about Marco, so yeah, why not? Eric has a sister."

"That's right." Kira raised her index finger. "She's listed as a contact in his employee file. We can get Angelo to give us the address. What about the police? Can't we ask them to do more?"

I dismissed the notion: "Lyman made it pretty clear he wasn't interested in pursuing this further unless we came up with something more. He's got tire tracks from a second vehicle, and I guess that's the only lead he's running on. So, for now, we're on our own with this."

She let out a frustrated sigh. "I don't know if this will lead anywhere, Dante. I don't know if we're wrong about Marco."

I reached out, placing my hand on her shoulder. "We won't know until we look into it. Then, if not, case closed. All right? The guy knows what I did. And I feel like, you know, there's more to his story."

Kira walked to her carrier bag, which rested on the dining chair, and pulled out a file. She returned to the kitchen island and dropped it on the counter. "Marco's file. Let's get to work."

My first call was to Lilibell's, the restaurant in Napa where Marco claimed to have worked. A woman answered with a cheerful greeting.

"Thank you for calling Lilibell's, how may I assist you?"

"Hi, yeah, I'm calling about a former employee of yours, Marco Devaney."

The line went quiet for a moment, and I thought I dropped the call. But I looked at the screen, and I was still connected. "Hello?"

"I'm sorry, I don't think we have anyone here by that name," the woman replied.

"No, I understand that. He worked there a few months ago. Marco Devaney?"

"I'm sorry, sir. I don't recall the name. We have a high turnover rate. Would you like to speak with a manager?"

"Yes, please," I replied, glancing at Kira with a raised brow.

There was a brief hold before a man with a deep voice picked up the line. "This is Zach. How can I help you?"

"Hi, Zach, my name is Dante Lucini. I'm looking for some information about a former employee of yours, Marco Devaney. I believe he was your sous chef a few months ago, maybe longer." There was that long pause again.

"Devaney. Yeah, what would you like to know?"

I looked at Kira and smiled, feeling like we might actually get somewhere with this. "We recently hired him as our head chef. And uh, well, this is probably a call that should've been made before we offered him the job, but we were in a bind."

"You hired Marco?" Zach asked.

"Sure did, about a week ago. He's been doing a great job, but I was wondering if you had any thoughts on him."

"I'm not sure what you mean," Zach replied.

"I guess, you know, like concerns." My smile faded as I got the feeling Zach was hesitant to speak. I set down my phone and placed the call on speaker, laying my index finger on my lips while Kira stood by.

"Concerns?" Zach began. "Well, laws dictate what I'm allowed to tell you, so . . ."

"Can we speak off the record? I can meet you in Napa if you'd like. I'm happy to take a flight." I wasn't, but this was important.

"Where are you located?" he asked.

"LA."

"Well, Dante, you're in luck. I'm flying to LA shortly. I have a meeting later today. I'll be there in about three hours with some time to spare before my appointment. Can you be available then?"

"Yeah, absolutely, that'd be great," I replied.

"Good. Meet me in Burbank. I'll send you the address of the hotel I'll be staying in tonight, and we'll meet in the lobby in a few hours."

"We'll be there, thank you, Zach."

"We?"

"My wife and I. We own the restaurant together," I added.

Zach scoffed. "Then it's a good thing we're meeting today. Look out for my text, and I'll see you both soon."

"Appreciate it, man, thanks." I ended the call, and with my hands pressed firmly on the countertop, I looked at Kira. "That was strange."

"Yeah, it was." She raised a brow. "He knows something."

CHAPTER 16: KIRA

As we drove into Burbank to meet with the owner of Lilibell's, it occurred to me that while Dante and I had been at each other's throats for months, we'd come together again. A time was, not that long ago, I wondered if we were going to make it. The stress, the grind, the money troubles. The suspicions. And I'd recently added to those suspicions myself now. It was shitty of me to want Marco to be the root of our problems. As though it would absolve me of my part in it.

I'd let my anger over what Dante had done drive my decision. And as I looked at him behind the wheel, I knew that if he learned about it, we were over. So maybe it was best to just get rid of the problem. To get rid of Marco.

All this proved to me that we still loved each other. Cared for each other. And cared about what happened to the people around us.

"This is it," Dante said, turning into the hotel parking lot. He held his phone and peered at the screen. "He texted saying he's in the lobby waiting for us. Let's go."

I wrapped my fingers around the car door handle, and with a deep breath, opened the door to climb out. Under a midday sun that grew warmer by the moment, I steadied my nerves. All we had to do was get to the truth. Was Marco someone we had to watch out for, and if so, what would happen if we tried to get rid of him?

The blast of cool air hit my face when Dante opened the door for me. I walked inside, my high heels clicking on the marble floor. It was a nice hotel — for Burbank. I looked at Dante. "We have no idea what this guy looks like."

He aimed a finger toward a group of cushy-looking chairs with a man sitting in one of them. "I'll bet that's him over there."

"How do you know?" I asked.

"Because he looks like he's searching for people." Dante turned to me. "Those people are us."

"I guess we'll find out." I followed him as he led the way toward the seating area.

"Zach?" Dante asked. "Zach Emory?"

"You must be Dante." The middle-aged man stood, wearing black dress pants and a white button-down shirt. He offered his hand and a smile that appeared almost sympathetic.

"Yes, sir. And this is my wife, Kira."

I leaned in and extended my hand. "Thank you for taking the time for us, Zach."

"Better to do this now before things get out of hand." He returned to his chair. "Sit."

Get out of hand? What did that mean? Whatever it was, it sure set the tone for this impromptu meeting.

"So, you hired Marco Devaney as your executive chef," Zach began, folding his hands in his lap.

"We did," Dante replied. "Our former head chef was let go, and Kira met Marco at a new restaurant that was under renovation. Sunset 717, I believe. One thing led to another, and now he's working for us." Dante shifted in his chair. "The thing is, our previous chef died in a car crash just days after Marco was brought on."

"I'm very sorry to hear that," Zach replied.

"Thank you." Dante raised a preemptive hand. "Now, I don't want to jump to conclusions, but—"

"After that," I cut in, not letting the accusation hang in the air, "other things started happening. Accidents in the kitchen, mostly to our sous chef."

Zach nodded and wore a knowing smile. "I see why you're here now." He scratched his stubbled cheek and drew in a deep breath. "Did Devaney do that to your arm?"

I glanced down, almost forgetting about the bandage. "No, that was an accident with our former chef."

He kept his gaze on my arm for a while before he finally turned his attention back to the conversation. "This is what I do know about Marco Devaney. He may be one hell of a talented chef, but the man's a liar."

Zach set his eyes on me and continued. "And what you're saying about strange things happening . . . we had similar things happen to us."

"Similar?" Dante asked. "You say he's a liar. What did he lie to you about?"

Zach scoffed. "How much time you got? Let's just say the man embellished his resume, for one. He had a two-year span where he claimed that he'd traveled to shadow some of the best chefs in Europe. Well, I read that and thought, great. Perfect. We need someone like that. So, I didn't question it." He placed his hand on his chest. "You have to remember, we're a Michelin-star restaurant, and he was exactly the kind of sous chef we were interested in. His resume indicated he'd worked at a few other places before that, which escape my mind now, so at the time, I didn't dig deep."

"Neither did we," Dante said, reluctantly.

"Exactly. Which, I think, is what Marco has counted on all this time. Complacency," he added. "We all know how hectic it can be running a restaurant, and when you see a guy like Marco cook these amazing dishes, you think, yeah, this guy knows what he's doing." Zach vacillated his gaze between Dante and me. "So not long after we brought him onboard, well, people started getting sick."

"Staff?" Dante asked.

139

"No. Guests." Zach shook his head. "We were in danger of having our star stripped from us. It would've meant the end. As it was, word about the illnesses had spread quickly. Yelp and all that bullshit. I couldn't prove it was Marco, of course. He was careful enough not to leave behind any evidence. But I'd worked with the rest of my kitchen staff long enough to know they weren't responsible."

"So you fired him?" I asked.

"Eventually." Zach pressed his elbows against his thighs and leaned over toward us. "To this day, I have no idea why he did those things, but listen to me. Get that man out of your kitchen, you understand? Get him out before he destroys you. I did, but only after nearly losing it all. Oh, and our head chef, who Marco worked for?"

Zach's face hardened as though he'd thought of a painful memory. I glanced at Dante and he back at me. Neither of us sure what he would say next. "What happened to him?" I asked.

Zach laced his fingers together and leaned back in the chair. "I don't know. He left one day, and we never heard from him again. Marco thought he would get the job, but something told me to get rid of him, so I did. And now, you need to do the same."

* * *

The fear was real. As we drove back into downtown LA, neither Dante nor I said two words to each other. We knew then that Marco Devaney was going to be a problem for us. Regardless, we had nothing new to take to the detective. More hearsay and nothing real. Except for the fear.

"What are we going to do?" I asked Dante.

His hands tightened around the steering wheel as he navigated through traffic. "We're going to fire him. Immediately."

"I'm sure he knows about the bribe," I said, using that as an excuse to not fire him. Not until I could be sure Marco wouldn't tell my husband what had happened between us.

140

"I get that, and we'll suffer the consequences. But at this point, I don't care. I won't risk something happening to any one of our staff, you, me, Angelo. No, this ends now."

I nodded, feeling my stomach tighten in knots. "It just doesn't make any sense to me. What could Marco possibly want that we haven't already given him?"

"How do you mean?" Dante asked.

"I get why he left Lilibell's. Aside from the fact that Zach wanted him gone, Marco wanted to be head chef. He wasn't given the chance. So why come work for us in that very position and attempt to screw us over? Dante, do you think he caused Eric's accident?"

"I don't know, babe. He had the job he wanted. Why go after the guy he replaced?"

I didn't have an answer.

Arriving at the restaurant, we walked into the kitchen and found Marco standing at the stove, his back to us. The kitchen was bustling with activity, cooks and servers moving back and forth, but we could feel all eyes on us as we made our way to him.

"Marco," Dante said, his voice firm. "We need to talk."

Marco didn't turn around, didn't acknowledge us at all. "Marco, would you please come into the office and talk to us? It's important," I added.

It was then that Angelo walked into the kitchen, capturing my attention. He approached us and I checked his eyes. They were clear. Still, this was more pressing, and Angelo . . .

"Can I have a word with you both?" Angelo asked.

Dante and I traded glances before I looked at my brother-in-law. "Can this wait?"

"No." And when he shot a look at Marco, I knew he was right. This couldn't wait.

"We can talk in the dining room." Dante led the way, and I followed him, alongside Angelo.

I could feel Marco's eyes watching us as Dante pushed through the swinging door from the kitchen to the dining area.

"What is it?" Dante asked his brother.

"Sit." Angelo gestured to a nearby booth. When we sat down, he began, "There's something you both should know."

Christ, what now?

"Whatever it was you two were doing today," Angelo said, "It's raised some concerns with Marco."

"I don't understand what you mean," Dante replied.

Angelo peered at him. "I mean, he knows."

"Knows what?" I asked.

"He knows about the bakery. About our parents." As Angelo kept his sights on me, I glanced at Dante, his shoulders sinking, his head lowering. "What are you talking about?"

It was then that the brothers seemed to be silently speaking to each other, as though some great secret existed between them. "What is it? You two are freaking me out. What about your parents?"

I knew they'd died in a fire at their bakery and that the insurance money helped us to move out here and start this place.

"That's it." Dante began to slide out of the booth. "This guy's getting fired right now."

"No," Angelo called out. "It's too late for that. I'm sorry, brother, but we're in this now."

Why had it suddenly felt like everyone was keeping secrets from me? I wanted to ask Dante what the hell Angelo was talking about, but the dinner service was about to start, and I was already behind on work because we'd been on a hunt for the truth about Marco, only to have more questions. Now, I wondered what in God's name was going on with my own husband and his family.

As I followed Dante back to the kitchen, my mind raced with questions. What did Angelo mean by *we're in this now?* What other secrets were being kept from me? And how could we possibly deal with the threat of Marco Devaney when we had everything else to worry about?

But as soon as we stepped back into the kitchen, all thoughts of secrets and family drama were pushed aside by

142

the urgent need to get through the dinner rush. The kitchen was a hive of activity.

In the midst of it all, Marco stood calmly at his station, his focus fixed on the task in front of him. It was hard to believe that this man I thought bordered on greatness had the power to end us. And I'd given him the power to destroy my marriage. I thought coming back here tonight would settle it for good. Consequences be damned. That was what Dante said. But clearly, some consequences existed he didn't want to face.

As the night wore on, the kitchen grew hotter and more crowded, the tension mounting with each passing minute. Every time a plate was sent out, we held our breath, waiting for the potential complaints to roll in, fearing Marco would employ the same tactics Zach Emory believed he had at Lilibell's. But to my surprise, everything seemed to be going smoothly. The guests were happy, the food was delicious, and the atmosphere was electric.

Even Marco seemed to be in a good mood, cracking jokes and chatting amiably with the other cooks. It was as if he had some knowledge that the rest of us didn't, as if he knew that everything was going to work out just fine. For him, maybe. But I still held my breath.

I found myself keeping a closer eye on Marco, trying to pick up on any subtle signs of wrongdoing. Any hint that he might reveal what we'd done.

He knew I was watching. The occasional glance my way. The crooked hint of a smile that played on his lips. He knew what Dante and I had done earlier — looking into his past. I don't know how, but he had to have known, and he knew he had the upper hand.

* * *

This all went back to the day I met Marco in that restaurant. So, this morning, I left the house early. Not even bothering to kiss Dante on the cheek.

In the early morning skies, drenched in brown haze and still air, I drove back to that place near the market. The upcoming Sunset 717. I had to track down the owner and find out what he knew about Marco. After all, this was a man who'd lent Marco a key to his restaurant and allowed him to claim it as his own. Maybe he had also been kept in the dark, but I had to know for sure.

I stopped by the market first, walking toward the man I'd met more than a week ago. "Good morning."

"Mrs. Lucini, if I'm recalling correctly," he said.

"That's right. How are you?"

"Doing okay." He spread out his arms over his boxes of fresh fruits and vegetables. "What can I get for you today?"

I moved in a little closer, scanning the area for eavesdroppers. Or maybe just making sure I was alone. "What can you tell me about the restaurant over there?" I aimed a finger toward the place. "Do you know who owns it?"

"Course I do," he replied. "Gentleman by the name of Tom Weaver. Good guy. Believe he's part owner of Brindi's as well. Why do you ask?"

"I was interested in who he's using for interior design."

"Didn't La Bianca's open only recently?"

"It did." I donned a smile, hoping to distract him for a moment while I invented a reason for my question. "But I thought if we wanted to expand to a second location, I'd love to know who he used."

"I see." He crossed his arms. "Well, he's usually there overseeing work. Sometimes stops by here, though I haven't seen him yet this morning. You might pop over and take a chance. If not, I'm happy to leave him a message for you. Like I said, he comes by to check out what we have on occasion."

I jerked my thumb over my shoulder. "You know what? I'll drive over there and see if he's in. Can't hurt, right?"

"Nope. Can't hurt at all. You be sure and stop back over if you decide you need anything today, Mrs. Lucini."

"I appreciate that. And call me Kira." I nodded and spun around, returning to my Mercedes.

Within moments, I'd arrived, and as luck would have it, it appeared someone was here. I stepped out and walked toward the door, which was propped open. As I entered, I noticed not much had been done since I was last here. I understood the pain he must've been going through getting crews lined up and permits in hand. I had no desire to go through that again.

"Good morning," a voice called out from behind me.

I turned around and spotted a tall, lean man with dark skin and hair. "Good morning. I'm sorry to barge in, but I noticed the door was open."

"That's okay, but as you can see, we're far from being open, if you're looking for a meal," he replied.

"Actually, I own a restaurant downtown, and I noticed this place as I left the market." I narrowed my gaze. "Are you Tom Weaver?"

His smile lit up the space. Gleaming white teeth, full lips, high cheekbones. "As a matter of fact, I am. And you are?"

He extended his hand, and I shook it. "Kira Lucini. Nice to meet you, Mr. Weaver."

His expression changed, turned almost blank. "Please, call me Tom."

"Tom. Call me Kira." *Oh yeah, he knows something about Marco, and he knows exactly who I am.*

"All right, Kira. What can I do for you, then?"

"You know, I was actually here a week or so ago. I'd met a man named Marco Devaney. He said he was the owner at the time."

"Is that so?" Tom scratched his stubbled chin. "Marco must've been trying to impress you. I've known him for some time and asked his opinion on the place. But he most definitely does not own it."

"So you know him well?" I asked, trying to sound casual about the whole thing.

"Well enough. He mentioned he'd gotten a head chef position at an Italian restaurant recently."

"That's right. And I was sure the owner at Brindi's recommended him. Was that you?"

"Uh, no. That must've been my partner."

"Okay. Well, anyway." I stammered. "I was wondering if I could ask you a few questions about Marco."

"You're here for a reference?" He choked out a nervous laugh. "Seems a little late, since he's already working for you."

"I am a little behind in my HR duties," I said, keeping things light. "I suppose I'm just now getting around to checking out his story."

"Is he not doing well for you?" Tom asked.

I raised my hands. "Oh, no, he is. No, it's not that. I guess what I wanted to ask was how you came to know him. Had you worked with him? I understood he'd been overseas for some time, studying with chefs in Europe."

His lips ticked up into a half-smile, but when he went quiet, and the smile faded, I felt unnerved.

"You know what?" Tom glanced over his shoulder. "I'm actually kind of busy at the moment. I'd love to chat with you about Marco, but how about you leave me your card and I'll shoot over an email reference? I am sorry about this." He turned around and walked toward the kitchen.

I stood there, stunned by his response. "What the hell?" I whispered. And before he disappeared, I called out to him. "Tom, if you can tell me anything about Marco, you'd be helping me out a lot. And I mean that."

He seemed to pick up on my desperate tone. I'd tried to say what couldn't be said, and he'd noticed. "Tom, if there's anything I should know . . ." I trailed off, hoping he would answer me. And when he stepped toward me again, I held my breath in anticipation.

"If I thought I could help you, Kira, I would. But I'm afraid I can't."

And then he was gone. I exhaled, feeling defeated and returned outside to my car. I slipped behind the wheel and sank into the driver's seat. First Zach Emory, and now Tom Weaver. Were they all afraid of Marco?

I slammed my head against the headrest, closing my eyes. "Damn it." But I quickly opened them when I heard a knock on my window. Startled, I let out a yelp. Marco stood outside, wearing a wide grin.

"Fancy seeing you here," he said leaning in close to my window.

I rolled it down. "Marco, what are you doing here?"

He stood upright again, shoving his hands into his pockets. "I should be asking you the same thing. Why are you here, Kira? Checking up on me or something?"

He appeared menacing, dangerous, and I was here alone. "No, I was at the market and decided to stop over to this place and see how things were going."

He leaned down, his elbows resting on the door frame. "Is that so?"

When he traced his index finger along my forearm, I grew unnerved. "Of course."

"Well, then, I guess you'll be going back to the restaurant now," he said.

"As a matter of fact, I was just about to leave."

He tapped on my door. "How about we grab a bite to eat first? Maybe we can pick up where we left off the other night?"

His meaning was clear, as was the look in his eyes. This was the price I would pay for crossing the line. "We talked about that, Marco. You know we can't do that again. It was a mistake."

He nodded with turned down lips. "I'm sorry to hear you say that, Kira. I mean, it's not like your husband hasn't done worse, right?"

"I'm sorry?" I asked. "What are you talking about?"

"You know what? It doesn't matter. I shouldn't be talking out of turn." He leaned close again. "Look, I get what happened between us can't happen again. I do understand that. I can't say I'm not disappointed, but I get it. And it really would be a shame if word got out, so you can count on me to make sure that doesn't happen." He gestured to his lips as though he was zipping them shut. "I'll see you later, Kira."

I smiled, rolled up the window, and pressed the ignition. He stood there, staring at me. I was under no illusion that what he'd just said wasn't a threat. He knew I was looking into his past, and now I feared he might tell Dante what had happened between us. Unless, of course, I stopped digging. As I reached the road and shifted into drive, I looked back at him through my rearview. Now, I was afraid.

CHAPTER 17: DANTE

She didn't know I was there, lingering out of sight while Marco stood at her car door. When Kira left this morning, I'd already been awake, on edge for most of the night over what Angelo had said. Marco knew what had happened when my parents died, something only Angelo could have revealed, no doubt, when he'd had a few drinks in him. He knew about the bribe.

This man, who'd only recently come into our lives, had managed to get under the hood and pull apart our fragile engine, piece by piece, waiting until we were nothing but a hollowed-out shell.

I'd checked Kira's location on my phone. Minutes later, I was up and out the door, heading her way, fearing she would search for answers about Marco alone. Turned out, I was right.

What I hadn't expected was to see him there. Marco must've known where we lived and had been watching us — watching her. What the hell were we up against? I'd been standing across the street under the awning of a liquor store, next to the outdoor ice freezer. The parking lot of Sunset 717 within my line of sight.

I'd watched her get into her car and then Marco turned up, appearing out of nowhere. It took everything in my power not to bum-rush the guy to get him away from her, but I didn't move. I wasn't sure what would happen. Would he get into her car? Would she get out?

Instead, Kira drove away, and I breathed a sigh of relief. Now, I watched Marco as he made his way to that restaurant where Kira had just come from. He entered the building, and something inside me stirred. I had a feeling that whatever was going on behind those brown papered windows involved my wife.

I had to make a move, and it had to be now. I stepped off the sidewalk, heading across the street toward the restaurant's entrance. With the windows covered, I easily approached without being seen. The door was closed, but a small sliver of glass was exposed between the two wrapped front windows. I shielded my eyes and peered in, but only for a moment. I didn't see anyone, but I heard voices. Indiscernible, but definitely coming from two people. The muffled voices continued to rise. One of them, I now recognized was Marco's.

"What did you tell her?" His deep cadence sounded through the glass. "You fucking owe me. I cleared the way for you to get this place, and this is how you repay me?"

"Cleared the way? You left me high and dry, or have you forgotten about that? I had to pull myself out of the hole you dug," the other man replied. "I can't believe you'd risk coming back here. I don't know what you think you're doing."

Coming back? I wondered. When had he'd been here before? From where I stood, Marco was tangled up in something bigger than Kira and me. Unless we were part of his plan. But what plan was that?

I'd been here long enough. Any longer and I risked being seen, so I hurried back to my car and climbed inside. Kira would notice my absence from the restaurant, but this couldn't wait. I had new questions for Detective Lyman. And a new reason to be worried for my wife. If this man had, in fact, told her things about Marco, then Marco might do more than just follow her next time.

The police station was only minutes away, and I had to confront Lyman about what I'd overheard. Maybe this would light a fire under his ass to take Marco Devaney seriously.

On my arrival, I hurried toward the front desk. "Excuse me, I need to see Detective Lyman. Is he available?" A different officer stood behind the desk this time and eyed me.

"Hang on and I'll find out." the officer made the call as I waited.

I grabbed my phone and opened Kira's contact. She'd be worried if I didn't at least text her, so I drafted a quick message to let her know I was running late, but that I was fine. I'd just pressed send when the officer called out to me.

"The detective will be with you in a moment, if you'd like to take a seat," he said.

I raised my hand, familiar with this part already. "Thanks. I'll wait over here."

Fortunately, Lyman didn't keep me waiting for long, and I noticed the look on his face as he approached. He thought I was about to waste his time again. To hell with that. I walked toward him with an outstretched hand. "Detective. Thanks for your time."

"As I mentioned before, Mr. Lucini, I am working to find the person responsible for Eric's death."

"I get that," I interrupted. "And that's not why I'm here. Not entirely." I shoved my hands in my pants pockets. "I went back to conduct that due diligence you mentioned. And, uh, look, Marco Devaney isn't who he says he is. He has a history in LA, and I think maybe a partner."

"A partner? In what?" Lyman raised a brow.

"I don't know, and I don't know the guy's name, but I think he's an owner in that new restaurant near the farmer's market. Sunset 717, I believe."

Lyman planted his hands on his hips. "Unless he's done something illegal, Mr. Lucini, I don't know what I can do for you."

I closed my eyes, keeping my frustration in check. "Can't you at least run a criminal background check on Devaney?"

"Not without cause, but you can. There are companies out there who will do that for you. Ask around. Lots of employers run backgrounds," he replied.

"Doesn't it bother you at all that Devaney seemed to turn up out of nowhere around the time my former head chef was murdered? Your words, Detective. Murdered."

Lyman tilted his head. "The two men had no connection to one another. So, I think the question I should be asking, Mr. Lucini, is why does Devaney bother you?"

* * *

It was clear to me that Kira and I were on our own. If I wanted Marco Devaney out of our lives, and to keep my own secrets at bay, then it was up to me to make that happen. I would have to go about this carefully. Methodically. I had no idea if he was responsible for what happened to Eric, but if he was, I'd be the one to prove it.

On my way back to the restaurant, I felt I was at least armed with more information than I had earlier. I also knew that Marco was watching us — Kira, more importantly. I walked through La Bianca's front door, and my brother's eyes locked onto me as he jumped from his barstool.

"Where have you been? Kira said she texted you, but you didn't respond."

"I sent her a message earlier." But when I pulled my phone from my pocket and looked at my texts, I noticed it hadn't sent. "What? I thought she got this. Is she in the kitchen?" I asked.

"Yes. Go tell her you're here, would you?"

"I will, but I need to talk to you for a minute." I grabbed Angelo by the arm and pulled him aside. "Look, I know the other night Marco talked to you—"

"I'd had too much to drink," he cut in.

What could I say to that? I glanced over my shoulder at the door to the kitchen, afraid someone might walk through. "Come over here."

We walked to a distant table and sat down, well away from prying eyes and ears. "Listen, Marco thinks he has a friend in you, and I want it to stay that way."

"I don't understand." Angelo knitted his brow. "He knows about Ma and Pop. How you were there, and . . . I messed up, man."

I watched my older brother's eyes glisten as he fought back his emotions. "Forget about that right now, okay? I have a plan, and I need your help. I need you to cozy up to Marco. At least, make it look like you're cozying up to him. He's smart, so he'll see through it if you don't sell this, you understand?"

"Yeah, I guess so. But why?"

"This guy likes to make himself look good, yeah? You're going to let him do that. Compliment him. Tell him what a great chef he is. Then he'll trust you, maybe say things he wouldn't say otherwise, you got it?" I leaned over the table and lowered my tone. "But Angelo, don't give him more ammo to use on us. Promise me that. Keep your wits about you when you're dealing with him. Can you do that?"

My brother was an alcoholic. Asking him something like this, something he might not have in his control, was setting him up for failure. Potentially, putting him in a dangerous spot. But I had no choice. Marco needed an ally in this restaurant, and I wasn't going to let it be Kira. Naomi was smart, but she had her own agenda. She wouldn't be interested in advancing Marco's.

Angelo hesitated, then nodded. "Yeah, I can do that. For you, Dante."

I put my hand on his shoulder. "Thank you."

"I think I'll go home and come back later. Give me a chance to sober up before I see the guy tonight." He looked down. "I'm sorry I've done this to you and Kira. I wish we could go back to the way things were."

"Me, too, brother. More than you know, but this isn't on you. Go on, then. I'll see you later."

I watched him leave, feeling a mix of guilt and determination. Guilt for putting him in this position, but determination to put Marco in a vice grip. The kitchen door opened, and Kira stepped out, drawing my attention. "Hey."

"Hi. Did you just get here? I texted you. I was getting worried."

"Yeah, uh, I had some things to do this morning. I'm sorry. I thought I'd sent you a text, but I guess I didn't." I raised my hands. "It's fine. I'm here now, and we're going to be fine."

"Where's Angelo?" she asked. "I thought I saw him out here earlier."

"He went home. We talked, and I think I got through to him about his drinking. Anyway, he'll be back later."

Kira gathered her hair in her hands, holding it to one side. That was her tell — fidgeting with her hair. That was how I knew she was worried.

"We're going to have to re-think things."

"What do you mean?" I asked.

"Him," she whispered. "If we fire him, he'll tell everyone about Oliver. And now there's this thing you won't tell me about your parents. What the hell is it, Dante? What more can Marco do to us?"

I wondered why she said nothing about her whereabouts this morning, or the fact that Marco had been there, too. What had the man in the restaurant said to her? She was right about one thing: now that I knew Marco had lived here in LA before, I had something to work with. Keeping him around, keeping an eye on him, maybe that was the best play. But what should I say to her now? About what I'd overheard, about going to see Lyman again? And now, my parents. Jesus, there was so much she didn't know.

"We have no way to know for certain what happened to Eric." Kira hesitated for a moment, looking like she wanted to say more.

"What? What is it, babe?" I asked.

"I don't want to be around him, Dante," she whispered. "You have to take care of this. I don't know how, but firing him will bite us in the ass."

She blamed me for all of it. I could see it in her eyes. I had no leg to stand on. The bribe, the blackmail. Shit, this *was* my fault. But something in her eyes made me feel as though she held something back, and I was sure it had to do with whatever had transpired this morning outside that restaurant parking lot.

Kira turned on her heel and pushed through the door into the kitchen. I followed her, feeling more alone than ever.

As we entered the kitchen, I saw him. Marco was back. I wondered for a moment whether he'd seen me outside that building. Had he seen me driving away, toward the police station? He had certainly seen Kira, and that was the real problem. A problem my wife was keeping to herself.

We locked eyes for a moment, both of us seeming to know something about the other. But rather than engage him in a conversation I wasn't prepared for, I diverted into the locker room.

Every staff member had their own locker, including me. I usually kept a spare suit inside, just in case something was spilled on the one I was wearing. I grabbed the handle and pulled it open when something fell from the top of my locker. "The hell?" It was just a blur until I looked down; it scurried toward my feet. "Shit!" I jumped back.

A rat squealed. Its claws scratched the tile floor as it tried to gain traction. I looked up again, that same scratching noise capturing my attention. And as I looked around the lockers, more rats poured over it. Five, ten, I had no idea.

"The fuck is this?" I stumbled back, almost tripping over the bench behind me. "Hey, I need some help in here!"

They scurried all around me, clawing at my shoes, running under the lockers, scattering like the gray, hairy, disgusting creatures they were. One of them ran toward me. I raised my foot, slamming down onto it. The sound it made when its guts spilled out forced bile to rise in my throat. Blood splattered on my shoes, landing on my socks and the hem of my pants.

Footfalls headed down the hall and Kira ran inside. "Wait!" I said, thrusting out my hand. "They're everywhere. We have to keep them from getting into the kitchen."

She started toward me and looked down at the floor, her face masked in revulsion. "Oh . . . oh, no. Oh, my God. What are we going to do?"

I looked down at the mess of blood and gray fur. My stomach heaved as the stench filled my nostrils. A small, flattened pile of rat lay before me, its innards dribbling down my shoes. "Goddamn rats." I looked at Kira, stunned. "We have rats."

Others must've heard the commotion, as the sound of footsteps seemed to sprint toward us. Marco appeared around the corner, and Naomi behind him, their cries alerting Amy to something happening at the room's entrance. Amy ducked under Marco's arm and stepped in from behind him.

"Are you guys okay?" Amy asked.

I stared at Marco, holding his gaze, and saw his eyes flicker with what I could've sworn was delight. "We need help. Rats are everywhere. Close the door. We have to stop them."

"Rats?" Amy shouted, closing the locker room door. She looked down. "There's one!"

"Kill it. Step on it," I called out.

Marco held her back. "I got it. I got it." He stomped on the rat, and another one came. He stomped on that one too.

I regained my balance, my shoes covered in blood and guts. "Kira, grab the broom and bucket. We'll force them into a corner and put the bucket over them."

"Got it." She hurried to the other end of the locker room and grabbed the equipment.

Meanwhile, Marco tried to stomp out each one. "They're everywhere. How the hell did this happen?"

I shot him a look. "You tell me."

Chaos erupted as we all tried to corral the rats, crowding into the corner to keep them from escaping to other areas of the locker room. I would've laughed if it wasn't so horrific. Rats in our restaurant. How could this have happened?

Well, I had a pretty damn good idea.

When we'd scoured the locker room, it seemed we'd captured all of them. "I'll take the bucket and dispose of them," I said. "Thank you, guys, for the help."

"This is bad, Dante," Amy said. "What if there are more in the dining room or the kitchen?"

"It's okay," I assured her. "I'm sure they were just in here." I walked around the metal lockers and pulled the section off the back wall. "I can't see where they came in." I looked back at her. "I'll call an exterminator right now, and have him check everywhere. They got here somehow, and I'll find out before we open."

Marco shook his head, a hint of a smile on his lips. "I don't know, boss. A customer sees one and that's it."

I kept my eyes locked onto his with a brief glance toward Kira. "That won't happen. You three need to get back to whatever you were doing. I got this."

Amy stood there a moment, staring at the bloody carnage. I placed my hand on her shoulder. "It's okay. I got it. Try not to let it get to you. I promise you won't see another one in this restaurant."

"If we did, Chef . . ." she began.

"Which is exactly why I'll be the one to handle it. Go on. I've got it." She finally retreated, and I looked at Naomi. "You, too. Try to put it out of your mind."

"Yes, Chef." She regarded me with a look of intimacy that made me feel guilty as Kira stood nearby.

When Kira and the others finally left, Marco remained.

"I said I've got this," I told him. "You need to finish prep."

But rather than leaving, he moved toward me. I firmed my stance, refusing to budge for this man.

"Dante, I think maybe we've gotten off on the wrong foot," Marco began. "We're not that different. We see what we want and take it, no matter the cost. Even if it means stepping over others in the process. Others who might have been more deserving."

What the hell was he talking about? Here I was, standing in the middle of a health inspector's nightmare, and he was talking about being like me?

"I don't see it that way, Marco," I replied. "I've worked hard to get here. Stepping on people, like all these goddamn rats, might get you to the top, but you'll be up there alone. That's not how I operate."

"Of course." He peered at the floor. "I hope you're right about this rat situation, and we won't find any more." Marco licked his lips and set his sights on me once again. "I want success for you and Kira more than anything. Trust me when I say, we're on the same page."

CHAPTER 18: KIRA

The mad rush to open for dinner was underway. The rats were gone, according to the exterminator. And after he filled in any gaps in the exterior walls, I felt better about opening tonight. Dante was certain Marco had done this. I couldn't disagree, not after this morning in the parking lot.

I wanted to tell Dante what happened, but how could I? Now, Marco had something on the both of us. We were being destroyed, and it was of our own doing. I could blame Dante for all of it. That would be easy enough. After all, he had ignited the spark. But I'd let Marco kiss me, touch me. I'd let him comfort me. Mostly out of anger at my husband, but that, too, was an excuse.

What would happen if we continued down this path? Letting Marco stay, tearing apart the fabric of our lives, our marriage, thread by thread, until nothing remained.

Something would have to give, and what Tom Weaver told me had set my plan into motion. If the police weren't going to help us, then I would take matters into my own hands.

It was clear from Tom's reaction that Marco had something on him, too. It seemed to be his game. But that meant Tom and Marco knew each other, had some sort of connection. Meaning, he had ties here in LA. Maybe I could track down those ties and learn more about him. A man like Marco Devaney leaves behind a trail of people who would want nothing more than to have their revenge. So, I was about to find out who his enemies were, and what they knew about him.

I stewed in my office for the rest of the dinner shift. I had no desire to see Marco, to be reminded of what I'd done. He could, at any time, reveal the truth to Dante, but he was waiting. Biding his time for the right moment. For what? I had no idea. Given his obvious talents, it seemed a shame things had spiraled the way they had. It didn't have to be this way.

I prepared to leave while Dante and the others stayed to clean up and close down the restaurant. I grabbed my bag and headed into the dining room where Dante wiped down tables and Angelo sat at the bar.

"I'm heading out, Ang. You okay?" I asked him.

He raised a glass of clear liquid. Could've been gin for all I knew. "Drinking water right now, so yeah, I'm good. Night, Kira."

I smiled at him and placed my hand on his shoulder. "That's great, Angelo. Good night. I'll see you tomorrow."

He nodded as I walked toward Dante. "I'm leaving. Everything okay here?"

"Yeah. I won't be far behind. Not tonight. I think I've had enough of this place for tonight." He leaned down to kiss my cheek. "Drive safely. And go straight home . . . please."

"I will. See you soon." I rested my hand on his cheek, noticing the concern in his eyes. We were both frauds in this marriage, and neither of us wanted to admit it.

I walked out to my car and slipped behind the wheel. Staring back at the restaurant that had consumed so much of our lives over the past seven months, it seemed unfathomable to think we were in jeopardy of losing it, and so much more.

The engine purred when I pressed the ignition. The headlights flicked on, and I shifted into reverse. As I looked back toward the building, I noticed Marco had stepped outside. He stared at me, his hand shielding the bright head-lights from his eyes. A crooked smile on his lips.

I shuddered at the thought of him watching me. I didn't want to give him any more power over me than he already had. I narrowed my eyes and sped off into the night, leaving Marco and the restaurant far behind.

The city was still alive with activity, but my mind was consumed with thoughts of how all we had was slipping from our grasp.

My phone buzzed with a text message. I glanced at it, grunting a little. *I was wondering when you'd turn up again.*

It was from the same unknown number that'd already sent me a warning. *Meet me at the deli on the corner of Wilshire and Alvarado*, it read. *I have information on a mutual acquaintance.*

That was in the MacArthur Park area, not far from where I now headed. The question was, could I trust this person? Whoever it was had only offered a vague warning. No name. Not how this person found me. Was it worth the risk? My pulse quickened as I considered the possibilities. Assuming this was about Marco, could this be my chance to finally get the upper hand on him?

I can do this. I'll stay safe. I continued on in the direction of the park.

The delicatessen was open twenty-four hours a day. And as I parked in the front, I could see through the windows that the place was practically empty. Empty except for the only man I could see sitting in a booth. He glanced through the windows as if looking for me. My headlights were on, and he couldn't see my face, but a half-smile appeared on his lips as he looked out. He seemed confident it was me.

He looked up as I entered and motioned for me to join him. I slid into the booth on the opposite side.

He clasped his hands on top of the table and peered at me. "You didn't listen to me the first time, so I figured I'd give it one more shot."

I took in this man, discerning whether he posed a threat. And while Lyman's appearance might as well have screamed he was a cop, I wasn't sure this guy was. Older, maybe in his fifties. White button-down shirt with rolled-up sleeves. No tie. From where he sat, however, I had no way to see whether he carried a weapon or wore a badge clipped to his belt. "Who are you?" I asked.

He shifted his gaze, as though we were being watched. I looked back at the counter to see only one worker. No one else within a mile of us, by the look of things.

"Robert Soto. I'm well aware of what Marco Devaney is capable of, and he's not one to be trifled with. You need to find a way to cut ties with him before it's too late."

"What if we can't?" I asked him. "What if he knows things that, were they to get out—"

"Then maybe it's already too late for you and your husband," he replied. "In either case, I have a piece of information that might help. Take it or leave it. But know that you won't hear from me again if you choose to ignore this."

"I won't. What is it?" I was eager to know what he had that could help us end this. But the source of this supposed information was from a stranger — I had no idea who he really was and where his interests lay.

"Marco Devaney is the prime suspect in the disappearance of Raymond Driscoll, the one-time head chef at Lilibell's in Napa Valley." He ripped open a sugar pack and dumped it into the cup of coffee that sat on the table in front of him.

Oh my God. Zach Emory's restaurant. "Disappearance? How do you know this? I understood he'd just stopped showing up," I said.

"I figured you'd already talked to Zach. Good. Then things are moving in the right direction." He took a sip from the mug. "And I know because I'm the lead detective on the case. I've been following Marco Devaney's movements for months since Mr. Driscoll went missing."

"Why didn't Zach mention there was an active investigation to find his chef?" I asked. "My husband and I spoke to him only yesterday. He'd said the man just took off. Never to be heard from again."

"That's been the official line for a while because we don't have any leads. But I've been working this on my own, keeping eyes on Devaney because I'm certain he knows something. And when I learned he'd moved out of his place in Napa and signed a lease here in LA, it wasn't hard to track him down to your restaurant."

I'd felt so stupid not knowing anything about Marco when he was clearly a dangerous man. "He knows people here, doesn't he? Tom Weaver? Have you heard that name before?"

"You hired a man you had no idea about," he said, looking smug.

I glanced down a moment. "If you're here to blame me for this, then . . ."

Soto rested his arm across the back of the booth. "You're right. This isn't your fault. My apologies. To answer your question, yes, Marco Devaney has connections to LA. And it's particularly important that you know this because his ties include your restaurant."

The server walked over to our table. "Can I get you anything, miss?" he asked.

I waved him off. "Thank you, but no, I'm good." When he left, I turned back to the detective. "My restaurant? How?"

"Devaney used to own your place. It was a restaurant before you bought it, correct?"

I felt the blood drain from my face. My head grew light, and my chest tightened. The past seven months of our lives flashed through my mind. From the day we knocked down the first wall to the day we opened, La Bianca's was ours. But it was his first? "Yes," I shook my head wildly. "It had been a restaurant when we bought it from the bank during an auction."

"It was Devaney's and his partner's, Tom Weaver — and it failed. The two lost everything. Not long after it shuttered, Devaney moved to Napa. And the rest, you already know," Soto added.

"He told Zach Emory he'd spent time in Europe, training with chefs," I said.

"I'm sure he didn't want Emory to learn that he'd lost his own place and made up some BS story. And like you, Emory didn't bother to check."

Weaver? I raised my eyes to the detective. "Tom Weaver owns another place now—"

"Sunset 717. I'm aware." Soto took another sip from his mug. "Funny thing, though, he's a partner in another restaurant. A place called Brindi's. Not far from your location, I believe."

"Yes, they were the ones who recommended Marco to us. Tom said it must've been his partner who offered the recommendation."

"Then I can only guess the reason Weaver agreed to do that was to keep Devaney from destroying what he has going on with his new place. I don't know what. But if I find that out, it could shed some light on my investigation."

It started to make sense now, but there were still pieces of the puzzle missing, like whether Marco had been involved in Eric's death. He hadn't known Eric. But as I considered the timing, he must've known Eric worked for us, then set a plan in motion to get rid of him, clearing a path for himself. "It was his way to get in," I whispered.

"What's that?" Soto asked.

I cleared my throat and returned my attention to the detective. "So he's come back to, what, buy us out? Screw us over and then lowball us into selling?"

Soto's face turned serious. "No, Mrs. Lucini. Marco Devaney is a particular kind of person. I've come to find out just how dangerous a man he is. I believe there could be a trail of bodies behind him. People who've gotten in his way over the years. So, no, he doesn't want you to sell. He wants you ruined. Maybe more. And trust me when I say, he'll stop at nothing to make sure that happens."

* * *

I returned home, shaken, and terrified. How could I have not known any of this? But I knew why. It was because I'd been taken by him. How ridiculous and juvenile to let myself be roped in by this snake. And what would I tell Dante? That he could go ahead and blame me for blowing up our lives? For losing every dime we had because I wanted to screw this guy? Even though I hadn't, I'd gotten close enough.

I walked inside our dark home, the lights sparkling through the windows that overlooked the city. Locking the door behind me, I slipped off my heels and walked in bare feet into the living room.

We had no choice now. Any attempts to fire Marco would not only destroy us, but possibly endanger our lives. All I knew right now was that Soto didn't have enough proof to arrest Marco. No one had any idea where Lilibell's chef disappeared to. Lyman had no proof of who killed Eric, and didn't seem to give a shit about Marco at all.

I turned on the side table lamp and dropped onto the sofa. Tears streamed down my cheeks. I felt helpless and alone. The weight of the situation suffocated me. I had to tell Dante, but how could I? How could I explain my stupidity? My selfishness? My hurt over his connection with Naomi, his lies about the bribe.

I slowly pulled out my phone and dialed Dante's number. The phone rang and rang, but there was no answer. I tried again, but still nothing. Panic filled my lungs. What if something had happened to him? What if Marco had done something to him, the way I was certain he had done to Eric?

No. No, I wasn't going to let this happen. I grabbed my keys and headed out the door. I had to find him and make sure he was safe.

I drove through the city in the middle of the night, heading straight for the restaurant. Every possibility played through my mind. Was Dante hurt? Kidnapped? Dead? But when I arrived, his car wasn't there. The lot was empty.

I reached for my phone again and tried Dante. "Please, baby. Please answer." And when he did, I nearly cried. "Oh my God. Where are you? I tried calling you earlier. I thought—"

"I just got home. Kira, where the hell are you? Are you okay?"

"I'm at the restaurant. I came back here . . ." My gaze shifted to the approaching headlights. "Uh, Dante, someone's here."

"Who? Kira, who's there?"

I let out a gasp. "It's Marco, but someone's in the passenger seat with him." It took me a moment, but I soon realized who it was. "Oh my God. Dante, it's Angelo. What the hell is he doing with Marco? What do I do?"

"Why would . . . that means he had to pick him up from his apartment. How did he know where Angelo lived? Why was he—"

"I don't know, but I'm freaking out right now. Should I call the cops?" I watched the driver's side door open, and Marco step out. He saw me and smiled. Then he moved around the car and opened the passenger door. Angelo spilled out. "He's drunk, Dante. Your brother's drunk."

"Get out of there, Kira. Right now. Just drive away," Dante insisted.

"I can't leave Angelo here alone with him. You have no idea who this man is. I'll call you back." I ended the call and stepped outside to join them. "Marco, what's going on?"

"I'm surprised to see you here, Kira," he said. "Shouldn't you be at home tucked up in bed?"

I had to scramble for a believable explanation. "I needed to take some money out of petty cash for the morning, and I didn't want to go out of my way to come here first." What the hell kind of answer was that? And more importantly, would he buy it?

"Why didn't you ask Dante before he left?" Marco pressed.

"I tried. I guess we just missed each other because he didn't answer his phone." Seemed plausible, but Marco remained stone-faced, and I had no idea if he believed me.

Marco grabbed Angelo by the arm and helped him around the car. I could see that my brother-in-law was drunk

166

off his ass. I was surprised because when I'd seen him earlier, he was stone cold sober. A first in a long time. What had Marco done to convince Angelo to drink tonight? "Why are you two here? Angelo, are you okay?"

"Kira! My favorite person in the whole world," he slurred.

At least he was okay. "Did you forget something, too?" I asked, casually walking toward them, wishing to God I'd had a gun in my purse, or even pepper spray.

"No, Marco said he wanted to make me a new dish. Wanted to try it out on me before he asked Dante to put it on the menu," Angelo replied, staggering as he leaned on Marco's arm.

"This late?" I swallowed down my fear, trying hard to keep my face from betraying me.

Marco shrugged. "I like to experiment, Kira. You should know that about me."

I nodded, trying to play along. "Well, yeah, sure. You know, I'd love to join you guys."

"Great." He smiled. "I'd love for you to sample the new dish with us."

Marco's voice was soft, but there was an edge to it that sent a chill down my spine. I couldn't leave Angelo, and the way I ended the call with Dante all but assured that he would arrive soon in any case. Things were about to go south, and I had no way to stop it.

I reached for my keys and headed toward the back door, opening the rear entrance to the kitchen. The alarm beeped, and I walked to the keypad to enter the code.

Marco switched on the kitchen lights. "All right then, I'll get to work. You two sit down over there. Watch a master in action."

I sat next to Angelo on the stools near the expo station. "You sure you're okay?" I whispered to him.

"Yeah, I'm fine." Angelo swatted away any notion to the contrary.

As Marco donned his apron and retrieved his ingredients, he continued. "You know, Angelo and I have had some really interesting discussions lately. And having you here now, well, there's probably some things you should know too."

"Oh yeah? What's that?" I don't think I sounded as laid-back as I wanted to.

Marco walked to the pantry to gather his ingredients. "Ang, you should tell her. Tell her about what happened with your parents at their bakery."

Angelo's face fell, as though he'd sobered up in an instant. "I don't want to."

"Oh, come on. I'm sure she'd like to know. You told me, and your own sister-in-law doesn't know? That's not cool. She's family."

Angelo bowed his head, and then slowly raised it, his eyes glinting with tears.

I laid my hand on his back. "It's okay, Ang, you don't have to say anything."

"Yes, he does," Marco shot back. "Go on, Angelo."

Angelo paused and drew in a shaky breath before continuing. "You know my parents died in the fire at their bakery."

"Of course. I was there, remember?"

"You were there?" Marco asked me.

"Not there at the bakery, but Dante and I were married, so of course I knew they'd died in a fire."

"Ah, but you see," Marco waved around his knife. "There's more to this story."

"They thought it was an electrical malfunction," Angelo continued.

"Right, I remember," I added.

Marco stopped chopping vegetables and put down his knife. "Now, that's not exactly how you told me it went down, Angelo. Why don't you tell her how the fire really started?"

I pinched my brow and looked at my brother-in-law.

"I told you that because I was mad at my brother," Angelo said to Marco.

Marco went back to the task of preparing a meal. "Well, that doesn't mean Kira shouldn't know, right? Doesn't she deserve to know?"

Angelo licked his lips and looked at me. "The fire department said the bakery caught fire in the back, where the flour was stored."

"Sure, of course," I said.

"And it's not the whole truth, is it, Angelo?" Marco pressed. "Why don't you tell her who was at the bakery shortly before it started?"

Angelo cleared his throat. "Dante was there. He was unloading a couple boxes of supplies that had come in late and put the flour close to an electrical outlet. But then he took off, thinking everything was fine."

"Okay." Dante never talked about the details of the fire. It'd always been too painful for him, and I never pressed him on it.

Marco raised his knife, pointing it toward me. "It's strange, don't you think, that your husband didn't tell you this? I mean, why not? Clearly, it was an accident. And didn't you guys get, like, a bunch of money or something from the insurance?" He shrugged. "I guess they figured it was an accident, too. But I don't think Angelo is so sure. Isn't that right, Ang?"

I turned toward my brother-in-law once again. "What does he mean?"

"Nothing. Nothing," Angelo replied.

Marco shook his head. "Tsk, tsk. He's not being honest with you, Kira."

I kept my gaze fixed on him. "Angelo? What are you not telling me?"

"I think Dante started the fire." The words spilled out of his mouth, almost incoherent.

My mouth fell ajar. "Why would you say that? If the fire department and insurance company didn't say that—"

"Because I knew he wanted to move here, Kira. He wanted to start a life with you here in LA and he needed money to do it," Angelo replied.

No, I couldn't believe what he was saying. "Are you telling me that you think Dante was responsible for the death of your parents? Why would you say such a thing?"

"Because it's true," Marco cut in. "Angelo told me himself the other night when he wasn't quite as drunk as he is now. To be honest, Kira, I'm surprised you didn't already know Dante had been there just a short time before the whole place went up in flames. What a thing to hide from your wife." He looked up at me. "Well, I suppose he also hid the whole bribery thing from you too, didn't he? And then there's you. You have your own secrets, don't you, Kira?"

I held Marco's gaze, knowing what he was about to say. I got up from the stool and grabbed Angelo. "We're leaving."

Marco slammed a pot onto the counter. The ringing of the aluminum echoed through the kitchen. "No, you're not. You're both going to stay right there."

The look in his eyes frightened me, and he went back to preparing the meal as if nothing had happened, as if everything was perfectly fine.

"This is something I picked up from a chef in France last year," he added, a smile on his face.

I mustered as much courage as I could and set my sights on him. "I'm sorry, Marco, but we aren't staying here. I need to get Angelo home. This will have to wait until tomorrow."

Marco stabbed his knife into the butcher block. "I said you're not leaving." His eyes turned black, but only for a moment. And then he smiled again. "Not until you've tasted this, Kira. Trust me, it'll be worth the wait."

The back door flew open, capturing my attention, and everyone else's, too. "Dante?"

He marched inside. "What the hell is going on in here? Kira, are you all right? Ang?"

"They're fine," Marco replied. "I'm just whipping up something new I created to test out on them. Well, just Angelo really, but imagine my surprise when I found Kira here, too? I thought, that's just perfect timing, isn't it? Of course, if I'd known she was here, I would've made it dinner for two."

My heart dropped into my stomach. "We're all right, Dante." I'd hoped he didn't pick up on Marco's comment.

170

Dante walked toward me and eyed his brother. I didn't know what to say to him. I didn't know what to do.

"Come on, we're going home," Dante said, placing his hand on my arm.

"This won't take much longer, I promise," Marco said. "Sit. Stay. Help them test out this new dish."

For a moment, I wasn't sure he would let us go, and I had no idea what would come out of his mouth next.

"It'll have to wait for another time, Marco. I'm sorry." Dante eyed me again. "Kira, let's go. Angelo can crash at our house tonight." He looked at his brother. "Right, Ang?"

"Yeah," he muttered.

"It's late, and we need to get home," Dante insisted.

"Yeah, okay. Let's go." And as we headed toward the exit, I looked back. Marco's face appeared stunned. I feared if we didn't leave in this moment, he would give away my secret. But as we slipped past him and toward the back door, he lowered his head, telegraphing defeat.

Dante held the door, glancing back. "Good night, Marco. Be sure to clean up when you're done."

CHAPTER 19: DANTE

The entire drive home, all I could think about was what Marco's intention had been tonight, and why he'd had my brother with him. Only hours earlier, Angelo was sober; he hadn't had a drink all day. Then he turns up wasted with Marco? It didn't make sense. And whatever happened in there turned Kira silent. She hadn't said a word since we left. Neither of them had.

I'd warned Kira on the phone to leave, but she didn't. She loved Angelo too much to leave him alone. God knows what would've happened had I not shown up.

"Come on, Ang." I shifted into park at the top of our driveway and stepped out to help my brother. Opening the rear passenger door, he held out his arm and I took it.

He struggled to look me in the eye, like he knew, no matter how drunk he'd been, that he'd messed up. I couldn't put the blame on him, though. This was on me. Marco was my problem, and I'd told my brother to insert himself into that problem.

I watched Kira step out of the car and head straight toward the front door without so much as a glance back. She'd already opened the door and left it ajar while I helped Angelo inside. It was almost two in the morning, and I'd been terrified that something had happened to Kira. It seemed she'd been terrified of the same thing. This wasn't how things were supposed to go.

"You know where the guest room is," I said to Angelo, closing the front door behind me. As I secured the dead-bolt, he stumbled into the hallway and disappeared into the corridor.

A single lamp burned in the living room as I entered. Kira was perched on the edge of the sofa, hunched over, holding a bottle of water with two hands. Her eyes fixed on the bottle.

"I have to tell you something, Kira." I made my way to the sofa and sat next to her. "Marco is hiding things from us. He has something going with Tom Weaver over at that new restaurant. I tried to tell Lyman he needed to look closer at it, but he insisted I had no grounds."

"Wait, how do you know this?" she asked.

This was the hard part — telling her that I'd followed her this morning. I peered down, rubbing the back of my neck. "I, uh, I tracked you down this morning. I knew you were at that restaurant. And I saw Marco, too."

She set her gaze on me. "You were there? You followed me?"

"Yes and no." I drew in a breath, thinking carefully how to best explain all this. And so I went into the entire situation. "I'm sorry; I was scared. I thought you'd go do something crazy or whatever, you know? Then to find out Marco followed you—"

"It's okay," she replied. "I'm not mad. This whole thing is crazy, and it's made us act crazy. I know you're afraid Marco will do something, and after tonight, you're right to feel that way. But I have to tell you something, too. You remember that text I got from an unknown number?"

"Of course."

Kira set down the bottle of water on our coffee table. "It was from a Detective Soto. He reached out to me again. He's investigating the disappearance of Raymond Driscoll. That's the name of Lilibell's head chef who took off. Apparently, he didn't."

"Lilibell's chef who up and quit? There's an investigation?" I asked. "Zach didn't say anything about cops being involved."

"That's because, according to Soto, this is sort of him running on a hunch. He has no evidence of anything. But he's looked into Marco, and he found him here, working in our restaurant. He's sure Marco's been watching us." She chuckled, but it sounded like she wanted to cry. "There's one more thing, Dante. I know the reason Marco came into our lives."

An ominous feeling that a monster-sized shoe was about to drop came over me. "Why?"

A tear streamed down her cheek, and she wiped it away. "He used to own our building . . . the restaurant it used to be. He was partners with Tom Weaver. And they lost it, Dante. Marco lost everything."

I closed my eyes, feeling like I couldn't breathe. "Now he wants it back. My God, Kira, that means he had to be involved in Eric's death."

"But how? That's what I can't seem to answer," she replied.

I racked my brain trying to find the connection... "I remember going for a smoke one night during dinner service, before we let Eric go. There was this car hanging around. No lights. It just sat there. I decided to check it out and when I walked over, it took off. I didn't think much of it then—"

"What does that have to do with anything?" Kira asked.

I hesitated, wanting to be sure. "It could've been Marco. According to this detective, Marco's been watching us, right? Making plans to worm his way into our lives?"

"I suppose, at this point, we can't put it past him. But he couldn't have known we'd fire Eric."

I raked my hand through my hair, ready to pull it out. "You're right." It was already happening. Our world, our lives were falling apart because of this man. Should I take the blame for my part? The bribe? Of course. Maybe he would've come up with some other plan to get us, but regardless, I was

174

no time traveler. I couldn't un-ring this bell. We were going to have to face this head-on. We needed a plan.

Kira gently sobbed as she sat next to me.

"We can fix this, Kira."

"How?" Her voice faltered.

"We know things now, too." I stood up, feeling a renewed confidence surge in me. "You said Marco's under suspicion for the disappearance of Raymond Driscoll. Now, if we can also tie him to Eric, too, we stand a fighting chance."

"The police haven't been able to do that, Dante. Soto thinks there could be others Marco's either disappeared, or God knows what. What makes you think we can find the proof? On top of running the restaurant, so we can keep paying our bills?"

She had a point, but I had a plan. "We keep the status quo. Let Marco think he has the upper hand."

"Which he does," Kira replied quietly.

"Yes, but we know more about him than he thinks. And the important thing here is to keep him from learning what we know because he'll go public with the bribe. He'll have nothing to lose by doing so." I paced a tight circle. "I can find out more about Driscoll. You say the detective — what's his name? Soto? He reached out to you; let's use him. He wants what we want."

"Okay," she said. "Then what?"

"We make sure Marco knows we need him there. That we know he has the leverage, and we're willing to accept that for however long he's willing to play this game." I stopped and peered at her. "Hopefully, long enough for us to get proof of what he's done."

Kira circled the coffee table to join me in the center of the living room. "We have to keep Angelo away from the restaurant. I love him, but he's too big a risk for us. And frankly, had I not turned up tonight, God knows what Marco would've done to him. Maybe Angelo would've been another Raymond Driscoll."

* * *

I took off early this morning, shortly after Kira left for the restaurant. I had a plan, and it started now. Eric's mother had called me yesterday about her son's upcoming funeral, leaving a message on my phone. I knew where Eric had lived, and that his sister had been staying there to help clear out his things. If I had any hope of making a connection between Marco and Eric's death, she could be that link.

As I drove down Interstate 10, exiting onto Venice Boulevard, I paid no attention to the jam-packed highways and hazy skies. I'd gotten used to it by now. LA had been a city I'd wanted to live in for years. It was a hub of culinary excellence. I'd wanted nothing more than to open my own restaurant here, to one day be recognized as the owner of a Michelin star destination. And we'd done it, Kira and me. The restaurant part, anyway. The cost, though, had been steep, much steeper than I'd ever imagined. So the idea of losing it all because of Marco Devaney — to hell with that.

The apartment building where Eric lived was several yards ahead. I made the turn into the parking lot and arrived in front of his first-floor unit. Jessica Castor was Eric's younger sister. I knew clearing out her brother's place was probably the hardest thing she'd ever done. I knew that because I'd been in her shoes. So, I wasn't sure where her head would be when I started asking questions about her dead brother.

I stepped out of my car and walked along the pathway until I arrived at the apartment. Number 1348. Taking a breath, I rapped my knuckles on the hollow-sounding door, wondering if she would hear it. But when footfalls sounded on the other side, and the lock clicked, I knew she was there, and the trip hadn't been wasted.

When she opened the door, I saw the face of a pretty young woman, drowning in sorrow. The shame I felt must've appeared on my face as she gazed at me with some measure of compassion. Did I deserve her compassion? No, I didn't think so.

"Good morning. I'm so sorry to come here unannounced—"

"Mr. Lucini," she interrupted. "What are you doing here?"

"I wanted to ask you a few questions about Eric, if I could. Do you have a minute?" The look on her face suggested reluctance, but I held out hope.

"Come in." She stepped aside. "I don't have a lot of time. I have to leave for work soon."

"Thank you so much." I walked into the small apartment that was well decorated. Pictures of Eric's family adorned the walls and bookshelves. One of Eric, in particular, with him in his chef's hat. I smiled.

"What do you want to know, Mr. Lucini?" she asked, folding her arms, and closing herself off to me.

"Do you know if Eric knew a man named Marco Devaney? Have you ever heard him mention that name before?"

"Doesn't sound familiar to me," she replied flatly.

I rubbed my bottom lip, thinking of how to better handle this. "I don't mean to sound indelicate, but have you been able to look at Eric's phone or email? I know how this must sound to you, but I've been talking with the detective who's trying to get to the bottom of what happened to Eric, and you see, there's a chance this Marco Devaney might know something."

"Eric's phone is in the hands of the LAPD, Mr. Lucini. And so is his laptop. If there's anything on them about this man you're interested in, then you should talk to them." She walked to the door. "Now, if you'll excuse me, I do need to leave for work."

Son of a bitch. Of course Lyman must've had Eric's things, and if he had found something about Marco, would he have told me? There had to be something else. Something I hadn't thought of.

"I understand, but may I ask you one more thing?"

"Yes," she said, holding the door open.

"Eric asked me for a letter of recommendation, which I provided to him on the night . . ." I trailed off, swallowing hard. "Anyway, were you aware of any jobs he had lined up? Anyone he planned to talk to?"

"A new restaurant that was opening," she began. "He was scheduled to interview with the owner that morning, but as we both know, he never made it to that meeting."

"No, of course. Um, do you recall the name of the person or the name of the restaurant?"

She raised her eyes as if thinking on it. "He said the man's name was Weaver, I believe. I think the restaurant was Sunset something or other. I can't recall now."

I held back the relief that swelled in my chest. "I see. Well, Jessica, thank you so much for talking to me. I should let you get on with the rest of your day."

"Goodbye, Mr. Lucini."

I walked out, the door closing behind me. I knew better than to think this was a coincidence. This was planned. And Marco had to have been the one who planned it. Whatever he had on his former partner was clearly enough to force his hand to make the call to Eric about a job.

I returned to my car and stepped inside, picking up my phone to call Kira. "Hi, it's me. Are you at the restaurant?"

"Yes. Marco and the others just arrived. Angelo's not here."

"Good. I'll make sure it stays that way. Listen, I'm leaving Eric's apartment now. I spoke to his sister. She mentioned Eric had a job interview with Tom Weaver."

"Oh my God," Kira interrupted.

"My thoughts exactly. Kira, this is the connection."

"That's how he's tied to Eric," she reiterated. "Tom Weaver. Somehow, Marco dragged him into this."

"He'd already set his plan in motion, not knowing we'd fire Eric," I said. "But given what we know about him, Marco doesn't do things half-assed. He wanted Eric out the way, entirely. This was how he chose to do it."

"The connection's there. Marco got what he wanted. As soon as we let Eric go, that was his opportunity, and he took it," Kira said.

"You think we can get Tom Weaver to come clean with us?" I asked, hoping for the impossible.

"He won't talk," she said. "Whatever Marco is holding over his head must be bad enough for him to keep his mouth shut."

"Well, shit. What can we do?" I clamped my hand on the steering wheel.

"Just come back to the restaurant and we'll figure it out."

I sensed an urgency in her tone. "Kira, is everything okay?"

"Yes, it's fine. Just get here as soon as you can."

I pinched my lips, feeling a knot form in my gut. "I'm on my way." My foot pressed down on the gas pedal as I made my way back to the restaurant. Something seemed off in Kira's voice, and now, thoughts swirled as to whether she was okay. But if the rest of the kitchen staff was there, then surely, she must be.

With traffic increasing, I was barely inching my way through. "Come on! Come on!" I slammed my palm against the steering wheel as cars slowed in front of me.

Swerving around into another lane, I passed them, hurrying toward the onramp. *On second thought...* Taking the freeway now would only delay me. *Surface streets it is.*

I'd considered going back to that restaurant to speak with Weaver. But if Kira was right and he refused, it would set off alarm bells for Marco. I couldn't risk that.

Finally, I'd arrived and pulled into the back lot. I scanned the cars to see who was here. It appeared everyone had been accounted for. Good. That meant Kira wasn't forced to be alone with Marco.

I jumped out of my car and pressed the remote to lock it, hurrying toward the restaurant's back entrance. I walked inside to find what appeared to be business as usual.

I looked at Naomi, and her head tilted. "Morning, Dante. Everything okay?"

She was at her station, prepping for the night's service as though nothing had ever happened. As though the burn on her hand was nothing more than a mild irritation, and the food poisoning she'd suffered had all been in her head. Was she in on it? Marco's plot to destroy our restaurant? Was it her way of getting back at me for leading her on?

Find Kira. Talk to her. That was all I needed to do right now, before I let my paranoia set in.

"Everything's fine. Thanks for asking." I walked by her, careful to hide my anxiety. "How are you feeling, anyway?" My glance shifted to Marco, who didn't acknowledge my arrival.

"I'm doing okay," Naomi replied.

"Glad to hear it." I made my way to the office and opened the door to find Kira at the desk. "Hey, babe."

She stood and pulled me into a tight embrace. "Thank God you're here."

I gently pushed her back, feeling that another shoe was about to drop. "What's wrong now?"

Kira aimed her finger at her laptop screen. "You'll want to see this."

I sat down at her desk to read the page she had on the screen. It was an *LA Times* article. And as I read it, I realized all was already lost.

The headline? *"New Restaurant Attempts to Bribe our Food Critic for Positive Review."*

CHAPTER 20: KIRA

The moment the article was released, our life as we knew it was over. When Dante called, I'd wanted to tell him over the phone, but I couldn't. Now, he stood over me, peering at the screen, his face masked in shock.

It took everything in my power not to march into the kitchen and confront Marco. He did this. Soto had warned me, but I thought getting rid of Marco would guarantee the restaurant's demise, as well as my marriage. One down. One to go.

The article was scathing, calling us out and demanding a boycott. Our reputation had been tarnished; our business would be ruined. Reservations we'd had for the next week were already dropping off like flies.

"This is a lie," Dante muttered, his eyes scanning over the words again. "That son of a bitch took my money. *Our* money."

I should've been furious at him for doing something so deceitful, giving Marco this kind of power, but I was no better. "The damage is done," I said, my voice shaking.

Dante looked at me with a mixture of rage and fear. "What are we going to do? Go after Marco now? This is his doing. We both know that."

"No, we can't," I said. "God knows what else he'll do, and he still has leverage. The more he talks about us to the press, the more they'll dig, and they might find things you don't want them to know. Eric's drug problem; Angelo and his drinking." There was more to it, of course. More leverage than I could reveal.

I took a breath to steady my nerves. "We have to placate him. What that means, I don't know yet." I suspected what that meant. "But we have to connect him to Eric's death or Driscoll's disappearance if we want him out of our lives before we have nothing left. It's time for damage control."

"How?" he asked.

It occurred to me then that Marco had done this to control me — to make me see that with a snap of his fingers, he could alter the course of our lives. "We have to buy ourselves time to connect the dots, or at least, give Detective Soto time to do it. We do that through me."

Dante looked at me with some misgiving. "What do you mean, exactly?"

"I mean, he clearly knows we've been snooping into his past. I'm sure that's what this article was about. A sample of what he could do to us." I considered our options. "I'll show him that this was your fault — the article. And that I'm on his side now. Dante, look, what happened, happened, all right? Marco prodded Oliver to make this public. God knows how. So the answer is for me to make it look to Marco like this was the final straw between us. That he can be my shoulder to cry on."

"No." Dante waved his hands as though he was a referee on a football field. "I won't let you get close to him, Kira. It's too dangerous. We both know what could've happened last night with Angelo."

"But it didn't," I said. "I can distract him, while you work to find the connection we need and take it to Lyman or Soto. What else can we do?"

I never thought I would find it so easy to lie to my husband. I could convince myself that Dante had lied to me plenty of times, even bringing about our current circumstance. But I was no better. This would change us when it all came to light. Could we survive it?

"Fire the son of a bitch," Dante shot back.

"If we fire him, he wins. This is our only chance, Dante." I studied his face to gauge his reaction before adding, "if there's one thing I have learned about Marco Devaney, it's that he's led by his ego. I'll give him the attention he wants, if it means keeping him from hurting us any more than he already has."

* * *

I'd steered clear of Marco as dinner service was set to begin. Facing him before I was ready could jeopardize the plan. The staff had seen the article. It was everywhere, and the problem couldn't be avoided. Dante had made an announcement that it was all a lie, and he would clear our names. But I saw the look in their eyes, a look that they weren't sure who to believe.

It didn't matter how great our food was, as many of our guests had raved on Yelp and the like. What mattered was that the owners were accused of bribery. That was what would stick in people's minds. Regardless, we had to proceed as usual. The only difference was that Angelo wasn't here. It was a relief, to be honest.

Dante had gone into the dining area to oversee the set-up. I finally got the nerve to step out into the kitchen. When I did, all eyes landed on me. But there was only one person I needed to see. "Marco, do you have a quick second?"

"Of course." He set down his spoon and walked toward me with a sort of swagger as though he knew we were beat. He wore a smug smile as he approached. "Everything okay?"

"I think you know it isn't," I said, holding open the office door. "Come in." He walked inside and I closed the door. "Why now? Why make this public now?"

He stepped closer, standing barely a foot in front of me. "Why stir up the past, Kira? Why go to Tom Weaver? If nothing else, I thought you at least believed I was a good chef."

"You are," I replied, taking a half-step back. "And I think it's time you and I come to an agreement."

He smiled. "What sort of agreement?"

I wasn't going to tell him I knew that he'd once owned this place. If he believed I was working with Detective Soto, there was no telling what he might do. "Dante screwed up. He didn't need to bribe anyone. But he did. You know it. We all know it. I guess I didn't think you'd be the one to make it public."

Marco raised his index finger. "You drew first blood, Kira. So, I suggest whatever it is you're about to say now . . . remember that I can do so much more damage."

I swallowed my fear, clasping my hands so he wouldn't see them tremble. "I know. So I'm here to offer you an olive branch. The menu is yours. Add whatever you'd like, in the hopes that it'll help dig us out of this hole. We need you to help us fix this, Marco."

"We?"

I saw a glint in his eye. "Me. I need you to fix this."

He appeared taken aback and yet intrigued.

I went on, "Whatever happened in the past, we will keep in the past."

He gripped my arm tighter than I would've expected. "Don't fuck with me, Kira. What's this really about?"

"It's about keeping this restaurant afloat. And you keeping your job. That's what you want, isn't it?" Of course, I knew what he'd wanted. He'd wanted this place to himself.

"The article is out. How do you plan to address that?" he asked. "Regardless of what I do with the menu, people will stop coming here, and soon."

"Oliver is lying, and the truth will come out. All we can do is hope customers have a short memory," I said.

He was silent for a moment, his eyes scanning the length of my body. I suddenly felt the urge to shield myself from him. "And you think I want my name associated with La Bianca's now? Convince me why I need to stay with you."

He wanted me to grovel. To beg him to stay and bail us out. I walked around my desk, making a show of thinking it over. I raised a seductive gaze at him. "And what would that look like? Pleading my case?"

I felt his breath on me now as he moved closer, nearly pressing me against the door. "You're a beautiful woman, Kira. You can't deny the attraction between us. I felt it when I touched you. When I kissed your lips."

I steadied my nerves. He stood too close, and I had to control my instinct to run. "If Dante finds out, we both lose. I won't deny the spark, but I can't give in to it, either." I placed my hand on his cheek, doing my best to convince him of my desire. "No matter how much I want to."

Marco snatched my hand from his face, squeezing it hard. "Are you lying to me, Kira?"

"No." I refused to let him see the pain he'd caused. If he knew how my heart was beating against my chest, fearing him, I was certain it would only drive him more.

Finally, he released his grip. "I'll come up with a menu. And so long as we keep out of each other's business, then maybe we can work out a deal, assuming La Bianca's survives this."

"Thank you."

He stood before me for several moments. I wasn't sure I'd completely sold him on this. But he opened the door and walked back into the kitchen. I nearly collapsed as he closed it behind him. He controlled us now. He controlled me. And the only thing that would stop him, was proof of his crimes.

* * *

Our bedroom was dark; the whirl of the ceiling fan hummed. The damage from the article hadn't hit yet. While it had been a slower night, customers still showed. Who knew what tomorrow would bring? But if the reservation system was any indicator, the dining room would be half-empty.

I peered at Dante, who seemed to be sleeping. Never mind. I wanted to keep to myself, anyway. Our marriage of only six years now hung by a thread, as did our livelihood. Maybe if I just told him that I'd let myself get carried away with Marco. For God's sake, I didn't sleep with him.

And it wasn't like Dante hadn't crossed the line before. I knew he had, and I'd overlooked it. Why? I blamed it on his job, and that we were only engaged at the time. Yeah, I didn't have much self-esteem when I was younger. When I'd seen the way he was with Naomi, I thought it would happen again. It made me want to get back at him. How stupid it all was now in light of everything. In light of murder.

It wasn't supposed to be this hard — marriage, life. Here we were trying to find proof that our head chef was a killer. It felt insane just to think it, but we were in a battle for our lives.

A noise outside startled me from my thoughts. It sounded as though something had hit our window. I listened, but after several more moments, I didn't hear it again. Must've been my imagination. Dante had either actually been asleep, or he didn't hear it. Either way, it stirred me enough that I now wanted a drink of water.

My phone lay on my bedside table, and I glanced at the time. Three a.m. It felt like I'd been lying in bed for a day, not three hours. I turned to see Dante on his side, facing away from me. He didn't move, so I climbed out of bed. In bare feet, I tugged on my long T-shirt, walking out of our bedroom, and entering the long hallway that led to the kitchen and great room.

I made my way through the darkness, knowing every inch of this house I'd wanted so badly. As I reached the kitchen, I opened a cabinet and pulled down a glass. The fridge was steps to the right, and I opened it, the light inside temporarily stinging my eyes.

I reached for the pitcher of filtered water and closed the door again. And as I poured the water into my glass, another sound captured my attention. This time, I was certain it came from our living room window. Fear caught in my throat.

Our house was built on a flat piece of land, but at the top of a hill. A steep drop of about fifteen feet in front of us was guard-railed.

Investigating the sound wasn't the best idea I'd ever had. Nevertheless, I told myself I couldn't live in fear. And the odds were good the sound came from an animal outside. A raccoon, or maybe a coyote.

I set down the glass and walked toward the living room, the tile floor cool under my feet. I glanced around the corner and saw nothing out of the ordinary. But as I stepped closer, I heard the sound again, this time more distinct. It was a tapping sound, like someone tapping their nails on my window.

My pulse quickened as I approached the window. The curtains were drawn, so I couldn't see anything outside. I paused for a moment, considering whether to pull them back.

I felt a tremor in the floor as I reached for the curtain. I caught my breath. A blast erupted, and a gust surged through our shattering window, blowing me back several steps. My arms instinctively raised to shield my face as shards of glass flew. A piece struck my cheek and I screamed. Stumbling backward, I tripped over a chair and fell hard onto the floor.

As I lay there, disoriented and in pain, I saw a figure move past the broken window, escaping into the night. I tried to sit up, my hand still pressed against my cheek, tears streaming down my face.

Dante rushed out. I heard him calling my name through the hall.

"Kira!" he shouted. "Are you okay?"

He appeared in the living room, seeming to search for me in the dark. When he found me lying on the floor, he rushed to my side. "Are you okay? Oh my God, what happened?"

I tried to speak, but my voice was nothing but a gasp. All I could do was point to the shattered window that now showed no signs of the dark figure.

Dante ran to the window. I heard his feet crunching on the glass. He looked outside. "I don't see anyone. No cars.

Nothing." He turned to me, his face etched with worry. "We need to call the police."

"No," I shot back. "It was him. I'm sure it was Marco. He was proving a point."

"What the hell kind of point was that?" Dante helped me to my feet and led me to the couch. He sat me down gently and reached for his phone.

I grabbed his arm. "No, you'll only make this worse."

"Kira, our fucking window was just smashed into pieces. Your face is bleeding. I'm calling the goddamn police."

* * *

Glass still covered our floor. The police arrived, and it was Detective Lyman who led the charge.

Luckily, my face was spared the worst of it. Only a few nicks and cuts. Didn't even need to go to the hospital. The glass was tempered, so it made more of a mess than caused any real damage.

Still, I knew who was responsible. We both did. And it meant that Marco wasn't going to go along with our plan — my plan.

Detective Lyman approached us as we sat on our sofa. He held a notepad as though he gave a shit about what was happening. His goal was to get the person responsible for Eric's death. That was great, but he needed to give Marco another look, especially now.

"Detective, my wife and I think that this was the work of Marco Devaney," Dante said.

"Why do you think that?" Lyman asked. "Did your wife see him? Do either of you have physical proof he was here? Did you see his car?"

"Okay, okay." Dante threw up his hands. "I get your fucking point, Detective. We can't prove it was Marco, no. Is that what you want to hear?"

Lyman sat down on the chair across from us. "Look, I'm sorry for what happened to you, Mrs. Lucini. But I gotta be honest with you, that article that came out . . ."

"You know about that?" Dante asked.

"Of course I do," he replied. "What I'm saying is with that, you've opened yourselves up to a bunch of crazies, okay? This could've been anyone. Anyone who feels like the rich get their way through bribes and whatever else."

"We're hardly rich," I said.

"That's beside the point." He gestured around. "Look at this place. Most people would kill to live here. What happened tonight was terrible, and we will do what we can to find whoever's responsible for it. But at the end of the day, this was simply destruction of property."

I pulled upright on the sofa, removing the gauze from my cut. "Did you know that Marco used to own our restaurant, Detective? And that he lost it, for whatever reason, and then moved to Napa?"

Lyman leaned back in the chair. He clearly had no idea what the hell I was talking about.

"And that Eric had an interview with the owner of Sunset 717, which, by the way, is owned by Marco's former partner," Dante added. "Doesn't that seem a little suspicious to you, Detective?" he pressed.

It was then that I noticed a shift in the detective's demeanor. I glanced at Dante, who seemed to pick up on it as well.

"Let me ask you something, Mr. Lucini," Lyman began. "I know you think I haven't been listening to you about Eric Castor and Marco Devaney, and all that, but I have. Trust me. And I've learned a thing or two about you, sir."

My face dropped as I looked at Dante, who remained stoic. What the hell was the detective getting at? Where was this going?

"Like how your folks owned a bakery for years in Brooklyn," he continued. "In fact, you and your brother worked there, isn't that right?"

"Yes," Dante replied, showing no emotion.

"That fire sure seemed suspicious, didn't it?" Lyman said, tilting his head, his lips raising into a half-grin. "Tell me, how did you two manage to get the money for this place? Or for the restaurant, for that matter?"

"What are you trying to say, Detective?" Dante asked. "Does this have anything to do with Eric's murder, or what Marco Devaney is doing to us now?"

Lyman pulled up to the edge of the sofa. "Here's how it looks to me, Mr. Lucini. It looks to me like you recently got yourselves some bad press. Bribery, if I read it correctly. And this was only a short while after you fired your head chef and then he died in a tragic car accident." He scratched his chin. "And you keep pushing this Devaney theory like he's the man responsible for it all."

"That's because he is," I shot back. "Whatever you think you know, Detective, trust me, you don't. Marco Devaney is a dangerous man, and he's coming for us. Now, are you going to do something about it, or should we?"

CHAPTER 21: DANTE

Last night made one thing clear — the cops were against us. Detective Lyman had the nerve to blame me for what had happened last night. How long would it be before Marco turned my staff against me, too? I could already feel their allegiance slipping away after learning about the bribe. Yeah, I knew that was on me: that fact was on constant replay in my head. I'd always considered myself a resilient guy, but I'd reached the end of my rope.

No one acknowledged my arrival this morning as I walked in through the back entrance. To be honest, I was surprised they'd turned up at all. I'd undermined them by paying for a rave review, assuming they weren't capable of getting one on their own merits. That wasn't how I felt at the time, but it hardly mattered. I was losing them, and if any one of them quit right now, we were up a creek for sure.

Kira was in the office, and when I stepped inside, the graze on her cheek reminded me of what had happened last night. "They ask you about that?" I closed the door behind me.

She pulled her attention from the monitor and turned to me. The look on her face, I'll never forget. Blame. My God, I was losing her too.

"I told them what happened," Kira replied. "I don't know how these next few days are going to play out, or whether they'll all stick around to see." She turned back to her work. "I logged into the reservation system. Come take a look."

"Do I have to?" I walked toward her while the screen populated. All I could do was laugh because it was so insane. I felt like I'd fallen into an alternate universe, or a bad dream I couldn't wake up from. "They've all canceled. Every one of them. We had been booked for two weeks straight."

"They're all gone," Kira said. "I have no idea if anyone will even show up for dinner tonight."

"We can hold out hope for those who don't read the *Times* or use social media." I raked my hand through my hair. "Have you seen him this morning?"

"No. I have no idea where he is, or if he'll come in." Kira's eyes glistened. "I'm not sure I want him to show. I don't know if I can go on with this . . ."

A knock sounded on the door, diverting our attention. "Dante?" the voice called out. It was our bartender, Gavin.

"Yeah, hey, what's up?"

"Sorry to interrupt." He thumbed back. "But there's a Detective Lyman out front asking for you."

I whipped back to Kira. "What do you think he wants?"

"I have no idea. He wasn't interested in what we had to say last night, so who knows?" she replied.

I followed Gavin into the dining room and spotted Lyman standing near the bar. "Detective, what are you doing here? Did you find out who busted our window last night?"

"Not yet, Mr. Lucini." He held out his phone and showed me a photo. "This was taken about two hours ago. Mr. Devaney showed up in the emergency room and claimed you assaulted him. Local PD was called in, and then I was informed a short while ago."

I looked at the picture. Marco's face was battered and bruised. A black eye, fat lip, cut chin. "What the hell is this? He said I did this to him?" I had to laugh at the sheer gall of this man. "Are you kidding me right now?"

"No, sir." He pulled out a pair of handcuffs. "I'm placing you under arrest for the assault of Marco Devaney."

He spun me around and clasped my hands together. "What the hell is going on? I didn't touch him. Detective, come on, you know I didn't do this. You were at my fucking house only hours ago." I looked over at Gavin. He understood my gaze and hurried into the kitchen.

While I was being placed in handcuffs, Kira rushed out to see me. "What are you doing? What's going on?" she shouted.

"Your husband is being placed under arrest for aggravated assault and battery of Marco Devaney," Lyman said, still securing the cuffs on my wrists.

Kira's eyes grew wide with shock. "What? That's insane. Dante didn't do anything. He was with me last night."

"Then why is Devaney claiming your husband attacked him early this morning?" Lyman asked, jerking me forward.

"I don't know, but it's a lie," Kira insisted, grabbing onto my arm as if she was going to stop him from taking me away. "You have to believe us, Detective. Dante is innocent. After what happened to us last night?"

Lyman pulled me toward the door. "Sounds to me like Mr. Lucini had a motive, then."

I felt a twinge of panic rise in my chest. This couldn't be happening. Not now. The restaurant teetered on the verge of collapse, and with me out of the way, what would stop Marco from coming after my wife? "Kira, call our lawyer. And don't let anyone else in here until he arrives."

Lyman led me out of the restaurant and into the back of his unmarked police car. As we pulled out of the parking lot, Kira stood in the doorway, tears streaming down her face. This was it. I was out of rope. So, what was I going to do about it?

* * *

The 77th LAPD precinct was a place I didn't want to see again, and yet, here I was. Only this time, I'd been placed under arrest. Lyman pulled me out of the backseat and led me to the entrance. The imposing structure had a linear design with stone columns along the front. He opened the door and ushered me inside. Voices echoed in the vast lobby. I'd been here enough times now, I thought the officers might start to recognize me. Nobody looked. Nobody cared. They were all too busy dealing with their own problems.

"You'll be placed in a line-up, Mr. Lucini," Lyman began. "And from there, you'll head into booking, where they'll take your prints and collect your belongings."

"Oh my God. You're serious about this?" I glanced over my shoulder at him as he pressed his hand against my back. "Don't I get to speak to my lawyer first?"

"You'll get the chance once you've been processed," he replied.

"I didn't do this, Detective. You know that. Look at what's been happening to my wife and me? Our chef was killed. You said yourself that you were looking at everyone, including Devaney. I don't understand what's happening right now."

Lyman came to a halt, stopping me in the process. He spun me around. We stood in the middle of the lobby. Officers, lawyers, criminals — they all walked by in a blur.

"Look, Mr. Lucini, Devaney was beaten to a pulp hours after you blamed him for breaking the window in your home. Your wife made it clear you two intended to take matters into your own hands. And now look where that's gotten you."

He started again, leading me down the hall. He was right. This was exactly what Marco wanted. This was how he intended to take us down. Divide and conquer. And now, Kira would be left alone to deal with the fallout. "Is he still in the hospital?" I asked.

"He was released earlier," Lyman said.

So, Marco was out. Kira was alone. And I would be sitting behind bars until we could get a lawyer to get me out on bail. She would have no choice but to put up the house or the restaurant as collateral. My guess was, she'd put up the restaurant. The house already had two mortgages.

I began to realize that Marco's plan to destroy us was going exactly as he must've predicted. After all, he'd gotten away with getting rid of Driscoll, and most likely, Eric. But it appeared he had a special place for Kira and me. We had something he wanted — our restaurant.

As I stood in the line-up, along with five others who didn't even remotely look like me, I felt humiliated. Maybe these other guys were innocent, too, but I knew that I was. And it would be hours before Kira could get a lawyer down here.

We didn't have one, unless the real estate lawyer who reviewed our purchase contract for the restaurant was qualified as a criminal defense attorney. My guess was, he didn't hold those credentials.

A voice came over the speaker. *"Turn to your left."* It sounded again. *"Turn to your right."* And finally, *"Numbers three and five, please step forward."*

I was number three and number five looked nothing like me. This was a sham. Marco Devaney stood on the other side of that mirror. I knew he did. If I could reach through it, I'd strangle him where he stood. That, at least, I could handle being charged with. Right now, murdering that man was well within my purview. Only now, I wouldn't get the chance. Not until I was out on bail.

We were finally led out of the room, and I was taken to a cell. I looked at the concrete bench, the black iron bars, the small window at the top. "This isn't right, man."

"Tell it to your lawyer," the officer replied, shoving me into the cell.

I sat down on the cold bench, dropping my head into my hands. I had no idea how long I'd been here, or how long I would remain in this cell. But what I did know, was that Marco Devaney was out, and I had to warn Kira. Angelo would need to step up and help. God knows if he could stay sober long enough to protect her, but we had no one else.

It occurred to me then that Kira and I had done a pretty good job at isolating ourselves. For the past seven months, that restaurant was all we had. Even our staff, as much as we liked them, we hadn't known long enough to get close to. Not long enough that we could ask them for help.

Eric, maybe, could've been that person, but he was dead now. I should've come clean with Kira about him. I should've done a lot of things that might've kept me out of this spot I was in now.

An officer arrived at my cell. "You have a visitor."

"Oh, thank God." I assumed my lawyer had finally arrived. But when the visitor approached, unless Kira had just gotten a law degree, I knew I was going to be in here for a lot longer.

I walked to the iron bars. "What are you doing here, babe? You should be at the restaurant. Did Marco show up? Don't let him in. Call the cops if you have to, but don't let that son of a bitch in, you got that?" Seeing the look in her eyes was the hardest part. Disappointment, a hint of regret, and fear.

She raised her hands to quiet me. "Look, I've managed to get a lawyer willing to take collateral."

"The restaurant?" I asked.

"No. I only needed enough for a retainer, for now."

That was when I noticed Kira rubbing her ring finger. Her wedding ring was gone. "No." I looked up at her. "Kira, no."

"I had to, Dante. We're broke. It was the only way. I can't let you stay here."

It was all I could do not to crumple to the floor right in front of her. This was all my fault, and she was paying the price for my mistakes. Just like my parents did.

"Has Marco contacted you?" I asked.

"No, I haven't seen him, and everyone knows not to let him in." She glanced around and leaned closer to the bars. "But we're all afraid, Dante. I think I need to close the restaurant for a few days. At least until all this is sorted out." Kira stepped back again. "Besides, after the article, I doubt many people will be coming in anytime soon."

What more could I say? She was absolutely right. "When will the lawyer get here? How soon can he get me out?"

Kira wiped a stray tear from her cheek. Her face appeared drawn and pale, and the cut on her cheek, while small, served as a painful reminder of what we'd been through. "He said he'd be here in two hours. It was the best I could do."

"What time is it now?" I no longer had possession of my phone, and they didn't keep clocks in the cells. I'd lost all concept of time, except that some light still came through the tiny window, so it must've still been daytime.

"It's 2 p.m. now," she said. "So, by four, he should be here."

Kira appeared to be holding something back. "What are you not telling me?"

She kept her eyes aimed at her feet. "You didn't do this, right? I mean, after last night . . ."

"What?" I rocked back on my heels. "No. Of course not. I was with you the rest of the night. You know that."

"And this morning?" she asked. "Before you came into the restaurant?"

"I swear to you, babe, I didn't hurt Marco. I don't even know where the hell he lives. This is all his plan. You have to believe me. You know what he's trying to do. Don't fall for it, like Lyman has. Please, I need you with me on this."

She nodded. "I'm with you. We'll get you out soon. In the meantime, I have to shut things down. It's the only way."

* * *

Waiting for the attorney to arrive felt unbearable. Every minute I was stuck inside this shithole was one more minute Marco Devaney could be plotting to come after my wife.

But now, as 4 p.m. arrived, I heard the heavy footsteps belonging to who I assumed was the officer on duty, and another set that trailed. "Please, God, let that be him."

I walked to the cell door and craned left. A man in a suit was barely visible behind the hefty man in uniform.

"Mr. Lucini, your lawyer's here," the officer said as he reached my cell door.

I stepped back, and he unlocked it, allowing the lawyer to enter. When he closed the door again, and walked away, I eyeballed the lawyer. He looked cheap. But cheap was all Kira's ring must've been worth.

The slight man with thin hair, dressed in a brown suit, offered his hand. "Mr. Lucini, I'm Hank Burrows. I've spoken to your wife and I'm here to represent you."

"How soon can you get me out of here?" I asked.

He moved toward the bench and took a seat. "I'll need you to sign a few things first, Mr. Lucini. And then I'm going to need you to tell me what happened."

"All right."

I sat down next to him, and he pushed a couple of sheets of paper toward me. I signed where he pointed, not even bothering to read the details. All I cared about was getting out of here and making sure Kira was safe.

"Now, tell me what happened," Burrows said, leaning in closer.

I recounted the events of the previous night and this morning, leaving nothing out. I told him about the article that was published, the accusations against me, and how Marco Devaney was trying to destroy us — and, possibly, blame me for Eric's murder.

Burrows nodded along, scribbling notes on a legal pad. "And do you have any evidence to refute these accusations?"

"Nothing concrete," I admitted. "But I can tell you that I didn't do it. I don't even know where Marco lives. So, how could I have gone to his house between the hours of 4 and 7 a.m.? And as for the article, it's all lies."

Burrows raised an eyebrow. "So you didn't bribe the food critic?"

I considered his question. Was it wise to lie to my own lawyer? I wasn't facing any charges for that — yet — but what I was facing was aggravated assault and battery, which was far worse.

"I'm trying to understand what it is I'm dealing with, Mr. Lucini," Burrows added. "You're going to have to be honest with me, here."

I licked my lips and nodded. "Yeah, I bribed him to give La Bianca's a good review, but the man took the money. The article says he went to his bosses after refusing, but that was a flat-out lie."

Burrows closed his notebook and set his eyes on me. "Okay, here's what I can do for you."

I leaned forward, desperate for some good news.

"I can get you out on bail for now, but we need to start gathering evidence to clear your name," he said.

"How much is the bail?" I asked, hoping it was something we could afford.

"Twenty-five thousand, or thereabouts," Burrows replied. "It's your first offense, so it's likely the judge will go easy on you, unless he learns about the bribery."

I scoffed. "I don't have that kind of money."

Burrows set down his pen and inhaled a deep breath. "Let me tell you how this is going to go, just so we're clear. If you want out of here, you and your wife will put up whatever equity you have left in your home or restaurant. I don't care which, but you might. And then, we'll get you out of here. Now, if you can't or won't do that, then you're wasting both our time."

"Okay," I whispered. "I've already got a second mortgage on the house. It'll have to be the restaurant."

"Good. Convey that to your wife, so she can get started on the paperwork." Burrows stood and grabbed his things. "I'll get going on my end and do my best to get you home by dinner."

He headed to the cell door and called out. "I'm ready." Only a moment later, an officer opened the door for him. He turned back to me. "The sooner your wife gets to work, the sooner we can get you out of here."

"Yeah. Thanks," I said, watching him walk out. The cell door slammed shut once again. I wondered what Kira was doing right now. She said the restaurant was going to have to close for tonight. That would cost us dearly. Then again, maybe not, thanks to the *LA Times*.

I leaned back against the concrete wall, closing my eyes. All I could see was Marco Devaney. But I couldn't put off the phone call any longer. I had to call Kira, first and foremost, to make sure she was okay. And then, to tell her we would have to put up the restaurant so I could get out of here. I called out for the officer. "I need to use the phone."

CHAPTER 22: KIRA

The kitchen appeared dusky with the signs of fading daylight scattering through the windows. The steel appliances and cookware caught the reflection of the few remaining rays. The soft hum of the air conditioners and refrigerators cut through the silence now that I'd sent everyone home. I wasn't sure if any of them would return. They'd watched their boss get hauled away in handcuffs, so they had reason to be concerned.

Now, I walked into our empty dining area that had once been packed with happy customers. They'd loved our food, our service; everything had been perfect. Until it wasn't.

Angelo was on his way, and I peered through the windows at the brown smoggy skyline in search of his arrival. I told him what had happened to his brother, and he sounded clear-headed. I was grateful because I needed him now more than ever.

The paperwork to put up the restaurant had been submitted, and I waited for the call from Burrows to tell me Dante was ready to come home. Soon, I hoped.

I hadn't seen or heard from Marco all day. But that meant I had no idea where he was or what he'd planned on doing. We knew him now. We knew what he'd done and why. Proving it, however, was another story altogether. I'd even begun to come to terms with what would happen when Dante found out what I'd done. It almost didn't matter to me now that my husband faced prison, while our world crumbled.

Angelo's car approached, the shine of its chrome trim bouncing off the front window. He parked and stepped out, heading toward the door. He saw me standing on the other side. I unlocked it and opened it for him. As he drew near, I offered a warm smile.

"You don't need to put up a front for me, Kira," he said.

I nearly burst out into tears at his words. He'd seen right through me. Angelo was a flawed man, but his heart was almost too big for his own good. "I don't know how we got here, Ang. I don't know what to do."

He pulled me close to his chest, wrapping his big arms around me. I wanted to melt. I wanted to give up, but I knew I couldn't. When I stepped back and set my gaze on him, I saw his pain, his concern. "What can we do?"

"Bring Dante home, for one," he said with firm resolve. "You two have taken care of me. Don't think I don't know that. It's been hard, you know, since our parents died. I haven't handled it well."

"Of course. That's completely understandable," I said.

"No. Not the way I've been behaving." His eyes reddened. "I screwed up, Kira. I let myself betray my own brother to a man who wants to hurt him — and you."

I put my hand on his shoulder. "We all make mistakes, Angelo." That sentence had never rung truer than it did now. "But we can make it right."

He looked at me with a glimmer of hope in his eyes. "How?"

"I want to contact Detective Soto. He's been looking into Marco for a long time, believing he had something to do with the missing chef up in Napa." I held up my hands. "It's a long story, and I'll fill you in on the details another time, but there might be something he can do to help."

Angelo looked hesitant. "Are you sure we can trust him?"

"I think so, yes."

"And right now, do we know where Marco is?" Angelo continued.

"No, and that's a problem." My phone rang and I looked at the caller ID. "It's Dante's lawyer. Hang on." I answered the line. "This is Kira."

"This is Hank Burrows. I thought I'd let you know that the paperwork has been processed, and your husband is free to leave."

"Thank you so much, Mr. Burrows. We're on our way." I ended the call and felt the knot in my stomach loosen. "Come on. We're going to pick up your brother."

I locked the restaurant doors and headed to my car with Angelo beside me. "I'll drive."

"I promise, I haven't had a drink since we were here with Marco the other night," he said. "I won't make that mistake again."

"I believe you, Ang, but I need to do this." I stepped into my car and waited for Angelo to get in.

As we drove to the station, my brother-in-law was silent, his eyes fixed on the road. I could see he felt guilt over all of it. But I didn't hold him responsible. This was the work of a sociopath. I knew that now.

When we arrived at the station, I saw Dante standing outside, his eyes downcast. He looked exhausted. I stepped out to meet him, doing my best to keep from crying. "Thank God you're out."

We started back toward my car when he noticed Angelo had stepped out from the passenger side. His hands shoved in his pockets, he shuffled his feet, trying to keep from making eye contact with his brother.

"I didn't expect to see you here," Dante said. "But I'm glad as hell you are."

"I want to help. I need to, brother." Angelo pulled Dante into a tight embrace.

"We should get back to the restaurant. I'd like to contact Detective Soto. We need his help." I slipped behind the wheel once again. And when the brothers were inside, I backed out of the parking lot and headed south.

The sun prepared to dip below the San Gabriel mountains. None of us knew what tonight would bring, but it was easy to imagine the lengths Marco would go. "Even if Lyman won't admit it, we know Marco was responsible for smashing our window last night." I looked over at Dante in the passenger seat. "And then he staged this assault. At this point, we have to assume he's willing to go to any lengths to break us."

"We know a hell of a lot more than he thinks we do," Dante said. "He's been watching us since we bought the restaurant. If it hadn't been us, it would've been someone else."

"How lucky are we?" I said, my tone laced with sarcasm. "If we don't prove you didn't assault him, the judge will put you behind bars. It'll be how he wins."

Angelo gripped the back of my seat and pulled up between us. "What about your phone, Dante?"

"What do you mean?" he asked.

"I mean, GPS. Didn't Lyman even look at it to see your location?" Angelo pressed.

"He did, and it showed I was home, but he said I could've left it at home for that reason or turned off the tracking."

"For God's sake," I scoffed. "What the hell's with that guy? Why is he fighting us?"

"Maybe Marco's got something on him too," Dante said. "That seems to be his MO."

"I don't think he's that smart. I think Lyman's lazy, and he has no interest in getting to the truth." I pressed the call button on my steering wheel. "Detective Soto."

The line rang over the speaker, and finally, the man answered. "Detective, this is Kira Lucini. We could use your help. I'm sitting here with my husband and brother-in-law."

"Hello, all," Soto replied.

"Marco Devaney got himself beat up and then blamed my husband for it," I continued, getting straight to the point. "Dante was arrested, and we just got him out on bail."

"I see," Soto replied.

"He smashed our living room window, too, last night," I added. "The cops don't believe us, and we have no proof. Detective, I'm afraid of what Marco will do next. Can you help us?"

There was a long pause on the line before the detective spoke again. "It's going to be tough for me to do that from here, Mrs. Lucini, but I'll make up some excuse with my higher-ups and be there tomorrow morning," he said. "We'll go over everything and try to build a plan of action. Until then, do what you can to steer clear of Devaney. I'll be in touch."

"Thank you, Detective," I said, ending the call.

Dante glanced at me. "I don't know what he'll do for us, Kira—"

"Hey, uh, guys," Angelo cut in, peering over his shoulder. "I think we're being followed."

I looked into my rearview mirror, blinded by headlights approaching fast. I couldn't discern the make or model of the vehicle, let alone who sat behind the wheel, but my gut told me it was Marco. "It's him. How did he know where we were?"

"Because he knew I'd been arrested. Probably waited for me to be released," Dante said. "Kira, just keep going. We're almost at the restaurant. If it's him, I don't think he'll have the balls to follow us there."

"I wish I shared your confidence." I turned onto the street where, only blocks down the road, was La Bianca's. The vehicle sped up behind us. "He's not backing off."

"Go faster," Angelo said. "We can't let him catch up to us."

"There's too much traffic. I can't go any faster," I replied.

Dante aimed his finger. "Kira, turn right here, now!"

I swerved around a corner, hoping to throw him off our tail, but he stayed right behind us.

"What the hell is he trying to do?" Dante asked. "There's people and cars everywhere around here, for God's sake. Go left, then make the first right. It'll take us back around to the restaurant."

I followed his instructions and turned left, then right. This street was a little quieter. I checked my mirror again. "Damn it. There he is." I tried to keep calm and focused, but my hands were shaking as I gripped the steering wheel. It was then that I heard an engine rev. "He's coming."

The vehicle charged ahead, moving beside us. "It's him, it's Marco!" His SUV swerved dangerously close, my small Mercedes rocking as he passed by. But he continued on, his taillights fading in the distance. "Jesus." I was out of breath when I looked at Dante.

His hand thrust forward, gripping the dash. "Stop the car, Kira! Stop the car!"

I slammed on the brakes, stopping at the entrance to our back parking lot. "What is it?"

"Turn in. I see something near the building."

I pulled into the lot, my headlights shining on the back entrance. "Oh my God." My lips quivered and my hands trembled.

Dante jumped out of the passenger seat and bolted toward the door. I heard Angelo hop out of the back.

"Wait!" I called out to him. But he didn't. He joined his brother, and then I stepped out. They were huddled near the edge of the dumpster, steps away from the stoop.

I stood frozen, Dante looking back at me. "Who is it?"

He walked back toward me. "Kira, don't."

"Tell me who it is, damn it!" I screamed, pushing him aside and making my way ahead. Angelo had squatted low, his eyes following me as I approached. And then I saw him. I lost my breath. My eyes welled, spilling salty tears down my face, stinging the cut on my cheek. I stood on shaky legs, my knees feeling as though they would buckle at any moment. "No," I gasped. "No, no, no."

I felt Dante's arms around me, but I shook him away. "No!" I cried, walking toward the body. I squatted beside him. Blood covered his face from the hole in his head. A gun lay next to his outstretched hand. I peered at Dante through watery eyes. "He didn't do this to himself."

206

"I know," he whispered.

I took in the lifeless form before me. Innocent and beautiful. "Jonah, I'm so sorry."

* * *

Flashing red and blue lights illuminated the night sky. Several patrol cars blocked the entrance to our parking lot. The busy street brought out onlookers as the police set up barricades to keep them back.

Detective Lyman had been called in. We told him what had happened, the description of the vehicle that chased us, and that we were all but certain it had been Marco Devaney. And that the chase had ended here, at our restaurant. We had seen the body of our young server, Jonah, with a bullet hole in his head, leaning against our dumpster.

And for the first time, I'd seen a hint of regret in the detective's eyes, as though he realized maybe he had been wrong. Maybe Dante hadn't attacked Marco, and that Marco had, in fact, broken our window last night.

And now this . . . a dead kid. Was it meant to look like a suicide? Because anyone who knew Jonah knew that wasn't possible. He'd been murdered, just as I knew Marco had been the one to pull the trigger.

We sat in the back of the restaurant, the three of us, trying to come to terms with the reality of the situation. I felt numb. First Eric, and now Jonah. How could we protect those around us? How could we protect ourselves? Because there was no mistaking it now: Marco would stop at nothing to get what he wanted.

I looked at Dante and Angelo, both of them shaken. "I don't know if Lyman is on our side, but we have to find Marco," I said, my voice barely above a whisper. "I won't let him get away with this."

Angelo took my hand. "The police will be after him now. He won't be able to hide for long."

"He won't hide," Dante cut in. "He'll come after us next."

"Detective Soto warned me, and I didn't listen. But I intend to listen now," I said.

"Kira, I don't know about this," Angelo continued. "Lyman — he seemed to realize this was serious now."

I looked around our beautiful restaurant. "We'll have to tell the staff what happened, and that we'll be staying closed for the foreseeable future." My eyes stung as Jonah's face flashed in my mind. His bright smile. His boisterous laugh. "We're through here now, but that doesn't mean Marco wins. He'll pay for what he's done."

* * *

When the scene was cleared, Dante drove us home. Angelo would stay with us until all this was over. However long that would take. We'd asked for the police to keep watch over our house. Lyman agreed, but I had no idea if he would follow through, or whether it would help. He'd refused to admit any wrongdoing in his actions, but I do think a part of him now believed we might actually be in danger.

I couldn't sleep as I lay in bed. My heart ached. I didn't know Jonah's family, but I couldn't help imagining their pain when that knock came on their door tonight. And then something else crept into my thoughts. "Dante?" I whispered. "Are you awake?"

"Yeah."

I felt him turn toward me. His face was cast in the dark shadow of our bedroom, but I could see his eyes enough to know they held pain and fear. Same as mine.

"I know this isn't the time, and maybe I was afraid to ask before, but I need you to tell me what happened to your parents in that fire. Angelo said things that night . . . when we were with Marco."

Dante sighed. "It's . . . complicated, Kira. And painful. You sure you want more of that now?"

"I want the truth, Dante. That's what I want."

He sat up, pulling the blanket around his waist. "If it'll give you some peace, I'll tell you everything."

I sat up, too, prepared to listen.

"The storage room of the bakery," he began. "That was where it started. It was early morning. Ma asked me to open for them because she had to take my dad to some doctor's appointment."

"I remember." I kept my eyes on him, watching them glisten with tears as he spoke.

"I guess I'd left the flour near an electrical outlet. Pallets of it had come in and I unloaded it for them, thinking I was doing my folks a favor. They said a spark due to some kind of electrical issue eventually came from that outlet, caught the flour on fire. It's highly flammable."

"Of course," I said.

"Yeah, well . . . So anyway, I left right after I opened up, just as my parents returned to the bakery that morning. I had no idea what I'd done. I thought everything was fine." He looked at me with an intense gaze that I'd never seen in his eyes before. "But I swear to you, Kira. It was an accident. I loved my mom and dad. I know Angelo realizes that too, but I think a part of him wonders. Or at least, blames me for it."

I laid my hand on his arm. "But it was an accident."

"Yes. And because they died, we're able to live here, and open our restaurant. A restaurant that we're about to lose."

CHAPTER 23: DANTE

When I woke up this morning, I was surprised to find Kira still lying next to me in bed. I half-expected her to have packed up her bags and left me in the middle of the night. I wouldn't have blamed her. The loss of Jonah wasn't going to be easy to overcome, and the fear that Marco could do more harm would be enough for any woman to want to break free from the man who'd brought on this crisis.

We were set to meet with Detective Soto and lay our cards on the table, hoping he could help us. Without it, where else could we turn? Lyman had begun to see the truth about Marco, but he still had a murder investigation to conduct with Eric, and hadn't yet spoken to Tom Weaver, who must've had more to say on the matter of Marco Devaney.

The house was still bathed in darkness with a hint of light from the rising sun spilling in around the kitchen as I entered. Our living room looked like we'd been preparing for a hurricane, the window still boarded. Then again, I supposed we had been preparing — for something.

Whether Kira had truly believed me about the fire, I had no idea. She said she did, for what that was worth. Angelo blamed me, even if he never said it outright. But for now, I couldn't dwell on the past. We had our restaurant to protect.

Our lives, and the lives of our staff, to protect. God, I didn't want to tell them about Jonah. But it wasn't fair to keep that from them. They deserved to know. And while the restaurant was closed, and they had no job to come to, I still considered them my responsibility.

I scooped coffee into the machine almost absentmind-edly, thoughts of Marco Devaney eating away at me. He was reckless, unhinged — deadly. He'd proven that he would stop at nothing to reach his goal, which was to destroy us. Why? Because it seemed he'd failed in the restaurant busi-ness, and we hadn't. Not until he came along.

I rubbed my eyes, feeling the exhaustion hit me hard. I couldn't remember the last time I'd had a full night's sleep. The weight of the world rested on my shoulders. Our world, anyway.

As the coffee brewed, I grabbed my phone, checking for any updates. Nothing new had come up, but I noticed a text from Eric's sister. My heart broke again for her as I read it.

Have you heard anything new? I miss him. I still can't believe he's gone.

I didn't force Eric to take drugs, but I'd let the situation spiral until Kira took action. And if it turned out Marco played some role in this, which I was damn sure he had, then I was still to blame.

The sound of footsteps pulled me from my self-indul-gent pity party. Angelo shuffled into the kitchen, his eyes bleary, and his hair a mess.

"Morning," he muttered.

"Morning." I poured him a cup of coffee. "How'd you sleep?"

He shrugged, taking the cup from me. "Not great. But I'll bet I wasn't the only one."

"No, you weren't." I took a sip from my mug. "We're meeting with Soto this morning. I hope to God he can do something to help."

Angelo scratched his protruding stomach. "And if he can't?"

"Then we keep fighting," I replied. "We can't let Marco win."

We sat in silence for a few moments, sipping our coffee and lost in our own thoughts. It wasn't until I heard Kira pad into the kitchen that I pulled my gaze from the window and looked over at her.

"Good morning," she mumbled, walking to the cabinet for a mug. "Any updates?"

Kira looked to me for answers, but I had none to give. "No. I checked the security system at the restaurant. Everything is still online."

"That's the first good news we've had in a while," she said, pouring the coffee into her mug.

I noticed her reach for her phone. Surprise appeared on her face. "What is it?"

"Detective Soto. He says he thinks he might have something on Marco." She looked up at me, her eyes full of hope. "They think they found Raymond Driscoll's body."

"Think?" I asked.

"He says they still have to ID the body, and it's in bad shape because of how long he's been dead. But given the location, he feels confident it's the chef."

"What does that mean for us today? We were supposed to sit down with him." Anger balled in my gut. "Are we on our own right now?"

"I think we might be," she replied. "But if what he's working on pays off, he'll track down Marco and arrest him. Then all of this will be over."

I held my mug between my hands and peered through the window again. "And after what happened to Jonah last night, what if Marco doesn't want to be found?"

* * *

Detective Soto's news was great — for him. Meanwhile, Marco Devaney was still here in LA. Kira and Angelo headed to the restaurant to freeze any ingredients that hadn't yet spoiled, in hopes we wouldn't lose the hundreds of dollars they cost. That hardly seemed important in light of what happened, but I think it was a way for her to process the loss of Jonah — staying busy like that. She'd insisted on making the calls to the staff about him, too. It should've been me. I knew that. But I'd been the one who made the calls when my parents died. I couldn't face doing something like that again, and especially for Jonah, who'd been just a kid.

Instead, my job was to work on getting Otis Oliver to come clean. Marco had threatened him into going public with the bribe, that much I knew for damn sure. And I needed him to give that juicy detail to Detective Lyman. All in the hopes that he would see the lengths Marco would go to take what was mine, including staging this BS assault, which would see me behind bars for more than a year, if convicted.

Marco had been smart, too, in making sure Jonah's murder looked like a suicide. A point-blank range bullet to the head. Powder residue on Jonah's hand. How or why Jonah had his gun on him, I couldn't possibly know, but he did, according to the cops. Regardless, it was bullshit to think for one moment that kid blew his own brains out. But I wasn't sure which way Lyman would lean on that.

I'd arrived at the offices of the *LA Times*, which had tight security. I couldn't get into the visitor parking lot without showing my ID to the guard at the gate. Frankly, I was surprised I wasn't on some no-entry list, but I got through.

As I headed toward the entrance, my plan took shape. They weren't going to just let me confront Oliver. No, I was going to have to take a more congenial approach to this. "Good morning," I said to the woman behind the front desk. "I'd like to see Mr. Oliver, if he's available."

"And you are?" she asked.

"Dante Lucini. Mr. Oliver knows me and our mutual friend, Marco Devaney." The mentioning of Marco was my way in. There was no mention of Marco in Oliver's lengthy denial of my so-called "attempted bribe," but no doubt he knew the name and would at least give me an opportunity to discuss our mutual problem.

"I'll see if he's here," she replied, picking up the phone.

For a moment, I couldn't be sure a couple security guards wouldn't show up out of nowhere and toss me out on my ass. But when she hung up the phone and looked at me, I figured I had a small chance at success.

"Mr. Oliver will be down in a minute."

"Thank you." I contained my smile, nodding politely before I stepped away. A fist pump in the air might've been too strong a reaction. I had to be cool about this. I had to think it through, because I would only get one shot.

Several moments went by, and I shuffled around the lobby floor, hands in my pockets. It wasn't until the elevator doors opened that I looked over to see him. Otis Oliver was heading my way. I looked at him and he at me. We both knew he was a lying son of a bitch, but I was the only one who paid the price for his lies.

"Mr. Lucini," he said, offering his hand.

"Mr. Oliver. How are you?" I asked, feeling like that was a stupid question.

"Doing well, thank you. Why don't you follow me, and we'll talk in the conference room down the hall."

I trailed him into the wide corridor that was flanked with offices and a few open-area workstations. Employee chatter surrounded me. Televisions were mounted on several walls, broadcasting the news. And finally, Oliver opened the door.

"Take a seat, Mr. Lucini," he said.

I entered the room. A conference table that sat about ten lay in the center. Leather chairs surrounded it. A large window that overlooked the city had blinds that were pulled up about half-way. "I think you know why I'm here, Otis," I said, taking a seat. I felt like I had the upper hand, but the way he looked at me made me question that assumption.

"I believe I do, Dante." He pulled a chair next to me. "I'm going to assume Marco Devaney has accomplished his goal."

"To ruin me and my restaurant?" I asked. "Yeah, you could say that. He's doing his damnedest to hurt my family

214

too. And I'm not sure how far he'll go, but if recent events are any indication, I'm gonna say pretty fucking far." I choked back my emotions for a moment. "One of my staff was found last night with a bullet in his head. A goddamn kid."

Oliver raised a brow. "Devaney did that?"

"I know he did. I just need to make sure the cops figure that out too," I replied.

"So what is it you think I can do for you?" Oliver asked. "I can't change my statement, if that was your purpose in coming here this morning."

Heat rose under my collar. "You took my money. You know you did. And I'm guessing I wasn't the only one. What's he got on you, huh?"

Oliver leaned back, shrugging a shoulder. "Enough."

I couldn't help but laugh at his audacity. "So you're not willing to do anything to make this right?"

"My hands are tied, Dante. Even if I could do something, it would undermine my credibility and wouldn't matter in any case."

"Now, see," I raised my index finger. "That's where I think you're wrong. You can go public about Devaney. Tell everyone he threatened you, and that was why you made up the story about me attempting to bribe you."

"The only thing I made up was the fact that I didn't accept your bribe. You still offered," Oliver replied. "And frankly, you just said you believed Devaney would go to extreme lengths to get what he wants. I'll be the first to admit that I don't want to know what those lengths are. If I go back on my statement, he'll come out with the other gifts."

"Gifts." I nodded. "Okay, so that's what this is really about. He's going to come out with a list of restaurants you've accepted these *gifts* from." I thought about how we could still salvage this and keep Oliver's hands clean. "So here's what we do. And I guarantee you, we'll both win."

Oliver leaned in. "I'm all ears."

* * *

Our shuttered restaurant was eerily quiet when I arrived. No one was in the kitchen, so I headed through the hall toward the dining room. "Kira? Angelo?" I called out, emerging from the corridor.

Kira walked over to me. "How'd it go?"

"He's not going to retract his statement," I said, glancing at my brother. "What have you two been up to?"

She looked at him. "Angelo's helped with the supplies. I made some calls. Everyone's in shock." Her eyes reddened once again. "What else did Oliver say? Is he going to do anything to help? I mean, he still took the money. Surely, we have some leverage there."

"Not with our current situation, but he agreed that, once Marco was out of the picture, dead or behind bars, he'd come forward to reveal that Marco had threatened him to make the statement."

"Once Marco's out of the picture?" Angelo shot up from the table. "We won't need the weasel's help then. He won't do anything for us to stop him now?"

"He will have a small part to play, which he has agreed to, in addition to making the statement after all is said and done." I widened my stance, shoving my hands in my pockets. "I'll tell Marco I want out. That I'd be willing to sell him the restaurant, as long as he doesn't come near you or any of us ever again."

Kira's face twisted with confusion and anger. "Hang on. First of all, how does this involve Otis Oliver? And secondly, that would require you coming face-to-face with Marco." She raised her brow. "Did you forget the man claimed you beat the shit out of him, and that you're out on bail because of it? Or how about the fact he likely murdered Jonah, and probably Eric, too? No. You're not doing this."

"Oliver's part is minimal, I'll give you that," I said. "He'll be the one to get in contact with Marco and set up a place to meet him. Because if I reach out to him, he won't respond."

"He'll respond to me." Kira held out her phone. "I'll text him. Forget about Oliver, at least for now. I'll set up a meeting in a neutral location — today."

I reached for her phone, taking it from her hand. "If you think I'm letting you go alone to meet with that psycho, you're mistaken."

She took back her phone. "I'll be the face of this operation, okay? You want to come along, fine. But you'll have to stay out of sight. He sees you, and he'll bolt." Kira darted her gaze between Angelo and me. "I'll tell him it's my idea to sell in order to get him out of our lives, and I have to convince you of it. No way he'll believe you want to sell to him. He'll smell the set-up a mile away. I can do this, Dante."

I took a deep breath and nodded. I knew she was right, even if my gut told me to keep her far away from Marco Devaney.

Kira quickly typed out a text message and hit "send."

"What did you tell him?" I asked, hoping we hadn't just made the biggest mistake of our lives.

"Like we just talked about," she replied. "Now, we wait."

We didn't have to wait long. His response came within minutes, and Kira's phone buzzed with a text message. She read it, but displayed no expression. "He wants to meet me at the old zoo loop trail in Griffith Park."

I considered the location. "There'll be plenty of people there. As long as you do this during daylight."

"Agreed," she added. "And you'll be able to stay out of sight."

Was I really going to use my wife as bait? "None of this works unless you get him to admit what he's done to us. And that by selling, he agrees to get the hell out of our lives. We need something to take to Detective Lyman."

"He won't admit to murder, Dante," she insisted.

"He just needs to admit to some wrongdoing. Our window, the false assault charges. You'll have to get him to say something like that if we stand a chance Lyman will bring him in for questioning. Now, I just need to convince Lyman to go along with this plan."

Kira held my gaze. "He hasn't been on our side since Day One of this nightmare, Dante. What makes you think he'll start now?"

* * *

Griffith Park was popular with hikers. It was the only reason I went along with this meeting — plenty of people would be around. Lyman agreed to come, with reluctance. I still couldn't figure out this guy's angle. Maybe Jonah's death forced him to open his eyes when it came to Marco Devaney.

The three of us huddled near the parking lot leading up to the trailhead when Lyman began: "Okay, Mrs. Lucini, I want you to call me now and then put your phone in your pocket."

"Got it." She dialed the number, and his phone rang.

He answered. "Good. Your husband and I will wait until he arrives, and we hear him on the call. Then, I'll head up the trail, making sure I stay back far enough to avoid being seen." He paused a moment. "Are you sure you want to go through with this? I could go up there and wait for him."

"No, it has to be me. You won't get him to talk, but I can," Kira said.

"Fair enough," Lyman replied. "Go. But keep me on the line."

Lyman and I watched her make her way up the trail. When she was out of view, I tapped him on the shoulder. "Let's go. We can't risk him seeing us."

We followed Kira's progress up the trail via the phone call. The wind rustled the leaves of the trees, and the occasional bird flew overhead, but there was no sign of Marco. I hoped this wasn't all for nothing. Still, just thinking about her having to face him made my chest tighten.

Kira's voice came through Lyman's phone, which he'd put on speaker. "I see him. He's coming toward me now," she said. "I have three hikers nearby. He won't try anything."

I didn't share her confidence, and I'd begun to regret this entire plan. We followed behind, keeping our distance, and listened in on the conversation. Marco sounded calm and composed as he spoke to her, but I knew better than to trust that calm exterior. He was a dangerous man, capable of murder. And my wife stood right next to him.

"You wanted to meet. Here I am."

I recognized the voice immediately and looked at Lyman. "That's Marco."

"I want to talk to you about the restaurant," Kira said, her voice sounding steady and confident. "I want to sell it to you — bargain basement pricing."

"So you said in your text," Marco sounded calm too. "I didn't think you and Dante were ready to give up so easily."

"I'm not giving up, Marco. I'm making a smart business decision. My husband and I want you out of our lives. You've destroyed our reputation. So if you think you can return La Bianca's, or whatever you chose to call it next, to its good reputation, then she's all yours."

I could almost hear the smile in Marco's voice. My fists clenched. Lyman raised a preemptive hand. He must've seen my rising anger. "Relax," he mouthed.

"I knew you were a smart woman, Kira. And I'm happy you finally see it my way," Marco said. "But, uh, given the present state of affairs, you'll be signing it over to me, free and clear."

"We don't own it, free and clear, Marco. You know that." Kira played along, and I could tell that she was doing everything in her power to keep the conversation going.

"Fine. I'll take over the payments," he said. "I can do that."

"What you did . . . coming to our home, smashing our window . . . and then telling the cops that Dante assaulted you, it didn't have to go that way. And Jonah? My God. Why?"

"I'm not sure what you mean," Marco said. "What happened to Jonah?"

219

"You know what you've done."

"What I know, Kira, is how good your lips tasted that night. How soft your breasts felt in my hands. Your nipples hard from excitement." He sighed. "Have you told Dante yet?"

I stared at the phone Lyman held in his hands. His eyes landed on me. I could feel them boring into my temple. My head dizzied. Sounds muffled. All I could hear was my heartbeat echoing in my ears.

I looked up the trail, searching for my wife. I needed to see her. I needed to know . . .

"I just need a little time to convince Dante to sell," Kira's voice sounded again.

I heard Marco snicker. "I see. And if he doesn't come around?"

"He wants you out of our lives as much as I do, Marco. He'll agree to it. The rest of it? Jonah and Eric? I guess that's for the cops to figure out, right? I want my family, and the people I work with, to be safe," Kira added. "If that means we give up, then that's what it means. But we do this? You can never harm us again. Us or anyone we know. That's the deal." She was quiet for a moment. "Your bruises seem to be healing nicely. Must've paid a lot to get someone to do that to you."

"I don't think I understand your meaning there, but sure, I have no problem keeping my distance. If that's what you really want," Marco said. "Once the deal is done, you'll get no more drama from me. You have my word."

"It's not enough," Lyman said, seeming to ignore the elephant in the room.

The phone went silent for another moment. Neither had spoken a word, and I could only wonder what was transpiring. Regardless of what I'd just heard, Kira's safety was all that mattered. "Should we go get her?" I took a step, but Lyman grabbed my arm.

"No. She's fine, Dante. Let her do this. We interrupt this thing, and there's no telling what might happen."

"Then I guess we're done here," Kira said through the phone.

The sound of what I thought had been Kira walking away from him, soon turned into more footsteps. It sounded like Marco was trying to catch up to her.

"Don't go to the cops, Kira," he said, his tone turning serious. "You won't like the consequences if you do."

Rage climbed in my throat. I wanted to sprint up that trail and put an end to that son of a bitch once and for all. I clenched my fists and took a step.

"Don't do it, Dante." Lyman squeezed my arm. "You'll end up back in jail. And you won't get bail again. She's okay. Kira's got this."

"Don't worry, Marco," she finally said. "I won't be going anywhere near them. If the cops come, it'll be because of your own mistakes. Not mine."

I listened as Kira began to move. "She's coming back down. We have to get back to the car."

Lyman gave me a slight nod.

We made our way back toward the corner of the parking lot, hiding behind a cluster of trees. And then I spotted her. She looked different. Her head hung, and her steps were slow. I watched her move toward us and we locked eyes. The entire exchange amounted to nothing. Marco had admitted to nothing. Except that wasn't all that had happened.

CHAPTER 24: KIRA

It was the look in Dante's eyes that broke my heart. I'd worn that very look before and knew exactly how he felt. To make matters worse, only part of the ill-conceived plan had worked. And not the part we needed, which was to get Marco to admit what he'd done, so Lyman could take him into custody. I knew it was a risk — going up there to meet Marco, knowing they were listening on the other end of the line. But I thought I could steer the conversation. Marco must've figured out I wasn't alone, and knew it was a way to push in the knife a little deeper.

Dante drove on as I looked through the sideview mirror. Lyman trailed behind us as we headed out of the parking lot. "Where do we go from here?" It was a question I was afraid to ask, but the silence was killing me.

"I don't know," Dante replied, keeping his eyes on the road ahead.

My phone rang and I answered the call, a glimmer of hope sparking in me when I noticed the caller ID. "Detective Soto, how are you?"

"Mrs. Lucini, I promised to contact you as soon as I knew anything."

"Please tell me you're ready to arrest Marco Devaney," I said.

"Not quite. We're still awaiting DNA testing from the body, first to confirm the identity, and then to get evidence as to who killed him. This could take time, Mrs. Lucini, you should know that. However, I did find some interesting information on Devaney's past. He was arrested for assault and battery ten years ago. The victim was his ex-girlfriend. She didn't press charges."

I felt my stomach drop. "Given what we know about him now, I suppose this shouldn't come as much of a surprise."

"Yeah, it sounds bad, I get that, but until I can make a solid connection, I want you to steer clear of him," the detective said. "We're getting closer to solving this case. I need you and your husband to hang on a while longer."

"He's not making that easy for us, Detective," I added. "If you or Detective Lyman can't scrape up enough to bring him in, I'm not sure what he'll do next."

"Mrs. Lucini, I have to insist you do not engage him. Do you understand what I'm telling you?"

Guess I wasn't going to tell him about the botched meeting I'd just had with him, which just so happened to include Detective Lyman. "I understand, Detective. Just please keep us posted. Thank you for the update." I ended the call and let my head fall back against the headrest.

"I take it Soto didn't have any news?" Dante asked.

"No, just more red flags we should've picked up on before hiring him. *I* should've picked up on." I turned to him. "We're going to have to talk about this, Dante."

He glanced at me with disappointment imbued in his gaze. Then his phone rang. "It's Lyman." He answered the call on speaker. "Yes, sir?"

"Thought I'd let you know that I reached out to Tom Weaver just now," Lyman said, his voice coming through the car speakers. "I'm going to meet him and see what he'll tell me about Devaney."

"Can we be there?" Dante asked. "Kira's already met him."

"Let me handle this, Mr. Lucini. This is what I do. If he can offer more insight, it'll help. I just need you and your wife to trust me on this. I'll keep you posted."

The line went dead, and I looked at Dante. "What are we supposed to do? Just wait and hope Tom Weaver talks?"

"That's the impression I get," Dante said. "We'll let him do his job. Weaver might be desperate enough to open up."

"Yes, but he scheduled an interview with Eric the morning he was killed. That has to mean something," I pleaded.

"Which is probably why Lyman is going to talk to him."

The car was quiet for the next several minutes. "Goddamn it, Dante, just say what you want to say."

"Did you fuck him?" He kept his eyes fixed on the road, refusing to look at me.

"No," I replied.

Dante made the turn up the hillside and arrived at our home. Cutting the engine, he turned to me. "I shouldn't have agreed to the meeting. I'm sorry I put you through that. But I'm not ready to deal with this right now."

"Okay." I reached for his hand. "What if Lyman isn't looking out for us, but his own interests? We need to protect ourselves. We'll wait it out for a while, then I want you to come with me and find out what Weaver knows. Find out what he told Lyman. If we get the same story from Lyman, then fine, he's doing what he needs to do. But if not?"

Dante glanced away as if in thought. "Then we'll talk to Weaver ourselves."

* * *

We waited in the parking lot of the farmer's market, which was already closed for the day. I saw Lyman's car parked in front of Tom's new restaurant. "I don't know when he went in. We could be here a while," I said.

"Then we'll be here a while," Dante added. "It's not like we have a restaurant to run anymore."

"I suppose not." I rested my head against the seatback on the passenger side, staring at the building where my entire life had been altered the moment I'd set foot inside it. I glanced back at the farmer's market, wishing I'd never been there that day, either. It was the result of yet another argument I'd had with my husband. We'd lost so much in so little time, but it was strange that I could hardly remember our lives before Marco Devaney. And only God knew what would remain after.

"The door's opening," Dante said.

I returned my attention to see Lyman stepping out. He glanced around, descending the steps and sticking a cigarette between his lips. His eyes narrowed as the sun seemed to blind him. And then he continued to his car. "Tom isn't following him."

"Good for us," Dante said. "It means he's still there. Now, we can find out what he told Lyman." He looked over at me. "And we'll know whether he's with us or against us."

Lyman soon drove away, and we waited a few minutes when I finally asked him, "Should we go in?"

"No time like the present." Dante opened his door.

I stepped out to join him, wondering if Marco had eyes on us. If he did, then whatever ruse I'd perpetrated against him would be over. We reached the door, and I turned to Dante. "He knows me. I'll start, okay?"

He raised his hands. "Okay."

I opened the door and stepped inside. The place seemed to be coming together, and for a moment, this felt normal. Then I remembered why we were here. "Hello?" I called out. "Mr. Weaver?"

Tom soon emerged, wiping his hands on a paper towel. His eyes changed when he recognized me. "What are you doing here?"

I stepped toward him with my hand gesturing out. "I'm sorry to bother you, Mr. Weaver. This is my husband, Dante. We'd like to talk to you if you have a few minutes."

"We saw Detective Lyman here a little while ago," Dante cut in.

"Yeah, he was here," Tom said. "And I told him everything I know."

I nodded. "Good. I was hoping you might tell us a few things. Because, you see, one of our waitstaff was shot in the head last night. A young guy, barely in his twenties."

"Jesus. I'm sorry. I didn't know," Tom replied.

"We know Lyman is working that case along with investigating the death of our former head chef."

"We've had a run of bad luck lately," Dante said. "Our friends have, anyway."

Tom glanced between us when I added, "We'd just like to ask you what you know about Marco Devaney, Mr. Weaver. Honestly, we're afraid if we don't arm ourselves with the truth about him, we're not sure what we'll be up against. I asked you before about Marco, and you said you couldn't help me. We've lost two people, Tom. We have to know what he's planning."

He turned away, as if regretting he'd made that choice. "Do you know what will happen to me if I tell you what I know?"

"Does that mean you didn't come clean with Detective Lyman about your relationship with Marco?" Dante asked.

Tom shot him a glance, but he turned his attention to me. "You know he used to own your restaurant, right?"

"We're aware of that now," I replied, picking up on the fact he didn't answer Dante's question. "Not at the time we hired him. We're desperate to stop him, Tom. Please — what can you tell us that will help us put an end to our nightmare?"

"He won't stop," Tom said, looking away from me. "Once he has you in his sights, you'll always be there until he gets what he wants."

"And what did he want from you?" Dante asked. "Money? A piece of your new restaurant? The whole thing?"

He licked his lips as if considering whether to continue. "I was his partner in the restaurant you now own. This was back before the pandemic. I put up some of my own money, Marco had some, and the rest we got from a silent partner,

Nate Conetta. But Marco couldn't keep the place going. Mismanaged everything he touched. It had nothing to do with what happened when all that COVID shit went down. He was an excellent chef, but couldn't cut it being an owner. So I cut bait. Lost some money. It wasn't easy at the time. Marco came at me pretty hard. Especially when he knew he was going to lose the place."

"What happened to Nate Conetta?" I asked.

"Good question," Tom replied. "Haven't heard from the guy since."

"How'd you escape untouched?" Dante asked. "You've got this place here now. How'd you get out from under Marco?"

"I had nothing more to offer him," Tom said. "No money. No restaurant. No standing at all. So, he went to Napa because, I don't know, I guess he knew some people up there." He pulled out a bar stool and sat down. "He'd been gone for a while, and I figured I was rid of him. But then you opened your restaurant and suddenly, there he was, back in my life. And he wanted a favor. Said I owed him."

"What happened to Eric Castor?" Dante pleaded. "Did Marco run him off the road?"

Tom coughed a little before reaching for a cup of water on the bar top. "He'd been watching Castor since he saw that you'd opened, knew he'd battled with addiction. Used that to his advantage."

Dante drew in his brow as if thinking about something. "What is it?" I asked.

He shook his head, appearing uncertain, but finally began, "That car I saw before we fired Eric, the one I mentioned?"

"Right." I turned to Tom. "Did Marco sell him the drugs, helping make sure Eric would be fired?"

"I have no idea. Once you fired him, Marco called on me for that favor. I reached out to Eric through some mutual acquaintances and asked him to meet me for an interview." Tom set his gaze to the window. "I think you know what happened after that."

"So Marco's been watching us since the beginning," I said, affirming my own suspicions.

"Just give him what he wants, Mrs. Lucini." Tom scoffed. "If he finds out I'm talking to you now, your lives won't be the only ones in danger."

I regarded him for a moment, sensing his fear. "Did you tell Lyman all this?"

Tom chuckled with some effort. "If I do, I'm a dead man. I might already be, because I'm not sure Marco intends for me to survive all this." He sighed heavily, his gaze fixed on the front window. "You want to know how to stop him?" Tom looked at me again. "You have to play his game. He's a master manipulator. He'll go to any lengths to get what he wants. But if you can beat him at his own game, then maybe you'll stand a chance."

I glanced at Dante, before turning back to Tom. "What kind of game?"

"He's been playing this game since the beginning," Tom said. "He's been pitting you against your husband. Marco got to Otis Oliver and demanded he go to the *Times* about the bribe your husband offered him."

"Oliver said in the article that he refused the money," I added. "That wasn't true."

"But because Marco knew about it, thanks to what happened to Eric Castor, he used it against Oliver, threatening to go public and insisting he had taken the money," Tom said. "All the while, he's been sabotaging your restaurant and making sure you fail, so he could swoop in and take everything from you, including your marriage."

It made sense now — the way Marco made me feel. Made me want him. It was no excuse; I was still the weak one. But I wondered if Dante could ever forgive me, as I'd forgiven him once.

"Out-manipulate him, Mr. and Mrs. Lucini." Tom eyed me up and down. "He's attracted to you. He told me that himself. Use that to beat him. And if you get the chance . . ." Tom hesitated. "Kill him."

* * *

228

If I was going to beat him at his own game, then I would have to steel myself in order to do it. We'd returned to Dante's car, neither of us able to speak.

As he drove away, I considered Tom's words. *Kill him.* And when Dante's phone rang as we reached Wilshire Boulevard, the words still reverberated in my mind.

Dante answered the call on speaker. "Detective Lyman. Have you spoken to Mr. Weaver yet?" He looked at me, both of us knowing the truth.

"He's a dead end, Mr. Lucini," Lyman replied.

I raised my brow as I looked at Dante.

"I'm in the car with Kira," Dante said. "Go on."

"I've issued an arrest warrant for Devaney."

Had I heard him right? "Sorry, Detective, this is Kira. I thought you said Tom Weaver was a dead end."

"Yes, ma'am, but given yours and Mr. Lucini's recollection of events regarding the vehicle that followed you, and then coming across the murder of one of your staff, I've taken that information to my captain. He gave the okay to draft the warrant. Talking to Weaver was supposed to be icing on the cake, but it didn't pan out. I need it to firm up the case, but with the warrant issued, we can go after Devaney now without further delay."

Turned out, I had been wrong about Lyman. Of course, we'd had Marco in our sights only hours ago, and having that warrant would've been helpful then. Still, what was done was done. "I'm not sure he'll meet me again. Not this soon, Detective. How will you find him?"

"I have a home address, and I'm issuing a BOLO on his vehicle. We'll see if we can't track down the son of a bitch," he replied.

"And can you protect my family, Detective?" Dante asked. "Can you send someone to keep watch at our home. At our restaurant? If we don't go through with Kira's plan, he'll know something's up."

"Well, here's the thing about that," he continued. "The best way for us to bring him back out into the open is for Kira to move forward. Unless I can track him down on my end, I have approval to set up an operation. It won't be just you and I out there. I'll have a team in place to bring Devaney in."

"So if I agree—"

"Kira, no," Dante cut in.

I raised my hand. "If I agree, you'll bring him in this time?"

"Yes, ma'am. You have my word," Lyman replied.

"Then I'll call him. He won't be expecting an answer so soon, so I'll have to think up something for that. And I'll let you know the time and place."

"Perfect. Keep me posted. And I'll do the same, in the event I strike gold first." Lyman ended the call.

"You think I'm going to let you talk to that man again, let alone see him?" Dante asked. "We don't need to now. They'll find him, if he has a warrant out. We're done with this bullshit. If I see that son of a bitch, I'll kill him myself."

"If we wait, we risk harm coming to our family, to our friends. No one will be safe until he's behind bars. I have to follow through with this, Dante. I want him put away, and to get you off the hook for the assault. I'm sorry, but this is what I have to do to help end this."

I reached for my phone and made the call. Marco answered.

"I'm surprised to hear from you so soon, Kira," he said. "Does that mean you have the paperwork ready for me to sign?"

"Not just yet. Dante is still processing all of this, but he is coming around. I just need you to give me a little more time," I replied.

"Then why are you calling me?"

"To tell you that I'm interested in making another deal — to buy me that time. A favor, if you want to call it that."

"You've piqued my interest," he said. "What kind of favor are we talking about?"

"The kind you've been wanting." My voice turned velvety soft. He was silent for a moment, and I wondered if I'd already blown it. I could feel Dante's eyes burning a hole in the side of my head. But Marco's ego was a delicate thing that required a gentle stroke.

"You'll have to be more specific, Kira," he said. "Tell me what you want. I want to hear you say it."

I closed my eyes, knowing my husband hung on my every word as he sat next to me. It was the nail in the coffin of our marriage, I was sure, but I had to keep playing. This was a game I could win. "I want you, Marco," I whispered. "I want to be with you. Just one night. And in exchange, you give me the time I need. The time to get everything in order so we can make this deal happen."

There was a long pause on the other end of the line. I looked at Dante, feeling guilty and embarrassed, noticing a tear fall down his cheek.

Marco was silent for too long. He hadn't expected this call, and seemed to try to figure out what my angle was. My angle was to find him. Plain and simple. If I didn't play it right, I'd lose.

"I'll meet you tonight. I'll text you the address," he replied. "And if the cops show, or Dante, or anyone else, I'll kill you, Kira. You, Dante, and your drunk brother-in-law. If you don't believe me, just think about Jonah and Eric."

* * *

We returned home, and I immediately set to work. Angelo was staying with us until this was all over. Dante had gone to find him in the kitchen to fill him in on what had happened.

I walked to our closet, stepping inside, and turning on the light. Shelves and hanging rods were mounted on every wall. The huge walk-in also had an island in the center with drawers for my jewelry. I touched my ring finger, longing for my wedding ring.

But what the drawers also contained was a gun. Legal and registered, Dante and I got it when we first moved here. We came from New York, which wasn't exactly a crime-free place. But we also heard how things were here, too. Never could be too safe. And this was the first time I'd ever considered taking it out of its case.

Dante appeared in the doorway. "What are you doing?" He looked at me and then the gun case.

His lips quivered and his eyes reddened. "It's okay," I replied. "Look, it's just a precaution, all right?"

"You don't know how to use it," he said.

I had always promised Dante I would get trained on it. He didn't like having it in the house and me not knowing how to use it. He was right about that. So, he walked over to me and keyed in the passcode. The box unlocked and he opened the lid.

With a deep sigh, he continued, "I'll give you a crash course."

CHAPTER 25: DANTE

The time and place had been set for Kira's meeting with a madman. A man who had touched her, kissed her. Bile caught in my throat at the thought of it. I didn't know what to say to her. Part of me had wanted to throw her out of the house. The other part remembered I was no saint. And then to hear Tom Weaver talk of Marco's intentions to drive a wedge through our marriage. Well, he'd succeeded in doing that.

Right now, however, I had to think about Kira's safety. I'd given her a quick safety lesson on the gun. I had no idea if she had the wherewithal to use it or use it accurately. I didn't know how this would shake out, but I had to at least see this through. She was right that it involved more than just us. Jonah was gone; so was Eric. Who would Marco take next?

Dusk had settled over the city as I peered through our kitchen window waiting for Detective Lyman to arrive. His plan was to keep a patrolman outside our home, and another who patrolled the area around our now-shuttered restaurant.

Our living room window was still boarded. An unsightly thing that some neighbors had asked us about. We gave them a sob story about vandals in the area. And now, they made sure their gates were locked tight.

Lyman was in charge of this operation scheduled for tonight, and my wife's life was in his hands. I'd never felt so useless as I did right now. I felt Kira's hand on my shoulder and turned around.

"Hey," she said. "Lyman should be here soon."

"Yeah. How are you holding up? Are you sure you still want to do this?"

She smiled that warm, compassionate smile of hers. "It's not like I haven't done this already. Another meeting with Marco to bring him out into the open."

"It's Lyman's job, Kira. You don't have to go through with this," I insisted. "I'd feel a hell of a lot better if you didn't."

"No, Dante. It has to be me. Now Lyman has a reason to arrest him. All I need to do is show up. That's the extent of it."

I shoved my hands into the pockets of my jeans. "I want more than anything for this nightmare to be over."

"I know you do, And it will be. Soon." Kira looked through the window. "There he is."

"Finally." I walked to the front door and let Lyman inside. "You have your people set up?"

He walked in. "I do. But I want to go over everything just so I know we're all on the same page."

"Fine. Follow me." I led the way into the kitchen where Kira waited. "Detective Lyman wants to go over the plans again."

She nodded. "Okay. Better safe than sorry."

* * *

I was always a firm believer in gut instincts, and right now, my gut was telling me this was a bad idea. But Lyman knew, and so did Kira, that Marco Devaney wouldn't give me the time of day, let alone meet up. I knew he wanted my wife, and that was the part that really stung, because at least for a while, she'd wanted him, too.

234

"We should head out," Lyman said. "Mrs. Lucini will drive. You and I will be in the backseat, staying low."

"Got it," I said, eyeing Kira. "You ready for this?"

Angelo wasn't playing a part in this game, thank God. I didn't need to worry about my entire family. But he wasn't happy about it.

"Dante, I want to be there. What if something happens?" Angelo asked.

"Then Detective Lyman, here, will call in his team. Right, Detective?"

"Yes, sir," Lyman replied. "I have two units on standby. We got this, Mr. Lucini."

I placed my hand on Angelo's shoulder. "Stay here. You'll be safe. There's a patrol car out front. I'll keep you posted as much as I can, okay?"

"Yeah, got it." Angelo turned to Kira and kissed her cheek. "I've never met a woman as brave as you. Please come home safe."

She smiled. "I promise I will."

Lyman started toward the door. "Let's head out."

Kira pressed the ignition after the two of us stepped into her Mercedes. I still questioned the plan, but Lyman was confident she would be safe, and his team would swoop right in and arrest Marco. If there was any other outcome, I don't know what I'd do.

She drove the car around our circular driveway and headed down the hill. Kira was quiet, and I wanted to say something, but what could I say? She wouldn't turn back. Not now.

"Head south on the 5, toward Lincoln Heights," Lyman said.

No one talked after that, not for several miles, and then Lyman aimed his finger ahead. "Turn right here. Another mile, cut the headlights."

When Kira made the turn, she continued down a scattering of large homes, finally killing the headlights. The street was pitch black. "This is the address Marco sent?" she asked.

"Yep. New construction. Maybe residential," I said. "Apartments? I don't know."

"Keep going about another five hundred yards or so. It'll be up ahead on the right," Lyman added.

I looked around for any place that seemed to be inhabited. "I don't see anything or anyone around."

"There he is." Kira's gaze shifted to the passenger window.

"Where?" I shot back.

"It's his car." She pointed to a dark Toyota SUV parked in an empty lot. "This is it. We're here." Kira looked back at us. "Do I just go in?"

Lyman had his phone to his ear. "We're here. Where are you?" He nodded. "Okay. Be ready. I'll keep you posted. Copy that." He ended the call. "The team's posted nearby."

"Nearby?" I raised my brow. "How nearby?"

"They can be here in less than a minute," Lyman said. "Calm down, all right? Mrs. Lucini's got this. He's not going to hurt her."

"You don't know that," I shot back.

"Dante, please. Don't make this harder than it is," Kira said, unbuckling her seatbelt. "Just let me get this over with."

CHAPTER 26: KIRA

The gun in my waistband kept poking my ribs as I walked toward the building. It was black out here. Black, and the air, cold. We'd driven several miles past Lincoln Heights toward Rose Hill. Homes were scattered throughout as we made our way. I spotted a small solar farm that, even in the dark, was surrounded by various flashing red lights.

But now, out here, I felt alone. Glancing back, I saw the car where Dante and the detective waited. Lyman had assured my husband I wouldn't be hurt. I wondered how he had been so certain when I, most definitely, was not.

I pulled back my shoulders, approaching the shell of a building, and walked through the first-floor door. Why they had installed the doors and not the windows was strange. Never mind that. Stay focused. Just get Marco to walk out of the building and Lyman will arrest him.

That seemed easy enough, but I'd promised him something. I'd promised him me. How was I going to get him out of there without delivering on that promise? And I know a part of Dante feared I might go through with it. My eyes stung and I cleared my throat, doing my best to stay strong. My life was at stake, and so was everything else.

Inside appeared to be framed-in rooms with electrical wiring spanning the studs. The concrete floors were covered in black marks. Finally, I spotted a staircase where light shone down. Not much light, just enough to see. "He's up there," I said to the empty space.

At least a handrail had been installed, so I clutched it, taking careful steps toward that light. As I climbed the stairs, a sickening feeling swirled in my gut. The staircase led to a hallway, still nothing but studs and wires.

The light appeared brighter near the end of it. Marco must have been in there, steps away. I stopped to listen, but heard nothing. I pressed my hand against my stomach as though that would help to settle it. Then, I checked the gun. Yep, still there. Would I dare try to use it? Yes, I would.

"In here, Kira," Marco's voice called out.

He'd heard me coming, so I started on again, reaching the end of the hall. To the right of me, a framed-in room and doorway. There he was, standing in the corner of that room, a construction light mounted on a tripod next to him. His face was doused in shadow, but I saw the look of amusement, like he was going to win this battle. Maybe so, but I wouldn't go down without a fight.

"You showed up," he said, standing with his legs wide apart, and his hands clasped in front.

"I told you I'd come, and here I am," I replied. If he could see my knees shake, he didn't let on. "Why did you want to come here? Doesn't seem to be the kind of place for what I had in mind."

Marco crossed the room to stand inches away. He loomed over me, a towering figure that sent fear through my body. His piercing green eyes, once so appealing to me, now felt like daggers as they inspected me from head to toe. He raised his hand and with his thumb, gently caressed my cheek. "You're thinking that if I touch you, that's your guarantee I'll play along."

I felt his hot breath on my face. He was close enough that were he to place his hand on my hip, he'd know I was armed, and survival might not be in the cards for me. "I just want you out of our lives, Marco. And if this is what it takes for you to give me the time I need to get Dante onboard, then I'm willing to make that sacrifice."

"Sacrificing yourself for your husband. Oh, I'm sure it won't be all that bad, once I'm done." He leaned toward my ear. "I think you might like it, Kira. Even if you won't admit it."

I steeled myself as I peered at him. "I know what you did, and I know who you really are."

"And your husband? Does he know who you really are? I'll bet he does now." He placed his index finger on his chin. "I wonder who exactly you think I am, Kira?"

"A liar. A killer. And worst of all, you're a failure, Marco," I shot back. "Dante never touched you. Never laid a finger on you. I don't know how you managed to get the shit kicked out of you, but I can only assume it was to get me to turn against him."

Marco touched his lips to mine, and I tensed, not daring to move even an inch. He'd closed his eyes while mine stayed open. When he pulled away, I quickly spoke up, "So we're in agreement? We'll finish this transaction, and I can leave."

He took a half-step back and stared at me. "You don't remember, do you?"

"Sorry?" I felt my pulse quicken, having no idea where this was going.

"I thought eventually it would come to you, given how close we've been." He sighed. "But it's clear I didn't make the same impression on you then as I seem to have now."

I racked my brain, wondering what he was talking about. "I don't understand."

He grabbed me by the waist and brought me against him, stealing my breath away from me. "I'm going to enjoy this much more than you know." His expression then changed; his gaze lowered and lingered on my waist before he let out a sinister smirk. "What do we have here? Did you think I wouldn't find this eventually? What was your plan,

Kira — get me close enough so you could shoot me?" He narrowed his eyes and licked his lips. "Good idea. Piss-poor execution."

I pushed him back, and the unexpected move forced him to stumble, nearly losing his footing. His grip tightened around my arm like a vice, trying to keep me from escaping.

"You're not going anywhere."

A desperate rage burned in me as I realized this may be my last moment of life; the gun was all that separated us now. I had to move fast if I wanted to get it away from his grasp before he killed me. My hand quickly slid down toward my waistband, grasping for the handle of the gun, and yanking it out in one swift motion.

But he was too close. I'd have to flick the safety and fire at his feet just to get him off me. My hand fumbled around the safety while Marco attempted to take hold of the gun.

"Give it to me now, Kira. This won't end well for you."

Marco's iron grip clamped down on my left arm, twisting it painfully until I cried out and released the gun to the ground. With a resonating clang, Marco kicked it across the room before slamming me into a corner. My head smacked against one of the studs as my body landed on the concrete floor with a sickening thud, sending stars to my eyes.

My vision cleared to see Marco pointing the gun at me, his finger against the trigger. Outside, Dante and the detective waited for us, but I'd failed in my efforts, and any chance at escape had dwindled. Tears streamed from my eyes. "What are you waiting for?"

CHAPTER 27: DANTE

Kira had walked into that building under construction and disappeared inside. Five stories. A few doors on the ground floor had been installed. When she'd disappeared, my throat had tightened, and my mouth had dried. I hadn't spoken a word to Lyman, but kept my eyes fixed ahead, praying for my wife to walk out of there with our enemy beside her.

And now, several minutes had gone by. Sweat formed on my brow even in the chilly night air. "Should we do something?" I asked Lyman. "It's been too long."

But the look on his face seemed to suggest Kira and Marco wanted to be together. He might as well have said, *they're fucking right now.*

"We just need him to walk out with her, then we've got him," Lyman replied. "Give it another five minutes."

I couldn't stand the thought of her there with him. She could be dead in five minutes. "No, if he's in there, what's the point in waiting, huh?" I opened the back door.

"Dante!" Lyman whispered loudly. "Wait."

"I'm done waiting. I'm going to get my wife." I closed the door and started toward the building. Soon, footsteps trailed, and Lyman caught up with me. "I'm not wrong about this. She shouldn't be in there alone," I told him.

241

I pushed open the door and the smell of sawdust filled my senses. We made our way up the stairs, listening for any noise that could give away Kira's location. As we approached the first floor, I heard a muffled sound. Voices. It was coming from one of the rooms at the end of the hallway.

I signaled for Lyman to follow me. I could hear Kira's voice, but she sounded different. Fear. I heard fear in her voice, and it made my blood run cold. And then I heard him. Marco was in there with her. I was going to end this right now.

I rounded the corner and stepped into the unfinished room. Kira was on her feet and spun around to me. "Dante?"

Her face lit up with hope. It was then I noticed a figure fleeing into another corridor. "Shit. He's getting away."

"Damn it!" Lyman hustled to follow him.

I ran beside him, determined to catch up.

Lyman made the call. "It's happening. Get over here now!"

Breathless, my mind racing with the thought of what Marco would do if he got away. There would be no more chances to entrap him. He would come for us. He would come for Kira to get back at me.

I could hear the sound of Marco's footsteps echoing through the empty building, getting fainter with every passing second. "Where's your team, man?" I knew I had to act fast if I wanted to catch him. I picked up my pace, running toward the exit, bypassing Lyman. As I turned the corner, I caught a glimpse of Marco running out the door.

"Go back, Dante," Lyman yelled. "I got this. Go check on Kira."

He was right. I had to make sure she was okay. I watched Lyman disappear, hot on Marco's trail, and I returned inside. I made my way through the hall again, calling out to her. "Kira, I'm coming." When I reached the room, she was huddled against the back wall, shaking, her face pale and tear-streaked. "Are you okay?" I asked, wrapping my arms around her.

"I'm okay. I tried . . . I tried to but—"

"Lyman's going after him," I cut in. "His team is close. They'll find him. There's no place for him to go."

"I'm so sorry," she continued. "Dante, he took the gun."

"I don't care about that right now. All I care about is that you're safe." Lyman didn't know Kira had been armed. I wished she would've shot Marco the moment she saw him.

"What are we going to do?" Kira asked, still sounding breathless. "He knows this was all a trap."

"Lyman and his people got this, okay? We'll go back to the car." I wrapped my arm over her shoulder, setting aside whatever had transpired between her and Marco, and we made our way down the stairs and out of the building. She came to a stop just as we stepped outside. I narrowed my gaze. "What is it?"

"He knows me," she whispered. "Somehow, he knows me."

"What? Of course he knows you," I replied.

Kira shot a look at me. "No, Dante. He implied we'd met before. How? Where?"

* * *

They'd searched for two hours, but Marco was gone. Lyman and his team had returned to the station. He'd requested Kira and I return with him, so we did, and now we waited in his office.

"Sorry to keep you both waiting," Lyman said, as he entered with a file folder in his hand. "We have alerts on his bank and credit cards, along with his phone. We will find him."

I glanced at Kira. "I hope you're right, Detective." I was going to have to admit that Marco was now armed. "There is one thing we need to tell you."

He sat down at his desk. "I'm listening."

The words lay on the tip of my tongue, but I hesitated to speak them. "Before we went to meet Marco earlier . . . I — uh — I gave Kira my handgun. Just in case."

Lyman turned stone-faced. "He has your gun?"

"Yes," Kira cut in. "I brought it for protection, and he overpowered me."

Lyman steepled his fingers and regarded her. "I get why you did what you did, but you should've told me. And then I would've said it was a mistake. You're lucky he didn't kill you with it."

"I know that, Detective," she said. "But what choice were my husband and I given? You weren't interested in helping us until Jonah was killed."

Lyman held his tongue. He'd wanted to say more, and I sensed that it was about what he'd heard at Griffith Park. Son of a bitch looked at my wife like she brought this on. "We're out of options," I said. "There's not a chance in hell he'll come out of hiding now, not until he's ready to make his final play."

"And what do you think that play is, Mr. Lucini?" Lyman asked.

I took Kira's hand in mine. "He plans on taking everything we have. Including us."

"Then I think the best plan now is for you two to re-open your restaurant," Lyman began. "Go on about business as usual and let me work on tracking down Devaney. We'll have ballistics back on the bullet that killed Jonah Evans, so when we do find him, I'll have enough to bring not only murder charges, but charges for attacking your wife tonight. You two need to step out of this now and let me do my job."

This guy wanted us to re-open our restaurant? The hell? "Detective, I have to step in here and just say that even if we could re-open, which we can't because we've let go our staff, we'd be sitting ducks. Marco would know exactly where we were and come for us," I said. "And we've had enough bad press that I doubt anyone would actually show up. I'm not sure where this is coming from."

Lyman pulled up in his chair. "Then I suggest you hire new people. Look, Mr. and Mrs. Lucini, you can sit in your homes, terrified of this man, or you can go on about your lives while I do my job to find him. I promise, I won't leave you hanging in the wind. I'll step up patrols in the area of your restaurant and your home." He leaned back. "The best thing you can do is to get on with your lives, or risk going bankrupt."

"Social media will help us to potentially bring some people back," Kira said. "But it won't be overnight."

I shot her a look. "Are you serious? You really think this is a good idea?" And then I saw something in her eyes. Rage. Not at me. Not even at Lyman. She was enraged by what Marco had done, all of it. Even putting thoughts into her head that he'd met her before. Trying to scare her. It was all part of his game, and she wanted to do this to prove he hadn't beaten us.

I set my sights on Lyman again. "I can't be the only one who thinks this is crazy. Are you asking us to do this because you think Marco won't show himself again, or because he will?"

CHAPTER 28: MARCO

We'd been locked in a battle of wills in that dark, empty shell of a room. I'd watched Kira tremble under the weight of her decision to come, seeming to wonder if she'd end up like Eric or Jonah. It had only reinforced my disgust for Dante, though — allowing his wife to be alone with me after knowing what I'd done to those he'd cared about. What I'd done to her.

I almost showed my hand. The temptation was strong, but I had to wait. I needed Dante there to see it. To realize he was at fault for all of it.

Besides, I knew she would never give herself to me, nor the restaurant. My attraction for her was obvious, but I was hardly gullible. I'd chosen a dangerous place where accidents could easily happen. The gun, however, was unexpected, forcing me to alter my plans. My mistake. One which would not be repeated.

I'd checked into a motel south of West Hollywood under a false name. And it wasn't the "Sunset Strip" or "Melrose Avenue" area either. No, just beyond that lay the kind of places that only took cash. The kind of places where kids sold themselves for twenty dollars.

The reality of the situation set in. In my desire to take back what was mine, and to make Dante pay, I'd gone too far. Left too much carnage in my wake. All they had to do was give up.

So where had that left me now? Get out of town while I still could? That would've been the rational thing, except rationality was long gone now. I'd never get back my restaurant, but I'd be damned if I let the Lucinis have it.

I slipped on my sunglasses as the sun rose in the sky, dabbing lightly against my cheek. The bruises were turning purple now. It had hurt like hell, but damn if it didn't look convincing.

Jonah's car was parked in a spot near my motel room, and I stepped inside. I'd taken the poor kid's keys after he went down. He'd been an easy target. Easier than I'd expected. We'd got to talking one evening, and I learned he enjoyed visiting the gun range for target practice, mentioning he'd owned a few guns as a hobby. Sometimes all it took was a friendly ear, and Jonah had needed one, apparently. Getting the gun to make it look like suicide? Damn kid didn't bother keeping them locked away in his apartment. What a shame.

It had taken some planning, maneuvering, but I'd managed to get my point across when Dante was released from jail. Jonah's death was a byproduct.

Now, I had one more loose end to secure. One more person who'd betrayed me in my quest to take back what was mine.

After the slog through traffic, I'd arrived at his house. Tom Weaver lived in the same home as when he and I were partners. He owed that to me, but I guess he'd forgotten how I'd helped him.

His car was in the driveway, so I figured he was home. The best way for me to get inside was to hop his fence and enter through the back. It was still early, and I knew the long hours he'd put into renovating his new restaurant, so I stood a pretty good shot that he'd be asleep.

As I walked into his backyard, I noticed a sliding glass door under the covered patio. The curtains were open, and I could see inside. The kitchen was to the right and on the left appeared to be the living room. No sign of him anywhere.

I raised the slider from its track and the lock easily disengaged, allowing me to open it. No alarm sounded. The old Santa Fe-style home was quaint, with a small kitchen and high-end appliances. Had to respect the man for his commercial-grade stove. I walked into the living room and to the hallway in front of me.

Keeping up my guard, I brandished the gun — the Lucinis' gun — and continued on. It would be much easier for blame to be placed on Dante that way. I stepped lightly, checking each room I came across, until finally . . . there he was.

Tom Weaver. A former partner. A former friend. A liar and betrayer who now lay in bed, unaware of my presence. Eyes closed, breathing short, quick breaths. "Tom. Tom," I said, approaching him.

His eyes fluttered open, and he turned his head just enough to see me. I noticed his eyes widen as he scrambled to get out of bed. "Hey, bud. How you doing?" I asked.

"What are you doing, Marco?" He got to his feet on the other side, reaching for the drawer of his nightstand. "Get away from me. Get out of my house."

"If you got a gun in there, don't bother," I said. "I'll take you down before you have the chance to grab it."

"Don't. Please, don't do this, Marco. You don't need to. The cops came to me. I told them nothing. I swear it."

"It's not the cops I'm worried about, Tom." I tightened my grip on the gun and tilted my head. "You talked to them, didn't you? No need to answer. I already know you did." I looked at his bed. "Lay back down. We're going to do this nice and quiet, all right?"

"No," Tom said, appearing defiant. "You want to kill me, do it right where I stand."

Gunfire would draw attention. Eyes would appear from behind closed doors as I made my escape, and I probably wouldn't get far. But one thing might help. "Well, if you insist."

I grabbed a pillow from his bed and held it over the end of the gun. A muffled shot fired. Feathers floated around me. Tom collapsed to the floor. "Sorry, man. It's just business."

I slipped out the way I came. As I reached the fence, I jumped it once again, landing awkwardly on my ankle. "Shit!"

A teenager was walking across the street and must've caught sight of me. I quickly stood as though I was supposed to be here. With AirPods in his ears and a phone in his hand, his glance was fleeting. Clearly, he hadn't heard the gunshot. I hobbled back to my car and slipped behind the wheel. No one set foot outside their homes. As usual, no one gave a shit, and I was in the clear.

* * *

My timing had to be right with Dante and Kira. Keeping eyes on them for a day or so would give me a sense of when to make my move. But I wasn't some novice, and I knew that sticking around LA longer than necessary would present a problem for me.

I walked into my motel room, tossing my bag onto the double bed that was covered in a dark blue comforter with more stains on it than I cared to think about. I sat down, setting my phone on top of the nightstand.

The buzz of the kill lingered, but that feeling wasn't something I ever craved. No, what I'd craved was to be the best. The sheer adoration from others for being the best. That was the real deal. The real high.

I grabbed my laptop and opened it, checking for news about me, first and foremost. No witnesses, or at least none that had come forward. Then, I searched for details on La Bianca's closure — the reason they put out to the public. Had they specified whether they would re-open? And what about the bribe? If I had the time to just let this play out, I would hardly need to intervene at all, but I was on a timeline.

CHAPTER 29: KIRA

The detective's idea seemed to place all the risk on Dante and me, and none on himself. He needed to solve his murder investigations and expected us to simply carry on with our lives, knowing Marco was out there. Would he really ensure our protection? I had no idea, because he hadn't exactly done the job to the best of his abilities, as far as I was concerned. Dante felt the same.

We prepared to leave Lyman's office, feeling betrayed by him once again. As we headed toward the door, his phone rang, and he answered. I grabbed Dante's arm to stop him, and we both turned back to see Lyman. The look on his face sent my mind to worry as he listened to the caller.

"Okay, yeah, got it. I'm on my way." Lyman ended the call and looked at us.

"What is it?" I asked him.

"Tom Weaver was found dead in his home."

Dante pulled me close as we traded glances. "What? He's dead?" I asked.

Lyman stood from his chair. "Apparently, one of his contractors doing work on the restaurant came to his house for a meeting. Found him dead in his bedroom. Gunshot to the chest."

"Oh my God." I couldn't take any more news of death. Tom had risked everything to warn us, and it got him killed. "Detective, this was Marco. You know that."

He looked at me, pressing his lips together, shoving his hands in his pockets. "You might be right about that, Mrs. Lucini. You and your husband should go home. I'll keep a unit parked outside your house. And whatever I said before — about your restaurant—"

"I think that option is off the table," I said.

"Yes, ma'am. I think it is."

* * *

Neither of us said a word when we arrived home. It was almost noon. We'd been up all night. Angelo had been sitting in the living room, waiting for us. He stood when he noticed us enter. "For God's sake, I've been waiting for one of you to call me or something."

He walked over to me, taking in my appearance. "Are you okay?"

"I'm fine, Ang." I looked at Dante.

"What?" Angelo glanced between us. "Is he gone? Is Marco gone?"

Dante headed into the kitchen. "He got away last night. Kira and I have been at the station with Lyman ever since."

"So, you risked everything and got nothing in return?" Angelo trailed Dante.

I followed behind him, feeling weak, scared, unnerved that somehow, I might have met Marco before, but it had eluded me. Maybe I'd had a stalker and never realized it. I glanced through the kitchen window. "Ang, have you seen a patrol car anywhere out front? I didn't see one when we pulled in, but maybe he's patrolling the area. Lyman is supposed to be sending someone."

"No, but I haven't exactly been looking." Angelo stood at the kitchen island, his beefy hands resting on top of the counter. "Do they have any idea where Marco might be? Is that why Lyman's sending a car here? Is he coming for us?"

Dante had swallowed almost an entire bottle of water before stopping to catch a breath. "I don't know, Ang. Lyman said we should go back to our lives, re-open the restaurant—"

"What?" He laughed. "Was he being serious?"

"Oh, yeah," Dante replied. "He was ready to wash his hands of all of it until the call came in."

"What call was that?" Angelo pressed.

"Tom Weaver, Marco's former partner, is dead," I cut in. "Someone shot him in his bedroom, and I'm sure we can all guess who that was. That changed everything." I walked over to the kitchen table and pulled out a chair to sit, staring out over the city, a thick layer of haze weighing down on it. "It seemed to me that Lyman finally realized the kind of man we were dealing with in Marco."

"What happens now?" Angelo asked.

I turned back to him, glancing at Dante, knowing his expression mirrored mine. "We wait."

* * *

All I could do was stare through our kitchen window, watching the unmarked police car that sat at the bottom of our long driveway. Dante had been on the phone with the bank and vendors, doing everything in his power to keep us out of bankruptcy and lawsuits. We were ruined. Our friends — dead. And now Detective Lyman was on the hunt for the man responsible.

If only I'd been able to pull the trigger before he got to me. This would've been over. Instead, we were holed up in our home, like prisoners. And there was still so much Dante and I weren't saying to each other.

I'd been terrified, standing before Marco in that building, a construction light in the corner of the room illuminating his face. He looked insane. A part of me wondered why Lyman would've let me go forward with the plan. At that moment, I hadn't considered it crazy, but that was exactly what it was — crazy. If Dante hadn't arrived when he did, I could be the one with a bullet in me instead of Tom Weaver. Instead of Jonah Evans.

What I wondered now was why Eric had been a target. He'd already been let go. Why go after him? I could pretend Marco wasn't responsible, but that ship had sailed. I could put nothing past him now, or the lengths he would go to get what he'd wanted.

I noticed Dante emerge from the hall, pocketing his phone as he headed toward the kitchen table. Defeat weighed down his shoulders as he shuffled. My eyes stung at the sight of him. He was a broken man, and I'd played a part in that. "What did the bank say?" I asked, afraid to hear the answer.

He dropped onto the chair and closed his eyes. "They expect payment as usual, or they'll put a lien on the house."

I nodded, feeling a lump rise in my throat. "Then I guess it doesn't matter what the vendors said."

"No." Dante looked down at his pocket and reached for his phone. It seemed a call was coming in. He answered. "Hello."

I didn't see the screen and had no idea who he was talking to, but when his expression changed, I bolted up in my chair. Was that a hint of a smile on his face? "Who is it?" I whispered.

He raised his hand, gesturing for me to give him a minute. "Yes, okay, thank you so much, Detective. Goodbye."

When his eyes glistened, I wasn't sure how to feel. "Was that Lyman? What did he say?"

Dante's chin quivered and then a smile appeared on his lips. "They got him, Kira. They got Marco."

* * *

Seeing was believing. I had to see for myself that Marco was behind bars. Dante and I returned to the LAPD for the second time today. I'd lost count how many times we'd been here over the course of two weeks. More than I cared to remember.

Lyman ushered us to his office. "Please, have a seat."

We sat down, wondering what the next step would be. Dante took my hand, both of us feeling assured we were finally going to get through this. Hopefully.

Lyman returned to his desk. "He's in processing now, and he'll be booked on suspicion of murder for Tom Weaver, and his attempted assault on you last night, Mrs. Lucini."

"So that's it? It's over?" Dante asked. "How were you able to prove he killed Weaver so quickly?"

I understood Dante's concern. After all, it seemed like Lyman had refused to lift a finger early on when we told him what we thought Marco had done. Now, all of a sudden, he was convinced Marco killed Tom Weaver?

Lyman leaned back in his chair. "Well, he used your gun. The bullet casing was recovered on scene, and I had a feeling, since he took the gun from Mrs. Lucini, he would use it in effort to lay blame on you. And he did. He made this one easy on us, Mr. Lucini. We tracked him down at his former partner's new place."

"Why would he go back there?" Dante asked.

"Money," Lyman replied. "We found him attempting to access a safe in the back of the building. He didn't get inside it, by all accounts."

I didn't care how they found Marco, just that they did. "What do we do now?"

"I'll need a statement on your last interaction with Weaver. What was said, and when. I'm working on a time-line of events and that will help. But after that . . ." He raised a shoulder. "You're free to go home. No doubt, Devaney will get a lawyer and an arraignment will be set. But in the meantime, I'll be working to make sure I have the evidence to prove without a doubt that Devaney killed Mr. Weaver."

I narrowed my brow. "What about Jonah and Eric? He killed both of them. You have to know that."

Lyman raised a pre-emptive hand. "In due time, Mrs. Lucini. This will all come together, and the evidence will start to roll in. Once it does, Devaney won't be seeing the outside of a cell anytime soon." He grinned. "It's over, Mr. and Mrs. Lucini." Lyman got to his feet. "I'll have one of my officers take your statements and then you're free to leave. Follow me."

I couldn't believe it. In fact, I was hardly able to stand. Was this really happening? Was this really over?

"Come on, babe." Dante helped me off the chair.

Lyman led us into the hall once again and from the corner of my eye, I saw him. Cuffed, dead-eyed. That was, until he saw me. Marco's lips spread into a toothy grin as we locked eyes. I stopped and Dante looked back at me.

"What's wrong?"

And then he saw Marco, too. For a moment, I felt him pull and take a step forward. "Dante, don't," I whispered.

It was then Lyman seemed to finally take notice of why we'd stopped. He hurried back toward us and ushered us away from Marco. "I'm sorry about that. I didn't think they'd take him into processing so quickly. Come on. Let's get you two out of here."

* * *

The first thing to do? Re-open our restaurant before we lost everything. The thing was, we had no staff. And whether any customers would return after the bribe fiasco was a big question mark.

But as Dante and I left the station, driving into the late afternoon sun, we felt free of the stranglehold Marco Devaney had had on us. We might still be ruined, our marriage all but over, but we were no longer frozen with fear.

Now, as Dante and I returned to the restaurant, Angelo met us there. He'd stood just inside the door, wearing a wide smile I hadn't seen in weeks.

"What took you two so long?" he asked. "Come on in. We have a lot of work ahead of us."

"We need to start making calls," I added. "Naomi first. We need her back, and we'll have to hope bygones can be bygones. I think the others will follow if they know she's back."

"And how do we pay everyone?" Dante asked.

"Breaking even in our first week is the only way we'll have enough for their salaries, and if that doesn't happen, then I don't know." I raised a shoulder. "I'm not even sure we have enough to pay to re-stock everything now."

"I still have a little on the line of credit," Dante said. "It'll have to do. And I'll make a call to Oliver. With Marco out of the way, he owes me."

"How soon?" Angelo asked.

"Before we can re-open?" I looked around the dining room. "A couple of days, if we hustle."

Angelo checked his phone. "If we're going to do this, we'll need immediate deliveries."

"They'll have been scheduled for the week already," Dante said. "I'll put together a list, and then, if you can help run some errands, between the both of us, we can have what we need by end of day tomorrow. At least enough to get us through the weekend."

"I can do that, but you might want to make sure we'll have staff," he replied.

My brother-in-law eyed me, realizing I was the one who would have to make the calls. The staff trusted me a hell of a lot more than they did Dante, especially after watching him get hauled away in handcuffs.

"Yeah, can't do this without them." I grabbed my phone and dialed Naomi's number. With the phone at my ear, I waited. "Come on, answer. Please, answer." The line picked up. I was a little shocked. "Naomi, hi. It's Kira."

"What do you want?" she asked flatly.

"I'd like to bring you back, if you're interested. We're aiming to re-open in two days." I regarded Dante a moment, unsure if I could pull this off. "Marco's out of the way now. He's been arrested, Naomi. And Dante is going to work with Oliver to fix that mess, too." I listened to her breathe on the other end of the line. "We need you, Naomi. It should've been you all along, and I'm sorry for that."

The line went quiet for too long, and I felt defeat clutch my throat.

"Me, too, Kira. I'm sorry for a lot of things," she replied. "But what about Jonah? The idea of coming back there after what happened . . . What will customers think?"

Jonah had never left my mind. Even when I faced Marco, holding that gun, I was doing it for Jonah, and for Eric. "I'm not sure how people will react to that. And you're right, it will be hard to re-open without him here." I looked around again. "This place won't be the same without him. But by doing this, by giving this another shot . . . I think that's what he would've wanted. Giving up wasn't in his nature."

"No, it wasn't." Naomi went quiet again. "Yeah, okay. I'll do it."

CHAPTER 30: DANTE

It had felt like the old days — my brother and I setting up tables. Angelo gathered the supplies. Kira had called every person we'd had on the payroll, pleading with them to come back. Some of them agreed.

Inside of forty-eight hours, we were ready to open again for the dinner shift. Would anyone turn up for it? I hoped so, because we were officially out of money and out of options.

The kitchen staff prepared all our signature dishes — steaming pastas topped with fresh herbs; crispy risotto cakes stuffed with creamy cheese; meaty lasagnas doused in sweet tomato sauce so thick you could spread it on a slice of bread.

Should I have let myself feel good about this when people I knew were dead? When Jonah and Eric were dead? The idea troubled me, and guilt weighed on my shoulders. Maybe even more than the guilt I felt over my parents. Kira and I conveniently ignored our own problems, too. Seemed we'd gotten pretty good at doing that.

"We're short on time," I said to Naomi as I approached her in the kitchen. "How are you coming along?"

"I got this, Chef," Naomi said. "I'll take care of the kitchen."

"Yes, Chef," I replied. Things would need to be aired out between us, but for now, we shared the same goal. She'd suffered at Marco's hands as well, and things could've turned out far worse for her.

Kira stepped out of her office and headed over to us. "Everything good?" she asked me.

"All good here. Naomi has things well under control."

"I'm sorry, Kira." Naomi blurted out, darting her gaze between us. "I'm not proud of my behavior. And after what you and Dante have just been through with Marco. I mean, the guy poisoned me. Tried to burn me." She looked at me for only a moment. "Anyway, I want to be here. I want to help. And I want to start fresh."

I turned to Kira, knowing full well this problem didn't rest on Naomi's shoulders, but mine. We all needed a fresh start. I just wasn't sure if it was possible.

My wife regarded me with a reserved grin and then set her sights on Naomi. "I want that, too."

* * *

We'd made it to the end of shift. Everyone had worked hard to make tonight happen, and we'd had fewer than ten tables at any given time. No way did we break even. I patted Angelo on the back as he wiped down the dining tables. He hadn't had a single drink tonight. In fact, it had been days, and I couldn't have been prouder. "Thanks, brother."

"Anytime."

I pushed through the swinging door into the kitchen. Most of the staff had cleared out. Kira was tipping out the two servers we'd had. Marie had come back, and recommended a friend who needed a job. We brought her on, too, unsure if we'd be able to keep her. Or any of them, for that matter.

Kira's lips curled into a gentle smile when she noticed me. "Hi."

"Back at you." I shoved my hands in my pockets. "We weren't anywhere near full tonight."

"No, but it's a start." She glanced at Naomi, who'd emerged from the hall, her purse slung over her shoulder.

"Thank you, Kira," she said. "I'm glad to be back. And I hope we can put all this behind us, including Marco Devaney."

"You and me both. Good night, Naomi. Get some rest. We're going to do it all over again tomorrow."

She smiled. "I hope so. Good night, Kira. Dante."

"Night," I said, turning back to Kira. "Looks like we're about finished. Should we get out of here?"

"Yeah, just give me a few more minutes?" she asked. "I just want to copy tonight's receipts, and I'll take it home to look at later."

As she turned around, I gently took her arm. "Listen, I know there's still a lot we need to deal with. Both of us have pushed aside our marriage, and it's suffered for it."

"I'm sorry, Dante," Kira said. "But I want to work on us. Can we do that?"

I felt Angelo's hand on my shoulder.

"We still need to clean up out there," he said, thumbing back to the dining room.

"Sure. Yeah." I turned back to Kira, but she'd already gone into her office. "Go through the closing list with me?" I asked him. "We let everyone take off already. Shouldn't take but ten minutes, and then we'll head out."

"Let's do it," Angelo replied.

I grabbed the checklist. "Okay, the back pantry is locked. I checked that already." I turned to him. "Take a look to see the ovens and cooktops are off. I'll check the grease traps, make sure they're clean."

We worked our way through the list while Kira remained in the office. It was late and I was ready to leave. And while I scanned the list for remaining items, I heard a gasp come from Angelo. I looked up and saw him hunched over, screaming in pain.

"Jesus! Ang." I rushed toward him, but stopped in my tracks.

Marco stood just inside the back door, clutching a knife. In an instant, I realized he had stabbed Angelo — and now he was coming for me.

"Don't come any closer," Marco said.

I reached out and grabbed the nearest thing I could, a frying pan, holding it up like a shield. I heard the office door open, and I turned back to see Kira emerge. "Run!"

CHAPTER 31: KIRA

Shock consumed me as Dante's words echoed in my ears. I looked at Angelo curled up on the floor, blood pooling around him. Marco stood at the back door, wielding a knife. How? How was he here and not in jail?

"Kira, run!" Dante repeated, holding a frying pan like a weapon.

There was only one place I could go if I hoped to bring back help. Instinctively, I darted toward the swinging door and into the dining room. It was dark, with only the light from adjacent buildings spilling in through the windows. I panted, aiming my sights at the front door. But it was locked and required keys to open it from the inside.

"Shit." My keys were on my desk, and so was my phone.

I ran to the door anyway, praying someone would see me or hear my calls for help. As I looked outside, cars drove by, but I saw no one on the street. Most of the places around us were closed. "Oh my God. Please, someone help us."

I searched for a place to hide while I figured a way out of this. Maybe I could find a weapon and help Dante fend off Marco. Tears streamed down my cheeks, clouding my vision. "The bar." Glass bottles could be used as weapons.

I stumbled toward the bar and could hear the sound of metal clashing against metal. The deep grunts of struggle coming from the kitchen. I couldn't tell who was winning. And I also knew that to sit here and wait for whoever emerged on the other side of that door wasn't in my nature. I couldn't leave my husband alone to fend off this monster.

My hands shook as I reached for a bottle of whiskey and pulled it off the shelf. I gripped it tightly, feeling the weight of it in my hand. I could do some damage with this.

Resolute, I returned to the kitchen to see the ensuing fight between Dante and Marco. I marched forward, the bottle of whiskey in my hand, ready to strike when Marco shifted his attention away from Dante. But as soon as he saw me, he changed course and came straight for me.

I swung the bottle at him with all my strength. He blocked it with his arm and thrust the knife to within inches of me. I dodged out of his way just in time before Dante yelled and tackled him onto the floor. The whiskey bottle smashed on the ground, spilling glass and booze everywhere.

Marco seemed unstoppable as he slashed his knife at Dante, who blocked each move with the frying pan. He was quick on his feet, but Marco kept coming at him with an intensity that left me terrified.

I heard a crack from the far side of the room and saw Angelo. He'd gotten to his feet, his shirt soaked in blood. But he stumbled, pulling down one of the metal carts. The crash reverberated in the kitchen.

Marco turned his attention to Angelo, and I hurried to Dante's side. "Come on, babe. Get up. Get up!" He lay on the floor, bloodied and beaten. And when I heard Angelo call out, I shot up again. "Oh God." Marco was coming for him. "No!" I screamed.

Dante tried to stand. "Go, Kira, Run. Get out of here!"

Angelo moaned and called out for Marco to stop. I slid my arms under Dante's shoulders and tried to pull him up, but he was too heavy. "Please, Dante. Get up!" I cried.

He managed to return to his feet and shoved me out of the way as Marco rushed toward him.

I stumbled backward, slamming into the metal shelves next to my office. I needed a weapon, something I could use while they tussled on the ground. I couldn't get to Angelo. I couldn't help him. Dante was fending off Marco on his own, and I had no idea how long he could last.

Finally, my fingers closed around something heavy and solid. A cast iron skillet. I brandished it in front of me. They were locked in a deadly scene. Dante's face was swollen and bloody.

"Stay back!" Dante warned me, his eyes never leaving Marco's.

But I couldn't let him fight alone. With a deep breath, I charged forward and swung the skillet at Marco's head. It connected with a horrible thud, and Marco stumbled backward. Dante took advantage of the moment and pulled Marco to the ground.

I watched in horror as they rolled around in a frenzy of fists, each one fighting for their life. I couldn't let Marco win. I had to do more.

With a steely determination, I stepped forward and raised the skillet high above my head. "Stay away from my husband!" I screamed as I brought it down with all my might, hitting Marco square in the face. Blood spurted from his nose and mouth as he collapsed onto the floor.

I stared at Marco's motionless body for a moment, wondering if he was out. But as I turned to look at Angelo, his chest barely moving, I realized we had only moments to save him.

Dante still reeled as he attempted to steady himself. I walked to Angelo and dropped to my knees beside him. "I'm so sorry, Angelo," I whispered. "I'm so sorry."

To look at him was to see someone on the edge of death. Blood covered his torso and had begun to spill out of his mouth. "Dante, we have to call 911."

Dante stumbled toward me, staring at his brother. We both sat there in stunned silence, the only sounds coming from Angelo's labored breathing as he clung to life.

As he reached for his phone, I heard the noise and peered back. "Dante! Look out!"

CHAPTER 32: DANTE

Kira's voice rang in my ears. Marco's steps lumbered toward me. I looked at my brother and then at my wife. "Go! Get him out through the back, now!"

I regained my footing and stood in front of them, guarding them with everything I had. If Kira could get Angelo out the back, maybe she could get help before Marco came charging at me. "Kira, go!" I demanded again, as Marco stood on shaky legs.

I couldn't look back at her. I wasn't going to chance taking my eyes off this man. Behind me, I heard Kira groan as it seemed she was attempting to pull my brother through the exit. Angelo was hanging on by a thread, that much I knew. If he died … no, no. I couldn't think about that.

I stepped forward toward Marco. "The cops will be here any minute."

Blood dripped down his face from the wound Kira left. He smiled through bloodied teeth. "No one's coming to help you, Dante."

Whatever energy I had was nearly gone. But as Marco stood in front of me, I knew that if he got past me, it was over for Kira and Angelo. So I gathered my strength and launched myself at him, bringing him to the ground once again. We rolled around, punching and kicking, the knife he still held slicing at my arms.

Finally, I managed to pin Marco, holding him down with all my weight. "I swear to God, I'll kill you." But he was relentless, and continued to struggle and squirm beneath me, his eyes blazing with rage. I took hold of his wrist, twisting it until he dropped the knife. It clattered to the ground, and I kicked it away.

Were they out? Had Kira and Angelo made it out back yet? I knew I couldn't hold Marco down for much longer. He struggled beneath me, so I raised the knife, ready to deliver the final blow.

He rolled out from beneath me in one swift move. "No!" I tried to stand, but my shoes slipped on the floor that was covered in blood and glass and whiskey.

Marco tried to get away, heading toward the door into the dining room. I grabbed the counter and pulled myself up. Exhausted, pained, I wondered why he'd gone that way . . . *Kira's keys.*

He must've snatched them from her desk. He was going to escape through the front. Hell if I was going to let that happen. I stumbled toward the dining room, snatching the nearest knife I could find. My heart pounded as I searched for any sign of Marco.

There. I caught a glimpse of him, just as he made it to the front door. He was fumbling with the keys, trying to unlock it.

I unleashed a guttural roar and charged forward. Marco turned to see me coming. I sidestepped him and slashed his side, causing him to stumble. He regained his footing and came at me again, but I was ready. I deflected his blow with my own. "You'll never hurt her. I swear to God!"

"I already got your brother, Dante. I'll get both of you, too," he said, his breathy words spilling from his bloody mouth. My heart twisted at the mention of my brother. I had been so focused on catching Marco, I'd almost forgotten Angelo could be dying right now. I had to get back to him.

He pushed forward, gaining ground on me before he punched me in the face. My nose broke under his fist.

I swung at him again, my movements fueled by desperation. Marco kicked me in the stomach, and I doubled over, gasping for air.

And in a stroke of luck, Marco lost his footing, tripping over his own shoes. I grabbed his arm, twisting it behind his back, then I pressed the knife to his throat.

"Dante?"

"Kira." I looked back at her. "What are you—"

Marco slipped out from my grip. The knife dropped from my hands. I watched helplessly as he hurled through the dining room straight at her, grabbing her by the throat.

"Get away from her!" I called out, trailing him by mere steps.

As I approached, Marco tightened his grip on her. Her eyes bulged and she struggled to breathe. "Let her go!"

"You should have killed me when you had the chance, Dante." He pressed the knife to Kira's throat, drawing a trickle of blood. "One move, and she dies."

I halted in my tracks, staring at him. I had to think of something, anything to save her. Why had she come back? I almost had him. "What do you want?" I asked. "You can't think you'll ever be allowed to walk free again. Not after this. I don't know how you got out of jail, but you won't leave here alive."

I looked in Kira's eyes. She was trying to tell me something, but I couldn't figure out what it was. Angelo? I wondered. Had he died? If help was here, the cops would've busted in by now. No, this was something else. She had a plan. But that meant I had to get Marco away from her. I had to hold him off a while longer.

With a deep breath, I stepped forward, my palms outstretched. "Let her go, Marco," I said, trying to keep my voice steady. "You don't have to do this."

Marco laughed. "Oh, but I do, Dante. You still don't know who I am, either, do you?"

I drew in my brow. "What?"

"I shouldn't be surprised you didn't recognize my name from the beginning. Even when I'd dropped hints, you still didn't remember stabbing me in the back."

My mind reeled, and Kira's face was masked in confusion. "I have no idea what you're talking about, but you need to let her go, you son of a bitch. Now."

"I was there that night," Marco continued. "You'd just been promoted to head chef at Michael's. He threw that Christmas party . . ."

"Oh my God," Kira said.

Marco chuckled. "Now she remembers. But to be fair, you were pretty tipsy. And I did look a little different back then. Guess I figured if I'd wanted to get a woman like you, I needed to up my game. So I ditched the glasses, took care of myself, learned a few things about what women like you wanted. But most importantly, I became the best chef in the city." He glanced at her. "We talked that night, didn't we, Kira? You flirted with me. Touched me, smiled that seductive smile of yours." He set his gaze on me again. "That job was supposed to be mine, you arrogant prick."

Michael's? I'd started there as a line cook. It was where Kira and I met. Then, I was promoted to head chef a few years later. Of course I remembered it. But not him. Marco wasn't there. Was he? "You didn't work there."

"No. You made sure of that. But I was at the party. Michael invited all of us who'd applied. A sort of consolation prize, I suppose. Not much of one, you ask me."

"That's why you're here? Because I flirted with you when I was drunk?" Kira asked.

I watched him tighten his grip on her arm. "Don't give yourself that much credit, bitch."

But it made sense to me now. Marco thought I'd beaten him. I'd gotten the position. Kira was a beautiful woman who paid him some attention, but she was my wife. Giving him more reason to come at me.

"And then Michael told you about this place, didn't he? I know he did, because I'd asked him for a favor — an investment. I shouldn't have been surprised he turned me down, waiting for my restaurant to fold," Marco continued, the knife still at Kira's throat. "He told you I'd lost it and that it was ripe for the taking, now that the bank had owned it."

"I had no fucking clue about any of this," I said. "I never knew this was your restaurant, and you know it. I didn't know Michael knew you existed, let alone that you ran this place into the ground. Are you telling me this is all because I got that fucking job and you didn't? That my friends are dead, and you tried to take my wife because you lost everything, and you blame me for it?"

Kira winced as he clutched her arm tighter. "No, Dante. That was just the tip of the iceberg. You don't deserve any of this. And you sure as hell don't deserve her."

I looked at my wife again. Her eyes darted to the side, toward the kitchen. But why? Now wasn't the time to ask. I would do it. I would find a way to push him back, back into the kitchen.

I walked forward. Marco drew in his brow, surprised by my action. He finally took a step back, but Kira winced in pain as he pierced her skin deeper with the tip of the knife. Blood trailed down her neck.

"Jesus." I held out my hands. "Don't hurt her." I took another step forward.

"Then don't come any closer, Dante, or I will slice her throat right in front of you." He leaned close and kissed her neck. Her blood stained his lips. "I can feel your desire, Kira," he whispered, keeping his eyes on me. "Did you tell him how good I made you feel?"

I watched Kira's eyes well, spilling over with tears. "Stop," I said, continuing to inch closer, almost imperceptibly.

He stepped back. Maybe a part of him didn't want her dead. Maybe he thought he could have her now. That wasn't going to happen, even if it killed me.

It wasn't until Marco glanced over his shoulder, appearing to gauge how close he was to the door, that I knew the moment had arrived. I charged ahead, shoving him through the swinging kitchen door. Kira fell to the ground in the corridor. Marco stumbled back until he fell just inside the doorway.

I remained standing, hovering over him when Kira called out to me.

"Lighter," she said.

"What?" There were only two ways out of this restaurant. The front door, which was locked. And the back exit through the kitchen, which wasn't. But Kira could get out through the front now, her keys lying on the floor right in front of it.

Without turning my gaze from Marco, I called out to her. "Your keys . . . get out."

"Lighter!" she yelled back at me. And then it dawned on me.

Getting around Marco, however, was another story. He lay on the ground, trying to pull himself up again, and blocked the path to the shelf where we kept the lighters. One of our stoves was tricky, the ignition switch played up on us. We used a lighter to turn it on. Kira's idea . . . it could work.

I kicked Marco, harder and harder, with all my strength, until he began to ball up for protection. Now was my chance.

I ran around him and headed straight for the shelf. I snatched a lighter from it and hurried toward the back door, stepping in the whiskey from the bottle she'd dropped. Along the way, I flipped on the knobs of the stoves. Gas began to hiss out of the burners.

Marco had returned to his feet as I went for the back door. Kira and Angelo stood on the other side, waiting for me. I needed my family more than I needed this restaurant.

As I reached the back door, I could hear Marco behind me, closing in quickly. I flicked the lighter, my fingers trembling.

Marco seemed to realize what I was about to do as he stood there with his hands up. His feet steeped in booze and the smell of gas around him. "Stop. You don't have the balls to do it, Dante. You love this place too much."

Fear laced his words. I turned to face him, my hand outstretched, my finger ready to press on the switch. My other hand gripped the door handle. In one swift motion, I flicked the lighter and tossed it into the kitchen. A giant fireball erupted as I spilled out, tumbling down the steps at the back door. I was on fire. I felt the heat, the flames burning my arms.

"Dante!" Kira ran toward me, rolling me around to snuff out the flames.

I heard Marco screaming in agony as the fire consumed him. I scrambled to my feet. "Get back! We have to move!"

Within seconds, I felt the fireball at my back. Kira and I were thrust forward from the blast. A whoosh of fire and wind.

We'd been thrown into the parking lot. My vision blurred, and my skin felt raw, but I saw the flashing lights of police cars racing toward us. My brother lay feet away, still appearing alive — just. "Angelo!"

"Dante, are you okay?" Kira pleaded.

I looked at her. "I'm okay. I'm okay. You?" Her shirt was partially burned off her shoulder and arm. The side of her face appeared black from soot. But otherwise, she appeared all right. And she was safe.

I stood and helped her up, walking toward Angelo. The heat from the burning building grew more intense. As I looked at it, the flames dancing higher into the night sky. Everything we'd worked for . . . "It's gone, Kira. The restaurant is gone."

She drew close to me. "But so is he."

* * *

The ride to the hospital with my brother seemed to go on forever. I sat next to him in the ambulance. Kira followed closely behind in her car. I was okay, despite the throbbing bruises that had emerged on my face. She was okay, once they'd put a bandage over the cut on her neck. But Angelo — he barely clung to life.

The paramedic had placed an oxygen mask over his face. The other tried to slow the bleeding from the wound in his gut. Angelo drifted in and out of consciousness.

I took his hand. "Please don't die, brother. Please." He turned his head toward me and tried to speak. "It's okay. Don't. Just rest. You're going to be okay, I promise."

The paramedic glanced at me, the look on his face suggesting my promise might be broken. But I didn't care. I wasn't going to lose Angelo. Not now.

As we arrived at the hospital, the medical staff rushed him into the emergency room. Kira and I stood outside, watching as they worked frantically to save my brother's life. The realization of what had just happened started to set in. Our restaurant, our livelihood, burned while we sat here. And yet, I felt relief knowing that Marco was finally gone, destroyed by the very thing he had planned to take from us.

But as the minutes ticked by, my relief turned to dread. The doctor appeared from the hallway, his face grim as he made his way toward us. I'd seen that look before. The firefighters who found my parents' charred bodies inside their bakery — they had worn the same expression.

The doctor removed his surgical hat. "I'm sorry. We did everything we could, but it was too late. He's gone."

Kira's hand covered her mouth, stifling a sob. I couldn't believe it. My brother, my closest friend, was gone. And it was all because of Marco. Anger and grief lit me up like I was on fire again.

"Oh, honey, I'm so sorry," Kira said, nestling her head against my chest.

I was numb, staggering in disbelief.

"I'm so sorry for your loss, Mr. and Mrs. Lucini," the doctor said, before turning to leave.

We stood there alone in the middle of the waiting room. Others moved around us, but I heard no one. No sounds at all, except for my mother's voice. "*Dante, you need to look after your brother. He's a good boy, but you've always been the leader.*" My lips quivered and tears streamed down my cheeks.

Kira took my hand. "Come on. Let's go home."

She tried to lead me toward the door, but I couldn't move. I stood firm, that fire in me growing hotter. And when she turned back to me, it took everything in my power not to punch a hole in the nearest wall. "Angelo's dead because of Marco." I fixed my gaze on her. "How the fuck did he get out of jail?"

CHAPTER 33: KIRA

It seemed impossible for me to comprehend that we'd lost not only Angelo, but our restaurant, too. For Dante, it had been his life's dream to open his own place, and I supported him. But losing his brother, knowing he was now the only one left in his family, I couldn't be sure what would happen next.

As I sat on the patio outside on this cool morning, over-looking a city that had just begun to awaken, I wrapped my hands around the warm mug and sipped on my coffee. It was all I could do last night to keep Dante from going to the police station to confront Lyman. I wasn't sure what he would do in that state of mind, and I didn't need him ending up behind bars.

But the question had played on repeat in my head. Marco had been in custody for the murder of Tom Weaver. How had he gotten to us? If he had been released, why were we not warned?

I hadn't heard whether they'd recovered his body yet, but there was no doubt he was dead. Our nightmare was over, but along with it, our dreams.

I caught movement from the corner of my eye and turned to see Dante enter the kitchen. From the look of him, sleep never came. Not that I'd gotten much of it either.

He shuffled to the kitchen cabinet and retrieved a mug, pouring a cup of coffee from the half a pot that remained. Dante shuffled outside to join me on the patio. Squinting at the hazy sky, he pulled out a chair next to me and sat down.

The silence between us grew. He was angry at me for not letting him go to the station last night. He'd had no sleep. I saw it in his face. "Babe—"

"Don't, Kira." He took a sip from his mug. "I intend to finish my coffee, take a shower, and go to the station to confront Lyman. This is his fault. My brother is dead because he let Marco walk free."

His phone rang as it lay on the table between us. I glanced at the caller ID and my stomach dropped.

Dante looked at his phone. His cheeks turned red, and his fists clenched. The screen displayed Lyman's name, and I looked at him, not knowing what he would do. He let it ring until it went to voicemail.

Moments later, a knock sounded on the front door. I closed my eyes, knowing it had to be Lyman, and if he was smart, he wouldn't be alone. "Dante, we have to answer that . . ."

My husband grinned, a strange, twisted grin, and got up from the chair. "I'll get it."

I jumped up, hurrying beside him. "Please, just stay calm, okay? Don't do anything that will get you into trouble."

He kept going. Whatever was about to happen wasn't going to be stopped by me. Dante seethed over the loss of his brother. And right now, Lyman was about to be his whipping boy.

Dante opened the front door, standing in a T-shirt and sport shorts. Detective Lyman stood on the other side, flanked by two officers.

Lyman raised his hands. "First of all, I want to tell you how sorry I am . . ."

"Don't you dare," Dante said. "You had him, goddamn it. You had him and you fucking let him go."

"That's not exactly how it happened." Lyman looked at me as though I could change Dante's mind. "Please, can we come in and go over all this?"

I reached out for Dante. "Hon, please."

He stood firm for another moment or two. No one said a word. Finally, Dante stepped back.

Lyman and the two officers entered. And before I could close the door, he'd already started talking.

"It was a technicality, Mr. Lucini. I had no control over it, I promise you. Devaney brought in a lawyer, spouted off some bullshit about wrongful detainment. And there was nothing I could do."

He shouldn't have said that. I looked at Dante, the fumes of anger practically billowing out of him. "You could've warned us," I said.

Lyman looked back at me. And when he did, Dante charged toward him.

"You son of a bitch."

The officers grabbed him, one holding each arm, pulling at him. "Stop," I said. "Stop it. He's done, okay? He's not resisting." I pleaded with Lyman. "Tell them to stop."

Lyman raised his hands. "Okay. Okay. It's fine. Everyone, calm down." He set his sights on Dante. "Mr. Lucini, you have every right to be pissed at me, but please hear me out."

I walked to Dante when the officers finally let him go. "Let him talk, please."

Lyman nodded and caught his breath. "I'd taken care of things on my end, still working on the case. Devaney's arraignment wasn't scheduled until today, but it'd been moved up. I wasn't made aware. I'd already gone home, thinking Devaney would be behind bars until I finalized the charges. I was still waiting on a key piece of evidence — prints — to prove he'd been inside Weaver's home. Anyway, I don't know what his lawyer did, but he got him out, pending charges."

While Lyman continued to explain, my phone buzzed with an incoming call. I looked at the screen and shot Dante a glance. "I need to take this."

I didn't tell him who was on the call, but I felt Lyman's gaze trail me as I stepped away. When I was out of earshot, I answered, "Detective Soto, hello."

"Mrs. Lucini, I got your voicemail. How are you and your husband holding up?"

I gazed back at Dante who still glared at Lyman, looking ready to kill him. "We're okay, all things considered. Lyman just showed up to explain how the hell Marco was let go last night."

"Okay, listen, I don't know if I'm too late on this or not, but whatever you and your husband do, do not mention me or my investigation."

"We haven't said anything, but I have to ask, why not?" I stepped a little farther away.

"Not over the phone. I'm heading your way now. I'll be in LA in a couple hours. Can I meet you two?"

"Yes, of course. We still have to go to the restaurant, and then . . ." I swallowed my emotions. "We have to start making arrangements for my brother-in-law."

"I'm so sorry, Mrs. Lucini," he said. "If I could've ended this sooner, please believe that I would have."

"No, I understand." That wasn't entirely true. I felt he, and especially Lyman, had failed us. "Call me when you arrive, and we'll set up a meeting place. Thank you, Detective." I ended the call, returning to Dante and Lyman, pocketing my phone as I arrived.

Lyman turned to me. "I was just telling your husband that an internal inquiry has been opened over what happened last night. It never should have gone down like that, and I'm so very sorry."

I looked at Dante, who appeared at the end of his rope. "If there's nothing else, Detective, we need to get to the restaurant and then take care of family."

"Of course," he replied. "Again, Mrs. Lucini, I am sorry for what has happened to you and your husband. I'll keep you posted."

* * *

We arrived at what was left of our restaurant. I didn't tell Dante that I'd spoken to Soto. He was in no place to deal with whatever Soto had to say. As I pulled up to the building, the worst of the damage contained to the kitchen, my emotions spilled over. I looked at Dante, stone-faced, just staring at it.

I gathered myself, knowing that this would be harder on him because Angelo died here. He died trying to protect me.

The firefighters had gone home, but when I glanced to my right, I saw a man who appeared to work for the fire department, but wore no gear. "Who is that guy?" I asked Dante.

"I don't know." He opened the passenger door. "The fire investigator, probably."

I joined my husband, and we headed toward the man with the clipboard.

"Excuse me?" Dante asked him. "Who are you?"

He held out a badge. "Harlan Reeves. LAFD chief investigator. And you are?"

"Dante Lucini," he said. "This is my wife, Kira. This was our restaurant."

"I'm sorry for your loss," Reeves said. "I'm here to determine the cause of the fire and was just awaiting clearance to enter. Did you receive a call from us?"

"No, sir," Dante said. "We've been with the LAPD detective in charge of our investigation all morning."

"Investigation?" he asked.

Dante went into detail on all that had happened and how Lyman came to be involved. Then I aimed my gaze at the building. "My brother-in-law, Dante's brother, died as a result. We were able to get him out of the building before it blew, but it wasn't enough."

"What can you tell me about the fire?" Reeves continued.

This was the part I wasn't sure we should answer. Dante had turned on the gas and barely escaped with his life. The accelerant was a bottle of whiskey I'd dropped. Did that mean we would be charged with arson? Without a lawyer, I had no idea, and risking our insurance not paying out on this would mean total bankruptcy.

Dante appeared ready to speak, but I reached out for his arm, and cut in, "This has been a long and difficult situation, Inspector Reeves. I think it might take some coordination with the LAPD for you to continue. We'd prefer to engage our lawyer before speaking with you further."

He removed his hat. The heavy mustache he wore ticked up as his lips raised. "I understand. I'm simply here to determine cause. I assume an insurance policy was in place."

"Yes, of course," Dante said.

"Then I'll begin my investigation without your help, if it's all the same to you. And when you have your lawyer at your side, I'd welcome any additional information you can provide." He walked toward the building.

"What was that about?" Dante asked me.

"I didn't want to admit that we were responsible for starting the fire," I replied. "Not until we can prove it was in self-defense. And then, I want to hear what Soto has to say first."

"What's he got to do with anything?"

I caught a glimpse of a vehicle approaching, and I recognized the driver inside. "That's him now. He was the one who called me at the house earlier. I didn't want to say anything until you had some time to clear your head. Anyway, he says he has something to talk to us about. I told him to meet us here."

We walked over to him, realizing the fire inspector hadn't taken much notice of the newcomer. I offered my hand. "Thank you for coming down, Detective. This is my husband, Dante Lucini."

"I'm so sorry about your restaurant," he said, shaking my hand. "Mr. Lucini, my condolences."

"Thank you," Dante replied flatly.

"You said you had something you wanted to talk to us about," I continued.

"I do." He paused for a moment, as if collecting his thoughts. "As you know, I've been investigating Marco Devaney for some time now in connection with Raymond Driscoll's disappearance. And since you've gotten involved, I've been able to consider other scenarios."

"Such as?" I asked.

"When I learned Devaney had returned to LA, I reached out to the LAPD. This was before we talked. I'd spoken to Detective Lyman, who didn't have any information on Devaney, but would, of course, keep me informed should news arise."

"But somehow, I doubt he did," I pressed.

The detective glanced at Dante, who'd remained close-lipped. He inhaled a deep breath before finally continuing, "After your home was vandalized, and you suspected Devaney, I started wondering why it was Lyman hadn't taken action: a restraining order, or even so much as questioning him about it. It got me thinking, why? So I started asking questions about Lyman. Turns out, his history with the department is . . . shaky . . . at best."

"Shaky," I said. "Well, after what we've just been through this morning, I suppose that doesn't come as much of a surprise. But forgive me, Detective, how does this involve me and my family?" I asked, feeling the frustration build. "You'd almost had enough to bring in Marco for Driscoll's death, but you didn't. And here we are."

"Yes, ma'am," he said, looking down as if ashamed. "There's nothing I'm sorrier for than that. However, I am here now to bring to your attention that, while I don't possess all the necessary details, I have reason to believe that Detective Lyman had been in contact with Marco Devaney on a few occasions."

That seemed to capture Dante's attention. "Was Marco paying him to look the other way? That sure as shit would explain a lot."

"When you mentioned to me Tom Weaver's murder, Mrs. Lucini, I made a request to the LAPD, outside of Lyman, for the phone records of Devaney. Told them it was in connection with my Driscoll investigation. They handed them over yesterday without a question. So, I dug deeper and found that Lyman had contacted Devaney. What was said in those conversations, I couldn't possibly know. However, one conversation occurred just hours before Weaver was killed."

"When Lyman and his people were supposedly searching for Marco after what happened to me in that construction site," I said.

"Lyman told Marco where to find Weaver?" Dante asked. "Why?"

"Told him where to find him, or cleared the path so that he wouldn't be interrupted when he did find him. I don't know which." Soto peered at both of us. "I believe you and your husband need to be careful around this man. In the meantime, I'd like you two to come with me. Trust me when I say, it'll be worth your time."

* * *

To my surprise, Detective Soto had a plan, and we were part of it. He had an in with the LAPD, and that contact granted him access to Marco Devaney's apartment. We followed a few minutes behind as we signed off on some paperwork the fire inspector handed over.

As I parked in front of the apartment building, a strange feeling came over me. I couldn't quite put my finger on it, except that I felt angered just by being there. Maybe because his place was so close to our restaurant, and we never knew . . . Never mind that now. If there was a way to tie Lyman to Marco and make him pay for what he'd done to my family, then I was all in. And I know Dante was, too.

"This is the place," I said, cutting the engine. "Second floor. Come on. Let's go." I started to climb out and noticed Dante had remained seated. "Hey, it's okay. You don't have to do this."

"I want Lyman to suffer. So, yeah, I do." Dante opened the door and stepped out.

The two of us walked up the concrete stairs to the second-floor unit. I knocked on the door and Soto opened it.

"Glad to see you made it." He held the door while I stepped inside. Dante followed closely behind. I already didn't like being in here. That anger I felt a moment ago only intensified.

As I looked around, I noticed a small sofa, a matching loveseat. Nothing on the coffee table. In fact, I didn't see much of anything except furnishings.

Then I noticed two suitcases. "He was planning to leave." I looked at Dante. "He wanted to finish what he'd started, and then he was going to take off."

"And he left this in an envelope with Lyman's name on it. Right here on the kitchen counter." The detective held a flash drive in his hand. "Must've been uncertain how things would play out last night and had this ready for the cops. Good thing we got here before they did."

"The son of a bitch didn't think I'd kill him," Dante said.

"My contact says Lyman and his team won't be here for about an hour, so I want to see what's on this drive, and anything else in this place that could tie the two of these people together. I have the phone records, so let's see what else we can find before LAPD gets their hands on things."

I watched the detective plug the flash drive into his laptop and begin to sift through the files. Dante and I stood by, anxiously waiting for any information that could help us prove Lyman was a bad cop, and let Marco go free to come for us last night.

As Soto clicked through file after file, I couldn't help but feel a sense of dread growing in the pit of my stomach. What if there was nothing here? What if we couldn't find enough evidence to tie Lyman to Marco?

But then, just as my anxiety reached its peak, the detective let out a low whistle and turned the laptop around to face us.

"Take a look at this," he said.

On the screen were emails, and a voice memo attached to one of them Devaney had sent to Lyman. "Can you play that file?" I asked him.

The detective opened it, and both Dante and I immediately recognized the voices.

"*You dragged me out here to the desert,*" Lyman said. "*What the hell do you want?*"

"*Thought you should see something,*" Marco replied.

The audio went quiet for a moment, and all we heard was the distant sound of birds flying overhead. Then Lyman spoke.

"*Where'd you get this?*" he asked.

"*That's not the question you should be asking, Detective. The question you should ask is what I intend to do with it.*"

Lyman scoffed. "*You can't prove I took that money.*"

"*No? I've got a friend who says you did. The money belonged to him. He says you took the cash and left the kilo of coke. I guess you weren't crazy enough to tangle with the cartels. Good call.*"

"*Your friend? Really? And you think anyone's going to believe the word of a felon over me? Go fuck yourself, Devaney.*"

As we listened to the conversation, I looked at Dante. "He sent this as a threat."

Dante nodded. "Marco recorded it as backup."

"*You know, I'll bet the higher-ups in your department will be interested in seeing this. Hard to dispute serial numbers on bills. Easy to trace,*" Devaney shot back.

"Blackmail," Soto cut in. "Devaney figured out Lyman was a dirty cop and used it to get his favors."

The audio went quiet once again. I thought it was over, but then Lyman continued.

"*You know, you could just walk away from these folks. Move on. Going this route will make you a lot of enemies.*"

"*I'll move on when I take back what was mine,*" Devaney replied.

Dante sighed. "How the hell did that guy dig up so much dirt on people?"

"It's not hard when you know the right folks in the LAPD," Soto replied. "Which, I assume was the case here. Hey, he got away with shit in Napa, too, so, he had plenty of help from bad people to get what he wanted. That's how it works with sociopaths."

It occurred to me then, the situations Lyman put me in with Marco. The park, the building under construction. "Oh my God. He was handing me over to Marco on a silver platter."

"So we would give up," Dante said. "That's it. We have him. We can take this to the authorities and get Lyman arrested."

"This is enough to bring Lyman in for questioning, at the very least," Soto added. "I'll take care of it. I'll have to tread lightly with LAPD. No telling how this is going to go over with one of their own involved."

"What about the rest of the files on the drive?" I asked.

The detective looked at the others, and then I saw the name. "Angelo? What the hell?" I shot a look at Dante. "What is this?"

"I don't know."

"Let's find out," the detective said, opening the file.

We listened as the conversation began. "It's Marco and Angelo talking," I said.

"Angelo mentioned to me that the two of them had talked when he was at the restaurant drunk the other night," Dante said. "Marco must've recorded the conversation."

I feared what was on that audio file, but it was too late now. I listened.

"*That's really awful what happened to your parents, Ang.*" Marco's voice sounded.

"*Yeah, it devastated both of us. Everyone thinks Dante was at fault.*"

"*Do you think that?*" Marco pressed.

I looked at Dante, who'd closed his eyes at the question.

"*No. I know Dante would never intentionally hurt our parents. And the fact is . . . I know it wasn't him because it was me,*" Angelo said. "*I caused it, not knowing my parents would be there. I knew they'd wanted to sell the place, because business had gotten bad, you know? They were losing money, and I figured, you know, insurance and all that.*"

"Oh my God." Dante placed his hand over his mouth.

285

"*So I turned on the gas oven, low, so the gas would come out slowly. And flour is so flammable, it wouldn't take but a single electrical spark, and the place would go up in flames. There was this one outlet that was tricky, you know? I was supposed to call the electrician to look at it, and I never did.*" Angelo sounded as though he had begun to weep. "*I didn't know Ma and Pop would be coming in so early. I'd already left, figuring things would take care of themselves quickly. I didn't even know Dante was going to be there at all. But he came in shortly after I left. That's why he thought it was his fault — he'd been the last one there. Then my ma and pop turned up and went inside. A flick of the switch and . . . boom.*"

Dante's face trailed with tears as he listened. I couldn't believe what we were hearing. All this time, Dante thought he'd been responsible for the fire. Even Angelo had let him believe that. But he wasn't. Angelo had done it.

"*When the insurance money came through,*" Angelo continued. "*I knew I had to give it to Dante. I knew he wanted to open his own place someday far away from New York.*"

"*So you gave it all to him?*" Marco said.

"*Yeah. I did.*"

The conversation went quiet for a moment when we heard Angelo's voice again.

"*I started hitting the booze pretty heavy after that. Can't seem to shake it now.*"

I placed my hand on Dante's shoulder as the recording ended. "I'm so sorry, babe."

"He knew all along he'd been responsible, and let me think I was," Dante said.

The detective stood up. "Listen, we'd better head out before LAPD arrives." He eyed us. "I have what I need. Do you?"

"I think so," Dante replied.

Soto was already up and preparing to leave when I noticed a look on Dante's face. "We should go."

He turned to me as if shaking out of his thoughts. "Right, okay."

We followed Soto out of the apartment. He'd secured the door behind him while we returned to the parking lot.

"Thank you, Detective," I said. "For everything."

"I'm sorry it took me so long," he replied. "I'll be in touch with you both soon." He carried on into the parking lot, climbing into his vehicle.

Dante still appeared upset as we returned to our car. Standing beside it, I regarded him. "Ang hated himself for what he'd done. I know you saw that. I did."

He fidgeted with the keys, looking right through me. "Yeah. I'll drive." Unlocking the driver's side door, he stepped in.

I walked around to the passenger side and slipped onto the seat. We were both quiet. I stared through the windshield at the apartment building. "We can get through this, babe. We've come too far not to."

It was then I noticed two police cars pulling into the parking lot. Another vehicle behind it. "That could be Lyman. We can't let him see us here."

And, as if a switch flipped inside Dante, he flung open his door and stepped out.

"What are you doing?"

He refused to answer. Instead, he marched into the parking lot until he stood directly in front of the unmarked car. It must've been Lyman by the look on Dante's face. I jumped out. "Dante, come on, let's go." But I was too late.

He pounded his fist on the driver's side window. The patrol cars in front of them came to a stop. One of the officers jumped out.

"Hey!" he yelled at Dante. "Step back."

The driver's side door opened, and Lyman emerged. "Oh my God. Dante, don't. Please." I started toward him, but he thrust out his hand and shook his head.

The two were face to face.

"My wife could've been killed by that psycho because of you," Dante said.

"What the hell are you doing here?" Lyman asked. "How did you even know—"

"You were willing to let her die to keep your dirty little secrets, you son of a bitch. You set him free to come at us. And for what?"

"You don't know what you're talking about, Mr. Lucini. Now, back the fuck off before you do something you'll regret."

My gaze shifted to the other officers, who were now approaching. Both palmed their weapons. "Jesus." And that was when I saw Dante's fist clench.

In one swift move, he threw a punch, landing it hard against Lyman's jaw. Blood spurted from his mouth as he stumbled backward.

Everything seemed to move in slow motion. I looked back at the officers. They'd drawn their guns.

"Hands in the air! Hands in the air!" one of them shouted.

Dante didn't move while Lyman regained his footing. "Tell them to back off or I tell them what you did."

Lyman rubbed his jaw, dabbing away the blood from his lips. "It's good. Back off. We're all good here," he shouted. "It wasn't personal, man. Now I suggest you and your wife get the hell out of here before those guys arrest you."

Dante smiled, even chuckling a little. "Go ahead and arrest me. They'll all find out soon enough."

* * *

Six Months Later

"Come on, Dante. We have to get down there," I said, pulling my purse over my shoulder. "We can't be late." I walked by the mirror near our front door and took another look at my dress. My baby bump was starting to show, and this dress didn't help with that. "It'll have to do."

My phone buzzed with an incoming text. I retrieved it from my purse and glanced at the screen. It was from Detective Soto.

Thought you should know, jury came back late today. Guilty. Lyman will be going to prison for a good long while.

I smiled, relief washing over me. It had taken Dante and I a long time to feel normal again. A lot of therapy, a lot of hard work. But this was the last page of a terrible chapter in our lives. And as I stood at the door, Dante finally arrived, dressed in his suit. "How do I look?" he asked.

"Like a restauranteur, and a little like a dad," I said, a wide grin on my lips. "Can we go now?"

He opened the door. "Yes, ma'am. By all means." He gestured for me to step out first, and I headed into the driveway toward our car. The city lights shone on this clear winter's night. But it was still LA, so I only needed a light wrap over my shoulders to keep out the chill in the air.

Dante stepped behind the wheel, and I climbed into the passenger seat of his Porsche. "Let's go."

He drove off, heading toward downtown. Tonight was going to be special. A grand re-opening. We'd worked hard to make it come together in such a short time, but it was done, and we were ready.

When the fire happened, we thought we'd lost it all. Angelo, the restaurant. All because of a man who desired revenge for something we had no control over — his own failings.

But what we hadn't known was that Angelo had taken out a substantial life insurance policy on himself. And he'd named Dante the beneficiary. It seemed his guilt had come out not only in his alcoholism, but in a way that he wanted to ensure Dante would have the resources he needed to continue in the restaurant business. Maybe even open a second one someday. Of course, he couldn't have known at the time all that would happen.

It turned out, Angelo saved us in more ways than one. This new restaurant? We decided on a name. "Angelo's." And tonight was the first night of the rest of our lives.

THE END

ACKNOWLEDGMENTS

Throughout my writing career, I have been blessed with love and support from my amazing friends and family. I would like to take this time to tell them just how much they mean to me. First of all, I must thank my husband, Paul, who often takes on our daily responsibilities, so that I may submerge myself when the words just keep coming. And it is my mother, Audrey, who I must offer my utmost gratitude and appreciation. A voracious reader my entire life, she has read every early draft I've ever written. Not a single book has been published without her input. Her dedication to my success is unwavering, and I would be lost without her.

And I have to say that this story would not have been possible if not for my son, Aidan. A young student, who has worked in many restaurants, it was his behind-the-scenes anecdotes that provided the inspiration for this book. Some of his tales were too good not to write about, and possibly embellish just a bit. Though I should clarify, no murders occurred in any of his restaurants.

To my dearest lifelong friends, Michelle, Missie, Sheryl, and Peggy. Each one of you has propped me up on your shoulders, carrying me through difficult times, reminding me that this journey is far from over, and great things still await.

Finally, I must thank my wonderful team at Joffe Books. The dedication and hard work you all put into making each story the best it can be is unparalleled. Special thanks go out to Publishing Director Kate Lyall Grant, who not only took a chance on this writer of detective tales, but also guided me into the darker, more ominous world of psychological thrillers. It was so much fun, and I can't wait to write another.

THE JOFFE BOOKS STORY

We began in 2014 when Jasper agreed to publish his mum's much-rejected romance novel and it became a bestseller.

Since then we've grown into the largest independent publisher in the UK. We're extremely proud to publish some of the very best writers in the world, including Joy Ellis, Faith Martin, Caro Ramsay, Helen Forrester, Simon Brett and Robert Goddard. Everyone at Joffe Books loves reading and we never forget that it all begins with the magic of an author telling a story.

We are proud to publish talented first-time authors, as well as established writers whose books we love introducing to a new generation of readers.

We won Trade Publisher of the Year at the Independent Publishing Awards in 2023. We have been shortlisted for Independent Publisher of the Year at the British Book Awards for the last four years, and were shortlisted for the Diversity and Inclusivity Award at the 2022 Independent Publishing Awards. In 2023 we were shortlisted for Publisher of the Year at the RNA Industry Awards.

We built this company with your help, and we love to hear from you, so please email us about absolutely anything bookish at feedback@joffebooks.com

If you want to receive free books every Friday and hear about all our new releases, join our mailing list: www.joffebooks.com/contact

And when you tell your friends about us, just remember: it's pronounced Joffe as in coffee or toffee!